George Francis Popham Blyth

The holy week and the forty days

Being a continuous narrative in the words of the Evangelists, constructed from the

four Gospels, Volume 2

George Francis Popham Blyth

The holy week and the forty days
Being a continuous narrative in the words of the Evangelists, constructed from the four Gospels, Volume 2

ISBN/EAN: 9783741198496

Manufactured in Europe, USA, Canada, Australia, Japa

Cover: Foto ©Andreas Hilbeck / pixelio.de

Manufactured and distributed by brebook publishing software (www.brebook.com)

George Francis Popham Blyth

The holy week and the forty days

THE HOLY WEEK

AND

THE FORTY DAYS.

———◆———

XXVII. *THE WALK TO GETHSEMANE. PETER WARNED.*

S. Matt. xxvi. 30–35; S. Mark xiv. 26–31; S. Luke xxii. 39, 31–38;
S. John xviii. 1.

WHEN Jesus had spoken these words, and when they had sung an hymn, they went out over the brook Cedron,

1. *an hymn.*—There is little doubt this was the usual song of thanksgiving which terminated the Paschal feast in our Lord's time. It consisted of Ps. cxv.–cxviii., which formed the "great Hallel," the second part of the Hallel (contracted from Hallelujah), or song of praise; the former part of which, Ps. cxiii., cxiv., was sung at the commencement of the feast. It is worthy of notice how constant is our Lord's use of the Book of Psalms, especially during the close of His life; they were to Him a manual of devotion, a "*prayer-book.*" He has thus left His blessing in the constant use of this portion of Holy Scripture, which has been so great a source of comfort to those in sorrow or in sickness; who have found, in every age, that under every trouble which is common to man, there is some gracious and appropriate devotion in the Book of Psalms.

2. *went out.*—See xxv. b. 27. Our Lord now leaves the Supper-room, in which, after rising from supper, He appears to have lingered to deliver His last address to His disciples, and to offer His last solemn prayer.

3. *brook Cedron.*—The word "brook" implies a *winter torrent*, the bed of which would be dry, or nearly so, in the hot season. Corn. à

into the mount of Olives.   Then saith Jesus unto them, All ye shall be offended because of Me this night: for it is written, I will smite the shepherd, and the sheep of the flock shall be scattered abroad.   But after I am risen again, I will go before you into Galilee.   Peter

Lapide mentions a tradition that as Christ was borne back across the brook, He was thrown headlong into it; and illustrates it by quoting Ps. lxviii. 1.   But he gives no good authority for the story.   The derivation of the word Cedron is by some said to be a Greek corruption of the Hebrew name, and so would mean " Cedars; " but by others a Hebrew origin is given, which signifies " darkness."   Farrar observes that the name which has been translated to mean Cedars, though there is no tradition of any cedar trees there, " is probably no more than a curious instance of the Grecizing of a Hebrew name; " and cites a parallel from 1 Kings xviii. 40, where the brook Kishon, when similarly Grecized, comes to mean " the brook of the Ivies."   See David's passage across this brook in 2 Sam. xv. 23–30.

4. *offended.*—In the usual sense of Christ proving a " stumbling-block and rock of offence " in the way of those who wanted faith.   They should all fall before the trial to which His cause should now subject them. They had " continued with Him in His temptations; " but now one had betrayed Him, and was gone out from them to return no more ; and all they that remained would fail in their duty, one denying Him, all forsaking Him in the presence of His foes.   Some writers place this warning before the farewell discourses, and in the Supper-room ; but the present arrangement is probably correct.

5. *written.*—Zech. xiii. 7.   There are several parts of this prophecy most significant of our Lord's present position.   (See Zech. xi. 12, 13 ; quoted Matt. xxvii. 9, 10.)   The context of the present passage is very striking, and makes it impossible to mistake the allusion to Christ: " Awake, O sword, against the Man that is My fellow, saith the Lord of hosts; " where the allusion to the humanity and the divinity of our Lord is distinct, as is also the fact that God ordained and sanctioned this submission of the Son to the sword of divine justice ; this slaying of the Shepherd in behalf of the sheep, in consequence of which they are scared and " scattered abroad," as sheep that have no shepherd.

6. *go before.*—The original word is sometimes used to express the action of an Eastern shepherd, who goes *before* His sheep when he takes them to pasture. (See John x. 4.) There is, no doubt, this meaning here ; and the connection between this promise of our Lord and the prophecy of the scattering of the sheep is thus marked ; Christ would gather again His little flock, and go before them, as their Shepherd risen from the dead, into Galilee.   If we accept this meaning of the word, we may reconcile the difficulties which arise on our noticing that, although

answered and said unto Him, Though all shall be offended because of Thee, *yet* will I never be offended. And the Lord said, Simon, Simon, behold, Satan hath desired

our Lord had said He would see the disciples in Galilee (which was full of disciples, and the familiar scene of so much of His ministry); yet we find Him appear repeatedly to them, in Jerusalem and its environs, on the day of the resurrection. (See P. II. i. 20). He thus appeared to them all; first to Mary Magdalene; then to the women who had gone to the sepulchre; then to Cephas; then to the disciples who went to Emmaus; then to the Apostles, Thomas being absent; then again to the eleven, Thomas present. After this He was seen in Galilee (John xxi. 1–24). The Apostles seem, in the interim, to have proceeded there in consequence of our Lord's direction; He "went before them" (as a shepherd before the sheep which follow him), but whether He went visibly before them, or, as seems more probable, gathered them in spirit, and so directed them, we know not. S. Luke (Acts i. 3) says, "He was seen of them forty days;" where the original word implies that He appeared at intervals during that period, on the scene of their former converse in Galilee, when He spoke to them of the things pertaining to the kingdom of God, and its constitution and progress, and their office and work in connection with it. It is probable that, shortly subsequent to His appearance at the Sea of Tiberias, He showed Himself to the Apostles, and to "above five hundred brethren at once," who were assembled with them, many of whom had doubtless been witnesses of His former labours (1 Cor. xv. 6), the same who are mentioned in Matt. xxviii. 17. Towards the close of the forty days the Apostles appear to have returned to Judea, where He was specially "seen of James, then of all the Apostles," gathered to His ascension. (See P. II. iii. 25, vi. 2, vii. 1–3, viii. 1, 2.)

7. *though all.*—In the A. V. of Matt. xxvi. 33, there is a mistake made, which is avoided in the A. V. Mark xiv. 29. We read, "though all *men* ;" the word "men," being in italics, is put in to supply the sense, which it curiously perverts. S. Peter does not say, "though all *men*," but "though all" (my fellow disciples) "shall be offended," yet will not I : his words are his reply to our Lord's declaration, "All ye shall be offended because of Me this night."

8. *desired.*—The original word is a strong one; it implies that he had made the demand, and had obtained it. This passage recalls the demand of Satan against Job (Job i. 6–12, ii. 1–6), which has often been looked on as a poetical allegory, but which, in the light here thrown upon it, must appear a revelation of truth. It is the certain doctrine of Scripture that God permits trial and temptation (urged under Satan's malign influence) to overtake mankind in order to prove them; but that also limits are imposed by His wisdom within which the trial may be made. (See 1 Cor. x. 13; James i. 2–4.) This

to have you, that he may sift *you* as wheat: but I have prayed for thee, that thy faith fail not: and when thou art converted, strengthen thy brethren. And he said unto Him, Lord, I am ready to go with Thee, both into

is, however, quite different from the temptations and trials, far greater in their number and danger, to which mankind subject themselves, by yielding to sins against which God's Word emphatically warns them.

9. *sift you as wheat.*—S. John seems to record this in the sequence of result, rather than of event; as SS. Matthew and Mark apparently give the anointing at Bethany just before the treachery of Judas. (See xxii. 8.) He would mark a connection with the strife amongst the disciples for pre-eminence: their want of humility gave a vantage-ground to Satan, of which he was prompt to avail himself, pride of heart being a spirit kindred to his own. This *sifting* tried them all; it carried away Judas altogether, and displayed the infirmity of Peter and of the other disciples.

10. *for thee.*—He had desired to have them all ("*you*" is plural), but Peter especially needed the shield of Christ's intercession; and therefore for him especially Christ prayed. And, lest he should be overwhelmed with sorrow for the depth of his fall, Christ graciously places on him the honour and duty of strengthening those whose fall had been less disgraceful than his own. There is the same kindness manifested in the risen Saviour's message to the disciples: "Go, tell His disciples *and Peter*"—especially him who needs, in his humiliation, an individual token of remembrance and love. (See P. II. i. 19.) But the injunction to Peter conveys a general lesson: those who have known the bitterness of a fall are, on their restoration, charged, as specially qualified, to strengthen the weak against the same errors into which they fell; they are most sensitive and alive to all the perils of temptation; and thus Christ's mercy gives them the true source of comfort and recovery to themselves, in bidding them guard and comfort others.

11. *fail not.*—Fail not utterly, beyond remedy. "And when thou art converted," penitent, and restored from the failure of faith over which you shall grieve and mourn, then recover your happiness and confidence in labouring to support the faith of others who have fallen with you, though less notoriously; who, had you been as strong in act as in profession, might not have fallen.

12. *I am ready.*—There is warm affection evident in Peter's reply, different, as light from darkness, from the sullen temper in which Judas sinned against his Lord. But there is that self-dependence and want of humility which must ever injure the cause of Christ. It is painful to notice this pride of heart in the warm-hearted devotion of Peter; he cannot think it possible that he should fall; he would dare the lingering despair of imprisonment, nay, even the sharp agony of death, before he would desert the cause which he had now heartily espoused.

prison, and to death. And He said, I tell thee, Peter, that this day, *even* in this night, before the cock crow twice, thou shalt thrice deny that thou knowest Me. But he spake the more vehemently, If I should die with

There is always the same danger, often the same sad fall, before those who, in excitement and rash zeal, vow everything to a cause whose cost they have not reckoned, and who know not the weakness of their own nature. They serve sadly to point the apostolic caution, "Let him that thinketh he standeth take heed lest he fall." We notice the contrast between the trouble of the Saviour's soul in His agony, and His thrice repeated and earnest prayer, and the presumptuous confidence of Peter, who had not counted the cost of fidelity, and had not measured either his own strength or that of the adversary.

13. *I tell thee, Peter.*—Our Lord only thus addresses Peter on this single occasion. In doing so He recalls the hour when He gave the name Peter (Matt. xvi. 18), on his confessing the name of Christ with a distinctness and faith which none other had shown; and in sad contrast to his then grand confession of Christ would be his base denial of his Lord. But the application of the warning, conveyed in this emphatic use of the name Peter, bears also the promise that, in a return to the bold confession of Christ, by which he had won the name, should lay his future strength, which (as regarded his own power) he had proved in failure.

14. *this night.*—The day was reckoned from six o'clock, or sunset, in the evening; consequently this expression, at the time our Lord spoke, limits the duration of Peter's constancy to about a hour or two. The cock crows at midnight; but the second time of crowing, just before the day dawns, is the usual time spoken of as "the cock-crowing." The Jewish watch, so called, forms the interval between midnight and daybreak. (See xviii. 119.) Peter, therefore, first denied our Lord within a very short time of his profession of singular fidelity; and then the second and third time, at a sufficient interval for him to have recovered from the cowardice into which he had been surprised. But, instead of this, he deliberately repeated his denial; and it was only when the cock crew the second time that he looked up and met his Lord's eye, and was shamed, and repented. How great must have been the comfort afforded to the penitent amongst the "lapsed," in the early ages, by this incident in Peter's discipleship!

15. *the more vehemently.*—Nothing but a sad and painful experience would convince Peter of his real weakness, and save him from a sadder and irretrievable fall in the future, by teaching him that he must depend only on his Lord. The Saviour thought for others, and showed this tenderness over the weakness and baseness of His disciples, in the very hour of His own absorbing agony. There never was unselfishness such as His.

Thee, yet will I not deny Thee in any wise. Likewise also said all the disciples.

And He said unto them, When I sent you without purse, and scrip, and shoes, lacked ye any thing? And they said, Nothing. Then said He unto them, But now,

16. *I will not deny.*—(See xxiv. *d*. 36, 37.) It is difficult to be certain that Peter was now cautioned for the second time. Many writers have concluded that there was only one such scene, and that it is recorded with variations, by the Evangelists. But the first of the cautions (for we consider them distinct), as recorded by the accurate S. John (ch. xiii. 38), is evidently placed in a different connection. He there wants to follow Christ at once, asking whither He is going, and professing his own readiness to give up life for His sake. This was just after Judas had gone out, and before the institution of the Lord's Supper, and the last discourses, and Christ's prayer. Peter's second and similar profession of devotion was on the way to Gethsemane, as the other three Evangelists record. S. John evidently supplements the account given by the other three, of this particular period of our Lord's life; they are perhaps more anxious to show the connection of one event with another, he to give the exact order of time where they had left it unsettled. It would be perfectly natural that our Lord should give this caution once; and then, noticing how entirely Peter had failed to take it home to himself, repeat it, as did Peter his profession, with increased earnestness. S. Augustine (and, after him, Greswell) thinks that there were three occasions on which our Lord foretold this fall. If so, the cautions would be three, the denials three, and our Lord's questions, after the resurrection, at the Lake of Galilee three.

17. *likewise.*—Here, as on several occasions, we find Peter had acted as spokesman on behalf of those who were not less devoted in their attachment, though less zealous in the profession of it.

18. *when I sent.*—(See Matt. x. 5–10.) Our Lord was now about to send His Apostles forth for the second time. Whilst they were with Him, He provided for their necessities and for their safety. But He reminds them of that first mission, and asks them if, whilst absent from Him, they had suffered any distress or privation: for then His protection had been with them, His Spirit had gone with them; they had needed neither money, nor clothing, nor food; all was arranged by His Providence. But now there would be no miraculous interposition in their favour; they would not find all things ready, and men's hearts towards them. They (and the rule extends itself to their successors in the Gospel mission in every age) must neglect nothing in providing for their own necessities; they would find His certain blessing on their endeavours, but no miracle would obviate the necessity of their onerous labours.

he that hath a purse, let him take *it*, and likewise *his* scrip: and he that hath no sword, let him sell his garment, and buy one. For I say unto you, that this that is written must yet be accomplished in Me, **And He was reckoned among the transgressors**: for the things concerning Me have an end. And they said, Lord, behold, here are two swords. And He said unto them, It is enough.

19. *no sword.*—Gk. "and he that hath not " (*i.e.* means to purchase), "let him sell his garment, and buy a sword." He who has a purse and money may buy this necessity for self-defence; he who has not, had better part with his spare garment, and buy it. This direction, coupled with our Lord's rebuke to Peter when he drew the sword in His behalf, has given rise to much perplexed comment. The direction appears to be a general one, to meet a general necessity; self-defence would be necessary and lawful for the protection of life. The Christian must not be an aggressor; but he must not throw away the life which is valuable in the service of his Master. The very attitude of self-defence is often sufficient; but the use of the sword, that is, of weapons of self-defence generally, may be resorted to. The urgency of the case is marked by the command to procure this sword of defence, even at the cost of the garment. Several of the German commentators have interpreted this spiritually, as "the sword of the Spirit;" but it is evidently as literal an expression as "purse, and scrip, and shoes;" and the reference to the requirement of those common necessities on the former occasion marks their literal sense here. It is noticeable that men and societies who advocate peace at any price, generally display a very sensible and literal regard to the injunction to provide "purse, and scrip, and shoes;" they are not amongst the poorest, the worst fed, or the meanest clothed of the Christian community. It is clear that our Lord, in this command, is not referring to any *present* need of arms in His own defence; but to the future generations of His disciples, and in correction of any expectation that they might be included in the terms of His primary commission to the Apostles. (See note 18.) "When the Prince of Peace bade His followers sell their coats, and buy a sword, He meant to insinuate the need of those arms, not their improvement; and to teach them the danger of the time, not the manner of the repulse of danger." (*Bp. Hall.*)

20. *have an end.*—They are now in course of immediate completion, and will forthwith be finished; it is therefore evident that our Lord did not propose any struggle against them on the part of His followers.

21. *two swords.*—These they now produce; not unwilling, perhaps, to show that they had thought of this necessity, being armed, like many

XXVIII. *GETHSEMANE. THE AGONY.*

S. Matt. xxvi. 26–36 ; S. Mark xiv. 32–42 ; S. Luke xxii. 40–46 ;
S. John xviii. 1, 2.

Then cometh Jesus with them unto a place called Gethsemane, where was a garden, into the which He entered, and His disciples. And Judas also, which betrayed Him, knew the place : for Jesus ofttimes resorted thither with

other travellers who feared to fall among thieves ; perhaps also somewhat in the spirit of the remark concerning the few loaves and fishes in John vi. 9 : " What are two swords, at such a crisis as this, and in the face of such foes ? " Their reply shows that they misapprehended the spirit of Christ's remark. He had said enough to show them that His submission to death was God's will and His own determination, and therefore to come to pass. He could not, therefore, be speaking now of the sword with a view to any change of purpose ; but, as they proved unable to receive His meaning, He did not now explain it, but left it to be recalled and made clear afterwards by the teaching of the Spirit.

22. *enough.*—Not merely enough for any present purpose, or euough to show them how unequally they would contend against the powers of evil by mere human might ; perhaps in some such way, at the moment, the disciples understood the remark. But it appears rather the remark of one who waived the subject, as being one that His hearers did not enter into, and which the present opportunity did not allow of pressing further.

1. *Gethsemane.*—(See App. XV.) The meaning of the word is an " oil-press ; " the enclosure called a *garden* was, no doubt, in this instance, an olive-yard. It lay at the foot of the Mount of Olives, just across the brook Cedron. An Eastern garden is generally an enclosure planted with shady trees, fruit trees, and flowering shrubs.

2. *knew the place.*—It was an aggravation of the treachery of Judas that he did not scruple to guide his confederates to this place, hallowed by many a remembrance of kindly converse with his Lord.

3. *ofttimes.*—Knowing what would happen on this spot, our Lord had consecrated it as a " place where prayer was wont to be made " by Him on many a previous occasion. Memories of things done on earth attach themselves strangely to localities : deeds of crime, or of heroism, or of piety, are imperishably connected with such places. And so there are places hallowed by converse with God, where prayer seems most natural, and where God's presence seems to linger. Such thoughts may consecrate even the particular place in a room where we

His disciples. And He saith unto the disciples, Sit ye
here, while I go and pray yonder. Pray that ye enter
not into temptation.

And He taketh with Him Peter, and James, and John,

are accustomed to kneel down in private prayer. God is everywhere;
but there seems to be both a special presence and a hallowed ground—
privileges, these, not to be despised.

4. *sit ye*, etc.—Not to be too literally understood. Christ told them
to *remain* there, whilst He went to prayer. At such a time there might
be hope that they would pray with Him, or watch over Him, keeping
a vigil of prayer near their Lord. He might have bidden them watch
in prayer, whilst He entered into the mortal agony of His Passion; but
He says simply, "Remain here, whilst I pray yonder;" leaving all
else to their sympathy and appreciation of the present crisis. He then
adds that for their own sake, as He had just forewarned them of their
weakness, they should pray against temptation.

5. *enter into.*—This seems at first a caution given to them all;
afterwards more specially repeated to the three disciples who were
privileged to be witnesses of His agony. The expression is a peculiar
one; it seems to denote a coincidence of the internal will with temptation externally presented to them. If they were watching in prayer,
this could not well be; the temptation might assail them, but they
would not enter into its snare. If they were careless and prayerless,
the temptation would involve them, body and spirit, and they would
fall. It was, therefore, not the temptation against which they were
to pray, so much as that they might not, by coincidence of will, enter
into it. There is the same distinction in the petition in the Lord's
Prayer; we are not taught to pray that we may never be tempted, but
that we may not be suffered to fall under temptation. Trial is
ordained for all; temptation is permitted to try all; our prayer should
be that we may stand firm against the temptation, and be victorious.
See James i. 12, who (*v.* 14) explains that the temptation to be
dreaded and shunned is when a man "is drawn away of his own
lust, and enticed."

6. *Peter, James, and John.*—St. Paul says of these Apostles (Gal.
ii. 9), they "seemed to be pillars." Peter, the foremost in profession;
and the two sons of Zebedee, who had declared themselves able to
drink of the cup of which He should drink, and to be baptized with
the same baptism with their Lord; John being the "beloved disciple,"
and perhaps the foremost in personal devotion to Christ. These should
be called on to do Him prominent service afterwards; and they are
now witnesses of His agony, that they may know that they have a
severe struggle before themselves, and that it cannot be maintained
in self-dependence. These three had before been specially honoured;
once, as witnesses of the first miracle of resurrection (Mark v. 37);

and began to be sore amazed, and to be very heavy; and saith unto them, My soul is exceeding sorrowful unto death: tarry ye here, and watch with Me. And He was withdrawn from them about a stone's cast, and

and, again, of the Transfiguration (Matt. xvii. 1), which should be a preparation for the victorious issue of the present humiliation, and for Christ's rising again.

7. *began*, etc.—Bishop Pearson says, "These words in our translation come far short of the original expressions, which represent Him suddenly, upon a present and immediate apprehension, possessed with fear, horror, and amazement, encompassed with grief and overwhelmed with sorrow, pressed down with consternation and dejection of mind, tormented with anxiety and disquietude of spirit." He who "bore our griefs and carried our sorrows" was, before, a man well acquainted with trouble. But there now fell upon Him the burden of the atonement of the sins of the world. The word *amazed* is a strong term; it expresses the horror and shuddering of His Spirit, as the prospect of death came upon Him who was "the Life;" and as the weight of human sin oppressed Him who was Himself without sin. He had to bear the punishment due to all sin, and to every sin; "the Lord had laid on Him the iniquity of us all;" and His mind shrank from contact with sin, and from the displeasure of God against it, and from the presence of death. For now Satan, who had "departed from Him for a season," returned, when every man's hand was against Him, and when God had awaked the sword of divine justice against the "Man who was His fellow" (see xxvii. 5), for the sin which He bore in making atonement for the sinner.

8. *unto death.*—See xvi. 15. Not merely that it appeared to Him that He must die under the pressure of this sorrow; but He required the ministration of an angel messenger from heaven, to give Him physical strength to bear it. Christ would not now, any more than in the wilderness, use His miraculous power for His own deliverance. He would not shrink from anything which was coming upon Him. But, though the strength necessary was supplied to Him to bear more than man could physically endure, the very agony of this sorrow, and the mental strain of the whole week, did its work upon Him; it brought about His death more speedily than could have been expected from the severe suffering of crucifixion. In six hours death came, although the sufferings of the crucified have been known to be prolonged beyond the ninth day. (See xxxi. 4, 36, 37, 54.)

9. *watch with Me.*—For their own sake. (See note 4.) But doubtless He, as man, appreciated the value of human sympathy, and desired it. The context shows this. (See note 10.)

10. *withdrawn from them.*—Gk. "torn away," as if He could scarcely endure to leave them at this juncture. The expression shows

kneeled down, and fell on His face, and prayed, saying,
Abba, Father, all things are possible unto Thee; take
away this cup from Me: nevertheless not what I will, but
what Thou wilt. And there appeared an angel unto Him

His deep reluctance to quit them; and further, His desire for their
sympathy. They were not, therefore, close witnesses of His ineffable
agony; in the clear moonlight they must, until sleep overpowered
them, have seen something of His gestures of suffering. They saw Him
first kneel down (Luke xxii. 41), and then, as the bitter waves of agony
rolled over Him, He threw Himself prostrate; "He fell on his face on
the ground." (Matt. xxvi. 39; Mark xiv. 35.) A close attention to the
words here gives much insight into the act of agony.

11. *this cup.*—(See xxix. 21.) The agony of His Passion, and the
death which closed it; *this cup* must never be forgotten in our
reception of its memorial cup in the Lord's Supper. It has been
often noticed how cheerfully many martyrs have gone to their death of
torture for the sake of Christ; and how many have even aspired to the
death of martyrdom, rather than to the life of witness in our Lord's
service; whilst Christ Himself seems bowed to the earth, and prostrated
in spirit, in the contemplation of His sacrifice. The reason is evident:
our Lord went to His death in perfect calmness and fearlessness, and
in all things that manhood could endure, or heroism inspire, He was
perfectly self-sustained. But none but He could know what death and
sin were to One who was sinless, and was the Lord of Life. Christ's
Gospel does not set a value on the affecting to depreciate or despise
realities of such profound gravity. Christ's example teaches us not
to hide (though not to parade) natural feeling; and therefore, though
Christ did not hesitate to die, there being no relaxation of His willing
submission, He would have been pleased had it been within what was
possible to God's righteous and just will, that He should otherwise
accomplish the mission of redemption. In Heb. v. 7–9, this prayer
and agony of our Lord's is noticed. It is said that Christ "was heard
in that He feared" (*i.e.* "by reason of his reverential awe"); His prayer
was accepted, and His reverential submission to the Father's will was
now, as ever, well pleasing in His sight, "who was able to save Him
from death," by the interposition of legions of angels for His deliverance from His enemies; but who had decreed that, "though a Son, He
should learn obedience by the things which He suffered." The result is
that He became "the Author of eternal salvation to all them that obey
Him," as He obeyed God. There is not that tone of triumphant confidence, in this prayer of His agony, which breathes in the great prayer
of intercession; but its issue has been the victory and the glory of
which He there spoke.

12. *what thou wilt.*—Thus Christ puts into practice, for our example,
the submission which He taught us to profess in prayer: "Thy will be

from heaven, strengthening Him. And being in an agony He prayed more earnestly: and His sweat was as it were great drops of blood falling down to the ground.

done on earth, as it is in heaven." We see here the exercise of the two wills of Christ, the human and the Divine will. (See xvi. 19.) The last was identically one with the Father's will; the other, by prayer and resignation, brought more and more intimately into coincidence with the Divine will. The passage has been the text of much controversy, especially during the prevalence of the Monothelite heresy (which asserted that there was but one will in Christ), which is here absolutely refuted. "Here He manifests a double will; one indeed human, which is of the flesh; the other Divine. For our human nature, because of the weakness of the flesh, refuses the Passion; but His Divine will eagerly embraced it; for it was not possible that He should be holden of death."

13. *an angel.*—In this we see Christ "made a little lower than the angels," who thus ministered to Him, "for the suffering of death." Though much of Christ's prayer was probably heard by the disciples, and the earlier part, at least, of His agony witnessed by them in the clear moonlight of that hour, the words "He kneeled down;" and, presently, He "fell on His face;" and, again, "He prayed more earnestly;" and the remark that the sweat of agony gathered on His brow, and fell in "great drops of blood to the ground"—are all touches of an eye-witness, details on which it is unlikely our Lord would speak. (See note 10). But they may not have seen this angel, who "appeared *unto Him.*" They were now in the deep sleep of sorrow and exhaustion; either He told them of this visitant, or the Holy Spirit revealed it for record in the Gospel of St. Luke: eyes asleep to the duties of the world are not likely to be cognizant of angel visitants. The means of relief which men feel in answer to prayer in times of trial and danger, or perplexity, is doubtless here made clear: it comes from heaven by the ministration of the angels, who minister, by God's command, to those who are heirs of the salvation which Christ wrought for them; to man an invisible, though a real, source of strength.

14. *more earnestly.*—He had now received the strength which He needed, to bear up against the strain of sorrow and agony, without being overcome by it; and so He contended more earnestly against the powers of evil. Ancient liturgies take up this watchword "more earnestly" as a call to prayer; it occurs frequently during divine service in order to rouse the congregation to closer and more fervent devotion. We meet with the same call in our Liturgy, where it is rendered in the words "Let us pray."

15. *drops of blood.*—Not merely the cold sweat of agony fell in large drops, but these were tinged with blood. There are instances

And when He rose up from prayer, and was come to the disciples, He found them sleeping for sorrow, and said unto Peter, Simon, sleepest thou? couldest not thou watch one hour? Watch ye and pray, lest ye enter into temptation. The spirit truly *is* ready, but the flesh *is* weak.

known in medical records, though they are very rare, of the same extraordinary experience; and they occurred in instances of the extremity of agony and mental distress. The fact of intense perspiration, in the cold of night, at this season of the year, would alone bespeak very great agony of mind. Bishop Pearson here applies Ps. xxii. 14, and remarks, "The heart of our Saviour was as it were melted with fear and astonishment, and all the parts of His body at the same time influenced with anguish and agony; well might that melting produce a sweat, and that inflamed and rarified blood force a passage through the numerous pores."

16. *for sorrow.*—Christ was strengthened and supported by the exercise of prayer: He went to the disciples to receive their sympathy, but He found them sunk in that peculiar stupor which masters those who have sustained some severe mental shock. It is well known how those under sentence of death, even if criminals, have frequently been roused, to go to their place of doom, from slumbers as profound and peaceful as those of children. Great sorrow, especially in bereavement, is frequently followed by the same unconscious sleep. But the disciples should have nerved each other against this depression and drowsiness; they gave way against Christ's example and His parting caution. Not even the request, "Watch with Me," affected them sufficiently to keep them waking.

17. *unto Peter.*—He must have felt the personal force of the question, "couldest not *thou* watch," as he had so prominently asserted his devotion; and he must have seen the danger in which he stood, when he could not sustain even so inferior a trial.

18. *one hour.*—Not perhaps a definite expression of time. Peter could not withstand a natural oppression for so much as one hour, in his Lord's company; how then could he endure the assaults of the powers of evil, and die a martyr's death in His cause, when Christ was removed from him?

19. *the spirit*, etc.—We need scarcely suppose (though some writers so observe) that our Lord says, "I know your inclination is good, and I can make allowances for your natural infirmity." He speaks not so gently of the want of faith and devotion they now displayed, a failure which might cost many their heavenly crown. But He cautions them that, even when the will is in union with the will of God (which theirs was not yet perfectly), the infirmities of the body offered great vantage-ground to the adversary. As man (though in

He went away again the second time, and prayed, saying, O my Father, if this cup may not pass away from Me, except I drink it, Thy will be done.

And He came and found them asleep again: for their eyes were heavy, neither wist they what to answer Him.

And He left them, and went away again, and prayed the third time, saying the same words.

Then cometh He to His disciples, and saith unto them, Sleep on now, and take *your* rest: it is enough, the hour

nature sinless, which they were not), He Himself felt how needful was earnest prayer to God, and thorough vigilance; and He spoke out of the force of His own experience of the *force* of temptation, in which He gave them His example of endurance. They had been too presumptuous in spirit to be approved as " ready; " and it could minister little strength to them, and to others in like need, to have allowance expressed for weakness, against which, however natural, they ought to have contended earnestly. Denial and desertion of their Lord followed, only too naturally, from self-confidence, and from want of watchfulness and of prayer.

20. *the second time.*—S. Matthew carefully marks the threefold prayer and contest, so coincident with the previous threefold temptation of our Lord. The second time He prays in more decided acquiescence with the trial before Him. The former prayer had evidently gained its response, and He was strengthened by communion with God. The disciples (for He returned to seek their sympathy and some proof of their devotion) were again in deep sleep; and they could not answer Him when He reproached them: they at least offered the humility of silence.

21. *the same words.*—We do not offend God by the repetition of set forms of urgent supplication, as our Lord's example lies in the use of " the same words " in which we have been accustomed to pray. And we may evidently gather that success in prayer is to be attained by repeated supplication for grace, which we may miss by asking only once that our petitions may be granted. The argument is strong in favour of liturgical forms; and, as our Lord's words on this occasion bear so great an affinity to those of the Lord's Prayer, we have a justification, if not the actual reason, for the repetition of that prayer in the services of the Church.

22. *sleep on now.*—There is some difficulty in the abruptness of expression here; but the sense appears to be, " It is too late now to urge you to pray with Me, and to watch; the time for this is past: sleep, therefore, if sleep you must and can. But the hour is come at last: look up! your Master is betrayed; the betrayer and his associates are upon us. Rise up at once, let us meet them!" We see and feel

is come; behold, the Son of man is betrayed into the hands of sinners. Rise up, let us go; lo, he that betrayeth Me is at hand.

XXIX. *THE BETRAYAL, AND APPREHENSION OF CHRIST.*

S. Matt. xxvi. 47–56 ; S. Mark xiv. 43–52 ; S. Luke xxii. 47–53 ; S. John xviii. 3–12.

And immediately, while He yet spake, cometh Judas, one of the twelve, and with him a great multitude, and officers with lanterns and torches and weapons, from the chief priests, and the. Pharisees, and the scribes and elders.

the transition of impulse which our Lord's brief words (evidently His exact words) clearly express. He speaks in sorrow and reproof, certainly not in irony, as some have said, to those whom He had brought there to help Him with sympathy and prayer in His hour of need, and who had so soon and so easily failed Him in the awful spiritual contest from which He had just come forth. They had neglected that prayerfulness which was even more necessary in their case than in His; they were not nerved to meet their own trials. The contrast between what He had Himself experienced, and their forgetfulness and apparent indifference of Him, was painful. But as He is speaking, the traitor and his band come into sight, close at hand ; and He feels how different is the imperfect devotion, but real attachment, of these chosen ones from the malice of His enemies ; and instead of leaving them to themselves, and going forth alone, He will have them with Him still. He "loved them to the end."

1. *multitude.*—All together a large number : foremost was the traitor, the most guilty, and the most to be pitied of those who were ranged on the side of Christ's enemies. There was also the band of soldiers, with their officers, whom Pilate had sent evidently on the requisition of the Jewish rulers, and on their misrepresentation of Him as a political offender ; they left nothing undone to prejudice His cause. There were also the Jewish officers of the Temple watches, "captains of the Temple," and many of the rulers and elders, and also some of their servants. They were armed, some with swords, some with staves or clubs ; and many of them bore lights, lest Christ should be hidden in the obscurity of night, amongst the deep shade of the olive trees, though the full Paschal moon was now shining.

Jesus therefore, knowing all things that should come upon Him, went forth, and said unto them, Whom seek ye? They answered Him, Jesus of Nazareth. Jesus saith unto them, I am *He*. And Judas also, which betrayed Him, stood with them. As soon then as He had said unto them, I am *He*, they went backward, and

2. *knowing all things.*—The perfect knowledge of Christ of everything that was before Him, and His voluntary submission, are carefully kept before us by S. John throughout his whole narrative.

3. *went forth.*—He came forward from the band of His disciples into the full light, to meet His captors. It is plain that He might, without exercise of supernatural power, have easily escaped in the indistinctness of moonlight, and under cover of His disciples; whilst His enemies, a disorderly multitude, most of them conscious of a cowardly and evil purpose, were groping about with their lanterns, throwing the distance into obscurity.

4. *whom seek ye.*—Critics have noticed this question as addressed to John's disciples, and again to Mary Magdalene, in the garden after the resurrection, as recorded by S. John i. 38, xx. 15; and have pointed out how the manifestation of Christ depended upon the earnestness of those who answered. There might have been, therefore, the same grace shown to His enemies, had they desired it; but their reply shows at once fear and insolence. They dared not to say, " We seek Thee ! " but they gave that name by which Christ was designated; not in their case, as in that of Philip, to distinguish Him when yet unknown, but derisively, as when they nailed His title to the cross.

5. *Judas also.*—S. John caught sight of him, so lately a disciple, now standing amidst Christ's enemies; and records his presence, as he noticed it, with horror.

6. *backward*, etc.—See Ps. xxvii. 2, xxxv. 4; Isa. xxviii. 13. Judas was amongst them, and probably now first experienced the power of Christ as manifested against those who rise up against Him. There appears to have been that divinity visible, which from time to time overawed those who came in contact with Christ; His bold and calm gesture, as He advanced singly towards them, and addressed them, and declared Himself, struck them with confusion; and at the awful words, " I AM " (see the Greek), they " stumbled and fell." They had often before been unable to lay hands on Him ; but now, at the moment when He stood unarmed before His enemies, it was clear that they were powerless in His presence, at His will. Farrar explains that this was the effect of His dignity, and of their bad conscience; and compares it with the effect of the calmness of Marius on the slave being sent to execute him. But the parallel is not correct. The slave had no bad conscience; his errand was in obedience to orders: but even had he

fell to the ground. Then asked He them again, Whom
seek ye? And they said, Jesus of Nazareth. Jesus
answered, I have told you that I am *He:* if ye seek Me,
let these go their way: that the saying might be fulfilled
which He spake, Of them which Thou gavest Me have
I lost none.

And he that betrayed Him had given them a token,
saying, Whomsoever I shall kiss, that same is He: take

had this, he would scarcely have hesitated. Nothing is gained to
the cause of truth, by trying to explain away, by supposed natural
causes and forced parallels, what prophecy foreshadowed, and what the
Evangelist evidently intends to represent as miraculous, in accordance
with his careful plan of showing the willingness of Christ to die.

7. *I have told you.*—The words seem to convey Christ's permission
to His enemies to advance and fulfil their purpose; and that He had
no intention of resisting them.

8. *the saying.*—He would have the disciples free, against whom some
of the multitude were probably advancing. He was thus thoughtful
for them in the moment of peril; and one meaning of His words in
John xvii. 12, is thus unfolded. But His chief anxiety was not for
their bodily safety, but that He knew them as yet unable to stand in
the hour of temptation: the danger was a spiritual one; they might
apostatize, and so fall beyond recovery, were they, at this moment of
weakness, tempted above that they were able to bear. And hence, as
His prayer was over them, so was His anxiety directed to their condition rather than His own; He would have them temporarily withdrawn from this peril, that they should not, in their moment of fiery
trial, so fail that they might not be converted and strengthened. He
thus found " a way of escape " for them; and presently they were
" able to bear " that which now was " above that they were able." The
lesson is one of Christ's constant faithfulness and mercy in dealing with
those whose infirmities He well knows, and whom His protection and
mediation guard.

9. *a token.*—The original word means "a concerted token," pre-
arranged between themselves. In this Judas outraged the common
sign of a friendly and hospitable greeting—an act of great hypocrisy,
as well as of treachery. The "kiss of Judas" has become the world's
proverb for the perversion of any office of friendship, or of friendly
courtesy, to purposes of malice.

10. *take Him,* etc.—The particularity of these directions almost
suggests the view which some writers have taken of the treachery of
Judas; namely, that whilst concerting with them about the token he
should give, and their action upon it, he did not expect that our Lord
would deliver Himself into the hands of the rulers, but that He would

Him, and lead Him away safely. And forthwith he came to Jesus, and said, Hail, Master; and kissed Him.

either pass out of their midst, and so escape them, as He had done before (see Luke iv. 30; John vii. 30, 44, viii. 59, x. 39), or declare Himself with power as the Christ. He therefore emphasizes his direction to the soldiers (being perfectly aware of Christ's power to free Himself), in order that he may appear to have done his best on their side, whilst he hails our Lord as his Master, with professed allegiance on returning to Him. If so, he was doubly false; false to his Lord, and false to his confederates in crime, playing traitor to both sides. The impression, however, generally conveyed by the record of the Evangelists is that Judas was not false to the rulers, and that he was determined that Christ should not escape, except by a miracle. (See xxii. 8; xxiv. *d.* 5.)

11. *he came.*—Critics are at issue as to the moment of Judas's act; whether it preceded or followed Christ's declaration of Himself. It seems more in accordance with Christ's voluntary surrender of Himself throughout, to suppose that He anticipated, and so rendered useless, the vile treachery of Judas (wicked plots often do so issue as to display the futile subtlety of their contriver); but that Judas determined to carry out his part, thinking, perhaps, that he still had his reward to earn, and so advanced to give the token. Judas knew our Lord well enough to feel sure that He intended now to deliver Himself to His enemies, and that therefore there was nothing further to fear from His power. But Christ was probably unknown by person to the soldiers at least, whose orders were to seize the man pointed out by Judas, according to the preconcerted signal. They had no orders to seize one who declared Himself, as Christ had just done. A devoted adherent might have personated, in order to save, his Lord: instances of such devotion are on record; and the execution of military orders was proverbially exact and literal in the Roman army. Judas therefore, either spontaneously, or urged by the Jewish officers, advanced and gave the sign. Some of the early writers have thought that Christ prevented recognition of Himself at first (as He did after the resurrection), and that only when He said, "I am He," He allowed Himself to be recognized even by Judas. But it is scarcely necessary to suppose that He thus hid Himself, as He sufficiently, without this elaborate proof, showed that He voluntarily gave Himself up..

12. *Master . . . kissed Him.*—On the use of the term "Master" by Judas, see xxiv. *d.* 7. The word *kissed* here means a warm embrace; so, in his anxiety and restlessness, the traitor overdoes the part he has undertaken. It is noticeable that, in the direction he gives to the soldiers, he uses a different term, expressive only of customary salutation. The A. V. in using the term "kiss" in both instances, does not express this distinction.

And Jesus said unto him, Friend, wherefore art thou come? Judas, betrayest thou the Son of man with a kiss?

Then came they, and laid hands on Jesus, and took Him. When they that were about Him saw what would follow, they said unto Him, Lord, shall we smite with

13. *Friend.*—Gk. "comrade." (See sect. viii. 27.) Our Lord does not ask this question expecting an answer, but as questioning the conscience of Judas, and conveying the reflection, For what a base purpose art thou here! His second question is to the same point, but more stern; probably on seeing that there was no trace of penitence in the heart of Judas, and as shrinking from the embrace of such a villain. There is no anger in it; but it is so simple a charge of the baseness of his treachery, and so direct an intimation of our Lord's perfect knowledge of the whole transaction, that it must have gone to the heart of one in whom there remained any good principle to work upon. Had there been this, had Judas shown any softening of penitence, we cannot doubt that even he might have found mercy from One who addressed him so gently. As He "looked upon Peter," so He spoke to Judas: the result was different, for there was great difference of heart.

14. *come.*—Gk. "art thou present?" The word does not simply express arrival on the scene, but presence in the company round Christ, and in order to do this particular act. It was surely a strange company for a disciple of Christ to be found in, and a direful purpose to fulfil. Some, however, explain the first question as a direction to fulfil or to declare the purpose for which he had come.

15. *Son of man.*—This title was emphatically our Lord's designation as the Saviour, and it is used here with a special intention. It is as if He said, "Judas, destroyest thou the Saviour, to the peril of the world's salvation, so far as thou canst peril it, and to the hazard of thine own soul's life?"

16. *then came they.*—The soldiers now appear to have advanced to take Jesus according to their orders, and probably seized Him; but they did not bind Him until He had yielded Himself. It is evident that though He manifested not such power as drove them away, yet, throughout the whole scene, He preserved (and the Evangelists carefully note it) His freedom of will. He put forth such power as, to the eye of faith, sufficed to express His possession of this freedom; and so, whilst He continued to speak to His enemies, they could not but suspend action to hear Him. Twice He put forth miraculous power; once when the multitude fell back and prostrate before Him, and again when He healed the ear of Malchus. It is clear, therefore, that His Divine might remained with Him, and that it could now, as ever, be exerted at will.

17. *shall we smite.*—There is a contrast here between the courage

the sword?　Then Simon Peter having a sword drew
it, and smote the high priest's servant, and cut off his

which the disciples, two only of whom were armed, displayed in the
face of this armed band, and the moral cowardice they evinced in
leaving Him in the hands of His enemies, so soon as His cause seemed
to droop before them.　This is especially noticeable in the instance of
Peter : without a moment's hesitation, he singled out a man of note
amongst the adversaries of our Lord, and struck him.　But he could
not bear the question of a maid-servant, an hour or two later.　This
cannot be unnatural, though it certainly seems so ; for we find a very
general inclination on the part of those professing Christianity, in all
ages, to fight at all hazards in defence of their religion ; whereas it is
equally clear that they very generally fear a few words of depreciation
or ridicule on this supreme subject, from those whose opinions, and real
worth, should not weigh for one moment in the balance against Christ's
cause.

18. *the high priest's servant.*—(See i. 32.)　The two first Evangelists, A.V., give " *a* servant of the high priest; " we should read " the
servant."　SS. Luke and John coincide in this.　S. John alone,
writing after the death of Peter, gives his name, and that of the disciple who struck him.　(See i. 32 ; xxii. 9).　Malchus seems either to
have been the only servant of the high priest present on this occasion ;
or, more probably, a servant of note, from his official position.　As
Peter attacked him, we may conjecture that he was as prominent
amongst those who came to take Jesus, as the high priest amongst
those who plotted against Him.　Peter appears not to have waited to
hear how his Lord would answer the question, " Shall we smite with
the sword ? " but to have acted with characteristic impetuosity,
though with a generous disregard of personal danger.　The opinion of
several of the early writers, concerning a spiritual interpretation of the
loss of the ear of Malchus, and of the act of his healing, may be expressed in these words of S. Ambrose : " The servant of the prince of
this world receives a wound on the ear, for he has not heard the words
of wisdom.　But the Lord restores the hearing ; showing that even
they, if they would turn, might be saved, who inflicted the wounds in
our Lord's Passion."　Some of the ancient writers further suppose that
Christ then healed not only the ear, but, as was so generally the case
in His miracles, the soul also, of Malchus.　It does not appear that he
afterwards took any part against Christ or His disciples, or attempted
in any way to avenge his hurt ; though one of his kinsmen recognized
and challenged Peter as being a disciple, he being present when
Malchus was struck ; but even he only charges the discipleship,
making no mention of what Peter did when he saw him present with
Christ in the garden.　The supposition has great probability.　S.
Augustine thus writes : " The name Malchus signifies ' about to reign ; '

right ear. The servant's name was Malchus. And Jesus answered and said, Suffer ye thus far. And He healed him. Then said Jesus unto Peter, Put up thy sword into the sheath: for all they that take the sword shall perish with the sword: the cup which My Father

what then does the ear cut off for our Lord, and healed by our Lord, denote, but the abolition of the old, and the creating of a new hearing, in the newness of the Spirit, and not in the oldness of the letter? To whomsoever this is given, who can doubt that he will reign with Christ? But he was a servant too, with reference to that oldness which generated to bondage; the cure figures liberty." Bede, and others, to the same effect. "Since the man had been hurt in laying rude hands upon His Body, the healing may be received as a merciful token that even unworthy communicants are not shut out from His mercy, and the benefit of the mysteries which they have profaned, except they persist in unworthiness." (*Keble.*)

19. *suffer ye.*—Much question has been raised on this remark. There are two main interpretations: 1. That our Lord spoke to the disciples, and so said, "Enough of this force; allow events to take their ordained course." But this seems unlikely, as His rebuke to Peter would suffice as a check to the disciples generally. 2. That He thus addressed the guard, "Allow Me this freedom; unhand Me whilst I repair the wrong done by My follower;" or, perhaps better, "Allow this injury to pass unavenged; I will redress it." It is noticeable that our Lord's last miracle was performed on the person of a declared and manifest adversary.

20. *put up thy sword.*—"Thy sword most alien to My cause." (*Bengel.*) There is no contradiction here with the permission given above (see xxvii. 19), to use the sword in self-defence. Our Lord uses the significant words, "*take* the sword;" it may not be *assumed* therefore, under pretext of defending the faith, without the warrant of God. The want of conformity to this command has produced many direful wars; the excuse of defending the faith has served to cover schemes of aggressive ambition and of personal vengeance, which those who have cherished them have hesitated to name straightforwardly. Our Lord would guard the Christian world against these unholy wars; and, recalling the Divine law of Gen. ix. 5, 6, declares the general rule that they should issue in the destruction of those who promote them. Williams suggests that the direction may be a check on the action of that Church which, under the claim to supremacy derived from Peter, has been so ready to ally itself with temporal power, and take the sword in defence of what it considers the faith.

21. *the cup.*—This question echoes the petition of our Lord's prayer in His agony. It is instructive to us to notice how soon, and how

hath given Me, shall I not drink it? Thinkest thou that I cannot now pray to My Father, and He shall presently give Me more than twelve legions of angels? But how then shall the scriptures be fulfilled, that thus it must be?

Then Jesus said unto the chief priests and captains of the temple, Be ye come out, as against a thief, with

thoroughly, the earnest prayer to God for strength to meet a trial, changes into the expression of steadfast determination to undertake it. Our Lord, who said, "If it be possible, let this cup pass from Me," now, in the face of danger, sees the utter impossibility of shrinking from it, and the unfriendliness of those who suggest such a course. Had the disciples kept their vigil of prayer in the Garden of Gethsemane as He did, how different must have been their conduct now! It is well for us to mark the contrast; it is so often verified in most lives.

22. *twelve legions of angels.*—Our Lord spoke to a disciple who had heard voices from heaven, and who had been with Him on the Mount of the Transfiguration. One so favoured would believe in the power which He asserts to be now at His disposal, even if he could not coincide with His determination not to exert it. A legion of soldiers numbered about 6000 footmen; the legions of angels could, at our Lord's desire, be brought against the legions of Rome. He seems to mention *twelve* as if to show how He and His apostles, twelve unarmed men against such a multitude, need not, if He so willed it, stand alone against their enemies: "They that be with us are more than they that be with thee." (2 Kings vi. 16.) This seems a preferable view to that sometimes given, which makes light of the fidelity of the disciples. "I can have twelve legions of angels to oppose the Roman force; what is the use of disciples striking in My favour?" The accents in the passage are on "*now*" and "*twelve legions of angels.*". Even *now*, in My humiliation, I have but to exert this power which is at My will.

23. *a thief.*—Our Lord has addressed the guard courteously, and Peter with reproof. He now turns to the chief priests, and the Jewish officers of the Temple guard, who were present here: they seem from the original word in Luke xxii. 52, to have either now *come forward* from the background, where they waited the action of the soldiers whom they had sent, and of the traitor; or else, just now to have *arrived* on the scene of action. The Scripture must be fulfilled; but that does not free these from the guilt of malice and cowardice. They had not dared to take Him openly and fairly, either on a charge of sedition, or of heresy, or of blasphemy, whilst He sat amongst them day by day, teaching publicly in the Temple, the most thronged place of resort, where any false teacher should have been at once apprehended. But now they come in the darkness of night, as men ashamed of their

swords and staves? When I was daily with you teaching in the temple, ye stretched forth no hands against Me : but this is your hour, and the power of darkness. All this was done, that the scriptures of the prophets might be fulfilled.

Then the band and the captains and officers of the Jews took Jesus, and bound Him.

evil errand, and after an intrigue with one of His own disciples, to take Him with treachery; they invoke the aid of the civil power, as if against a felon. Their deed was unworthy of the nation they ruled, of their own high position, and of the religion they professed. It was written of Christ, that He should be "numbered with the transgressors;" but our Lord did not submit to be so vilified without protest. As Isaac Barrow says, "He did, it seems, as a man loathe to be prosecuted as a thief;" and He pointed out that if the sword was unnecessary on the part of His followers, so was it an outrage to take up arms on the part of those who brought their array of weapons against Him, who had done no wrong.

24. *daily.*—During the past week especially, and also whenever Christ was in Jerusalem, He constantly, daily, visited the Temple to teach the people. The rulers feared the people too much to take Him openly in their sight.

25. *your hour.*—The hour permitted to you by God, who, until Christ's hour came to be offered for the sins of the world, would not suffer your malice to prevail. This was emphatically an hour of the power of darkness, well typified by the dead of night, under cover of which they executed their treacherous purpose against Him who was "the light of the world."

26. *all this*, etc.—(See i. 14.) Our Lord Himself had just made the same reference to the Scriptures; it is noticeable how carefully the accordance of the events of this time with the declarations of Holy Scripture is pointed out. The types and prophecies of the Scriptures centre in the sacrifice of Christ; and the Evangelists, therefore, take especial pains to direct attention to the ancient Scriptures, that, in all that transpired, there was but the fulfilment of prophecy concerning Him. Nothing happened that was not foreknown; the malice of man effected nothing in wantonness : the "remainder of wrath did He restrain," who assigned the bounds within which "the heathen so furiously raged together," and "the rulers took counsel together against the Lord, and against His Christ." (Ps. ii. 1, 2; Acts iv. 27, 28.) Some attribute these words to Christ Himself, not the Evangelist; if so, they would be S. Matthew's variation of His words alluded to above.

27. *the band.*—The soldiers of the Roman guard, acting under the direction of the Jewish officers and rulers, and with their personal aid,

Then all the disciples forsook Him, and fled.

And there followed Him a certain young man, having a linen cloth cast about *his* naked *body;* and the young men laid hold of him : and he left the linen cloth, and fled from them naked.

now advance and execute the orders, as to which they appear to have suspended action whilst Christ continued to speak to those around Him. (See note 16.) Emphasis is evidently laid on the fact of their all combining to seize Christ. The eagerness of the Jews to aid in this gave opportunity to the disciples to effect their escape.

28. *fled.*—So fulfilling His words that they all should be offended that night because of Him, in the distress of His cause, and should be scattered like sheep bereft of their shepherd. (See xxvii. 4, 5.)

29. *young man.*—Bishop Jeremy Taylor thinks that this was S. John ; but he could not well have been any one of the disciples, because they had all fled; and although Peter and John, and perhaps others, so far recovered themselves as to appear again presently whilst Christ was on trial before the high priest, yet it is unlikely they would have so speedily returned. Besides, this young man "followed *Him,*" not the multitude; and that so evidently that the guard perceived it, and would have seized him as a partisan of Christ. There is a strong tradition that this was S. Mark, the writer of the Gospel which records this incident, who thus modestly mentions his own presence as an eye-witness. (See also xxiii. 6.) Bengel, comparing Matt. xi. 8, notices the fact of his wearing a *linen* cloth as a proof of wealth; and this might agree with the notion of Mark being the young man, as he possessed a competence. There is also a tradition that this was Lazarus, who had preserved his grave-clothes in memory of his resurrection, and was now wearing them, having ran out hastily on hearing of the apprehension of Christ. This tradition appears to rest on the probability that Lazarus, being wealthy, would be possessed of the *sindon* (linen garment), which is, of course, likely, and on the propinquity of his residence; but what happened so far from Bethany would scarcely be known there so speedily, and at night, especially as Christ and His captors had come from Jerusalem to the scene of action. It is pure supposition that Lazarus would preserve his shroud as a remembrance of the grave; it is at least as likely that he did not. Besides, the *sindon* is not mentioned of Lazarus, but only in this passage and in several places of Christ's sepulture. It was not merely a burial shroud, but a costly robe of linen, worn under other circumstances, given probably to Christ as being the most costly material, appropriate to the occasion.

XXX. *JUDICIAL PROCEEDINGS AGAINST CHRIST.*

S. Matt. xxvi. 57–75; S. Mark xiv. 53–72; S. Luke xxii. 54–62;
S. John xviii. 13–27.

(*a.*) *Christ before Annas.*

S. John xviii. 13, 14.

And they that had laid hold on Jesus led *Him* away
to Annas first; for he was father-in-law to Caiaphas,

1. *Annas.*—Annas was a man of great distinction amongst the
rulers. He had held the office of high priest himself, and is said to
have been now held by the Jews as high priest *de jure*, as he was
so by the order of the Divine law. His position and great experience
made it right and natural that his counsel concerning Jesus should
first be asked; and it must have been given to the effect that legal
measures should be adopted against Him. The Romans had deposed
Annas, and preferred his son-in-law, Caiaphas, who was now the
actual high priest, to that dignity. Annas, therefore, held a prominent position, and was personally an object of interest and sympathy
to the Jews. S. Luke couples his name with that of Caiaphas (Luke
iii. 2), as if they were exercising a conjoint authority. In Acts iv. 6
he is styled the high priest, and had possibly been reinstated in office.
His influence was considerable with the Romans, even in his degradation; for it is recorded that he was able to procure the office of high
priest for no less than five of his sons. Corn. à Lapide quotes the
statement of S. Augustine, that his house stood on the road which
Jesus must pass on His way to the palace of Caiaphas; and also says
that Judas directed the band there, as there he received the stipulated
thirty pieces of silver. From this we gather at least the ancient
opinion that Christ was not detained for examination before Annas.
(See xxx. *b.* 1.)

2. *Caiaphas.*—This man was utterly unworthy of his sacred rank.
The mention here of his unwitting prediction calls our attention to
the fact that our Lord's judge had predetermined His death. It was
an extraordinary prophecy (John xi. 47–53). At a council held at
Jerusalem by the rulers, after the great miracle of the raising of
Lazarus, they expressed fear lest the Romans should be stirred into
action against them, in consequence of the popular excitement in
Christ's favour. They did not speak honestly; they much more feared
the loss of their own personal influence. But that which they afterwards affected to fear through Christ, came upon them through their

which was the high priest that same year. Now Caiaphas was he which gave counsel to the Jews, that it was expedient that one man should die for the people.

(*b.*) *Christ before Caiaphas (preliminary).*

S. Matt. xxvi. 57 ; S. Mark xiv. 53 ; S. Luke xxii. 54 ; S. John xviii. 19–24.

Now Annas had sent Him bound unto Caiaphas the

own rejection of Him, and their support of false Christs. So also the counsel of Caiaphas, on the same occasion, that they had better put Christ to death, justly or unjustly, rather than run the risk of the danger they professed to fear, became prophetic. In the exercise of his high office it was permitted him to prophesy unwittingly, of the death of Christ in behalf of Israel and of the world, and for the union (as S. John interprets) of all mankind. The counsel thus given was entirely characteristic of the man ; it was utterly unscrupulous, in subversion of justice, hypocritical, and it displayed an adroit abuse of popular passion to justify a cold and murderous design.

3. *that same year.*—The Romans had brought this holy office into great contempt. By God's law it was held for life ; under the Roman governors it had become almost an annual appointment, to which, for bribe, or for political reasons, or sometimes on the plea of treason, they advanced new candidates at pleasure. Their excuse must be the utter worthlessness of those, who abused the highest and holiest office to promote their own personal interests, and to stir up party feeling and sedition ; who made the office contemptible to the heathen, for all religious associations, and a centre of danger and suspicion through the power it gave them of arousing popular excitement.

1. *had sent.*—These words may be rendered, " And Annas sent Him bound to Caiaphas," or as they are given in the A. V., where the marginal reference from John xviii. 13 to *v.* 24, and to Matt. xxvi. 57, together with the important marginal explanation at *v.* 13, sufficiently show the opinion of the translators. The verse has given rise to a very difficult controversy, the more perplexing because there is almost a balance of opinion on either side. It is contended, on the one hand, that the passage (John xviii. 19–23) contains the account of an examination of Christ before Annas, and that *v.* 24, in the natural order, and rendered as above, " And Annas sent Him," etc., closes the account. On the other side, it is asserted that there was no examination before Annas, but that Christ was at once sent forward to Caiaphas by direction of Annas. (See xix. *a.* 1.) It is impossible to enter into the

high priest. Then took they Him, and led *Him*, and

arguments of the case fully. In preferring the latter view, it may be explained, that the taking of Christ before Annas was a natural and courteous act towards one who was, by right of descent, the high priest. It was natural also, because Annas had used his influence to compass Christ's death, and was a prime agent in the plot of the rulers. It is scarcely necessary to suppose, with Farrar and others, that he, being the high priest's deputy, was the proper person to hold a preliminary examination. It was, however, overruled by God that in this way the real high priest should be asked to give his sentence for, or against the cause of Christ; and he gave it against Him. Thus were all the representatives of the Jewish people unanimous in His rejection. S. John alone notes the fact that Christ was taken before Annas; and it is remarkable that, whilst in his Gospel " Caiaphas is carefully styled the high priest," Annas is never so styled by him. So that his account of the hearing of Christ by the high priest, would really seem to be the same which the other Evangelists distinctly say was an examination before Caiaphas. Again, Peter's first denial is placed by S. John, as by the other Evangelists, in the high priest's palace. The difficulty caused by this is explained, by the advocates for the examination before Annas, by saying that Annas and Caiaphas occupied jointly the high priest's official palace, and therefore that Christ's being led away to Caiaphas, was merely His being led from one apartment to another. But there is no authority for this supposition; and it is not perhaps likely that the Romans would allow this probable source of rivalry, between the supporters of the real high priest and of their own nominee, even if those two high dignitaries, as near relations and friends, could reside together. It is certainly unlikely that Roman officers would take their prisoner for judgment before one whom they had officially deposed, though they might yield to the Jewish officers and rulers, so far as to allow of His being led before Annas for reference. We must notice S. John's explanatory statement that it was *because he was father-in-law to Caiaphas,* not because he had been (and was, in right of Divine law) high priest, that Christ was taken before Annas. Dean Milman says, " The house of Annas was the first place to which Jesus was led, either that the guard might receive further instructions, or perhaps as the place of the greatest security; whilst the Sanhedrim was hastily summoned to meet at that untimely hour, towards midnight, or soon after, at the house of Caiaphas." From Mark xiv. 53 we see that they must have been ready for the summons, and speedily gathered together. (See note 3.)

2. *bound.*—He was bound in the garden by His captors; but His being now sent away bound expresses the acquiescence of Annas in the proceedings against Him, and perhaps implies a more decided imposition of bonds than was possible in the hurry of capture. It has

brought Him unto the high priest's house : and with
him were assembled all the chief priests and the elders
and the scribes.

And Simon Peter followed Jesus afar off, even into
the palace of the high priest; and *so did* another
disciple : that disciple was known unto the high priest,

a further significance in the present instance, as in the preceding
verses (John xviii. 22, 23) it is stated that an officer of the high
priest struck Jesus, a wanton and cowardly insult to one who was
bound. Christ was again sent bound by the rulers to Pilate, after the
examination before the Sanhedrim, perhaps this time in chains. A
prisoner would naturally be secured; and therefore there seems to be
a marked particularity in this repeated mention of Christ being bound,
on these several occasions, by the officers and rulers of the Jews.

3. *high priest's house.*—The official residence of Caiaphas, where the
rulers were assembling, or where most of them already assembled. It
is clear that no very formal summons was required; they were all
ready beforehand for the mock trial, whose issue they had predetermined. Though Christ was not brought immediately before them,
but privately examined first before Caiaphas, whilst they were gathering, yet all was over before the legal hour for the opening of Pilate's
court. (See xxx. *d.* 1.) This preliminary examination must have
occupied almost an hour, that being the interval mentioned between
the first and third denial by Peter. The great council itself might not
sit by night; it was therefore necessary to make the formal assembly
as late as might be. Yet the impression on reading the Evangelist's
words is distinct, that before any ordinary notice could have been
circulated amongst the rulers, and at an hour most unseasonable and
unusual, they were all promptly gathered at the palace of Caiaphas.

4. *afar off.*—Peter's attachment to his Lord would not suffer him to
leave Him altogether; he kept at a safe distance, but watched his
opportunity, and got into the palace with the crowd who had taken
Jesus.

5. *another disciple.*—Generally supposed to be S. John himself.
How he obtained this influence in the high priest's household is not
known; but the position of Zebedee his father, though a fisherman,
was no insignificant one in his own country; and it may be that, as a
fisherman, S. John had become known to the household of the high
priest. Though it is only stated that " this disciple was *known* to the
high priest," yet his acquaintance was recognized in the household,
and his word sufficed for Peter's admission. The servants of the high
priest were known to S. John by name, and in their relationships; he
alone mentions the name of the servant whose ear Peter cut off, and
also that it was his kinsman who identified Peter. We notice here the

and went in with Jesus into the palace of the high priest. But Peter stood at the door without. Then went out that other disciple, which was known unto the high priest, and spake unto her that kept the door, and brought in Peter. And he went in, and sat with the servants, to see the end.

Peter's First Denial.

S. Matt. xxvi. 58–70; S. Mark xiv. 54, 66–68; S. Luke xxii. 54–57; S. John xviii. 15–18.

And the servants and officers stood there, who had made a fire of coals; for it was cold: and they warmed themselves: and Peter stood with them, and warmed himself.

And as Peter was beneath in the palace, there cometh

boldness of the disciple who "went in with Jesus into the palace of the high priest:" he had recovered much of his confidence and allegiance to his Master; and it is evident that he did not go there in any disguise—he was known as a disciple of Christ. Most probably he did not put himself forward, but kept apart within the hall; but yet the fact of *his* requesting admission for Peter, was the reason why the damsel who kept the door looked on him with suspicion, and watched him. (See note 8.) The act of kindness which now brought Peter within the range of temptation, was a mistaken one; but it was the act of one who was not the least ashamed of his position as a disciple of Christ. Elsley, with Grotius and Whitby, think that this was not S. John, as being a Galilæan, and therefore suspected. Grotius thinks he was the master of the house where our Lord kept the Passover; but the conjecture is less credible than the tradition in favour of S. John.

6. *a fire.*—This was the cold season in the Holy Land, when the night air is extremely keen; the guard had therefore lighted a fire in the open courtyard ("*hall*"), within the palace, and were gathered round it. Peter stood amongst them; perhaps hoping to escape notice by not keeping aloof from them, and perhaps to gather anything they might say concerning Christ. But here he stood, or sat, in comfort amongst his Lord's enemies, whilst Christ was in tribulation at their hands. He was now in the direct way of temptation.

7. *beneath.*—The audience-room in which Christ stood before the high priest opened out upon the courtyard, from which it was reached by a flight of steps, as is common in the East. Those around the fire were within view, and within hearing probably, of what went on

one of the maids of the high priest, the damsel that kept the door, and when she saw Peter warming himself, she looked earnestly upon him as he sat by the fire, and said, This man was also with Him: thou also wast with Jesus of Nazareth. But he denied before them all, saying, Woman, I know him not: I know not, neither understand I what thou sayest. And he went out into the porch; and the cock crew.

The high priest then asked Jesus of His disciples, and

within. The word translated "*palace*" really means a court open to the sky. Eastern houses are frequently built in a quadrangle round such a court. It was in this court that Peter was, near the fire kindled by the guard. (See **xxx.** *c.* 24.)

8. *he denied.*—The circumstances of the first denial, as gathered from the four narratives, appear to be these. The maid-servant, who admitted Peter at the request of a known adherent of Christ, suspects him of being a disciple; for this reason, or because she might have seen him with Christ in Jerusalem, as he was always prominently near Christ's person. In the exercise of her duty as porteress, rather than perhaps in any hostility against Christ (no *woman* is ever mentioned as His enemy), she watched the demeanour of the man she had admitted. He was not quite at ease, like a man actuated by dangerous impulses; he might do something which would bring her into trouble for admitting him; so she watched him warming himself, as he "sat *towards the light*" of the fire (for this is the exact force of the original). She is convinced he is a disciple of Christ, and presently remarks aloud before the guard, "This man was also with Him;" and then, addressing Peter directly, "Art not thou also" (*i.e.* as well as John) "one of this man's" (pointing to Christ) "disciples?" Shrinking from so many contemptuous and hostile faces, and ashamed at the word of the maid-servant, he turned to her and, in most express terms, denied Christ before them all. "Woman, I know Him not!" nay, more, "I know not, neither understand I what thou sayest." And then, to avoid further question, went out of the courtyard, from the firelight, into the darker porch. At that moment (though apparently, in his preoccupation and distress of mind, Peter did not notice it) a cock crew. Bede remarks that "Christ is denied not only by the man who says that He is not the Christ; but also by him who denies that himself is a Christian. Therefore Peter denied Christ Himself when he denied that he was His disciple."

9. *the high priest.*—Caiaphas. (See note 1.)

10. *disciples . . . doctrine.*—Not merely of the twelve Apostles: the question was rather, Who, of what rank, and in what numbers, were His adherents; and what was it that He taught them to expect in

of His doctrine. Jesus answered him, I spake openly
to the world; I ever taught in the synagogue, and in the
temple, whither the Jews always resort; and in secret
have I said nothing. Why askest thou Me? ask them
which heard Me, what I have said unto them: behold,
they know what I said.

Himself, and from His cause? What offers did He make them? The
object of the high priest was to form some pretext for a charge that,
throughout the land, from Galilee to Jerusalem, he had his partisans;
that, in fact, a secret society was in existence under Christ, hostile to
the Roman rule. The doctrine of a Messiah reigning on the throne of
David, could, of course, be represented as a claim subversive of the
sovereignty of Rome.

11. *I spake openly.*—We must distinguish the occasions on which
Christ replied to those who sat to judge Him, and on which He
refused to reply: they are very significant. He replied whenever
His silence might be misunderstood, or might lead to any false conclusions, as in this instance; and whenever there was any hope that
good might be received from Him, as in the first examination by
Pilate. (See **xxx. *d.* 11-19, 22.**) He was silent whenever merely
malicious questions were asked, or false witness adduced; to such He
would not condescend to reply, whether asked by the rulers, by Herod,
or by Pilate. There was no need to defend Himself in such cases,
and no good could arise from His doing so; no misconception could
result from His silence. His reply here, against the insinuation that
He was the head of a secret and dangerous confederation, was to the
effect that such a thing was simply impossible; for He had never
taught in secret, but always publicly, in the places of most public
resort, in the synagogue in every town, and in the Temple at Jerusalem; the whole nation had been His audience and His witnesses.

12. *always resort.*—Some MSS. have, "from all sides resort," and
some, "whither all the Jews resort."

13. *they know.*—To question Jesus Himself about any secret confederacy was futile: He appealed to the public voice of the thousands
of His audience, as one who ever taught in public. Jerusalem at this
time was full of such witnesses; multitudes were also there who had
been healed by Him, and they would of course be the most attached
and intelligent of His followers, and the most capable of speaking to
His doctrines. Christ had been before the nation three years, and His
leading claims were notorious, and generally understood. There was
an unconscious admission of neglect of duty on the part of Caiaphas
in asking such a question now; the Sanhedrim, as a religious tribunal,
ought long ago to have examined and decided concerning His claims.
Christ's reply, "Why dost thou question Me" on these points? must

And when He had thus spoken, one of the officers which stood by struck Jesus with the palm of his hand, saying, Answerest thou the high priest so? Jesus answered him, If I have spoken evil, bear witness of the evil: but if well, why smitest thou Me?

Good Friday.

(*c*). *Christ before the Sanhedrim.*

S. Matt. xxvi. 59–68; S. Mark xiv. 53–65; S. Luke xxii. 66–71.

And as soon as it was day, the elders of the people

have exposed to Caiaphas the obvious impropriety of such interrogation. There was the same fair assumption of right, in His case, that there was also in that of John the Baptist; those whose special duty it was to pronounce upon the claims and ministry of both, had, by their long silence, and indeed by their refusal to pronounce against them, sanctioned them. In our Lord's reply to Caiaphas, His use of the pronoun "*I*," and its position in the sentence in the Greek, is decidedly emphatic. Christ sees the intention to twist His words into a confession of sedition, and He says, "*I* spake to the world; these here present are witnesses; everything said by *Me* was perfectly public: *you* may choose to colour differently what I said plainly."

14. *struck Jesus.*—Christ had answered with perfect respect for the office of the evil judge before whom He stood. He had but refused to criminate Himself, and had appealed to the public as His witnesses, from this prejudiced and informal examination. The officer seeing the high priest baffled, and being no better disposed towards Christ than he, answered by a blow. It was a cowardly outrage upon a bound prisoner, and a disgrace to the presence and tribunal of a judge. Such an act was no reply at all to the just demand advanced by Christ, for the impartial examination of competent witnesses.

15. *Jesus answered.*—His words are gentle, and doubtless they were accompanied by some gracious gesture, in reply to the violence of this servant. Were our Lord's words evil, they were surely not rightly met by an insolent and angry blow. Let the high priest, instead of permitting such an outrage upon the forms of common justice, point out under what law He had offended; He was a prisoner, bound and in their power. But if, as was the truth, He had spoken well for His own defence, and fairly and respectfully in answer to the charge and suspicion urged against Him, how utterly inexcusable was such violence; how unworthy of the presence in which He stood! But "in His humiliation His judgment was taken away!"

and the chief priests and the scribes came together, and led Him into their council, saying, Art Thou the Christ?

1. *their council.*—The Sanhedrim, the great council of the Jews, was composed of seventy-one members, who were—the high priest; the chief priests, or heads of the twenty-four courses of the priesthood, as established by David, and restored after the Captivity; and the elders, being other elected members, men of repute for learning in the Scriptures, or venerable for position: these were usually men of advanced age. The council of seventy elders assembled in the wilderness under Moses, is said to have given the germ of the Sanhedrim; though that council does not appear to have been a permanent institution, or to have been continued beyond the time of the sojourn in the wilderness. Jewish history gives no account of its reconstitution; but this is generally supposed to have taken place after the Captivity, if not later than the Maccabæan period. From the New Testament we gather its importance, and venerable dignity, and its supremacy in all religious causes amongst the Jews. The power of life and death is said to have been taken away from the Sanhedrim, about three years before the Crucifixion, but on this point there is doubt; at any rate, the council did not scruple occasionally to take advantage of popular frenzy, or other means of evading the Roman law, as when they caused Stephen to be stoned. But when they put Christ to death, it was convenient to them to take advantage of the Roman power, partly through fear of popular odium, partly because they did not dare to exceed their limits of authority whilst the Roman governor was residing in Jerusalem during the feast. (See **xxx.** *d.* 7.) There is no parallel in the world's history to the position of the Jews, as the guardians of a religion delivered by God Himself; nor to the office of a tribunal, composed of the chief officials connected with the Divine service, and of the most eminent students in the Divine law—a tribunal whose especial province it was to deal with matters relating to religion. Nor does the history of the world afford any such instance of supreme injustice and perjury, as that of this court (being composed of such members, and intrusted with such an office), in consulting secretly to put Christ to death, in prejudging His cause, in preparing false witnesses for a mock trial, and, on their failure, extracting from His Divine claims a charge of blasphemy; and the shifting back the capital charge to one of treason against Cæsar. As they did this with their eyes open to the wrong, or, at least, wilfully closed against the right, we can only explain their conduct in the words of our Lord to them: " Ye are of your father the devil; and it is your own will to perform the works of your father: he was a murderer from the beginning, and he never kept in the truth."

2. *the Christ.*—John the Baptist had assigned this character to Jesus; He had also Himself claimed it, and had supported His claim

tell us. And He said unto them, If I tell you, ye will not believe: and if I also ask *you*, ye will not answer Me, nor let *Me* go.

And all the council sought false witness against Jesus to put Him to death; and found none. For many bare false witness against Him, but their witness agreed not

by appeal to prophecy, by His doctrine, and by His miracles. The council ought therefore, from the first, to have decided the point on which they now interrogated Him. But they appear rather to be thus putting the question, prearranged in their programme for Christ's condemnation; one which they knew He would not refuse to answer, and to which He would probably give an answer which they could easily call blasphemy. On the failure of this, as first proposed by them, they had recourse to their false witnesses, ready to hand even at that hour of their sitting, which was irregularly, if not illegally, early; when again these failed them, the high priest put the original question as an adjuration. (See note 10.)

3. *if I tell you*, etc.—Christ shows the council that He perfectly understood the nature, and the motive, of their question. It was not in order that His claims might be properly examined, and, when established, accepted as the commands of God; it was not in order to believe the truth, that they asked to know it. He knew also that, if in reply He questioned them, on points which His claims included, they would, as they had before done, refuse to answer. Nor would they release Him, whether His claims were now established, or, for want of their official decision, postponed. Christ was brought before them for one sole end, His condemnation, under official forms. He would, therefore, neither be heard in His defence, nor acquitted for want of evidence. "In His humiliation His judgment was taken away."

4. *ask you.*—*i.e.*, "interrogate you;" as He did with reference to the witness of John, or concerning David's ascription of Divinity to his son.

5. *false witness.*—Amongst all the thousands who had heard Him preach, and had received blessings from Him, or been healed by Him, there was not one brought forward to speak in His favour; for any true and fair witnesses must have established His innocence. False witnesses were therefore prepared, and produced; but their witness afforded no pretext for condemnation : they contradicted each other.

6. *agreed not.*—The law required that there should be two or three witnesses, and provided against false evidence (Deut. xvii. 6, xix. 15-19) in any case which might involve a sentence of death. Many now presented themselves to give evidence against Jesus; but the testimony of no two was found to coincide, sufficiently for the merest

together. At the last came two false witnesses, and
said, This *fellow* said, I am able to destroy the temple

show of justice. Who these witnesses could have been, we are at a
loss to conjecture; for Christ made few enemies amongst those to
whom He preached. They may have been adherents of the rulers,
who were indeed His foes, and probably men who had little personal
knowledge of Christ Himself.

7. *this fellow*.—The word "fellow" is not expressed in the original,
but is an excellent equivalent to the contemptuous use of the pronoun
which precedes it; the witnesses betray their animosity and partisan-
ship, in their disrespect to Christ. The saying now brought forward,
was uttered by Christ early in His ministry, two years or more before
this. It is likely, from the remark of the rulers to Pilate in Matt.
xxvii. 63, that they had some idea of Christ's meaning in this instance,
which is recorded in John ii. 19, and was addressed to themselves.
Wherever else our Lord speaks of His resurrection after three days, it
is to the disciples. We may perhaps gain some insight into this dis-
agreement of the two witnesses in this case, by referring to the
account in Mark xiv. 58, where they state that Christ said, "I will
destroy this temple made with hands; and, within three days, build
another, made without hands." Christ did not really say, either "*I
am able to destroy* the *temple of God*," or "*I will destroy* this temple;"
nor did He speak of rebuilding. His words referred not to what *He*,
but to what *they* should do: "Destroy (*ye*) this temple, and in three
days I will raise it up." Thus, they were to be the destroyers, He the
rebuilder. The figure of the nation, or of individuals, as a spiritual
temple, was a sufficiently familiar one in Scripture; only a perverse
ingenuity could twist it into an idle threat of violence, impossible by
one man, against the Temple of God's worship. Besides, if these
"blind guides" themselves decided that an oath sworn by the Temple
might be perjured (Matt. xxiii. 16), it could not be more sinful to have
said what Christ was alleged to have said. "Even a vain-glorious
boast of destroying the Temple could not be capital; especially being
attended with a promise of rebuilding it in three days." (*Whitby.*)
Dean Milman's view of this charge is thus strikingly expressed: "This
misapprehended speech struck on the most sensitive chord in the
high-strung religious temperament of the Jewish people. Their
national pride, their national existence, were identified with the inviola-
bility of the Temple. Their passionate and zealous fanaticism on this
point can scarcely be understood, but after the profound study of their
history. The fall of the Temple was like the bursting of the heart of
the nation. How deeply this speech sank into the popular mind may
be estimated from its being adduced as the most serious charge against
Jesus at His trial; and the bitterest scorn with which He was followed
to His crucifixion exhausted itself in a fierce and sarcastic allusion to
this supposed assertion of power." (See xxxi. 12.)

of God, and to build it in three days. But neither so
did their witness agree together. And the high priest
stood up in the midst, and asked Jesus, saying, Answerest
Thou nothing? what *is it which* these witness against
Thee? But He held His peace, and answered nothing.
And the high priest answered and said, I adjure Thee
by the living God, that Thou tell us whether Thou be

8. *stood up.*—Farrar notices, that the full import of the original here
implies his " starting up from the judgment seat, and striding into the
midst—with what a voice, and with what an attitude, we may well
imagine."   The high priest seems beside himself with vexation at
the failure of his special witnesses, and shows it in his menacing and
angry attitude.   He affects astonishment that Christ will not condescend to examine, and reply to those whose falsehood is best refuted
by allowing them to expose themselves. Had He replied to the high
priest's question, " What is it which these witness against Thee?"
He could only have said, in one word, "*Falsehood.*"   To the judge, so
evidently partial, so manifestly chagrined at the miscarriage of evidence
Christ declined to break that dignified denial of silence.

9. *held his peace.*—Gk. " remained, or continued silent."

10. *I adjure thee.*—The margin of the A. V. here gives a reference to
Lev. v. 1, which is quoted by many writers, as forming the rule for
this strange and solemn adjuration. The law referred to is that of a
witness put on solemn oath before God, to declare the whole truth so
far as he knows it.   The reference, therefore, is not a perfect parallel.
It would have been so had the high priest adjured the *witnesses.* It
was, however, enough to him, if he could make Christ give witness
against Himself in this way. But it is possible that a solemn adjuration in God's name, on the part of the presiding judge, may have been
grounded on this particular law; so perhaps Joshua adjured Achan.
The high priest thus invokes the living God, in whose Name he
adjures Christ to declare Himself in plain terms. He well knew that
Jesus would not give occasion for misconception or misrepresentation,
by declining this solemn challenge ; and he was prepared to brand His
answer as blasphemy.   He therefore, instead of putting Him on oath
as to the charge of sedition, or of doctrine, puts in this awful form the
question, which the council seems to have put to Christ less formally,
when first placed before them ; that being the point on which they had
determined to condemn Him, and which they had failed to establish
by false witness. The scene exhibits the height of audacity, profanity,
and malice. One who reverences the great name of the Almighty,
and the mission of His Divine Son, must shudder at the recital of this
crowning sin on the part of the rulers of the Jews.

the Christ, the Son of God. Jesus saith unto him, Thou hast said : nevertheless I say unto you, Hereafter ye shall see the Son of man sitting on the right hand of power, and coming in the clouds of heaven. Then said they all, Art Thou then the Son of God? And He said unto them, Ye say that I am.

11. *the Christ, the Son of God.*—This shows how well the rulers could have answered our Lord's question, as to how David's son, the Christ, could be David's Lord.

12. *thou hast said.*—Thou hast rightly stated what I am ; a Hebrew idiomatic equivalent for " I am."

13. *nevertheless.*—And further (though the declaration be as unwelcome as that of My Divinity), hereafter (*i.e.* hereupon, from this date) you shall see the fulfilment of Daniel's prophecy (ch. vii. 13, 14). The spiritual kingdom of the rejected Son of man shall be established with power for ever ; and beyond this, at the last day, your eyes shall see Jesus enthroned as Christ at God's right hand, in His second and glorious advent. The triumph of Christ's kingdom has dated from the dark hour of His Passion. Many of those His judges lived to see the rise of the Christian power, which they could not crush, and which, under the Apostles, spread wide over the earth. They lived to see the destruction of their Church and nation, by the very power for whose sake they professed to reject, and into whose hands they delivered, their Saviour to die, under circumstances which must have reminded the most thoughtless, who thus survived, of the words of Christ. And there remains yet before them all that certain vision of Christ's glory, and the final establishment of His cause at the last day ; for this, like all our Lord's words of prophecy at this season, has successive developments of fulfilment.

14. *they all.*—The whole council takes up, doubtless in excitement and with violence, the question of the high priest. To them collectively, as to him personally, our Lord spoke with unmistakable plainness. They had apparently caught our Lord's reference to Daniel, and therefore probably use the words " Son of God " in a more solemn sense, than Caiaphas had at first suggested in putting them ; not as meaning a distinguished Son of God, or prophet amongst men, but as the Divine Son of the " Ancient of Days," who, though styled by Daniel (after Christ's own designation of Himself upon earth) the " Son of man," they knew to be the Son of the Most High God. Our Lord's distinct reply to them is, therefore, equivalent to His saying, " In the fullest sense of the words, ye say truly ; I am indeed the Son of God." They evidently considered the two titles, " Son of man " and " Son of God," to indicate the promised Messiah.

Then the high priest rent his clothes, saying, He hath spoken blasphemy: what further need have we of witnesses? behold, now ye have heard His blasphemy. What think ye? And they all condemned Him to be guilty of death.

15. *rent his clothes.*—This was a highly significant act on the part of the high priest. The law (Lev. xxi. 10) forbad him to rend his clothes, though this may specially refer to occasions of mourning, and to official robes; yet it would certainly attach more than ordinary importance, to any occasion on which he acted contrary to the letter of the law. Caiaphas, in his pretended horror at what he was bold enough to call blasphemy, did this, which on other eventful occasions had been done with marked effect. The Bible margin furnishes two parallel instances, of the elders of the Jews, and the king rending their clothes, when the honour of God's name was blasphemed (2 Kings xviii. 37, xix. 1). The exigence of the time, and the spirit with which they were actuated, were in strong contrast with this act of the high priest. But it had also another significance, one which Caiaphas little intended; for we may see in it a parallel to the rending of the garments of the prophets Samuel and Ahijah (1 Sam. xv. 27, 28; 1 Kings xi. 30, 31), and note that the high priesthood was rent that day from the house of Aaron, and from the Church of Israel. It is dangerous for wicked men to challenge the coincidence of Scripture parallels, as they may do so in illustration of their own fall. This act of the high priest (as was no doubt intended) excited the whole council to frenzy; and no voice could have been heard, even if any were raised, in defence or explanation of Christ's declaration. The Jewish Rabbis had a rule, that whoever heard blasphemy against God's name should rend his clothes. The high priest, we see, did this; but the rest, though unanimous in condemning Christ to die, do not appear to have considered the charge of blasphemy a reality worth the rending of their garments.

16. *blasphemy.*—Never was such blasphemy spoken on earth as now, when these evil sons of men charge the Son of God with blasphemy, because He speaks of His Divine claims, and declares that the kingdom of God is amongst them. They reject it and Him, and lay against Him the most awful charge that can be brought against man; which presently, with ready facility, they abandon before the Roman governor, for one which he will consider of more importance, though equally false.

17. *witnesses.*—Caiaphas was relieved to find that it was no longer necessary to continue those humiliating transactions with false witnesses. To himself, and to his evil colleagues, his words mean, " We may now dispense with the attendance of prepared witnesses; Jesus has sufficiently entangled Himself in our net." We may imagine the triumph of the remark, and the gesture of the man.

And the men that held Jesus mocked Him, and smote
Him. And some began to spit in His face. And others,
when they had blindfolded Him, struck Him on the

18. *guilty of death.*—No words can do justice to this scene. The
contempt of justice; the parody of its forms; the arraignment of the
Son of God before the tribunal of man, of the "Judge of all the earth"
before the bar of His creatures ; the Saviour refused by the lost; God
blasphemed by man's impious charge of blasphemy; "the Lord our
righteousness" branded thus as the worst of sinners; the Lord of life
condemned to die;—these, and many other such contrasts, combine to
present these rulers of the Jews to us as terribly sublime in iniquity,
princes of darkness. They are associated with spiritual powers of evil
in our Lord's words : "This is *your hour,* and the power of darkness."

19. *the men,* etc.—The sentence of the Sanhedrim is spoken; and at
once the officers attached to it, and the guard, begin to offer violence
and insult to their prisoner. The hour is yet early for the completion
of legal forms, though the court has sat in defiance of custom, and has
passed its sentence, and has risen. (See note 2.) Whether the acts of
personal malice now perpetrated were done in open court, or in some
interval during which Christ is in the hands of these ruffians, whilst
His judges transacted certain formalities of their court connected with
their sentence, it is hard to say. But they were certainly done with
the approval, and probably commenced in the presence, of the rulers.
As Christ was conducted by themselves to Pilate, they could not altogether have left Him. The insolence of many is summed in that act
which is the height of personal insult in the eyes of Oriental nations ;
they *spat* upon Him, and in His face, which conveyed ceremonial
uncleanness among the Jews (Numb. xii. 14). Others combine ridicule of His claims as the Christ, and as a prophet, with personal injury ;
they blindfolded Him, and struck His face, and bade Him declare, in
the spirit of prophecy, the name of him that did this wrong. The
Evangelist gives these as representative of numberless profane and
cowardly insults; and points out the real blasphemy of those who
offered them to Jesus, though they had condemned Him of blasphemy
against God. Such scenes of personal wrong would disgrace any
court of justice, however criminal the condemned sufferer ; but in the
case of Christ, whether we consider what He really was, or even the
claims of His ministry upon the people for His countless acts of real
goodness done to them, they must stamp the Sanhedrim and its under-
lings with an indelible infamy.

20. *blindfolded.*—Greswell points out that, when blindfolded and
struck on the face, Christ must have been bareheaded ; and states, on
the authority of Philo, that "to remove the covering of the head from
an accused person when brought to trial, especially in cases of a more
aggravated description, was a practice amongst the Jews:" and con-

face with the palms of their hands, and asked Him, saying, Prophesy unto us, Thou Christ, Who is he that smote Thee? And many other things blasphemously spake they against Him.

Peter's second Denial.

S. Matt. xxvi. 71, 72; S. Mark xiv. 69, 70; S. Luke xxii. 58; S. John
xviii. 25.

And Peter stood and warmed himself. And after a while a maid saw him again, and began to say to them

siders it "a critical proof that Jesus was now, and had been before, formally put upon His trial." The scrupulosity of the rulers, in doing their deed of murder with all customary forms of justice, is characteristic of them; and it gives the fullest deliberation to their act of rejection of Christ.

21. *Peter stood.*—S. John (who had broken off his narrative to give the first denial in the order of its occurrence, and then resumed it) now returns to the sad story of Peter's fall, where he had left him standing amongst the guard, round the fire in the open court. He had, indeed, on being first challenged, stepped back into the porch from the full light of the fire; but now again he was either standing amongst them as at first, or on the outside of their circle.

22. *a maid.*—There is an apparent difficulty in the variety of accounts of this second denial of Peter. S. Mark says that "a maid saw him again;" the original implies *the same* maid as that spoken of before, or at least *the* maid on duty at the door. S. Matthew says "another maid saw him, when he was gone out into the porch;" S. Luke, that "another" (masc.) "saw him;" and S. John, that they charged him with being Christ's disciple. To these severally, although at the same moment, Peter spoke some word of denial. We may, perhaps, reconcile these accounts thus: After the first denial Peter had gone out into the porch; but presently the maid, who had seen him and pointed him out whilst within the light of the fire, noticed him again, and expressed her conviction that he was a disciple. This attracted the attention of another maid-servant, her companion, who was busy about the porch (S. Matthew notices that this maid was there, and S. Mark had said above that Peter had retired into the porch), and she also declared her conviction that Peter was with Jesus. Peter turned round to her also and repeated his denial. (The original here, Mark xiv. 70, implies reiterated denial.) And then, perhaps, several persons took up the charge, and challenged Peter (or it may be that St. John's word "*they*" includes only the two maids and

that stood by, This is *one* of them. And he denied it again. And when he was gone out into the porch,

the man); and he then passionately and earnestly declared, with an oath, that he knew nothing of Jesus. These several questions must have occurred almost simultaneously, and the reply to them forms one denial; voice after voice attacked Peter, and he, as S. Mark (Gk.) expresses it, "kept denying" the charge. Some writers have seen a conflict in these accounts, which almost impugns the veracity, quite the accuracy, of their witness. But really the reverse is the truth. All the Evangelists are most anxious to narrate this scene, so discreditable to one of the twelve; and this alone argues their fairness, and anxiety to set before the world the instance of accepted penitence which it affords. And these differences of account, so naturally reconciled, show great independence of testimony, and the freedom of the Evangelists from any desire to write in such a way as to support the account given by each other. S. John, writing so much later than the three first, merely thinks it necessary to show us that several persons attacked Peter, and that he repeated his denial, by saying that *"they"* charged him with being a disciple of Christ. We must guard against the notion that there were more than three occasions on which Peter denied Christ.

23. *to them.*—That is, to those officially present, the officers and guards who stood around. Such a remark to these persons, would be more likely to compromise Peter, than if they were spoken to unofficial hearers; and therefore he was the more moved to denial.

24. *the porch.*—The residence of the high priest was probably built in a quadrangular form, like many large Eastern houses, with an open court (translated *"palace"* in Matt. xxvi. 58, 69, and other places), which was generally open to the sky, but could be covered over with an awning. There were few windows, and those of small size, on the outside of the house; but inside, opening on to the court, were verandahs, into which the rooms looked; and in the upper story, often, latticed verandahs. In such a house in India, belonging to a wealthy native gentleman, I witnessed the recitation of a Sanscrit poem by a celebrated reader. The open court was gained by a passage through the house itself, which formed the ample recessed porch; within and about which were many servants on duty, and attendants on the guests. The audience, more than one hundred in number, were accommodated on seats placed opposite the reader, who occupied a small square stage ornamented with silver. The lower chambers of the house opened into the verandah surrounding this court; the upper rooms opened into an upper verandah, part of which was latticed; and there, and elsewhere, behind a curtained screen, were stationed the ladies of the family and neighbourhood, who evidently were greatly interested in the scene below. Over the whole, was a large awning to

another maid saw him, and said unto them that were
there, This *fellow* was also with Jesus of Nazareth.
And another saw him, and said, Thou art also one of
them. And Peter said, Man, I am not. They said
therefore unto him, Art not thou also *one* of His disciples?
And again he denied with an oath, I do not know
the man.

Peter's third Denial.

S. Matt. xxvi. 73–75 ; S. Mark xiv. 70–72 ; S. Luke xxii. 59–62 ;
S. John xviii. 26, 27.

And about the space of one hour after, another con-

keep off the sun, which, even at this time, the cold season, was
powerful. Such an awning, of a more permanent and strongly constructed form, or, more probably, the use of the upper verandah over
such a stage as I have mentioned, might afford explanation of Mark
ii. 4 ; Luke v. 19. The lower part of the house itself, its porch, courtyard, verandah, and wide chambers opening on to it, very much realized,
to my mind, the scene in the palace of the high priest.

25. *this fellow.*—See note 7.

26. *with an oath.*—Peter, distressed and frightened by the repeated
charges against him, and finding that a simple denial gained him no
credence, asseverates with an oath. So determined was he in his
denial of his Lord, and so ashamed of His falling cause.

27. *one hour after.*—During this time Christ had been before the
Sanhedrim, exposed to the malevolence of His judges, and insulted by
the perjury of the false witnesses, the blasphemy of the high priest,
and the mock sentence. The guard were probably now treating Him with
ignominy, and thus His cause seemed to have quite gone down before
His successful foes. There is, in this denial also, the same apparent
want of harmony, but real truthfulness, which we notice before
(note 22). SS. Matthew and Mark give the general voice against Peter,
and the detection of his provincial accent ; S. Luke tells us that one
man especially noticed this. Peter seems to have been off his guard ;
an hour had elapsed since his former denial of his Lord, and he had
not again been challenged. But now this man notices the peculiarity
of his northern accent, as he conversed with those about him, and
points it out as a suspicious circumstance ; to which, no doubt, some
abstraction or, perhaps, excitement of manner, or particularity of
interest in the trial, contributed. He is convinced that a Galilæan
would only have been present amongst them as a partisan of Jesus.
This causes another man (as S. John states) to look carefully at him

fidently affirmed, saying, Of a truth this *fellow* also was
with Him : for he is a Galilæan.　And Peter said, Man,
I know not what thou sayest.　One of the servants,
being *his* kinsman whose ear Peter cut off, saith, Did
I not see thee in the garden with Him?　And they that
stood by said again to Peter, Surely thou art one of
them ; for thy speech bewrayeth thee.　Then began he
to curse and to swear, *saying*, I know not this man of
whom ye speak.

And immediately, while he yet spake, the second time
the cock crew.　And the Lord turned, and looked upon

and he now recalls, though with some hesitation, the presence of
Peter in the garden at Gethsemane.　The confusion of the apprehension of Christ, and the distraction of moonlight and torchlight,
may have made the identification somewhat difficult, but yet this
man recognizes him as the disciple who injured his kinsman Malchus ;
and he could probably have said more than he did on the subject,
had he chosen. (See xxix. 18.)　Peter denies, anxiously and hotly.
Then the general voice of all, alleging the Galilæan accent, declares
that his very speech convicts him.　And then follows the emphatic
iteration of denial, with the additional aggravation of oath and imprecation.　Peter had thrice denied his Lord : and as the words of his
perjury died upon the ear, the cock gave forth his shrill proclamation
of the daybreak ; and this time Peter heard it, and terrible conviction
of his sin seized upon his mind, as the words of the Saviour smote
upon his memory.　He turned and met the Saviour's eye.　And now
the bonds of the Evil One were broken ; he hurried forth, not in remorse to die, but penitent.

28. *the second time.*—That this was the second time, is remarked
only by S. Mark.　All the Evangelists have mentioned this crowing
of the cock ; it had before escaped the especial notice of almost all who
were near, until the repetition of the crowing gave it significance.
Some of the early writers see the office of the preacher of repentance,
or even of the Holy Spirit, symbolized by the cock-crowing ; he is
thus calling the sinner to remembrance, and saying, "Awake to
righteousness, and sin not."

29. *the Lord turned.*—Jesus, too, had heard the crowing of the
cock ; and He turned round, and looked towards Peter, for whose
weakness and sin He was grieving.　If He turned round amongst
those who were buffeting Him, the sight must have been a sad one
for Peter.　If, as some have thought, He was now being led from the
council chamber, across the court, to the palace of the governor, His
sacred person bore the marks of vile treatment and ignominy.　In

Peter. And Peter remembered the word of the Lord, how He had said unto him, Before the cock crow twice, thou shalt deny Me thrice. And he went out, and when he thought thereon, he wept bitterly.

Christ is led away to Pilate.

S. Matt. xxvii. 1, 2; S. Mark xv. 1; S. Luke xxiii. 1; S. John xviii. 28.

And straightway in the morning the chief priests held

either case, His condition, and the glance of His eye, were eloquent of reproach to Peter's mind. But it is evident that there was no anger or contempt in Christ's glance towards him; Peter must have read in it the knowledge of all that had passed, during the two or three hours, since he had sworn extraordinary fidelity, and Christ had rebuked his presumption and foretold his fall. But there must have been also forgiveness in His look, for Peter instantly became penitent, and heart-broken; and thus his grievous fall became the stepping-stone to renewed strength, and a truer courage for the avowal of the faith of Christ hereafter. There could not be despair possible for one so penitent; for, at the same moment that he thought on Christ's words, he remembered also that He had said, " I have prayed for thee." Peter learnt his own weakness, and, at the same time, the strength of Christ.

30. *thought thereon.*—The original term has been the subject of much criticism: it may mean he " covered himself in his garment " in passionate sorrow, or he "flung himself" out of the hall, or into deep grief. The sense of the A. V. appears to be the best. Impetuosity is so much a characteristic of Peter, that the former renderings have many advocates; but Peter was now heart-stricken, his feeling was a deep and permanent one, and his thoughts were wrapped up in the contemplation of his great iniquity. He "thought thereon " before "he wept." Peter was a changed man, in the experiences of that hour; he had learnt to know himself, and also to know Christ; he was in the first agony of that conversion, whence should come the gift of power to strenghten the infirmity of his brethren.

31. *straightway.*—Without delay, as soon as practicable and legal, in the morning, a new and formal council is held to deliberate on their sentence of death, and specially to decide upon the mode of effecting it; probably with closed doors, and whilst Christ remains in the hands of their ruffianly band. They would very much prefer to escape having the popular odium of Christ's death upon themselves; this would be averted if the sentence was seen to be a Roman one, by the governor's order. And though they might secretly, or in some

a consultation with the elders and scribes and the whole
council against Jesus to put Him to death : and when
they had bound Him, the whole multitude of them arose,
and led Him away, and delivered Him to Pontius Pilate
the governor.

tumult, have murdered Jesus, they preferred to fall back on their
want of power to put any man to death. They were well aware that,
if Christ were put to death by Roman law, it would give to His cause
the aspect of sedition: He would seem to be one of the number of
false Christs. They had also certain scruples about defiling themselves
with blood at the festival; therefore, they determined finally to take
Him before the governor. But they knew that a Roman, who cared
nothing about questions concerning their law, would not enter into
a charge of blasphemy. The Romans had incorporated too many
national deities into their own Pantheon, and tolerated too many
contending sects, and rival schools of philosophy, to care much what
divinity any man honoured, or the contrary; or what religious sentiments he professed. Pilate would only take cognizance of political
or criminal charges arising out of religious questions; they decided,
therefore, to prefer a charge of conspiracy against the government.
This was not exactly a new charge, as some writers suppose, but
another aspect of the charge of blasphemy. The Jewish people would
never rise against Christ, if only accused of planning' insurrection
against Rome; they rejected Him because He would not do this.
The rulers, therefore, represented to the people that Christ had
blasphemed God, and the law, in His religious teaching, and therefore
was no Messiah: to the governor, that His peculiar religious
views were dangerous; that He had an organization throughout the
country, especially in the populous and disaffected districts of the
northern division; that He claimed royal honours, and therefore was
an enemy to Cæsar. Thus, to a group consisting of Jewish people
and Romans, such a group as might surround the governor's tribunal, they preferred the charge, Jesus "hath blasphemed God, and
the king."

32. *bound him.*—(See xxx. *b*. 2.) These may have been chains, or
stronger bonds than before, or with a cord round the neck; for with
the daylight, the chances increased of a popular rising in His favour,
and of rescue. It was well also to stamp Him as a dangerous malcon-
tent in the eyes of Pilate.

33. *the whole multitude.*—How carefully is expressed the united
action of the priesthood, Rabbis, teachers, and elders, the rulers
spiritual and temporal of the nation, against the person and claims of
Christ; the very word rendered *"delivered"* has in it a sense of *betrayal*.

34. *Pontius Pilate.*—The character of this man was notorious, as
an oppressive and unscrupulous ruler. He held the office of Procurator

Judas hangs himself.

S. Matt. xxvii. 3–10 [Acts i. 18, 19].

Then Judas, which had betrayed Him, when he saw

in Palestine, under the Prefect of Syria. His residence was at Cæsarea, it being unadvisable to have the Roman standards, and the religious observances which took place about the governor, introduced into the holy city. Pilate, soon after his entering upon his office, attempted to change this, and nearly caused an insurrection. He was now at Jerusalem on account of the festival, when there was always danger of some outburst of fanaticism. He was capable of violent and sanguinary acts (Luke xiii. 1). On one occasion he seized the Corban (the treasure in the Temple) for public works, being in want of money to construct an aqueduct; but he did not care to lend himself to the Jews in their oppression of Christ. (See App. XVI.; and xxx. *f.* 13.) He had no interest to serve by Christ's death, and his superstition inclined him not to take part against Him. But in the end he found himself unable to prevail against the Jews: the circumstances of his previous political life formed a strong chain upon his actions; he did not dare to break with the Jews altogether. It is often thus, that the fetters of past errors bind one who would fain do right. Pilate was weak and timid by nature; the Jews knew him well; and they had little doubt of being able to gain from his fears, and want of moral courage, what he was at first inclined to deny to them. He ruled in Judea about four years after the death of Christ; and then was ordered to Rome, to answer the complaints the Jews had made against him, and was deposed, having been in office about ten years. He is said by some to have died at Vienne on the Rhone, by his own hand; others say that he lived for some time in remorse and solitude, upon the mountain, near the Lake of Lucerne, which bears his name, and that he drowned himself at last, in the small and gloomy lake upon its summit. All accounts seem to coincide in the fact of his suicide; though possibly that was occasioned by the worldly trouble of his evil life, rather than by any remorse he felt for the death of Christ, though such a connection would be sure to suggest itself to early writers, who would justly infer the retributive providence of God's justice. Bishop Ellicott's sketch of his character is excellent: "Pilate was a thorough and complete type of the later Roman man of the world. Stern but not relentless; shrewd and world-worn, prompt and practical, haughty, just, and yet, as the early writers correctly perceived, self-seeking and cowardly; able to perceive what was right, but without moral strength to follow it out; the sixth Procurator of Judea stands forth a sad and terrible instance of a man whom the fear of endangered self-interest

that He was condemned, repented himself, and brought
again the thirty pieces of silver to the chief priests and

drove not only to act against the deliberate convictions of his heart
and his conscience, but further, to commit an act of the utmost
cruelty, even after those convictions had been deepened by warnings
and strengthened by presentiments." Through all time his name goes
down to posterity, even on the lips of little children, with the brand,
" He suffered under Pontius Pilate."

35. *when he saw,* etc.—Judas had not anticipated all that followed
from his act. This did not, however, at all excuse his sin; for who
ever does anticipate all the evil consequences which may result from
his particular crime? The theory which represents Judas as expecting
that Christ would deliver Himself, or declare Himself as the Messiah,
is pleasant and plausible; but it is not supported by any hint in
Scripture that Judas entertained such romantic, though mistaken
views. There is nothing said of him from which we can receive the
impression, that he was one of those who held (with his particular
attention to his own advantage) the general principle, that it is allowable to do evil that good may come. Few men are altogether bad;
f w but have some better motives mingled even with bad actions; and
Judas, so long a disciple, must have had such. But they do not better
his character; they must have been founded on a misconception of
Christ's mission, resulting from the imperfection of his own devotion.
If he intended less than the death of Christ, he was also guilty of
treachery towards the rulers. (See xxix. 10.) He truly does not appear
in a much more moral guise, if we suppose that he did not imagine
that Christ would be put to death, but would be forced to declare
Himself; he would thus betray Christ, deceive the rulers, and be
himself ready for any grander opportunities for making gain, on the
extension of Christ's influence. But, of all passions, avarice is perhaps
the most degrading; it is a master passion, and " the root of all evil; "
and it is quite in accordance with the ordinary characteristics of
avarice, that Judas was capable of selling his Lord, and sacrificing, or
hazarding, His cause for the most paltry gain. It is equally in accordance with the experience of crime, that he should feel remorse as soon
as he had attained success; that he would now give the world to undo
the mischief he had done. He awakened to a sense of the enormity of
his sin; his petty gains lost their attraction the moment his attention
was diverted from their pursuit; and the consequence was remorse,
not repentance—thorough self-reproach for his folly, not that contrition
which turns to God for forgiveness, and gains pardon. He could not
bear the misery of his own conscience; he could not lay it upon the
Saviour, for his misconception of Christ drove him from Him; and, in
the possession of Satan, he hurried to destroy himself. He is the type
of many a suicide.

elders, saying, I have sinned, in that I have betrayed the innocent blood. And they said, What *is that* to us? see thou *to that*. And he cast down the pieces of silver in the temple, and departed, and went and hanged himself.

36. *I have sinned.*—This seems (as Origen notices) like a momentary impulse of penitence; and Judas certainly tried to undo what he had done; not, however, for Christ's sake, but for his own. He went not to Christ for pardon—he had no faith in His mercy, and atonement—nor to Pilate to clear Him; but went to tell his fellow conspirators, the chief priests, what they were equally aware of, that Christ was innocent. Judas had not been a witness, and therefore his testimony, though important to the world as that of one who had been a constant companion of Christ, had no weight with reference to the proceedings which had been concluded in the Jewish courts. His bargain had been to betray Christ, and he now makes restitution of the blood-money; but neither he, nor the chief priests, had then spoken of His guilt. He now declares his sin, and his remorse, for which the rulers care less than nothing. Their heartless reply (and a more fiendlike and cruel repulse never drove sinner to despair) that Christ's innocence, and the traitor's remorse, were nothing to them, but simply his own concern, was the last blow that made the self-accusation of Judas insupportable to him. The contrast of his remorse with the penitence of Peter is most striking. Peter turned at once to Christ, and met His eye already looking for him; he knew his Master well enough to trust to His pardon. Judas turned away from Christ, and sought comfort from his associates in sin; and finding none, hurried despairingly to die. He is the only man concerning whom the place "prepared for the devil and his angels" is spoken as "his own place." We have seen the loving way in which Christ tried to turn this disciple from his crime. God had foretold the death of Christ; but it was not a necessary part of His plans that the soul of Judas must perish. We cannot at all doubt that, had Judas repented and turned to Christ for pardon, the mercy showed to others would not have been denied to him. Judas was not the one man to whom mercy was denied; the one to whom salvation was impossible; the only one for whom Christ did not die, a failure therefore in the perfection of His redemption. He threw away his own soul in the face of constant and repeated efforts for his salvation. (See xxix. 13.)

37. *innocent blood.*—The word "*blood*" is forcible here; it marks the consciousness of Judas that his crime has proved one against the life of Christ.

38. *in the temple.*—The original specifies that inner part of the Temple in which the priests (now probably engaged in preparation for

And the chief priests took the silver pieces, and said,
It is not lawful for to put them into the treasury, because
it is the price of blood. And they took counsel, and
bought with them the potter's field, to bury strangers in.

the Paschal services) officiated, and to which they alone had access;
into this, across the barrier, he threw the money. The fact of his
doing this seems to imply, that some of those with whom he had made
his iniquitous bargain, had already hurried back from the council
to their official duties in the temple, which were especially urgent on
this day. Dean Milman, however, thinks that the chamber *Gazith*,
the usual place of meeting of the council in the Temple, was the scene
of this transaction.

39. *hanged himself.*—In the Acts of the Apostles (i. 18), it is said
that "falling headlong, he burst asunder in the midst, and all his
bowels gushed out." The usual, and the simplest, explanation of this
is, that the rope broke with his weight, and that he fell down some
considerable distance, and was ruptured and torn open by the fall.
An old tradition says he was crushed and disembowelled by a waggon
which happened to be passing; it is quoted by Papias (Fragment III.),
who was a hearer of S. John, and also by other ancient writers. It
is valuable as affording, if not (as it probably does) the true explanation, yet a means of reconciling the difference between the accounts
in S. Matthew and the Acts; showing that, whilst one gives the cause
of death, and there leaves the subject, the other alludes to the horrible
after-consequences, which were notorious and memorable.

40. *not lawful.*—Not lawful to put the price of blood into the
treasury of God: but not unlawful to strike an infamous bargain for
the betrayal of Christ's life; to hold a mock trial, with all its shameful
incidents, supported by false witnesses; to condemn falsely to death;
and then, with their hands full of all this iniquity and blood-guiltiness,
to hurry back to their duties, sacrificial and ministerial, before God.
Our Lord's words are true concerning them: "Ye strain at a gnat
and swallow a camel."

41. *strangers.*—It is noticeable how scrupulous they are about so
small a sum; it is worth a consultation, and so they "take counsel,"
and the result affords a characteristic touch of prejudice and spite.
This money is blood-money, and therefore must be put to no good
purpose. The season reminds them of the many foreigners in Jerusalem,
who have come up to witness the feast of the Jews; some of these
die at the holy city, where their very presence is a defilement, and
their interment in Jewish ground an offence. But a cemetery, appro-
priately accursed by its circumstances of purchase, will be most
admirably suited to the necessities of Gentile burial; and whereas
the Lord would give His life a ransom for His people, they will only
allow its price to purchase a burial-place for dead strangers, after that

Wherefore that field was called, The field of blood, unto this day.   Then was fulfilled that which was spoken by Jeremy the prophet, saying, **And they took the thirty**

place has been defiled by the suicide of His disciple; hence "the field of blood" is set apart as the burial-place of aliens.   They did not notice that they unwittingly realized the words of the prophet, in which the references to the casting down of the money in God's House, and to the potter, are significant.   In the Acts, it is said that "he purchased a field with the reward of iniquity."   S. Peter (who is speaking oratorically, but the truth of whose view cancels the misconception of the subtle rulers) probably means, that all Judas acquired by his iniquity was the field of evil omen, which was bought with what really proved to be *his* blood-money; it remained associated with his crime and memory, as "the field of blood."   Greswell, however, considers that there were two distinct fields, and that he had actually purchased the one before his death; but his immediate remorse, and its quick action, seem conclusive against this supposition. The way in which S. Peter speaks, evidently connects this field with the fate of Judas; it might be that he killed himself upon that very ground, or that he fell from a height upon it, and very probably was himself buried there.   The ground itself, already worked out as a potter's field, would be useless for most purposes, and therefore easily purchased; whilst the association of it with Judas's death, may have suggested its purchase with his money.   This would reconcile the apparent difficulty, that the Evangelists represent the field as branded with its name of ill repute, from its being purchased with the money of Judas; whilst in the Acts it is said to have already gained that name, from its being the scene of his horrible end.   Corn. à Lapide, quoting several authors, gives an interesting sequel to this subject. He says that a large quantity, many shiploads, of the earth of this "*field*" was brought to Rome, by order of the Empress Helena, and placed near the Vatican mount, and formed into a cemetery for the burial of strangers.   The earth was said to have the property of very speedily reducing those who were buried there to dust.   It was known as the "Campus Sanctus."   It would be strange if Rome, whose passion for relics is boundless, should thus possess the dust of the traitor.   Forster says, "The Aceldama," or "field of blood" (*still* so called since the Evangelists wrote), continues to be a public burying-place; and a large chamber, excavated in the rock, remains the common charnel-house of the poor and unhonoured dead of Jerusalem.   If the former account is true, of course the site remains, and may still be so used.

42. *Jeremy.*—The words are not found in Jeremiah, but in Zechariah (xi. 12, 13).   The mistake is of little consequence, but it has exercised the ingenuity of many writers, in explanation.   The two most worthy

pieces of silver, the price of Him that was valued, whom they of the children of Israel did value; and gave them for the potter's field, as the Lord appointed me.

(*d.*) *Christ before Pilate.*

S. Matt. xxvii. 11–14; S. Mark xv. 2–5; S. Luke xxiii. 2–7; S. John xviii. 28–38.

Then led they Jesus from Caiaphas, unto the hall of judgment: and it was early; and they themselves

of remark are the suppositions, that Zechariah incorporated words originally uttered by Jeremiah, which is quite possible, and has a Jewish tradition in its favour; or that the quotation is from memory (as the inaccurate way in which it is quoted suggests), and given under the general head "Jeremiah," who, it is said, was considered by the Jews as the first of the prophets. The supposition of error of early copyists is too convenient to be worth much notice, except when supported by the variation in the *oldest* MSS.; it is, however, a coincidence, that the ancient Syriac version gives "by the prophet," without specifying a name. But Bishop Hall remarks, "The testimony is plainly cited out of Zechariah, and yet is in ancient copies alleged under the name of Jeremiah; which doubtless happened by the writer's mistaking of the abbreviations '*Zriou*' for '*Iriou*,' as I have seen it in a very old manuscript."

43. *valued.*—Set their contemptuous price on.

1. *it was early.*—The Roman magistrates sat from about nine o'clock, in the Prætorium, or "hall of judgment," and it is not likely that Pilate would sit much earlier. But he had doubtless been warned of the capture of Christ, on the preceding night; his wife's dream may have been the result, so far as it came of natural causes, of the news brought to her during the hours of sleeping. The Roman guard was probably told off with his permission; he was not therefore surprised, but ready to receive the rulers. He was also desirous to see Christ, of whose wonderful deeds he must have been fully informed, as he had ruled in Judea during the whole of His public ministry. For these reasons he may have shown himself at the hall of judgment when "it was early," to meet this venerable but malevolent assemblage. The present proceedings, however, do not seem to have been quite formal and judicial. Pilate's first examination of Christ has somewhat the aspect of a private inquiry, like that of Caiaphas before the hour when the Sanhedrim assembled. S. John, who notices the early arrival

went not into the judgment hall, lest they should be defiled, but that they might eat the passover.

Pilate then went out unto them, and said, What accusation bring ye against this man? They answered

of the rulers at Pilate's residence, seems to have been a personal witness of the proceedings against Christ, from first to last. These preliminary matters must have taken up some time; and probably the usual hour had arrived, when Pilate formally entered upon the trial of Christ, and listened to evidence against Him. By this time also the officers and scribes of the court would have assembled, and the people gathered round the governor's palace. Pilate's official residence, during his presence at Jerusalem, was in the splendid palace built by King Herod.

2. *the passover.*—This sentence has given rise to very much comment. (See xxiii. 1.) It gives great support to the argument, that the Passover had not as yet been partaken of by the majority of the nation, and that, therefore, Christ and His Apostles anticipated the usual day, in partaking of the Last Supper. There is, however, a further question suggested as to the meaning of the word "*Passover*" here. It could scarcely have been the Paschal lamb itself, because they would only have been unclean until the evening, through entering a Gentile dwelling. They might have been unclean at the time of slaying the lamb, but that might have been undertaken by another member of the household. It would appear, therefore, to have been the mid-day meal of rejoicing; that of the peace offerings, or "Chagigah." Elseley instances the opinion of Le Clerc, Bochart, and others, that the Jews had already eaten the Passover, on the same day as Christ, and that these were victims offered during the Paschal week; but the conjecture is too general to be very valuable in reconciliation of the principal difficulty.

3. *went out.*—Pilate was not a man to bear calmly this submission of himself to the religious prejudices of a people who held it defilement to enter his house, and yet who required him to perpetrate a judicial murder in their stead. (See also Acts xxv. 15.) Both as a Roman, and as a governor, he must have felt the humiliation; the more so as the Jewish rulers behaved with considerable insolence in his presence. The whole scene throughout gives instances of this feeling. Bishop Ellicott notices that Pilate, being a Procurator only, had no Quæstor to conduct the examination; he therefore did it in person. Tittmann, however, says that he went out to pronounce sentence; evidence being heard within the Prætorium, sentence pronounced outside. (See App. XVI.)

4. *what accusation.*—They evidently expect of Pilate that he will at once ratify their sentence, and put Christ to death, without further inquiry. This was contrary to the law of Rome, which we find enunciated more distinctly in Acts xxv. 16. Pilate's reply is to the

and said unto him, If He were not a malefactor, we would
not have delivered Him up unto thee. Then said Pilate
unto them, Take ye Him, and judge Him according to
your law. The Jews therefore said unto him, It is not
lawful for us to put any man to death : that the saying
of Jesus might be fulfilled, which He spake, signifying
what death He should die.

effect that he is prepared to try the prisoner, against whom the leaders
of the Jewish nation appear in accusation. He will not, however,
take their word and position, as a sufficient reason for a sentence without
a hearing, nor be the executiouer of their sentence. (See App. XVI.)

5. *if he*, etc.—They answer with considerable temper and haughti-
ness. What did Pilate suppose induced them to appear thus before
him, the chief magistrate with power over life? What else than a
malefactor could *their* prisoner be? They are consistent throughout
in prejudging the cause of Christ, and desiring judgment against Him
on the part of all others.

6. *take ye Him*.—If you have nothing else against Him, you had
better judge (Gk. "condemn") Him by your own laws ; your demand
is not within the scope of Roman justice. (App. XVI.)

7. *what death*.—(See Matt. xx. 18, 19.) The right of life and death
not being theirs (see **xxx.** *c*. 1), their saying this shows that they had
brought Jesus there for capital sentence. The Gentile world must
take part in the death of Christ ; the guilt of the world is as universally
represented, as was Christ's redemption universal ; Jew and Gentile
unite in presenting the offering of His blood before heaven. The
reservation of capital sentences to the Roman emperor, and the nature
of the Roman punishment of death, combine to verify the word of
prophecy. But there is here an apparent difficulty. The Jews did not
hesitate to stone Stephen, and to attempt the lives of S. Paul and
of others ; were these infractions of the law, which they dared on the
strength of a popular outbreak? In the case of Christ, they charged
Him with treason against Rome, in order to force the Roman power
to undertake the responsibility of His death. Dean Milman thinks
it "difficult to define the extent of the power which was in the hands
of the Sanhedrim at this time. Herod had exercised the supreme
power, but it is not clear that the Romans had deprived them of what
remained to them. If the power of life and death in civil cases, was
taken from them, it is probable that that of executing capital sentences
in religious cases may have remained to them ; though, from the great
unwillingness to exercise it on the part of the Pharisees generally, it
may have fallen into disuse." Some of the ancient writers incline to
this view, and interpret "it is not lawful for us to put any man to
death on the day of the Passover." He suggests also "that they did

And they began to accuse Him, saying, We found this *fellow* perverting the nation, and forbidding to give tribute to Cæsar, saying that He Himself is Christ a king.

Then Pilate entered into the judgment hall again, and called Jesus: and Jesus stood before the governor: and

not know whether the Romans would permit them to execute capital punishment, especially on a criminal accused of rebellion." It seemed best to disavow a power, which the multitude, or the Roman governor, might question, and which, exercised on the feast day, might bring odium on themselves. It was preferable to place this responsibility, if possible, upon Pilate. Dean Burgon thinks the advice of the old man Annas was, that this odium of Christ's death should be put, if possible, on the Romans.

8. *we found.*—The word here has a judicial air: they would have Pilate suppose that they had detected, and found Christ guilty of this treason, a matter which it was scarcely within their province to take cognizance of. They could not, however, have come before Pilate with the accusation, "We have found Him blaspheming." The charges they allege are singularly wanting in truth; whatever is literally true in them, is so by distortion of the real truth. Christ might be said, from their point of view, to be perverting the nation, inasmuch as He taught truth, in opposition to the glosses taught by themselves; by which He turned all true hearts from them to Himself. There was no truth at all in the second item of accusation; as His decision, in opposition to their opinion, was that it was not only necessary, but right, to give tribute to Cæsar. (See ix. 18.) He did say that He was Christ a King; but not, they knew, with any reference to temporal royalty, or the subversion of existing sovereignty in the land. The charge would not admit of proof, but the rulers intended to offer none; they expected that their influence would overrule all else, and in the end it did so. It is singular that their delivery of Christ on a charge of refusal of tribute, suggests Him to be the very Messiah they professed to want, namely, one who should throw off the Roman yoke.

9. *called Jesus.*—Pilate left the rulers standing outside the hall, into which they were too scrupulous to enter. He then summoned Jesus before him, and examined Him privately. The fact that Jewish rulers were bringing up a prisoner, on a charge of refusal of tribute to Rome, was in itself suspicious, as Pilate knew the temper of the people he had for some years governed; they were always ripe for insurrection upon this question. It was, in fact, a general maxim of theirs, that God's people should not pay tribute to the Gentiles; so far Christ could have said no more than many another, and their delivering Him up for such a reason was singular. Pilate, too, knew a good deal of Christ's

the governor asked Him, saying, Art Thou the King of the Jews ? Jesus answered him, Sayest thou this thing of thyself, or did others tell it thee of Me ? Pilate answered, Am I a Jew ? Thine own nation and the chief priests have delivered Thee unto me : what hast Thou done ? Jesus answered, My kingdom is not of

character and pretensions, and His influence with the people ; but still the charge was one which must be carefully examined.

10. *art Thou,* etc.—He asked with mingled pity, scorn, and surprise, "Art *Thou,* so friendless and in such extremity, the King of the Jews ? "

11. *sayest thou this.*—The rulers had clamorously urged this charge, which of course both Christ and Pilate had heard ; and it was therefore on their assertion, that Pilate asked the question. Our Lord seems to address some inward conviction and opening in Pilate's heart, to which He might unfold the truth. The whole of Pilate's conduct is consistent with there being some secret lurking desire to know what is right, struggling with his consciousness of wrong-doing. His better nature seems to rise against the evil and scepticism habitual to him, which forced it down. Our Lord therefore asks, "Sayest thou this of thine own heart's desire to know the truth, or merely as echoing the voice of the rulers, who raised the charge against My claim, which they have refused to acknowledge ? " The answers of Christ to Pilate's questions, as contrasted with His silence or stern bearing towards the rulers, are very striking ; and show to what difference of feeling on the part of His interrogators He responds. (See note 22, and xxx. *b.* 11.)

12. *a Jew.*—Pilate's Roman pride rises on this reply ; what had he to do with *Jewish* hopes and aspirations ? His words are not, however, the calm and stoical reply of one to whom the matter was supremely indifferent ; the voice of Christ has probed his innermost feelings, and unhappily his pride is instantly in arms against the master touch which he recognizes. Pilate turns off from the inner meaning, and falls back upon the terms of accusation by the Jews. Christ, in demanding "Sayest thou this of thyself ? " had asked the question as to whether, as the governor, Pilate had any charge against Him ; and Pilate's reply is, in fact, an admission that there was no charge on the part of those entrusted with the peace and administration of the country, but merely this accusation (its value was notorious) on the part of the Jews. So men fence off a question which disagreeably touches their conscience, by answering to its literal terms.

13. *done.*—Pilate will have nothing to say to the intricacies of Jews' distinctions. He despises the subtleties of their theological schools, and the presumptuous assertion of sanctity, which forbids their entry into his house. He does not, therefore, ask to know their definition of a

this world : if My kingdom were of this world, then
would My servants fight, that I should not be delivered
to the Jews : but now is My kingdom not from hence.
Pilate therefore said unto Him, Art Thou a king then ?
Jesus answered, Thou sayest that I am a king.   To this
end was I born, and for this cause came I into the world,
that I should bear witness unto the truth.   Every one

king ; nor does he care to give his own. With the practical sternness
of one (and that a Roman) sitting in judgment, he demands what
Christ has *done*, to justify this accusation : if it is true, He must have
committed Himself in action ; and it is this he demands to know.

14. *My kingdom.*—Christ waives the second, and replies to the
former question. His words show, more distinctly than those of the
governor, that there was something working in Pilate's mind, to which
Christ desired to appeal, with the view of leading him on to a higher
conviction, and to salvation. It was obvious that Christ did not aim
at establishing any earthly dynasty. Though a royalty *in* the world,
and supreme and universal within it, His kingdom was not *of* this
world. It must absorb into itself all the kingdoms of the world, and the
glory of them, in virtue of its Divine origin ; but, being a purely
spiritual kingdom, it is no rival of any earthly sovereignty. Pilate
must have known, had there been any armed confederacy of which He
was the Head ; and if there had been such, Christ's servants would, of
course, have fought in His favour against His enemies. The very fact
of no such defence having been made, was sufficient to disprove the
political charge.

15. *now.*—*i.e.* from this very circumstance, it is clear that Christ
advanced no claims to worldly sovereignty.

16. *art Thou.*—(See note 10.) Thou, a prisoner and in bonds, with
every influential voice of Thine own people against Thee—art *Thou* a
king ?

17. *thou sayest.*—There breathes the majesty of Christ's Divinity, in
the words of His reply. He, who had prior and eternal self-existence,
was born amongst men, incarnate in humanity ; and He " came into
this world " (there is assertion of spontaneous will and action in this
phrase) as a King, to erect the throne of a universal kingdom. All
mankind err from the truth ; and therefore Christ was born to establish the kingdom of truth. Christ, as the one authoritative witness to
absolute and infallible truth, must be supreme and sovereign within
that kingdom—the King, therefore. This, and the words which follow,
contain the "*good confession*" alluded to in 1 Tim. vi. 13.

18. *bear witness.*—Not as an ordinary teacher ; but as God's own
Son, personally present to bear witness to God's truth, with authority.
He was not here on any mission merely to teach a religion, different
from other religions.

that is of the truth heareth My voice. Pilate saith unto Him, What is truth?

19. *every one.*—These are the subjects of the kingdom; every one whose heart inclines to the truth must recognize the royalty of Christ. (See also John viii. 47; iii. 33.)   This was Pilate's opportunity; Christ's words gave to him an opening, which his own mind partly discerned; and well would it have been had he seized it !   The truth would have made him free from all those fetters which sin, and his unworthy fear of the people he governed, fastened upon him. Christ never thus spoke to men in whose hearts there was no responsive chord, which might answer rightly to His words. He never spoke without aim. Certainly He discerned in Pilate that honesty and hopefulness which, long stifled, might haply be roused into life. But, alas ! he did not offer himself as a seeker of truth, a subject of the kingdom of Christ. His habitual scepticism returned, and he broke off the subject, as he had done before. (See note 12.)

20. *truth.*—Pilate had partaken of the polish of a Roman education ; he had heard the philosophers of various schools of Grecian and Roman thought, argue about truth. They all professed to know it, or to seek it ; but none gave any more satisfactory definition of it than another. And now, in the bitterness and sarcasm of one who chose to assume, that the truth of which Christ spoke, was only a Jewish aspect of the great question, worth no more than, if so much as, those of his own philosophical school ; his pride rises again, and forces down every better and more hopeful feeling. As he asks this question, carelessly, scornfully, or bitterly, he rises from his tribunal. He has ascertained enough to be convinced that Christ is no political offender, but rather the leader of a school of thought, of which the rulers disapprove ("he *knew* that for envy they had delivered Him "); and as for His kingship, he attached no dangerous significance to the claim—all the philosophers proclaimed themselves kings of men, in their superiority of wisdom. Thus he closes his examination, and the subject. He does not see that he now refuses the grace of One, at whose sovereign bar himself must hereafter stand. He made that election now, which involved him in all the troubles which the condemnation of Christ entailed; and there are not a few indications of the unrest and indecision of his mind, and of its struggles against the expediency, which mastered him. We need not affirm that remorse for this particular act of his purposeless life, induced him to cut it short at last by his own hand; but we may here see the turning-point, where he had been brought to the moment of decision, and put the truth aside. Dean Milman says, "That the peace of a nation or the life of an individual should be endangered on account of the truth or falsehood of any system of speculative opinions, was so diametrically opposed to the general opinion and feeling of the Roman world, that Pilate, either in contemptuous mockery, or with the

And when he had said this, he went out again unto the Jews, and saith unto them, I find in Him no fault *at all.*

And the chief priests accused Him of many things: but He answered nothing. And Pilate asked Him again, saying, Answerest Thou nothing? behold how many things they witness against Thee. But Jesus yet answered nothing; so that Pilate marvelled. And they

merciful design of showing the utter harmlessness and insignificance of such points, inquired what He meant by truth; what truth had to do with the question of life and death, with a capital charge brought by the national council before the supreme tribunal."

21. *I find.*—The same word is used by S. John, as that which, in S. Luke, expresses the finding of the Sanhedrim. (See note 8.) The result of Pilate's examination is thus placed on record. He went out to the Jews, who were waiting his return, and declared, that of the charge of disaffection and disloyalty, and therefore also of sedition, he *found* Christ perfectly guiltless. He did not, as he ought to have done, at once add the official order, of release of the innocent and outraged prisoner.

22. *many things.*—Not apparently worth stating, certainly not worth Christ's answer; and unsupported even by the testimony of false witnesses. Christ only answered upon trial, when He was questioned by one who had some sincerity in him, as was the case with Pilate, or when His silence could be misrepresented, as in the case of the high priest; on all other occasions He was uniformly silent. This now excited the surprise of Pilate, as Christ had so recently spoken to himself with the greatest readiness. Christ did not even appeal to him against the rulers, or take advantage of any favourable impression He had made upon him; nor did He even point out the injustice of calling on Him again to plead, after sentence of acquittal had been formally pronounced. Pilate, however, noticed His bearing; and he was quite able to appreciate the malevolence of the Jews, and the worth of their charges, which were the less pleasing to him, as he had just delivered his sentence in Christ's favour. Pilate's question, "Answerest Thou nothing?" seems to express his persuasion that Christ *could* answer and refute them. But He is now silent, even when addressed by the governor, since his question is merely the pressing of the charges of the rulers.

23. *yet answered nothing.*—Gk. "He no longer answered anything." What He had to say He had already said, and it was no part of His design to plead for His life, or to make any defence, except where the truth was at issue.

were the more fierce, saying, He stirreth up the people,
teaching throughout all Jewry, beginning from Galilee
to this place. When Pilate heard of Galilee, he asked
whether the man were a Galilæan. And as soon as. he
knew that He belonged unto Herod's jurisdiction, he sent
Him to Herod, who himself also was at Jerusalem at
that time.

(*e.*) *Christ before Herod.*

S. Luke xxiii. 6–12.

And when Herod saw Jesus, he was exceeding glad:
for he was desirous to see Him of a long *season*, because

24. *the more fierce.*—They redoubled their accusation, both in force
and point; but in their excitement they overreached themselves. They
pretended a conspiracy, which they represented universal in Judæa, as
well as in Galilee. There had been an insurrection under Judas
of Galilee (Acts v. 37), sufficiently recently to make it worth while
to colour their statement, by referring to a district where disaffection
was always ready for a leader. Their mention of Galilee now gives
Pilate, as he thinks, an opportunity for getting rid of them, and at the
same time of showing a courtesy to Herod, the native sovereign in
whose jurisdiction Galilee lay. He therefore sent Christ to him.

25. *sent.*—A legal term; he *remanded* Him for Herod's hearing.

1. *Herod.*—This was Herod Antipas, son of Herod the Great,
Tetrarch of Galilee, who had been reproved by John the Baptist for his
aggravated adultery, and had imprisoned and then beheaded him. He
still continued his evil life. Though Christ had been so long in his
dominions, he had never seen Him; though, as a matter of curiosity,
he had long desired it. He had been accused by the Pharisees to our
Lord (either falsely, or as his own contrivance to get Christ out of his
territory) of intending to kill Him (Luke xiii. 31); but Herod had
never taken any trouble about seeing Christ; and we may well imagine
that his anxiety to see Him was much crossed by the fear of His
reproof, and of the interest of the people in His teaching. Herod was
now at Jerusalem for the Passover, being nominally a Jew.

2. *glad.*—There was not in his gladness any single aspect of piety.
His character had deteriorated since he heard John with gladness, and
"did many things" in consequence of his exhortations, and was sorry
for the fatal consequences of the rash oath which caused John's death.
The Saviour was never more ready to make offer of His grace, than
during the season of His Passion and death. "The secrets of many

he had heard many things of Him; and he hoped to have seen some miracle done by Him. Then he questioned with Him in many words; but He answered him nothing. And the chief priests and scribes stood and vehemently accused Him. And Herod with his men of war set Him at nought, and mocked *Him*, and arrayed Him in a gorgeous robe, and sent Him again to Pilate.

hearts were then revealed." But there was brought to light no secret feature of hopefulness in Herod's case, to which Christ could address Himself. He knew Herod's character well—its unredeemed wickedness, its meanness, and its *apery* of the vices of the court of his paramount lord, Cæsar. The "leaven of Herod" was our Lord's proverbial designation of that worldliness and scepticism, which spread so evil an influence within his dominions (Mark viii. 15); his craft, treachery, and meanness won from Him the contemptuous brand, "That fox" (Luke xiii. 32), our Lord's sole word of personal invective. He only wanted, from motives of vulgar curiosity, to see Christ display that miraculous power of which he had heard so much; and he flattered himself that Christ, in His low estate, would readily embrace the offer of doing some mighty work before him.

3. *questioned.*—Not so much judicially, as with curiosity; hoping to draw from Christ some account of Himself, and His powers and claims, for his own gratification. To a man hardened in such sin as his, so utterly without principle, or religious reverence; idly and sceptically inquisitive; asking such questions as trifled with the supreme sanctions of truth, Christ had not one word to offer. The malevolent rulers had followed Christ to Herod's presence, and repeated there the clamorous and groundless accusations which they had advanced before. And no doubt upon Herod, as a Jew, they urged their charge of blasphemy. Herod, better able even than Pilate to judge of these matters, evidently disregards them utterly.

4. *men of war.*—Herod made a vain affectation of military display, which contrasted somewhat ridiculously with the insignificance of his real power, and which, it is said, formed one principal reason for his eventual deposition, and banishment by the Romans. Herod had a number of these troops with him at Jerusalem, and he did not disdain to associate himself with them, in their contemptuous treatment and mockery of Jesus.

5. *gorgeous.*—(Gk. "white," or "shining.") Some think that this was a purple robe of royalty, one of Herod's cast-off garments, which the sense of the word would bear; and that it was the same robe which was afterwards used in mockery of Christ, by the Roman soldiers. But, though purple was the Roman imperial colour, that of Hebrew theocratic royalty is said to have been white; and this, therefore, may have

And the same day Pilate and Herod were made friends together : for before they were at enmity between themselves.

(*f.*)   *Christ again before Pilate.*

S. Matt. xxvii. 15–32 ; S. Mark xv. 6–21 ; S. Luke xxiii. 13–25 ; S. John xviii. 39–xix. 16.

And Pilate, when he had called together the chief

been such a robe, and peculiarly derisive of the claims of Christ's royalty. Others again think, white being the colour of the robe assumed by Roman *candidates* (hence the word) for high office, that Herod thus derisively decorated the candidate for the throne of David; but this explanation is the less probable, as it presupposes an acquaintance, on the part of the Jews generally (else the satire would miss its point) with those customs of Rome which Herod himself affected. He "now sends forth Christ robed royally, to show Pilate that such a pretender to a throne deserved no heavier punishment than ridicule or contempt, from the Tetrarch of Galilee, or from the Procurator of Judæa." (*Bp. Ellicott.*)

6. *made friends.*—The cause of this enmity is not certainly known ; it was probably caused by some stretch of authority on Pilate's part, which had touched the vanity of Herod. Such an act as the slaughter of the subjects of Herod, under circumstances of unusual violence, though probably not without some justification (Luke xiii. 1, 2), may have been the cause of quarrel. Greswell thinks that the sedition of Barabbas had just taken place, and that there had been bloodshed, both of Jews and Roman soldiers; and that the scene of this had been partially in the Temple, where some innocent Galilæans, who were sacrificing there, were slain during the tumult. Without fitting in the affair of Barabbas, it is quite as likely that these Galilæans were political agitators; but their summary massacre by Pilate, under such circumstances, might well cause a quarrel between Herod and Pilate. Pilate now seems to have taken the opportunity of offering a courtesy, convenient to himself, in sending Jesus, as a subject of Herod, to him for judgment; the more marked, as Christ's ministry had been really as much in Judæa as in Galilee, and He was by birth of Bethlehem. Pilate, therefore, might have decided the case himself. Whether or not we consider that S. Luke suggests this, as an occasion and manner of their renewal of amity, he certainly does point out the significance of this alliance between rival political powers, as confederate against the Christ; not, perhaps, that they made friends on purpose to oppress Christ, but their doing so seems to have arisen out of the circumstances of that oppression. (Cf. Ps. ii. 1, 2, with the inspired comment by S. Luke in Acts

priests and the rulers and the people, said unto them,
Ye have brought this man unto me, as one that perverteth
the people : and, behold, I, having examined *Him* before
you, have found no fault in this man touching those
things whereof ye accuse Him : no, nor yet Herod : for
I sent you to Him ; and, lo, nothing worthy of death
is done unto Him. I will therefore chastise Him, and
release *Him*.

Now at that feast the governor was wont to release

iv. 25–28.) We notice also a close parallel here to the association
between the rival religious sects, the Sadducees and Pharisees, and of
both with the Herodians (in this case *purposely*), to entangle Christ
with subtle questions.

1. *called together*.—The passage details a formal and official proceeding. Pilate, going out from the judgment hall to the Jews, as
before, but seating himself upon a "judgment seat," calls the rulers
around him ; and with them "*the people*" also, to whose sense of
justice he might look for support against the evident malevolence of the
rulers. The formal aspect of this court would still the excitement of
the multitude, with whom the rulers had affected to make themselves
one. Pilate then rehearses the charges laid against Christ; and, passing
over his private investigation, and speaking only of his more formal
examination and decision, points out that Herod has taken the same
view with himself, and that it is therefore out of the question to condemn Christ capitally, upon these charges.

2. *before you*.—This examination had been open, before them all.
Pilate lays no stress upon the private hearing ; as, though it greatly
influenced his own mind, it had not taken the place of formal proceedings, after the usual manner, and probably at the time appointed
by law for the sitting of the procurator's court.

3. *unto him*.—Or "by him." This expresses the decision of both
their courts, upon the evidence offered. Herod's action must have
thoroughly convinced Pilate that nothing need be feared politically from
Christ. (See App. XVI.)

4. *chastise*.—Pilate would have saved himself much had he now, at
least (see xxx. *d*. 20), acted on the decision so clearly expressed in the
foregoing words, and released Christ publicly. But here he shows that
weakness which the Jews had calculated on, and were prompt to detect
and turn to account. (See xxx. *c*. 34.) As Christ was innocent, He
should not have been condemned to the scourge. Pilate, in so sen-
tencing Him after deliberate acquittal, committed a palpable injustice,
and betrayed his fear of the rulers.

unto the people one prisoner, whomsoever they desired.
And they had then a notable prisoner called Barabbas,
which lay bound with them that had made insurrection
with him, who had committed murder in the insurrec-

5. *one prisoner.*—It is conjectured that this was a very ancient
Jewish custom, and was observed in honour of the Passover, because
Israel was permitted to escape out of the prison of Egypt. Such a
custom was in keeping with the spirit of the law. The Roman practice
in this case was probably as old as their occupation of Judæa; and it
was an act of grace consonant with the usage of nations. Pilate takes
skilful advantage of this, and hopes that the popular voice may compel
him to release Christ, which he feared to do upon his own sentence of
acquittal; or, if not, may so support the action of the rulers as to make
it expedient to sentence Christ. To make this more certain, he offers
two names for release, to the people's choice. (See App. XVI.) "Of the
extent of the crime of Barabbas we are ignorant; but Pilate, by selecting
the worst case—that which the people could not but consider the most
atrocious, and offensive to the Roman government—might desire to
force them, as it were, to demand the release of Jesus. Barabbas had
been undeniably guilty of those overt acts of insubordination which
they endeavoured to infer as necessary consequences of the teaching of
Jesus." (*Milman.*)

6. *Barabbas.*—The name of this criminal, which means "*son of the
father*," together with the fact of his mention as one who had committed
insurrection, very much favours the supposition that he was no common
robber. By a strange coincidence this man bore (according to Origen,
and with the support of some ancient MSS.) the name of "*Jesus
Bar-abbas.*" He may have been a false Christ, and therefore, in the
eyes of the Jews, somewhat of a patriot—a character which would
atone for many of his excesses and crimes. A parallel to such a
character might be found in some of the guerilla chiefs of lower type,
in Spain and other countries, where the government has been unsettled,
or which have been under occupation of a foreign force. These in one
sense show themselves heroes, whilst they are otherwise undoubted
ruffians. They disgrace a good cause with crime, and often assume
patriotism in excuse for license. In this view Jesus Barabbas would
be (as Archbishop Trench points out) a hideous caricature of the true
Christ Jesus, the Son of the eternal Father; and the choice of the
multitude, ever quick to discover coincidence of name or circumstance,
is, even allowing for the influence of the rulers, something awful and
marvellous.

7. *insurrection.*—Insurrection against the Roman yoke would, of
course, be professedly an attempt in favour of national deliverance.
The Jews hoped this was to be the glory of the Messiah's advent; and
their choice is significant in this aspect.

tion. And the multitude crying aloud began to desire *him to do* as he had ever done unto them. But Pilate answered them, saying, Whom will ye that I release unto you? Barabbas, or Jesus which is called Christ? For he knew that the chief priests had delivered Him for envy.

When he was set down on the judgment seat, his wife

8. *began to desire.*—This was the usual demand at the feast, as the original in S. Matthew expresses. But whether the multitude (who, as S. Matthew observes, were now gathered together) raised the cry with any desire to free Jesus, it is difficult to say. It may well have been the thought of the friends of Christ, setting in motion the popular will. If so, their thought found an echo in Pilate's heart, or they detected his object and promoted it. It opened a new chance of doing what he knew to be right, without compromising himself with the rulers. He now brings forth two names, between which he thought there could be no question.

9. *Barabbas, or Jesus,* etc.—(See note 6.) Some old MSS. read "Jesus Bar-abbas, or Jesus which is called Christ." These MSS. are not, perhaps, of sufficient authority to establish the reading; but Origen speaks of it as if it were the common reading of his day. If it be the true one, it places the true, the Christ, and the Antichrist in strange contrast indeed. But it shows, at the least, that the significance of the name of the robber chieftain had received very early recognition in the Church; and it is quite likely that he bore, or had assumed, the same personal name as our Lord.

10. *he knew.*—The ill feeling on the part of the rulers was notorious. It had grown as Christ's ministry advanced amongst the people, and had been a check to any great manifestation in His favour. Pilate was, no doubt, perfectly aware of this; and now that Christ and His enemies came personally before him, he recognized the innocence of the one and the extraordinary malevolence of the others. To his mind their "envy" ("*jealousy,*" rather) of Christ's public reputation and success, and of His marvellous powers, would be more distinctly in view than any real appreciation of the contest between good and evil, truth and falsehood, Divine and human doctrine.

11. *his wife.*—This must have occurred here, in the order in which S. Matthew gives it, whilst Pilate was waiting for the reply of the people. The Romans were very superstitious on the subject of dreams; they held especially true those which came towards morning, and Pilate was likely to be much impressed by them. He accordingly labours with increased diligence to release Christ, avoiding, however, the obviously right and manly course, of judicially ordering the immediate discharge of the innocent prisoner. We see that Pilate's wife was convinced of the justice of Christ's cause and character, and

sent unto him, saying, Have thou nothing to do with that just man : for I have suffered many things this day in a dream because of Him.

But the chief priests and elders persuaded the multitude that they should ask Barabbas, and destroy Jesus. The governor answered and said unto them, Whether of

did not hesitate to express her opinion, which was greatly strengthened by the experience of her dream. Without there being the least *necessity* for attaching any supernatural character to this dream, which admits of explanation, as it followed on the agitation caused by the tidings brought to the governor's palace at night (see xxx. *d.* 1); yet the significance of dreams in the history of the Bible, and notably in the earlier portion of S. Matthew's Gospel, renders it highly probable that this may have been one of the warnings which God gave, of the great sin of the rulers against Christ. It was at once a mode of warning consonant with heathen notions, and was also a principal way in which God had made known His will in the land of Israel in early times, and, more recently, during the childhood of Christ Himself. Some ancient writers, indeed, have expressed their conviction that this dream was a device of Satan, and sent by him to prevent the crucifixion of Christ, by the influence of Pilate's wife upon the mind of the governor, as he now saw that the crucifixion of Christ would win the real triumph of His cause, and the redemption of man. But this (though a remarkable thought) is not the opinion of the most reliable of the early writers, who consider it a warning sent by God; and we certainly do not gather, from the narrative of the Evangelists, any impression of Satan's agency being exerted to prevent, but certainly to advance and multiply, the terrors of the crucifixion. Tradition gives the name of Pilate's wife as Procula Claudia, and notices her kindly feeling towards the people of the land. There was the pleasing belief, in very early times, that she afterwards became a Christian. Hers is the only human voice directly raised in our Lord's behalf, during the whole of the proceedings against Him.

12. *persuaded.*—From Matt. xxvii. 20 it would seem as if the people hesitated, and were silent, and as if Pilate had a chance of success in Christ's behalf. But the chief priests were intently on the alert; they had not much time for action, but still enough to complete what their emissaries had already been doing during the last two days. (See ix. 21.) Whilst Pilate was attending to the message of his wife, which thus came at an unhappily critical moment, they probably represented that Barabbas, with all his crimes, had boldly pronounced in the popular cause, whilst Christ had refused the position to which they had called Him, and disappointed their hope of His assuming the sceptre of David. (See App. XVI.)

the twain will ye that I release unto you?   They said,
Barabbas. And Pilate, willing to release Jesus, answered
and said again unto them, What will ye then that I
shall do *unto Him* whom ye call the King of the Jews?
And they cried out again, Crucify Him. And he said unto
them the third time, Why, what evil hath He done?   I
have found no cause of death in Him: I will therefore
chastise Him, and let Him go. And they were instant
with loud voices, requiring that He might be crucified.
And the voices of them and of the chief priests prevailed.

When Pilate saw that he could prevail nothing, but *that*
rather a tumult was made, he took water, and washed

13. *willing to release.*—The Evangelists mark these three special,
and other, efforts for the release of Christ. (See App. XVI.; and xxx.
c. 34.) Pilate did not doubt that the popular voice would rise in
favour of Christ; and their demand would justify him against the
complaints of the rulers, should they dare to complain to Rome. Great
must have been his astonishment and consternation, when they accepted
the two names proposed for their choice, and, without hesitation, preferred Barabbas. He then tried to recall the enthusiasm of three days
ago, and reminded them how they had hailed Jesus as " the King that
cometh in the Name of the Lord." There is, in his way of putting the
question, the appearance of being utterly astonished, and at a loss;
" What is it then your pleasure that I shall do to Him whom ye yourselves call the King of the Jews?" What *can* be done in His case?
The title, however, passes from his lips with some irrepressible scorn of
themselves and their King. They neither explain nor reason; they cry,
in the frenzy of excitement, " Crucify Him." (See Isa. v. 7.) Pilate
last appeals to their sense of justice, and terribly his question tells
against himself; but, seeing no response in their faces, he repeats his
first intention of releasing Christ, after a chastisement which he hoped
might satisfy the people, but to which he had no right to doom an
innocent prisoner. (See App. XVI.)

14. *prevailed.*—They saw Pilate's irresolution and fear, and their
voices grew outrageous and menacing; there seemed no slight probability of an outbreak; and, as such considerations must always compel
one in whom irresolution and want of principle meet, they prevailed
over Pilate's sense of justice, and dignity, and right. S. Luke's word
" prevailed " is not the same in the original as that of S. Mark immediately following in the text. The former means to overpower and
predominate; the latter, merely to help, or to effect anything beneficial—
a mild term.

15. *took water.*—This was undoubtedly a Jewish custom (Deut. xxi.

his hands before the multitude, saying, I am innocent of the blood of this just person: see ye to it. Then answered all the people, and said, His blood *be* on us, and on our children.

6–9; Jer. ii. 22); and Pilate had not known the Jews so long without noticing their addiction to the washing of hands. But it was not exclusively Jewish. There are many instances of such a washing in classical authors, which show that it was a ceremony common to the old world. The fact that it is always associated with circumstances of solemnity, gives a strong weight to the act on Pilate's part, as expressive of his conviction of Christ's innocence, and of his unwillingness to give sentence against Him; which is further enhanced by his general recklessness in shedding blood. The wonder is, that Pilate would go so far as to perform this public and solemn, but hypocritical, lustration, and yet not have the moral courage to give an order to the armed force around him, to release the prisoner, or to convey Him for safety to Cæsarea. (See App. XVI.)

16. *this just person.*—The echo of his wife's words. The justice of Christ's cause shines the clearer for the black injustice and wrong, which pronounces Him innocent, and punishes Him with the most guilty.

17. *all the people.*—This awful imprecation seems to have been unanimous and national. The reckoning of Josephus makes the number of people present at this feast about 3,000,000; and this embraced the adult population of the whole country. Representatives of the country generally must have been present here, so that we cannot fairly consider the rejection of Christ as merely the act of the people of Jerusalem, or attribute less than a national character to it. If the majority of the people took no part in the act in which they were adequately represented, certainly there was no attempt, on the part of any section of that majority, to protest, interfere with, or condemn an act which was carried out in the most public place and manner, at a season of such a gathering of the nation. Thus to invoke upon themselves the consequence of their act is terrible enough, but to entail the curse upon their children shows determination, malice, and frenzy appalling to contemplate. Christ had been pronounced innocent by Pilate; and it must have been evident to every Jew that the real charge against Christ was waived by the rulers, as one which could not be sustained. There was, therefore, the greatest audacity in such a cry to heaven in such a case. It was the boldest invocation of God's award that ever people raised to heaven. And, when we consider what Christ was, and was known to be, and what He had been before the people during His ministry, we must own that it was also the most impious. The world does not contain the record of a doom so terribly verified. The events of the destruction of Jerusalem are described by

And *so* Pilate, willing to content the people, gave sentence that it should be as they required. And he released unto them him that for sedition and murder was cast into prison, whom they had desired; but he delivered Jesus, when he had scourged *Him*, to their will, to be crucified.

Then the soldiers of the governor took Jesus into the common hall, called Prætorium; and gathered unto Him the whole band *of soldiers*. And they stripped Him, and

Christ as "great tribulation, such as was not since the foundation of the world to this time, no, nor shall be;" and the shadow of this doom still rests upon the children of those who invoked it.

18. *to content.*—A very contemptible exhibition of the mind of a ruler. It has always been the sign of decay of power, and moral weakness, that the principle of government became the keeping the people quiet at any price, and by concession of everything to their passion and clamour. The sovereign people soon perceive their power, use, and abuse it. Pilate's concession did not maintain him in authority; the voice of discontent arose against him, until it made itself heard at Rome, and caused his disgrace. (See xxx. *c.* 34.)

19. *desired.*—The word is designedly severe. We find it again used (Acts iii. 14.)

20. *scourged.*—This was not quite the same punishment as Pilate before proposed, to "*chastise*" Christ and release Him; that word, in the original, is also milder than the term here used. The scourging here spoken of was, very commonly, a portion of the punishment of crucifixion; it was a terrible torture, and one inflicted generally on slaves. The scourges were thongs loaded with sharp bone or metal, causing fearful laceration and bruises; and it was by no means rare that the criminal expired under the infliction.

21. *whole band.*—This scene of mockery and insult must have been one in which very many were engaged; at the least, the whole of the guard around Pilate's residence, if not (as the original will allow) the whole cohort, the tenth of a legion. Christ was set at nought and rejected by the Gentiles. Pilate was now occupying the old palace of King Herod, to be ready for any outbreak; and had with him a strong force, sufficient to repress insurrection, certainly sufficient to enforce justice. These men were gathered to Jesus at the call of their comrades, in whose custody He was, in the great open court of the palace. There they enacted this shameful act of mockery, unworthy of armed and brave men, disgraceful to the governor. In their centre stood the weary and tortured prisoner, bruised and lacerated with their scourges. And some tore His clothes from Him, and put upon His shoulders a robe

put on Him a purple robe. And when they had platted
a crown of thorns, they put *it* upon His head, and a reed
in His right hand : and they bowed the knee before Him,
and mocked Him, saying, Hail, King of the Jews ! And
they spit upon Him, and took the reed, and smote Him
on the head.

Pilate therefore went forth again, and saith unto them,
Behold, I bring Him forth to you, that ye may know that
I find no fault in Him. Then came Jesus forth, wearing
the crown of thorns, and the purple robe. And *Pilate*
saith unto them, Behold the man !

of caricatured royalty; others bound a circlet of sharp, strong thorns
upon His brow, in mockery of some royal diadem, or of the imperial
laurel crown; and into His hand they forced a reed as a sceptre. And
then, with every gesture of insolence and scorn, they bowed the knee before
the King thus apparelled, crowned and sceptred; and, in bitter derision
of the people whom they hated, and over whom such a King should reign,
cried, " Hail, King of the Jews ! " And then, in depth of contempt,
they spat upon Him—a loathsome insult (see **xxx.** *c.* 19); and, as His
hand refused to grasp the sceptre of such degradation, though He
patiently bore their outrages, they took it, and smote Him on the head,
driving down the thorns of their crown into His flesh.

22. *purple robe.*—This may have been the one used before (see **xxx.**
c. 5); or, as the word rendered " *robe* " means a soldiers' cloak, it may
have been the scarlet cloak of a Roman soldier or officer, which they
made to serve their purpose.

23. *no fault.*—Pilate again carefully and formally expresses his
decision that Christ is without blame, bringing Him forth unsentenced,
from within his hall of audience, where sentence else had been pronounced; and, supposing He had afforded any ground for the hatred
of the rulers, what He had already suffered was surely sufficient atonement. Pilate may have thought it possible that, though innocent
of real guilt, and persecuted by malicious and envious foes, yet he may
have given some reason for the animosity manifested against Him; and
even thus they should now be amply satisfied.

24. *Behold the man.*—There is little doubt that Pilate sought thus
to excite the pity of the multitude. He hoped that, when they saw
One, so lately the object of veneration and regard, thus humbled, some
voice would be raised in His favour; and that the people would at last
call for His release. He speaks as if he himself felt the sadness and
pitiableness of the sight. There is no scorn now in his words, as he
presents Him to the people, thus suffering, humiliated, and patient.
But Pilate little knew the significance of his own words and actions;

When the chief priests therefore and officers saw Him, they cried out, saying, Crucify *Him*, crucify *Him*. Pilate saith unto them, Take ye Him, and crucify *Him:* for I find no fault in Him. The Jews answered him, We have a law, and by our law He ought to die, because He made Himself the Son of God.

When Pilate therefore heard that saying, he was the more afraid; and went again into the judgment hall,

for he then presented before God and before men, both Jews and Gentiles, "*the Man*," representative of our race, offered up as a sacrifice and atonement for the whole of the sinful race. Had he had the faith of John, he might fitly have used his words, "Behold the Lamb of God, that taketh away the sin of the world."

25. *crucify.*—The rulers anticipated the popular voice, and led it. The very sight of Christ, thus degraded and tormented by man, excites their deeper hatred. They hasten to prevent any hope on Pilate's part, by the word which they repeated as a constant cry, "Crucify!" (See App. XVI.)

26. *take ye Him.*—He speaks in irony, and in anger; let them perpetrate this judicial murder themselves, if they chose, and if they dared. Again he repeats his official acquittal of Christ, as a reason why he will have nothing to do with the case. He may also intend to convey to them, that, if they do venture upon the crime, he will be silent, and will not interfere to prevent their infraction of the law.

27 *we have a law.*—The rulers consider Pilate's last words as a final refusal to crucify Jesus on the charge on which he had so repeatedly pronounced Him innocent. They decline the challenge to break the law on their own responsibility. They now fall back on the sentence of the Sanhedrim, under the law of Lev. xxiv. 16, which awards death for blasphemy. The Romans had assented to the general maintenance of Jewish law; and on this principle they now take their ground.

28. *the Son of God.*—The title "*sons of God*" was rather generally applied in the O. T.—for instance, in Hos. i. 10; and even that of "*gods*" was used of those "to whom the word of God came;" and therefore, according to Christ's argument, might be more justly applied to those who by their works showed obedience to that word (see John x. 33–36), where, as the Jews were not able to enter into the profundity of His claims, He condescended to take lower ground, in proving their error in imputing blasphemy to Him. It is evident, however, that they here used the title in no general sense, or in that lower sense permitted in Scripture; but that they charge Christ with assuming the rank of the Son of the living God, in the fullest and highest sense. Nor are they unconscious either of Christ's real claim, or of His right to assume the title.

29. *the more afraid.*—He had felt before the extraordinary power of

and saith unto Jesus, Whence art Thou? But Jesus
gave him no answer. Then saith Pilate unto Him,
Speakest Thou not unto me? knowest Thou not that
I have power to crucify Thee, and have power to release
Thee. Jesus answered, Thou couldest have no power *at
all* against Me, except it were given thee from above:

Christ's personal presence, and that it was no ordinary man who stood
before him as a prisoner; but his pride stifled any better impulse
of his heart towards Christ. Now, however, that the Jews mentioned
this as His true claim, Pilate felt increased awe, and an undefined dread
of what might be the result of that day's trial. He knew well the old
mythological stories of Greece and Rome, and perhaps saw no difficulty
in the thought that "the gods have come down in the likeness of men,"
as in Acts xiv. 11. Christ had done no miracle in his presence; but
the circumstances of His capture, and His bearing before His accusers,
were all extraordinary, and sufficient to invest Him with awe to any
mind not prejudiced against Him, nor carried away by excitement.

30. *whence art thou.*—Of what origin? with special reference to the
title "Son of God;" and possibly to what Christ had said before, "My
kingdom is not from hence." To this question our Lord gave no reply.
Pilate deserved none. He did not ask to know the truth for the truth's
sake, but in consequence of his fears and superstitions, and in the
irresolution of his mind. He had before avoided the subject of truth,
and closed the opening which Christ afforded. Christ's silence is
conclusive as to the spirit in which Pilate asked this question.

31. *unto me.*—The emphasis rests on *me*. In the original, the order
of the words is, "Unto me speaketh Thou not?" Evidently Pilate's
pride, which so often rose in the way of his better impulses, was touched
now, whilst he looked on Christ in His misery, in such a crisis between
life and death, awaiting the word of fate from his lips, and yet refusing
to plead, or sue for favour from him. "He was unwilling to answer,
lest He should clear Himself of the charge, and be acquitted by the
judge, and so the gain resulting from the cross should be done
away." (*Bede.*) And there was no personal message now which Pilate
could receive.

32. *I have power.*—These are words of self-condemnation, for Pilate
does not say that upon the decision of the law, or the sentence of justice,
depends Christ's fate; but that his will, with or without consideration
of these, decides the case. They were also a false profession, for he *dared*
not use his power to release Christ.

33. *from above.*—Not from any official superior, as the Prefect of
Syria, or the emperor; but from God direct. The words are true, if we
interpret them by S. Paul's language (Rom. xiii. 1–4) concerning the
origin of earthly power; but they have a special reference to this par-

therefore he that delivered Me unto thee hath the greater
sin.　And from thenceforth Pilate sought to release Him:
but the Jews cried out, saying, If thou let this man go,
thou art not Cæsar's friend: whosoever maketh himself
a king speaketh against Cæsar.

ticular case, namely, that God had, in His wisdom, entrusted the power
of condemning Christ to Pilate, in accordance with His everlasting
purpose.　For "it was in regard to that originally supreme authority of
God His Father, and to His particular appointment on that occasion,
that our Saviour did then freely subject Himself to those inferior and
subordinate powers, as to the proper ministers of Divine justice.　Had
He suffered in any other way, by any private malice or passion of man,
God's special providence in that case had been less visible, and Christ's
obedience not so remarkable.　And if He must die by public hands, it
must be as a criminal, under a pretence of guilt and demerit.　There
must be a formal process, how full soever of mockery and outrage;
there must be testimonies produced, however false and groundless;
there must be a sentence pronounced, although most partial and
corrupt.　For no man is persecuted by authority, without some colour of
desert; otherwise it would cease to be public authority, and become
private violence.　The prosecutor would then put off the face of a magistrate, and appear as a murderer or a thief."　(*I. Barrow.*)

34. *therefore.*—"Since God has entrusted to thee this power, though
thou hast sin in thy conscious abuse of the principles of law and
justice, and of moral responsibility in the exercise of it, yet he who
knew more of My nature and claims than thou, and yet knowingly
delivered Me to thy power, Caiaphas, the president of the Sanhedrim,
has sinned more deeply than thou."　Caiaphas had the sin of plotting
against One whose actions, teaching, and object he was well able to
appreciate; and whose claims, and their coincidence with the witness
of prophecy, he understood.　Where he did fail to understand, his was
the ignorance of one who wilfully closed his eyes to the fulness of
light, seeing that the light was there.　The sentence may refer also to
Judas, Annas, Herod, and to each one of those who had combined to
deliver Christ to Pilate.　It is astonishing (and even Pilate felt awed by
it) that there was such majesty of utterance and judgment in one who
stood there scored with the furrows of the "ploughs" (Ps. cxxix. 3),
and bedecked with the trappings of mock royalty.　He remarks on the
guilt of those who had severally used the power entrusted to them
against Him, and apportions their respective shares of sin, with far
greater calmness than Pilate had shown upon his tribunal.

35. *thenceforth.*—With resolution at last.　Pilate could stand no
longer against the voice of superstition or conviction which oppressed
him.　(See App. XVI.)

36. *Cæsar's friend.*—This is supposed to have been an official title of

When Pilate therefore heard that saying, he brought Jesus forth, and sat down in the judgment seat in a place that is called the Pavement, but in the Hebrew, Gabbatha. And it was the preparation of the passover, and about the sixth hour: and he saith unto the Jews,

courtesy, by which the higher magistrates of the empire were addressed; but the denial of his title menaced Pilate with a complaint against his administration, and particularly for pardoning a political prisoner against the voice of the people. The present emperor, Tiberius, was notoriously jealous, and severe with his lieutenants, upon any suspicion of their loyalty; and the charge would probably be a fatal one to the prospects of a man like Pilate. The complaints of the Jews hitherto had met with every attention at Rome; and there was a probability, terrible to Pilate, that he would not be more leniently dealt with than Herod and Archelaus.

37. *the Pavement.*—This seems to have been a space covered with tesselated pavement of costly description, upon which the judgment seat of the procurator was placed, when he gave sentence in solemn cases. From its Hebrew name, "*Gabbatha*" (that is, "hill," or "high place"), we may infer that it was raised ground; or, at least, an elevated platform. It stood in the open air, outside "the hall of judgment," where causes were heard. Julius Cæsar set the example of taking about with him one of these squares of mosaic pavement; and it is likely that many of the Roman governors of provinces did the same. The representative of the majesty of Rome placed his throne of judgment upon this beautiful and costly work, many large specimens of which have been preserved to our own times. Pilate now again takes his seat with formality; and orders Jesus to be brought out from the hall, where he had retired with Him for private colloquy, and to be placed before him for his sentence.

38. *the preparation.*—This was not the preparation *for* the Passover, to which festival it had no particular reference, further than that it was a day of universal solemnity as occurring within this hallowed week. The preparation was of weekly occurrence; it was the preparation for the sabbath, and it was commonly spoken of as "the preparation" simply. "The preparation *of* the Passover," therefore, is the preparation of the sabbath within the Paschal week. The day, therefore, was Friday. (See xxxii. 2.) Norris quotes Brown, "who, in his 'Ordo Sæculorum,' shows astronomically that in this year, A.D. 29, the Paschal full moon fell on Friday, 18th March, and adopts this as the date of the crucifixion; and this agrees with the constant tradition of the first five centuries, that Christ suffered in March, in the consulship of the Gemini." The Jewish date was the 14th day of Nisan.

39. *sixth hour.*—Mark (xv. 25) says it was the "third hour" when

Behold your King! But they cried out, Away with *Him*,
away with *Him*, crucify Him. Pilate saith unto them,

Christ was crucified ; and the three Synoptical Gospels give the crucifixion as far advanced by the sixth hour (Matt. xxvii. 45 ; Mark xv.
33 ; Luke xxiii. 44). There is here an undoubted difficulty. Some
writers, following the authority of ancient MSS., read " third hour "
instead of " sixth ; " and are satisfied that the error crept in through a
very early MS. This is, of course, possible; but, unless such errors can
be clearly demonstrated by the authority of undoubtedly genuine MSS.,
it is not a satisfactory, though an easy, way of solving the difficulty.
Others declare that S. John, writing for the Churches of Asia, does not
adopt the Jewish or Roman computation of time, but that of Asia,
which, they say, was reckoned from midnight. This may be true, but
would bring the crucifixion rather too early. There are several notices
of time to guide us. Christ had been examined before the high priest
before daybreak, before cock-crowing, and before the Sanhedrim " as
soon as it was day ; " the consultation as to His death took place " in
the morning ; " " it was early " when He was placed before Pilate, who
examined Him privately before the formal opening of his court (xxx.
d. 1) ; and then publicly, on the accusation of the Jews ; He was then
sent to Herod ; and then the subsequent proceedings before Pilate,
owing to his irresolution, must have occupied considerable time. It is
difficult to suppose that all this took place by " the third hour," *i.e.*
nine o'clock. Another explanation is, that the Jews specified the third,
sixth, and ninth hours, which gave name to the four watches of the
day, and did not generally mention time very exactly ; and therefore
that, whilst S. Mark says it was the *third* hour, he refers to the whole
period before the sixth, reckoning forward. S. John does the same,
reckoning backward ; so both agree. This might fix the time some-
where between the hours of ten and eleven, which would harmonize
with all accounts, and is at least as satisfactory as assuming that error
exists. The question, however, confessedly retains its difficulty.
There is one other explanation, which has the support of Ignatius
(Longer Epp.), who says, " At the third hour He received the sentence
from Pilate ; at the sixth hour He was crucified." If this passage
stands as genuine, we have the explanation of a disciple of S. John
himself ; but if not, it is exceedingly ancient. The interval between the
sentence and its execution is supposed to have been spent in making
preparation for the crucifixion, and in the release of Barabbas ; matters
which must have taken up much time.

40. *Behold your King !*—Pilate apparently still endeavours to bring
about Christ's release. He shows Him to the people in the thorough-
ness of His humiliation, and suggests the absurdity of executing such
a one on the charge of aspiring to the throne. Seeing, perhaps,
that there were some who wavered, or who had some national pride

Shall I crucify your King? The chief priests answered,
We have no king but Cæsar.

Then delivered he Him therefore to be crucified. And
when they had mocked Him, they took off the purple
robe from Him, and put His own clothes on Him, and
led Him out to crucify Him.

Christ bearing the Cross.

S. Matt. xxvii. 32 ; S. Mark. xv. 21 ; S. Luke xxiii. 26–32 ;
S. John xix. 17.

And as they came out, they found a man of Cyrene,

against the degradation even of a Jewish pretender to the royalty which
all desired should be restored, or perhaps some who remembered Christ's
deeds of mercy, he puts the question once more, in different form. But,
if the people for one moment relent, the chief priests prevent any
expression of pity ; and thus Pilate's last appeal only elicits the most
thorough rejection of Christ in the character of the king. They speak
words as prophetic as those of Caiaphas, concerning the expediency of
giving one man over to death for the nation ; for they never again were
nationally offered by God, the King, the Messiah whom they rejected.
They had " no king but Cæsar " whilst they remained a nation, and in
rebellion against his sovereignty they were destroyed as a Church and
nation. The saying of Christ is often verified in the experience of
human life : " By thy words thou shalt be justified, and by thy words
thou shalt be condemned " (Matt. xii. 37). Men often thus unwittingly
pronounce the sentence in their own case, which God refuses to pronounce, but which the Judge will verify at the last. (See App. XVI.)

41. *delivered.*—Pilate no longer struggles against their determinate
will. This is his final order, to carry the sentence of crucifixion into
execution.

42. *the robe.*—The scarlet robe of mockery. (See note 22.) It is not
said also that they took off the crown of thorns ; and some of the early
writers assert that this remained upon His brow as He hung upon the
cross, as artists, in all ages, have depicted. The Jewish priests and
mob now took their turn in mocking Christ, and then they led Him
away to execution.

43. *came out.*—Execution took place without the city (Num.
xv. 35; Acts vii. 58; Heb. xiii. 12). As Christ suffered not within the
limits of the Jewish city, so we see that the efficacy of His saving
death is world-wide, without limitation or restriction of locality—a point
pressed in the latter passage.

44. *a man of Cyrene.*—They met Simon entering the city, as they

Simon by name, the father of Alexander and Rufus, coming out of the country, and on him they laid the cross, that he might bear it after Jesus. And there followed Him a great company of people, and of women, which also bewailed and lamented Him.

came forth from the gates. Cyrene was a part of Lybia, or Africa, which was attached to the Roman government of Crete, to which island it was somewhat adjacent. It was extensively colonized by Jews, who had a synagogue at Jerusalem (Acts vi. 9), to which they resorted when business or worship called them there. We find some of them present, and beholding the effusion of the Holy Spirit on the day of Pentecost. Some appear to have become Christians, and, after Stephen's death, to have preached the Gospel to the *Greeks,* who were probably Gentiles, not merely Hellenists or foreign Jews (Acts xi. 19, 20, xiii. 1). The names mentioned here are found in the Acts, and that of Rufus (Rom. xvi. 13) is identified with the son of this Simon. Both he and his mother were Christians, and therefore there is probability that Simon also, now or eventually, was a follower of Christ. It is his special distinction to have thus shared the burden of the cross of Christ. Basilides propounded the monstrous heresy that Simon was crucified instead of Christ. The word used for "*compelled*" is a Persian word, signifying the pressing of horses or men to the king's service.

45. *after Jesus.*—Bearing the cross was a degradation which formed part of the sufferings of the crucified. Christ was now too much exhausted by long vigils, and by His agony, to bear the weight alone. It appears, therefore, that whilst He bore the upper portion, the foot of it was laid upon Simon, who so bore it "after Jesus;" or he may have borne it at intervals instead of Christ. "Take up thy cross and follow Me," is Christ's monition to those to whom He will give afterwards a share in His glory. We must bear the cross with Him therefore; and it is a thought of comfort that our crosses may be crosses of Christ, and that, if we are bearing them patiently for His sake, He is bearing them with us.

46. *company.*—Not of disciples, but of ordinary spectators. There is always a curious throng attendant on the execution of a sentence of death; and the circumstances of Christ's life and ministry must have attracted very many "to that sight." Many of the women in this company, as they beheld Christ, and the two malefactors who were condemned to die with Him, going to their terrible death, bewailed His melancholy condition and prostration of strength. Many of them remembered His deeds of love and mercy; perhaps by His touch, and at His word, they had "received their dead raised to life again" from the living death of incurable disease; and they did not hesitate now to show their sympathy with Him, though they did not confess or espouse His cause.

But Jesus turning unto them said, Daughters of Jerusalem, weep not for Me, but weep for yourselves, and
for your children. For, behold, the days are coming, in
the which they shall say, Blessed *are* the barren, and
the wombs that never bare, and the paps which never
gave suck. **Then shall they begin to say to the mountains, Fall on us; and to the hills, Cover us.** For if
they do these things in a green tree, what shall be done
in the dry?

47. *Jesus turning.*—The gesture is noticed. Christ always arrested
the movements and attention of those who guarded Him ; when He
had words to speak, they must stay and listen. (See xxix. 16.) He
now bids these women not to mourn for His sufferings, but for their
own future misery, should they be involved in the destruction of their
city. The exhortation is that gospel cry to repentance and obedience,
which He had uttered from the first ; and it contained the offer of mercy,
that the fate He foretold should not fall upon them if believers.

48. *the days.*—Those foretold in His great prophecy, delivered on the
Mount of Olives.

49. *they shall say.*—It has been noticed that Christ does not say, " *Ye*
shall say." Some of those who heard Him might not live to see those
days ; some might happily embrace His faith, and so escape the doom
of those who refused to believe. But those shut up within the city,
during those days of terror, would bless the lot of those who were
spared the agony of parents beholding the misery from which they
could not save their children, and which would come within the lifetime, and upon the children, of those who heard Him.

50. *fall on us.*—(See Hos. x. 8.) There is a repetition of this in
Rev. vi. 16, where the scope of the prophecy is enlarged to include all
who have refused Christ as their Saviour ; and they are represented as
desiring to escape from " the wrath of the Lamb," of Him who was
now being " led as a lamb to the slaughter." This, therefore, is the
sad cry of the lost, who discern that ruin is upon them, and that it is
too late for salvation. There was a literal fulfilment of our Lord's
words ; for, in the siege of Jerusalem, numbers took refuge, and were
destroyed, in the excavations under the city.

51. *green tree.*—This is a proverbial expression. (See Ps. lii. 8.)
Christ is the green tree, the tree of life ; the unbelievers are the dry
and withered branches (see xxv. *c.* 9) ; and, more immediately, the
dry tree is the dead Jewish Church. If God permits such sufferings
to come upon the righteous, who are engaged in His direct service,
giving proof of the vitality of their union with Him by their works
of faith, " where shall the ungodly and sinner appear "—where shall the
wicked, and all who reject and who forget their Saviour, stand, when He

And there were also two other, malefactors, led with Him to be put to death.

XXXI. *THE CRUCIFIXION.*

S. Matt. xxvii. 33-44; S. Mark xv. 22-32; S. Luke xxiii. 33-43;
S. John xix. 17-27.

And when they were come to the place, which is called Calvary, that is to say, being interpreted, the place of a skull, which is called in the Hebrew Golgotha, they

appeareth? Elseley and Bishop Goodwin give another interpretation, perhaps of more immediate application to those to whom our Lord spoke: "If the Romans crucify Me in this way, during peace and prosperity, what will they do to the nation when they come upon them as bitter foes?" that is, whom rebellion has rendered suitable for destruction.

52. *two other, malefactors.*—The punctuation here is important. There is a separation between the "two other," which were "malefactors," and Christ; the plural "others" would have made the sentence more clear to modern readers. These two *malefactors* were, no doubt, men of the band of Barabbas, whom we read of as a prisoner in company "with them that had made insurrection with him" (Mark xv. 7). We might suppose, from the difference in their disposition, that one had followed him as a leader of desperadoes, for the chances of plunder which he offered; the other, perhaps, from purer and more heroic motives, followed him as a false Christ. (See notes 6, 7, 9.) Pilate may have ordered their crucifixion with Christ, if followers of Jesus Barabbas, to anger the Jews for their preference of their leader to the true Christ.

1. *a skull.*—Calvary is the Latinized form; Golgotha, the Hebrew equivalent. Why the place should thus be named, it is difficult to say. There is an old tradition that Adam was buried here by Shem, which has been dwelt on by early writers, as being a significant fact that the first Adam and the second Adam should meet in death, upon the same place. There is also a tradition that, in the Garden of Gethsemane, where our Lord's Passion commenced, Adam eat the apple of temptation, by which disobedience man fell. Another explanation is, that this was the place of public execution, and that the name was derived from the skulls of the criminals put to death or exposed here; but it is not "the place of *skulls*," and, if even the usual place of execution, it was contrary to Jewish custom to leave human bones exposed. A third (apparently the most reasonable, certainly the best supported) is,

gave Him to drink wine mingled with myrrh: and when He had tasted *thereof*, He would not drink. And there they crucified Him, and the malefactors, one on the right

that this was a low rounded hill, the form of which bore some resemblance to a human skull, and formed a slight eminence. The reason for the name, however, remains a matter of debate. There has been great question as to the identity of the site pointed out in modern times with that of the true Calvary. One of the objections seems to be that it now lies within the city. But the importance of the place itself would soon bring the modern city round it. Without entering into arguments beyond the compass of a note, it is exceedingly probable that the site has been correctly maintained by constant tradition. (See App. XV.) The period most possible for error would be that prior to the time of Constantine. It may reasonably be hoped that the progress of modern research may place this interesting question on a satisfactory and permanent footing.

2. *wine ... myrrh.*—S. Matthew gives "vinegar and gall;" the *vinegar* being the sour wine of the country, and the *gall* either added to the myrrh, or as being typical of extreme bitterness. S. Matthew speaks in the words of Ps. lxix. 21. It is probable that the draught was drugged with other herbs, as the effect of myrrh alone would not be particularly stupefying; for it is generally agreed that this was the usual draught given to those condemned to die on the cross, in order to deaden their sensibility to pain. This might, indeed, in the end prolong the period of suffering, as, if really an anodyne, it would lessen the first shock to the nervous system. But it seems to have been given to Christ from some kindly motive. Farrar says that charitable women in Jerusalem prepared these opiates for criminals, and that the custom was founded on a rabbinical interpretation of Prov. xxxi. 6.

3. *tasted.*—He first tasted; and whilst thus accepting any intended kindness, He deliberately declined what He perceived was intended to prevent His experiencing the full bitterness of pain, by the stupefaction of His natural senses; nay, by tasting, He accepted the bitterness, of which, by refusing to drink, He denied Himself any mitigation.

4. *crucified.*—This punishment is generally considered to have been that in which the extremes of agony and degradation were combined. That death, therefore, which by common consent includes these extremes, comprehends, and is representative of, all other deaths that man can die; thus, as well as in the stead of all, Christ "tasted death for every man," and conquered death in whatsoever form it can assail man. The cross was of several forms. That on which our Lord was crucified consisted of one upright, with a transverse bar; the upright being continued above the transverse, as it bore the superscription or title "*over His head*," which was written by Pilate (Matt. xxvii. 37; Mark xv. 26; Luke xxiii. 38; John xix. 19). The sufferer was some-

hand, and the other on the left, on either side one, and Jesus in the midst. And the scripture was fulfilled, which saith, **And He was numbered with the transgressors.**

Then said Jesus, 𝕱𝖆𝖙𝖍𝖊𝖗, 𝖋𝖔𝖗𝖌𝖎𝖇𝖊 𝖙𝖍𝖊𝖒, 𝖋𝖔𝖗 𝖙𝖍𝖊𝖞 𝖐𝖓𝖔𝖜 𝖓𝖔𝖙 𝖜𝖍𝖆𝖙 𝖙𝖍𝖊𝖞 𝖉𝖔.

times bound with cords, sometimes nailed to the cross, as in the case of Christ: "They pierced His hands and His feet" (John xx. 25). After He was fixed to the cross, it was placed in a socket prepared in the ground for it, and made fast. This caused great agony, by bringing the weight of the body, with a sudden shock, upon the lacerated hands and feet. Intense thirst and inflammation aggravated the sufferings of the crucified, which often lasted until the third or fourth day, and were known occasionally to last as long as the ninth day. Although His life and death were subject to His own will (John x. 18), yet the distress of mind, and excessive fatigue, and previous injuries, naturally shortened our Saviour's sufferings. Without being sustained by a miracle, He could not, humanly speaking, have survived the protracted strain and agony which death thus terminated. Crucifixion was a Roman, not a Jewish, punishment, though known also to other ancient nations.

5. *Father,* etc.—"Give time and opportunity for repentance, that they may live to see, and reject their error." This is the first of our Lord's "*seven words upon the cross,*" and was probably spoken as they made Him fast to the cross, or erected it in the ground. It sums up, in His example, that great doctrine of the forgiveness of injuries, which He preached so constantly, as a necessity of our acceptance with God. It is a very general and comprehensive prayer; there is, however, a limitation. It is "because they know not," and therefore "*if* they know not what they do," that Christ prays for forgiveness for His murderers. The soldiers were amongst these; some of the council, also, "had not consented unto the deed of them" who compassed His death; many of the multitude around did it "in ignorance" of the deep sin against Heaven in which they were actors. Christ would not have His death revenged upon them; He would rather that they should be converted, and the grace of penitence bestowed upon them, and the blessing of His forgiveness sealed to them. If ever Christ's prayer is effective—and we know that God heareth Him always (John xi. 42)—we may suppose that urged upon the cross must be so. And truly it was not without fruit. If "the blood of the martyrs is the seed of the Church," how much more the blood of Christ? The confession of the penitent malefactor, and of the centurion, were first-fruits from Jew and Gentile of His prayer in death. But the prayer must extend to include all those who, in after ages, "have crucified the Son of God

And Pilate wrote a title, and put it over His head on the cross. And the writing was, JESUS OF NAZARETH

afresh," in the wickedness of their ways, for whose salvation Christ died. It would probably not include those whose sin remained, because they declared their consciousness that *they saw* (John ix. 41). Such were Caiaphas, and many of the rulers. "There is a sin unto death," and, when it is consummated, it must place the doer beyond the effect of this prayer. Certainly none who knew most fully the enormity of their sin, even the rulers, "had they known it" (in all its consequences), "would not have crucified the Lord of glory." "Through ignorance they did it" (Acts iii. 17); but, though S. Peter might charitably admit this palliation of their error, it would not avert the sentence of God's wrath against those who wilfully transgressed, and adhered to their transgression of the rule of right which they did see, and who deliberately closed their eyes that they might, so far as was possible, keep themselves in ignorance of the exact truth. The whole passage in Heb. vi. 4–6 is to be considered with reference to this crucifixion of our Lord by those, who, though blessed with the illumination of the heavenly gift of God's Spirit of knowledge of the truth, sin against light, determining not to see. For all but such as these, our Lord has prayed that God would forgive them their share of that sin for which He must die; and, therefore, their share in His death. "Nor must we imagine that here He prayed in vain; but that in those who believed after His Passion, He obtained the point of His prayers. It must be remembered, however, that He prayed not for those who chose rather to crucify than to confess Him, whom they knew to be the Son of God; but for such as were ignorant what they did, having a zeal of God, but not according to knowledge." (*Bede.*) The forgivingness of Christ is very striking, in contrast with the natural impulse to call down punishment and vengeance upon those who do us wrong. It is a lesson of universal application: for, if Christ could pray for forgiveness for those who crucified Him, and put Him to an open shame, surely the lesser offences of our neighbour, which are not against our life, must be included in the law of forgiveness, which teaches men to forgive and pray for even their murderers and slanderers.

6. *a title.*—A technical term, denoting the designation, or description, of the crucified. S. Mark also terms it "the superscription of His accusation;" S. Matthew simply "His accusation." Pilate, partly in scorn of the Jews, who had forced him to exhibit such irresolution, cowardice, and injustice, placed upon the cross the title which they desired to repudiate; partly, perhaps, in the conviction, that, in some mysterious sense, Christ's claims were true—that He was worthier of royalty than they of such a King,—published to the world His rightful description. It was all the more distasteful to the rulers, because of the declaration that their King came out of Nazareth. The rulers

THE KING OF THE JEWS. This title then read many of the Jews: for the place where Jesus was crucified was nigh to the city: and it was written in Hebrew, *and* Greek, *and* Latin. Then said the chief priests of the Jews to Pilate, Write not, The King of the Jews; but that He said, I am King of the Jews. Pilate answered, What I have written I have written.

Then the soldiers, when they had crucified Jesus, took His garments, and made four parts, to every soldier a part;

perceived the mockery of the Romans, and, whilst they wished Christ to be derided, as they also derided Him, they did not wish that the title "the King of the Jews" should be held up for ridicule; for they did not mean what they said, "We have no king but Cæsar;" but they wished Pilate to write that Christ was put to death as a false pretender to that title.

7. *Hebrew, Greek, Latin.*—One, the language of the nation of the promise; the second, that of universal literature; the third, the imperial language of the world. Most ancient and modern writers point to this, as significant of the universal dominion of Christ the King, and of the world's interest in His salvation. Pilate did not intend so much; but he truly described the office of Christ. His obstinacy of disposition, and unwillingness further to gratify those who had so humiliated him in his own consciousness, prompted his refusal to alter what he had written; and thus Jesus, before men and angels, received, in death, the designation which the Jews, to their ruin, refused to acknowledge. Greswell supposes that "the inscription on the cross of our Lord was legible from the city;" but the words of the Evangelists scarcely bear this construction. Unless the cross was immediately below the walls, and the writing of enormous size, it would be impossible. (See note 17.) But many of the Jews, coming in and out of the city, at this season so crowded with residents, must have been arrested by the sight, and read the title.

8. *his garments.*—They had first humiliated Him by stripping Him of His clothes, which, save a linen girdle, which was usually left, became the perquisite of the executioners. The under garment, being woven, could not be divided, but was awarded by lot. To the eye of the beholder, there must have been a strange contrast between the agony of the patient Saviour, who hung above them upon His cross, and the recklessness and heartlessness of those who were dividing and throwing the dice for the disposal of the garments which He had worn— those garments, on the very touch of which healing power had been so often conveyed to the faithful sufferer who sought His grace. And yet, as they thus acted, to the distress of those who, standing by His cross, or afar off, beheld His sufferings, how minutely was being fulfilled the

and also His coat: now the coat was without seam, woven
from the top throughout. They said therefore among
themselves, Let us not rend it, but cast lots for it, whose
it shall be: that the Scripture might be fulfilled, which
saith, **They parted My garments among them, and for
My vesture did they cast lots.** These things therefore
the soldiers did. And sitting down they watched Him
there.

words of Scripture which, centuries before, had exactly described this
scene! The prophetic words, "they stand staring and looking upon
me," express *His* humiliation, "who bore *our* shame," on this degradation.

9. *four parts.*—The ancient writers have seen, in this division, the
sharing of the Saviour's righteousness amongst the quarters of the
world; whilst the woven robe, which might not be divided without
destruction, denotes that the Church of Christ's righteousness is one,
and catholic: it must embrace every one, and its unity must be maintained—schism is ruinous to its unity. There is, in some of the earlier
writers, a disposition to trace type and allegory in every Scripture
incident, to a point which often obscures the simple and literal truth;
but none can question the devotion of those who search the hidden
meaning of all that concerns Christ's death, when every incident is
significant, and when the finger of prophecy has pointed to the group
of soldiers, at the foot of the cross, as acting their careless part beneath
the searching eye of Divine Providence.

10. *fulfilled.*—Of course, the soldiers did not do this that they might
fulfil a prophecy of whose existence they were wholly ignorant; but
their actions unconsciously verified the word of God. This illustration
of the way in which prophecy finds fulfilment, is a valuable one.
(See i. 14.)

11. *watched.*—This was simply the fulfilment of the ordinary duty
of the guard, who sat down to await the full execution of the sentence
in the death of our Lord, and to prevent rescue or interference on the
part of His friends. But how evidently this gesture of ease and
carelessness impresses itself upon the eye witness who describes it! It
is one of the details of the picture of the Crucifixion which strike the
heart of him whose whole interest is absorbed in the scene; and who,
as he regards it, knows that the true interest of the world is centred
in the crucifixion of Christ, and that the earnest regard of the angel
world is also bent upon it. Everything, whether in the foreground or
in the background of the picture; whether in contrast or in harmony
with the central figure of the Saviour; as scorn, hostility, or pity is
displayed; as rejection or belief actuate those grouped around; all
these, in every minutest incident, are invested with unspeakable
importance in the great scene before the eye. (See note 8.)

And the people stood beholding. And they that passed
by reviled Him, wagging their heads, and saying, Ah!
Thou that destroyest the temple, and buildest it in three
days, save thyself. If Thou be the Son of God, come
down from the cross. Likewise also the chief priests

12. *that passed.*—There was a great crowd of spectators who stood
beholding; many of them, apparently, in silent concern, or, at least, not
joining in the violence of the rulers and other bystanders. Later on
we are told that they "came together to *that sight;*" but many also
were coming and going to and from the city—for the day was one of
great importance, and, at this hour, of bustle, for multitudes were
now engaged in preparing the Passover. These took readily the lead
of the rulers, and reviled the Saviour. S. Luke xxiii. 35 connects the
insolence of the people with that of the rulers, "The rulers also *with
them* derided Him." Their scornful gestures on this occasion are
foreseen in Ps. xxii. 7. Their exclamation, rendered, "*Ah!*" stands
for a world of gibe and vulgar insolence. As so much of their occupation on this day was connected with the service of the Temple, they
are prompt to point out how firm it stood in its beauty, whilst Christ
was dying on the cross. Their words of contempt show that they had
been tutored by the rulers, who had brought forth these words of our
Lord, and distorted them by the mouth of false witnesses. But there
seems a peculiar malice in them, if they understood that "He spake
of the temple of His body" (a familiar and general figure), and now
applied them to Him in this meaning; though the crowd around might
otherwise interpret them. (See xxx. c. 7.)

13. *if Thou be,* etc.—He had called on God, as His *Father,* to forgive
them. Here is their retort. But we see that their malicious words are
not only due to the rulers, but to Satan also; for we recognize the very
words in which he first taunted Christ to save Himself from hunger—no
mere coincidence, at such a moment, and under such circumstances.
As Satan had entered into Judas, so had he also entered into these
men; and there is to Christ's ear the laugh of the arch-fiend, recalling
the temptation in the wilderness. He who had "departed from Him
a season" was present now: it was "their hour, and the power of
darkness."

14. *chief priests.*—These leaders of religious thought and ceremonial
were not ashamed to disgrace themselves, publicly, by this outrage upon
one whom they had succeeded in bringing to death by judicial murder.
But they do it to their own cost. In their choice of bitter taunts, they
commit themselves to the statement, "He saved others;" therefore
they have crucified a *Saviour.* It is noticeable that they do not
address Christ directly, like others who were mocking Him. There
seems a consciousness of villainy upon them; and their courage goes

mocking *Him*, with the scribes and elders, said, He saved others; Himself He cannot save. Let Him save Himself, if He be Christ, the chosen of God. If He be the King of Israel, let Him now come down from the cross, and we will believe Him. **He trusted in God; let Him deliver Him now, if He will have Him** : for He said, I am the Son of God.

And the soldiers also mocked Him, coming to Him,

no further than talking jocosely and scornfully at Him amongst themselves, as the original of S. Mark xv. 31 distinctly expresses. No doubt, also, they thus strengthened themselves in their decision that He was not the Saviour, as He would not now save Himself.

15. *we will believe.*—They had no longer the power, neither had they the desire, to do so; the sentence of judgment had already passed upon them. (See xvii. 5, 6.) S. Jerome attributes the cry, "Come down from the cross," to the instigation of Satan, who now perceived that Christ upon the cross was truly a conqueror. (See also xxx. *f.* 11.) And we cannot but consider this as a temptation of Satan, through their lips—an unavailing and despairing effort against the Saviour, even at the last, and in the agonies of His death. It was a public renewal of that former proposal to gain credit as the Messiah, by precipitating Himself from the pinnacle of the Temple before the eyes of the people, who, seeing the miracle of His deliverance, would be inclined to believe. But it was not such a challenge as this which could move Him, who was now "enduring the cross, despising the shame." It is a law of temptation, that, once successfully resisted, it presents itself in feebler force; and, therefore, these words of the rulers' scorn have not the vigour and subtlety of Satan's original temptation. But they are truly fiendish in their origin; and they must have had their force at such an hour, as urged against One who was utterly exhausted by the weariness and the agony of His Passion. We need not be surprised that Satan, who had only "left Him for a season," when vanquished in the wilderness, should be present and busy at the closing scene. And if Satan lacked vantage-ground to tempt (for, as the Saviour declared, "the prince of this world cometh, and hath nothing in Me "), yet truly he did not want the malicious insolence which dared to stir up old and painful memories of past assaults, to wound Christ's spirit with the recollection of past pain and indignation in His last moments; nor did he want willing agents, through whom to press his malice and wrath. He did not see that he did but strengthen Christ, by stirring up the recollection of past victory.

16. *the soldiers.*—They, too, followed the lead of the Jewish rulers. Jews and Gentiles were thus again united against Him. These offered Him some of their sour wine, as it were some royal draught, and

and offering Him vinegar, and saying, If Thou be the King of the Jews, save Thyself.

The Penitent Malefactor.

S. Luke xxiii. 39-43.

And one of the malefactors which were hanged railed on Him, saying, If Thou be Christ, save Thyself and

urged Him to issue a royal decree for His own deliverance. But theirs was a far less malicious taunt; they only mocked one whom they thought worthy, in His humiliation, to be called king of such a people as the Jews; and who, though rejected by these Jews, was condemned for aspiring to contest Cæsar's sovereignty. For the similar but kindlier act of one of them, veiled, perhaps, by the echo of like words, see note 33.

17. *and one.*—This narrative is peculiar to St. Luke. If we take the words of SS. Matthew and Mark literally, we should suppose that *both* the malefactors at first *reviled* Christ; but that one of them, struck with His patience and goodness, repented of having done so; whilst the other, with an accession of insolence, went on to *blaspheme* Him. This might be; but there are sufficient instances in the N. T. of the use of the plural in an indefinite sense, to explain this statement, without supposing that the penitent malefactor reproached Christ at all. He may have called on Him, if indeed a Saviour, to save them. But with regard to the other man's malicious conduct, it was, indeed, a transgression of what appears to be a sort of rule of the fellowship of suffering, when even he took up the taunts of the crowd against Him who shared his death, "and cast them in His teeth;" for there is generally found some mutual kindliness amongst those who are "in the same condemnation," and whom the world has doomed and abandoned. The term "malefactor" is more rightly descriptive of these criminals than the word "thief." The original word does not mean a common and petty *thief*, but one to whom a more general term might be applied. (See xxx. *f.* 6, 7, 9, 52.) Tradition, in one of the apocryphal Gospels, gives the name of the penitent malefactor as Dysmas, and speaks of his having preserved the life of the Virgin and Child on their flight into Egypt. Greswell thinks that these two men were crucified looking west, and Christ looking east; such a position being favourable for what passed between them on the cross. He considers that this would account for the legs of the malefactors being broken first, as the soldiers came to them before coming to Christ; and he states that the title on the cross was legible from the city walls (see note 7), and, therefore, that the cross of Christ must have been turned towards them. The position of the cross may have

us.   But the other answering rebuked him, saying, Dost
not thou fear God, seeing thou art in the same condemnation?   And we indeed justly; for we receive the due
reward of our deeds : but this man hath done nothing

been as he describes, though the same object would be attained if
Christ's cross was a little behind or before the other two; or if, as
painters represent, it was somewhat higher.   The last assertion is
scarcely credible, considering the height of the walls of Jerusalem, and
the space occupied by bystanders around the cross.   The ancient
writers notice that the position of the two malefactors, on Christ's right
hand and on His left, indicates the separation of believers and
unbelievers, especially in the final judgment.

18. *fear God.*—Man had done his worst against them—therefore
they have no more to fear from men; but this criminal recognizes still
the power of God—the state hereafter.   He acknowledges the justice
of the sentence by which he dies, perhaps not as man's just sentence,
but as the award of God's justice against his sins.   He had probably
followed a false Christ (xxx. *f*. 52), and, under his banner, allowed
himself to be led into acts of rapine and lawlessness, perhaps of murder
also.   In clear contrast with his own career, he beheld the goodness
and mercy of Christ, whose prayer he had just heard, of whose
acquittal by Pilate he was probably aware; and he discerned the malice
of the rulers against Him.   If this man was a follower of Jesus
Barabbas as a false Christ (and the fact of his crucifixion argues him a
political, rather than a criminal, offender); crucified, perhaps, that Pilate
may show his bitter scorn of those who rejected such a King of men
as Christ, and chose such a vulgar ruffian as Jesus Barabbas—as, in
strange coincidence, the pseudo-Christ was named (see xxx. *f*. 7)—he
must have aimed at better things than he attained to under such a
leader.   Perhaps he now saw in Christ the realization of the excellence
to which he aspired.   It is difficult to account for the fact of one who
in sincerity sought a Christ when our Saviour was on earth, finding
only Barabbas, though the Saviour's name and deeds were so familiar
in the land.   But it would appear that he never had come into contact
before with Jesus, or, at least, not so as to have had opportunity to
discern His saving character.   He had been brought up in the belief
that the Messiah must come with arms and force of human conquest;
and it is the nature of error to hold men back from the truth.   Elseley
notices the remonstrance of this man with his fellow-criminal, as
showing some anxiety for his salvation.   This is probable; for why,
otherwise, should he rebuke him, and not rather content himself with
expressing his own different sentiments by turning to Christ?   This
view would mark an additional excellence in his case, and another
aspect of faith.

amiss. And he said unto Jesus, Lord, remember me when Thou comest into Thy kingdom. And Jesus said unto him, 𝕺𝖊𝖗𝖎𝖑𝖕 𝕴 𝖘𝖆𝖕 𝖚𝖓𝖙𝖔 𝖙𝖍𝖊𝖊, 𝕿𝖔-𝖉𝖆𝖕 𝖘𝖍𝖆𝖑𝖙 𝖙𝖍𝖔𝖚 𝖇𝖊 𝖜𝖎𝖙𝖍 𝕸𝖊 𝖎𝖓 𝕻𝖆𝖗𝖆𝖉𝖎𝖘𝖊.

19. *into Thy kingdom.*—This should be "*in* Thy kingdom." The faith of this man is marvellous. None had believed Christ under such circumstances as these. He saw the vision of Christ's kingdom, even when He hung upon the cross in mortal agony, with the impress of death upon His countenance; and, in his faith, he begged that Christ would grant him pardon and acceptance when He came forth from death, a conqueror, and in the glory of His eternal kingdom. We notice that the conditions of the Gospel proclamation of mercy were met in his case; he repented, and believed the Gospel. The offer of salvation came to him in his last hour, and he embraced it at once, and was saved. It is clear, therefore, that there is hope of mercy even at the hour of death, when only repentance and faith are possible, and when there is no time to amend the errors of the life past, by a new life of obedience. What is granted in one case may be granted in others; but it is necessary to remember the often-quoted caution that "there is one instance given, that none may despair; and one only, that none may presume." But we must also see that the assurance often grounded on this case is not a correct one; it does not teach directly the acceptance of a "deathbed repentance," in the ordinary sense of the expression; that is, the acceptance of the contrition of one, in his dying hour, who has wilfully or negligently postponed repentance until then. With regard to such cases, there is hope in the general rule that, wherever God grants the grace of repentance, He gives the offer of mercy. But the case of the penitent malefactor is not such a one. It is not likely that he had ever spurned, or postponed, the offer of Christ's mercy; but his example is rather one of the glad acceptance of grace immediately it was offered, which, in his case, was the hour of death. Like the case of the labourers in the vineyard, he had his offer in the eleventh hour, and accepted it; quite a different thing from the case of those who had the offer earlier in life, and constantly, but who have put off repentance until "the eleventh hour;" to whom neither the call of these labourers, nor of the penitent malefactor, gives (as is sometimes supposed) any special warrant of hope. This malefactor gives example of a wonderful *faith*; the ordinary "deathbed repentance," of *contrition* for a life of extraordinary neglect, wilfulness, and want of faith. Bishop Goodwin remarks that the penitent thief was familiar, as a Jew, with the idea of a life hereafter, and of a Messiah coming in His kingdom.

20. *to-day.*—Not only when Christ came in His kingdom of the future, but at once, he shall have his portion with Christ. There seems much tenderness in the words, "*with Me.*" Christ accepted the

Christ commends His Mother to John.

S. John xix. 25-27.

Now there stood by the cross of Jesus His mother,

man's devotion and faith, as a King and as a Saviour. But there is, further, in these words, the acceptance of the one human heart which owned His cause, and spoke up in His behalf at this crisis. This could not but be a grateful homage to Christ as *man*, as one who never slighted, but ever warmly welcomed, human friendship and sympathy. Thus the ancient writers point out that Christ upon the cross foreshows His enthronization as Judge. He dispenses acceptance and condemnation to the types of those who shall be ranged hereafter upon His right hand, and upon His left.

21. *paradise.*—The word is a Persian one, and means a pleasure-park of great, though limited, extent, like that surrounding a royal palace. It was used by the Jews to signify the state into which the soul entered after death—a state of being of which they had but an indefinite idea. It was, however, a place of protection from accident or trouble—the guarded and happy residence of the children and servants of the "great King." There His servants, the angels, passed to and fro upon His embassy; for it was not the inner palace of His presence, but the outer garden of His residence. There were rivers of coolness and beauty—rivers of life, and the choice trees (Rev. ii. 7) which adorned and shaded the approach to His palace. In fact, paradise was more than a restoration of primæval Eden. To the Christian, it is Hades; but the Hades of the blest, where the souls of the righteous await, in the repose of happiness, their resurrection to eternal life. We know that it is not heaven itself, because Christ did not ascend into heaven until after His resurrection. His saying, " To-day shalt thou be with Me in paradise," makes certain the fact that there is an intermediate state of rest between earth and heaven, where the souls of the righteous await the resurrection of the body. We are not received into a perfect place of bliss whilst in an imperfect state of being. The Jews had another name for paradise—"Abraham's bosom." To their mind, Abraham was not only the father of their nation of believers, and greater than any other who had passed into the unseen world; but equally the father of the blessed beyond the grave. (See essay " The Descent into Hell.")

22. *the cross.*—It has been noticed how distinctly the Crucifixion brings into prominence the principle that the cross of Christ has ever proved the touchstone to human hearts. We see how strangely the Crucifixion itself brings out the leading failings or excellences of those who were concerned in it, or present at the time; how they approached

and His mother's sister, Mary the *wife* of Cleophas, and

Christ only to be revealed in their true light. The evil are prominent in evil action ; the good range themselves on the side of Christ ; even the timid, who had not before professed Christ openly, are strengthened and decided. It is still the same. The name of Christ holds together a vast number of those who are thoroughly identified with His interests; multitudes, also, who would reap the advantages of Christianity in this world, but who aspire no higher. Directly the cross of Christ, as the emblem of self-denial or trouble, lays its shadow before them, there is an immediate and decided separation : the true-hearted gather to the front of danger and trial, the faint-hearted waver and stand aloof. This principle descends into individual experience, where there is no point of general interest at issue, in which the Church or the multitude are concerned ; for there is ever the same separation in the tastes and preferences of daily life, as the command or service of Christ bars self-indulgence, and demands obedience. There is also another view of the cross. We may notice how it typifies all virtues and graces, all joys and hopes, all sorrows and sympathy, all provision made for relief of human misery, all opposition to wrong, every crusade against sin in its every form, all service beneath Christ's banner, everything connected with our career on earth, which Christ included in the command, " Take up thy cross and follow Me ; " all deeds of mercy and goodness, all endurance in suffering, all glory of victory.

23. *His mother.*—From the way in which this is introduced, we can scarcely suppose that "the three Marys" had been there from the first. It may have been that, after S. John, who appears now in charge of them, had seen the conclusion of the trial, and the act of crucifixion, he went to tell the women what was done, and brought them forth to the cross of Christ. Had they been there at the first, we should not, perhaps, have read the words, " when Jesus saw His mother ; " they suggest her having just arrived on the scene. It was truly a sad trial for her who had loved her Son deeply ; and who had, during all these years, pondered in her heart His divine sayings, and the declarations of God concerning Him ; and had understood, better than most others, the nature and truth of His claims. He now, at the last, provides for her future comfort, for so long as she remains upon earth ; and for ministration to her of the truths of spiritual life. He thus manifests His care and love for her in the very agony of death. It had been declared that " the sword should pierce through her own soul also," when the sword of God's vengeance " awakened against the man that was His fellow " (Luke ii. 35 ; Zech. xiii. 7). It is not written that her faith failed her now ; it is unlikely that it did so ; though her mother's heart was pierced with more than natural grief, as she saw Him dying. She is only once again mentioned in Scripture (Acts i. 14). There is little doubt that Joseph was at this time dead, and

Mary Magdalene. When Jesus therefore saw His mother,

that she had no children but our Lord, and no near relative. Lightfoot remarks that if " the brethren of Jesus " (see note 24) were even sons of Joseph by a former wife, as some have thought, they (not S. John) would have been the fittest to be charged with the maintenance of his widow. Tradition places his death prior to the marriage of Cana in Galilee ; and if, as some modern critics think, Salome, the mother of John, was the sister of Mary our Lord's mother, we see how natural a charge (as well as from his character and devotion how suitable) was this now made to the beloved disciple, who had also been the nearest and most constant in attendance on our Lord during these hours of darkness. But see note 24, and App. XVII.

24. *Mary . . . of Cleophas.*—This should be " *Clopas*," and is generally identified with Alphæus, the father of " James, and Joses, and Simon, and Judas," our Lord's " brethren ; " and is said to have been the brother of Joseph, and therefore the reputed uncle of Christ. His son Simon, or Simeon, is said by Eusebius to have been made Bishop of Jerusalem after James, by the joint consent of the surviving Apostles, as being the nearest relation of our Lord. Clopas is supposed to have died before our Lord's public ministry commenced, in which case he cannot be the same as Cleopas of S. Luke xxiv., as is often said. SS. Matthew and Mark say that Mary, the mother of James and Joses, was present near the cross ; and if Alphæus and Clopas are identical, this Mary would be the same spoken of by S. John, as " Mary, the wife (now probably *widow*) of Clopas ; " and by the other Evangelists as " Mary, the mother of James and Joses." Many writers further identify her with the sister of our Lord's mother, here men- tioned. But there is some question whether our Lord's mother's sister was this Mary, the wife of Clopas, mother of James and Joses, or Salome, mother of S. John (see note 23) ; and, therefore, it is difficult to decide whether there were *three* women standing near the cross, as is generally supposed, namely, 1. Mary, our Lord's mother ; 2. Mary, her sister, wife of Clopas ; 3. Mary Magdalene ; or, 1. Mary, our Lord's mother ; 2. her sister Salome, mother of Zebedee's children, called also Mary, in a fragment (questioned) of Papias (see App. XVII.) ; 3. Mary, wife of Clopas ; 4. Mary Magdalene. The question turns on whether the words, " his mother's " sister, refer to Mary, wife of Clopas, who is next named ; or, without naming her, to Salome : in the former case three, in the latter, four, must have been present. There is also a difficulty in exactly identifying this group, as given by S. John, with those given by the other Evangelists ; but they may have been viewed at different times. It is possible that our Lord's mother was led away by S. John from this scene of sorrow ; and the group may have been re-formed afterwards ; as her name does not occur amongst those who were present when Christ died. There thus appear to have been other

and the disciple standing by, whom He loved, He saith
unto His mother, **Woman, behold thy son!** Then saith
He to the disciple, **Behold thy mother!** And from that
hour that disciple took her unto his own *home*.

Christ dieth.

S. Matt. xxvii. 45–53 ; S. Mark xv. 33–38 ; S. Luke xxiii. 44–46 ;
S. John xix. 28–30.

Now from the sixth hour there was darkness over all

ties than those of their discipleship which united these holy women
who stood near the cross of Christ.

25. *Mary Magdalene.*—(See note 50.)

26. *Woman.*—Our Lord never addresses her as "mother." He
makes clear (and the Evangelists distinctly express it), the great
separation between Himself and her—a distinction which has been lost
sight of in the exaltation of the Blessed Virgin to divine honours. But
the term our Lord uses is, in the original, one of great respect; and
we may be assured, as spoken at this time, of infinite tenderness also.
He glances now at S. John, who was standing near her, and desires
her to look to him henceforth as being in the place of a son, to support
and protect her, and to minister to her the mysteries of the eternal life,
during the remainder of her days upon earth. And then he gives the
same charge to the beloved disciple, as the strongest proof of His love,
and the greatest honour He could confer on the Apostle. It has been
beautifully explained that our Lord uses the term " woman," to show
that she is the true type of all that is womanly and good ; that He did
not wish to point her out to the insolent crowd as His mother ; and
that such an address would, at this moment, only have intensified her
sorrow for her Son.

27. *from that hour.*—Many writers think that S. John led her away
at once from the painful scene of the Crucifixion, and that she was not
present when our Lord died (note 24). It is likely that this was
the case, though the words need not imply so much. If so, however,
S. John returned to the cross, when he had placed her in safety (John
xix. 35).

28. *unto His own.*—The word " *home* " is not the original, which, in
its indefiniteness, is of wider application. It expresses that in all things
which were his on earth, he acknowledged her claim ; he took her not
to his home only, but to his heart also, and fully adopted the relationship bequeathed to him by his Lord—that of a son towards a mother.
" Unto his own what ? Was not John one of those who said, ' Lo, we
have left all and followed Thee ' ? He took her to his own, *i.e.* not to

the land unto the ninth hour. And about the ninth hour, Jesus cried with a loud voice, saying, **Eli, Eli, lama sabachthani!** that is to say, **My God, My God,**

his farm, for he had none, but to his care, for of that he was master." (*Augustine.*) (See **xxv.** *e.* 37.)

29. *from the sixth hour.*—On the difficulties connected with the time as given by the several Evangelists, see sect. **xxx.** *f.* 39. This darkness continued from about noon to the third hour in the evening. It could not have been caused by an eclipse of the sun; because no eclipse could last so long, and no eclipse is possible with the moon (as during the Paschal week) at the full. The darkness could only affect such a portion of the earth as then enjoyed the light of day; but there is no reason for assigning a wider meaning to the words "all the land," than to "all the world" in Luke ii. 1, namely, all the land of Judæa—*the* land, "the glory of all lands" to the thought of the Jew; indeed, it is only necessary to the truth of the narrative that we should understand that all the land near Jerusalem should be so darkened, though we may well suppose a wider limit. It was evidently a miracle, and one in contrast with the bright effulgence of heavenly glory in which proclamation was made of the Saviour's birth. And if ever the sun was darkened by the interruption of the ordinary laws of nature, it had reason to be so, when the Son of God, who made the worlds, was dying upon the cross for human sin, crucified by wicked hands of lawless men. We may suppose how deep silence fell now upon all around the cross; and how conscience smote the wicked, as during that plague in Egypt when the darkness "could be felt," when Nature refused to look upon their evil deed. (See i. 30.) This was the "hour of the powers of darkness," and doubtless they were busy now.

30. *Eli, Eli*, etc.—S. Mark gives a Syro-Chaldee form, Eloi. This mournful cry broke the stillness of that terrible darkness. We cannot tell the horror of sin and the misery which was upon the soul of the Saviour, when such words burst from His lips. They are not the cry of bodily agony, but of oppression of spiritual life. The world's sin lay upon Him; He had "made His soul an offering for sin," and He felt (that man might never feel it, and as man never could feel it) the distress of the Divine displeasure against the sins for which He had given Himself up to die; for they lost nothing of their heinousness in God's sight, because they were laid upon Christ. The terrors of the judgment were upon Him, and the awe of God the Judge. He now "tasted of death for every man;" not the mere "shuffling off this mortal coil," but He perceived the bitterness of the sinner's death that never dies. We cannot fully understand this mystery of His sufferings; but we may thank God, who "has commended His *love* towards us, in that Christ died for the ungodly." There is, in the language of

why hast Thou forsaken Me ? Some of them that stood there, when they heard *that*, said, This *man* calleth for Elias.

After this, Jesus knowing that all things were now accomplished, that the scripture might be fulfilled, saith, **I thirst.** Now there was set a vessel full of vinegar : and

this cry, one word of hope. Our Lord is not alone; the Father is with Him, though He bears the Divine judgment; for He says, " *My* God ! " Although He stands in the sinner's stead, He can still say that. It has been proposed to read, " why *didst* Thou forsake Me ? " as if the shadow were passed even before Christ thus spoke.

31. *Elias.*—It has been questioned if this was entirely spoken in mockery. Some writers recall the expectation that Elias should come and restore all things; and suppose that, in the horror of the darkness, and with their knowledge of the reality of Christ's truth, some of the rulers were struck with fear that Elias was now being summoned by Him. Some of the bystanders may have felt such alarm. A comparison of Mal. iv. 5, 6, with Joel ii. 1, 2, 31, might suggest such an awe. But the general opinion is that they mocked His distress, as the Psalms foreshowed; choosing to understand the word " Eli " (God) as " Elias," a misunderstanding almost impossible, unless intentional. The words must have been spoken by Jews, for they alone would be familiar with the name of the great prophet Elias; and there is not one single word or deed recorded, throughout the whole history of the Passion and crucifixion, which can help us to think that any of the Jews showed any other spirit towards our Saviour, than that of mockery and cruelty. There was no fear of man or God; no softening towards Christ, in any degree.

32. *all things.*—Generally, all that the Father gave Him to do in the prosecution of His commission to earth; and, specially, all prophecies and types fulfilled, and the whole purpose of God accomplished with regard to the incarnation, earthly life, Passion, and death of Christ.

33. *I thirst.*—The Scripture (Ps. lxix. 21) had foreshown this thirst of Christ, and it was now fulfilled. Excruciating thirst is one of the natural consequences of crucifixion; our Lord felt it, and He noted the fulfilment of prophecy, the last remaining to be verified, in His demand. It is an expression of our Lord's humanity which might have touched the hearts even of those who had crucified and mocked Him; for the cry of those who thirst is one of the most sacred claims in the East, and one which our Lord, in His consecration of the common obligations of life, has graced with the blessing of the Gospel (Matt. x. 42). But His demand was most inhumanly mocked by the rulers. One of the Roman soldiers, indeed, was prompt to respond to it; and at once dipped a sponge in a vessel of the soldiers' wine, and

straightway one of them ran, and took a spunge, and filled *it* with vinegar, and put it on a reed, and gave Him to drink. The rest said, Let be, let us see whether Elias will come to save Him.

held it up to Him upon a stalk of hyssop, and put it to His mouth. It is his distinction to have done the last act of kindness to the dying Saviour; it was accepted by Him, and, by our Lord's rule, he would not lose his reward. But the rulers scoffed at His distress, applying their miserable play upon the name of Elias; and would have prevented the act of mercy, saying, "Let Him alone, until we see if Elias will save Him!" The soldier, if we take Mark xv. 36, literally, seems to have repeated their words; but, if he did so, he did not desist from his act of kindness. Bishop Ellicott supposes that this man, who had joined in mocking Christ, does this act now in compassion; but that, on the rest trying to hinder him, he persists, under cover of mockery, in performing it; running up with the sponge, and saying, "Let me alone; let us see if Elias will come." This is very ingenious; and, considering the unanimous spirit of mockery which actuated the by-standers, it is possible he may have pretended to scoff, in order to be able to do a deed of pity amongst these merciless men; but the idea is one which would scarcely present itself to an ordinary reader, as a natural explanation. It seems, however, clear that he was pitiful, whilst they were scornful. There may have been, in their words, some reference to John the Baptist, also put to death, of whom Christ had declared to the multitudes (Matt. xi. 14), "If ye will receive it, this is Elias which was for to come." And then the taunt would imply that this, *His* Elias, could not come to save Him whom He had declared to be the Messiah; they had now done to both "whatsoever they listed." The draught now taken by our Lord, strengthened His parched lips to pronounce the two other "words" which remained to be spoken. Stier here sees a spiritual significance in the words "I thirst," with reference to the thirst of Christ's spirit to fulfil the word of God, and to appear in His presence (Ps. xlii. 2), and as conveying to us the general lesson to thirst after righteousness.

34. *a reed.*—S. John says this was hyssop, the stalk of which would be about fifteen or eighteen inches long; quite sufficient to reach the mouth of Jesus, as the height of the cross was not very great. The ancient writers attach significance to everything in connection with the crucifixion of Christ; and, certainly, the coincidence of the scarlet robe of mock royalty which Christ had worn, and the hyssop here mentioned, with the "scarlet wool and hyssop" of Levitical sacrifice (see Heb. ix. 19), is remarkable. A bunch of hyssop was that with which the blood of the first Paschal lamb was sprinkled, on the lintel and doorposts of the houses of the children of Israel in Egypt, that the destroying angel might pass over them.

When Jesus therefore had received the vinegar, He said, **It is finished**. And when He had cried again with a loud voice, He said, **Father, into Thy hands I commend**

35. *it is finished.*—(See note 32.) The original word here rendered "finished," is the same before rendered "accomplished." This is our Lord's declaration that all connected with His mission as a Redeemer was finished; His own sufferings and example, all God's will, all the prophecies which heralded His earthly career, all that concerned our salvation, was complete. His was a perfect work, whether looking back upon the necessities of past ages; of that in which He lived upon earth; or future, to the end of time. Not one thing remained now to be done which ever had been, or could be, required of the Saviour, in the interest of any soul of man. Looking at Christ's work in connection with our salvation, as a finished work, we must see that, so far as we have "to work out our salvation," ours should be, like His, a perfect work; "forasmuch as we know that our labour is not in vain in the Lord." We need not, however, shrink from the thought of perfecting our work after His example; for when He says, "It is finished," He includes all that we could not ourselves do, and the power to finish all that we can do; and we have the assurance that "He that hath begun a good work in you will perform it unto the day of our Lord Jesus Christ."

36. *a loud voice.*—The mention of the loud voice is suggestive of the power which our Lord retained over His life. (See note 45.) The draught of vinegar had relieved extreme exhaustion; but, though He was at the point of death, and, in all ordinary cases, such a cry would have been physically impossible, He could not die but by His own will. He was not mortal by the law of sin by which Adam's transgression bound himself and his descendants (see App. XVIII.); for Christ was without sin. No man could take from Him His life. He had "power to lay it down, and had power to take it again " (John x. 18); and this power was manifested in His last cry—He spoke with a voice of preternatural force. Bishop Beveridge notices this as an especial proof that He died by the permission of His own will, and as His own voluntary act; and instances the conviction produced in the mind of the centurion, "who could not but from thence conclude that He was indeed the Son of God, in that He did not die as others do, by having their souls forced from their bodies; but by sending it forth Himself, voluntarily, and of His own accord." The free-will act of Christ in death, cannot be too carefully marked: because if He could not Himself help dying, He could not save us from death; if He could not raise Himself from the grave, He could not raise us; if He required a Saviour, the Father, for Himself, He could not be a Saviour for us. The whole depends upon the literal truth of His assertion in John x. 17, 18.

𝕸𝖞 𝖘𝖕𝖎𝖗𝖎𝖙: and having said thus, He bowed His head, and yielded up the ghost. And the sun was darkened;

37. *Father*, etc.—This was the seventh and last word from the cross. Our Lord now calls upon God, and surrenders into His hands the human spirit which He had received from Him, as the last act of pious submission to His will. We cannot entirely penetrate the mystery which closes round the world beyond the grave; but this much seems generally agreed, that Christ now completed the act of death by the severance of His human spirit from His body in the natural course of suffering; neither, however, being separated from that Divine nature into which He had taken manhood, and which, at His will, reunited them presently; for the Godhead of Christ was never more parted from His manhood, after His once taking of the manhood into God. (See App. XIX.) Though the soul and body, His manhood, were severed from each other, both the body which lay dead in the grave, and the soul which ranged the spirit world, were equally, as before, conjoined with His Divine nature. The body remained, therefore, incorruptible in the grave; "it saw no corruption." The spirit passed into the unseen world, and there appeared as one of the spirits of the righteous dead. This consequence of death was fulfilled by Him. But, being alive in His spirit, He went and announced amongst these spirits the victory He had proclaimed on earth—"it is finished," with regard to salvation, in the hope of which they rested. (See Essay, "The Descent into Hell.") As all have to pass into this unseen world, except those who are alive at His coming again, there is set before us the example of His piety in committing the soul, not, as He did, with power, but in faith and hope, as Stephen expresses His dying trust, "Lord Jesus, receive my spirit" (Acts vii. 59).

The "seven words upon the cross" are gathered from the several accounts of the Evangelists, none of whom give the whole seven. Bengel has an excellent remark, which may have a wide illustration in the harmonious variety of the Gospel narratives: "There are seven words in the four Evangelists, all of which not one has recorded; whence it is plain that these books are four voices, which produce symphony when heard together." For convenience of reference, the seven words are these:—1. "Father, forgive them, for they know not what they do!" (Luke xxiii. 34). 2. Verily I say unto thee, To-day shalt thou be with Me in paradise" (Luke xxiii. 43). 3. "Woman, behold thy son! Behold thy mother!" (John xix. 26, 27). 4. "My God, My God, why hast Thou forsaken Me!" (Matt. xxvii. 46; Mark xv. 34). 5. "I thirst!" (John xix. 28). 6. "It is finished!" (John xix. 30). 7. "Father, into Thy hands I commend My spirit!" (Luke xxiii. 46).

38. *bowed . . . yielded.*—(See note 36.) Words apparently designed to express the free will and power which rested in Christ; they well convey the dignity and majesty which He put forth in the act of dying.

and, behold, the veil of the temple was rent in twain from

S. Augustine argues, " If Christ's power was so great in laying down His life, what must be the power of His coming again ? " It is clear that, in the course of nature (for He had permitted to Himself the exercise of the law of death), He must now die. He had borne as much as a human body could bear, unassisted miraculously ; although, as Olshausen observes, to His body " appertained a possibility, not the necessity, of death." He had refused all means of mitigating the pains of death, the anodyne offered to Him. (See note 3.) He would suffer all that was laid upon Him ; but He could only live longer by the exercise of supernatural power, and there was no reason for such an exercise. All was finished. But yet the act of death awaits His will ; and thus He bows His head in acquiescence, and yields His life. Bishop Pearson thus sums up the article of the Creed, " He was dead : " " I do really and truly assent unto this, as a most infallible and fundamental truth : That the only begotten and eternal Son of God, for the working of our redemption, did in our nature, which He took upon Him, really and truly die, so as, by the force and violence of those torments which He felt, His soul was actually separated from His body ; and although neither His soul nor body was separated from His Divinity, yet the body bereft of His soul was left without the least vitality. And thus I believe in Jesus Christ which was crucified and dead." Greswell says that, " in this separation of His soul from His body, our Lord did not wait for the natural progress of dissolution, but exerted His Divine power in anticipation of the effect ; the reason of which was the necessity of so timing His death, that, in all the circumstances which took place afterwards, the Scriptures might be fulfilled, as they had been fulfilled before." This cannot be accepted. In the first place, Scripture prophecy expresses the Divine foresight of things which will eventually happen. Christ never either performed works, or " *timed* " them, merely so as to fulfil Scripture. And, again, to say that Christ exerted His Divine power to hasten the event of His death, would be (if not to give colour to suicide), at least, to contravene the constant habit of His life, never to exert such power to spare Himself inconvenience or suffering. He had just given a special instance of this in His refusal of the medicated potion. How could Christ's example give strength of endurance to man in extremity of mortal agony, if, for any reason, He exerted Divine power to stay it ? The truth is that Christ died, when He allowed natural causes to take effect in His case ; and God's statement in prophecy is as accurate by *anticipation*, as any other statement of history. The idea of Christ *timing* His actions to fulfil prophecy, throws discredit on the whole subject of prophecy ; it would cease to be " the more sure word " of Divine witness.

39. *the sun.*—(See note 29.) This seems to express the hiding of

the top to the bottom; and the earth did quake, and the
rocks rent; and the graves were opened; and many

the light of day, and of the principle of light and of life in nature;
that the darkness was not the covering of the earth with mist or cloud
—not the shrouding of the earth, but of the sun. It is not quite a
repetition of the account of the three hours' darkness, but the specifica-
tion of its character.

40. *the veil.*—The best comment on this extraordinary occurrence,
is that in the Epistle to the Hebrews, in which is shown the spiritual
signification of the veil, namely, the extension of the offer of life, and
its connection with the death of Christ. (See Heb. vi. 19, ix. 7–12,
24–26, x. 12–14, 19–22.) This occurrence took place at a moment
when it must have been seen by numbers of people. This was the
day of the Passover, and the preparation for the sabbath; the Temple
must have been crowded with worshippers, and numbers of priests
would be ministering there; some offering incense, probably, because
it was about the hour of evening sacrifice. Though the mysterious
darkness covered the city, there was light in the Temple sufficient for
the awe-stricken worshippers to discern that the great veil, which
separated the holy of holies, was rent in its full length, without
visible agency; and now, for the first time, were revealed to sight the
mysteries of the inner sanctuary. Forster gives the thickness of this
veil as one foot, and its length, sixty feet; and notices that it was rent
from the top downwards, instead of from the bottom upwards, as would
have been the case by any natural agency, whilst it was hanging in
its place. We can scarcely over-estimate the deep impression such an
occurrence would make, although it is narrated in so few words by the
Evangelists, as being secondary in importance to the great fact of
Christ's death. Several writers trace a connection between this event,
and that spoken of in Acts vi. 7, " a great company of the priests
were obedient to the faith; " and, without some cogent reason, we
should be at a loss to account for so blessed a change amongst them.

41. *the earth,* etc.—This was no ordinary earthquake from natural
causes. The earth had felt the ruin of the Fall, and was cursed for man's
sake; it now shuddered at the death of its Maker. There are other
instances in Scripture, from Gen. iv. 11 downwards, of the sympathy
of the powers of nature with great events. (See i. 30.) Modern
travellers have noticed the extraordinary clefts and fissures in the
rocks, near the scene of the crucifixion; and, though there is now no
reliable testimony which connects them with what the Evangelist
states, the coincidence of the *fact* is very remarkable. They are
evidently not the effect of any ordinary earthquake, similar traces of
which might be noticed elsewhere. It is not likely that rocks rent
here at this time, should have closed again.

42. *the graves.*—The convulsions of nature probably opened the

bodies of the saints which slept arose, and came out of the graves after His resurrection, and went into the holy city, and appeared unto many.

graves of these dead; and not one or two, but "many bodies of the saints which slept," were raised to life again. It has been supposed that these were patriarchs, prophets, and saints of the Old Testament; but it seems, rather, that they were saints who had been believers in Christ, for they were personally known to living survivors in Jerusalem. But they did not rise till the third day, after Christ's own resurrection. Naturally so; for, as the early writers observe, He must be Himself " the *first-fruits* of them that slept." They appeared to many chosen witnesses in Jerusalem, who must have divulged the truth, and who could have contradicted any wrong assertion on this point, at the date at which the Gospel of S. Matthew was written. Had the holy city been (as some say) figuratively that spoken of in Rev. xxi., it is likely there would have been some early tradition concerning their entrance into heaven, rather than into Jerusalem; but the supposition is of later origin. Who they were, who were thus selected as Christ's witnesses, we know not. S. Matthew, who alone records the fact, is the Evangelist to the Jews, who would be most intimately concerned and interested in this event; but he only mentions the bare fact, and that by anticipation of the order of the occasion. Farrar says that the earthquake displaced the great stones which covered the tombs; and, "it seemed to the imaginations of many, to have disimprisoned the spirits of the dead, and to have filled the air with ghostly visitants, who, after Christ had risen, approached to linger in the holy city." What does this mean? S. Matthew says nothing about *spirits* filling the air, and *lingering* in the holy city; nor is there any air of mystery and unreality about what *he* says. It is a pity to evade a difficulty in this shadowy fashion. The statement of S. Matthew is made as distinctly, and as gravely, as any other connected with the crucifixion. But further than this, we know nothing of these saints; the mystery which, in all cases, surrounds the inhabitants of the world beyond the grave, forbids our nearer approach to them. It has been supposed that they rose with their bodies of the resurrection, and went with Christ into heaven. This was the opinion of some of the most eminent of the early writers. It seems, perhaps, unlikely that these saints, who rose with Christ, would be doomed to die again. But we *know* no more concerning them than concerning Lazarus, the widow's son, and the daughter of Jairus, whom Christ raised from the dead. Tradition asserts that one of these, Lazarus, did die again. The cases, however, of these saints are not exactly parallel. The former, at any rate, were not raised to life by Christ with a spiritual, but with a natural body; and we are told nothing of the body in which these were raised.

43. *the holy city.*—The term is remarkable as used, at this moment,

Impressions of the Crucifixion.

S. Matt. xxvii. 54–56 ; S. Mark xv. 39–41 ; S. Luke xxiii. 47–49.

Now when the centurion, and they that were with him, watching Jesus, saw the earthquake, and those things

of a city which had just accomplished the darkest deed ever wrought upon earth, and against which Christ had pronounced so heavy a doom. There seems to be a great sanctity attaching to persons, places, and things set apart for God's service. He is ready to accept, and slow to reject, such devotion of that upon which His name is called. The principle seems to be a general one; innumerable illustrations might be cited from Scripture.

44. *the centurion.*—The guard under his command were greatly awe-stricken and impressed; some, perhaps, superstitiously, but others, probably, in a more effective manner. They had no Jewish prejudices to blind their conviction; and they must have noticed that the voices of the Jewish scoffers were stilled by the terror of the signs which had occurred. But the centurion was the most decidedly and really convinced. The earthquake, and the darkness, and other circumstances of awe, excited "fear," or reverence, in them all: but especially the "loud voice," being not that of a dying man, but of one having power, impressed him strongly with a conviction of the Divinity of Christ; and he acknowledged the hand of God, not of the gods of Rome, but of the God whom Christ invoked. He did not scruple to acknowledge the "righteousness," that is, the *innocence* of Christ, and the justice of His cause; and so the further admission comes naturally (though, from a heathen, not the less candidly): if He is an innocent and just man, He must be what He asserted, and what nature acknowledged Him to be in the face of man's denial; "truly this man was the Son of God." The words could not have been spoken in their fullest sense, because the centurion did not know God; this occasion being a revelation of Him to his mind. But no doubt he meant that the God he now glorified, and whose Son he owned Christ to be, was the true God, in opposition to all false gods. The Jews had tauntingly said, " *If* Thou be the Son of God!" Christ had, to His mind, proved that He was the Son of God. Tradition gives his name as Longinus, and states that he afterwards preached the faith of Christ, and suffered martyrdom in His cause. We may surely hope that God would clearly manifest to this man of candid mind, and noble confession, the full knowledge of the Saviour, whom, whilst rejected by His own people, and put to death, he had yet confessed before the men whose opinion he valued— the men of his own nation and command.

that were done, and that He so cried out, and gave up the ghost, they feared greatly; and he glorified God, saying, Certainly this was a righteous man : truly this man was the Son of God.

And all the people that came together to that sight, beholding the things which were done, smote their breasts and returned.

And all His acquaintance, and many women were there beholding afar off, which followed Jesus from Galilee,

45. *that he so cried out.*—(See note 36.) The fact of the great cry before death, so impossible under ordinary circumstances to those dying upon the cross, and the evident power with which Christ laid down His life at His own will, were more convincing to the mind of the centurion, than even the miraculous attestation of nature.

46. *to that sight.*—The phrase is a very descriptive one. This multitude was a curious and gaping crowd, many of whom had nothing better to do than to come to see "the sight" of the crucifixion. They were not unaware of the claims of Christ, but they had little sympathy with them, and were quite careless of all but the interest of the moment ; probably their highest expectation was "to see a sign" from one who had wrought so many deeds of wonder. But these, too, were conscience-stricken and ashamed, and convinced of the evil deed which had been done, and of the righteousness of Christ; they smote their breasts with sadness and remorse, and returned, heavy and dejected, to their homes. Perhaps some of them would fain have recalled the terrible imprecation, " His blood be on us and on our children." We may hope that some returned penitent for their share in this deep sin, and open to conviction of the truth ; for upon the preaching of Peter, so shortly afterwards, in one day, about three thousand souls were added to the Church of Christ (Acts ii. 37–41). These sightseers, the centurion, the guard, the faithful women, the penitent malefactor, are all instances of the power of Christ's cross as the touchstone of human hearts. (See note 22.)

47. *His acquaintance.*—A general term, including all who were favourably disposed towards Him, and reckoned themselves as disciples; who had had many opportunities of knowing Him, and of being benefited by Him. Probably there were some of His Apostles, and some of the seventy, amongst them, with many others who followed His steps. Many of them also were doubtless of the number of those who had raised their voices in His favour on His triumphal entry into the city a few days before (See i. 23); these are spoken of as "the whole multitude of the disciples" (Luke xix. 37).

48. *afar off.*—With the exception of S. John, we do not read that any of the disciples had ventured near the cross : the eleven had not

ministering unto Him : among which was Mary Magdalene, and Mary the mother of James the less and of Joses,

all recovered from the terror of their dispersion in the garden of
Gethsemane.   But some of the women, now "afar off," had stood near
the cross shortly before.   It does not appear that they were driven
away; it is scarcely likely that, if they were permitted to stand near
whilst so many voices were mocking our Lord, they would be driven
off when the darkness fell, and the voices of malediction were stilled,
and conscience was moving in many a breast.   It has been suggested,
and with great probability, that Mary Magdalene, and Mary the mother
of Joses, retired when our Lord's mother was conducted away by
S. John; and, if so, these two, at least, remained amongst the number
of faithful who stood within sight, watching earnestly the end.

49. *ministering.*—Our Lord and His Apostles so entirely gave themselves to the work of His mission, that frequently they had "no
leisure, no, not so much as to eat."   They had, therefore, no time for
the exercise of the calling by which most of them had formerly earned
their living.   We know, from Luke viii. 2, 3 (where the full phrase,
"ministered unto Him *of their substance,*" occurs), that our Lord
availed Himself not only of their personal services of kindness and
attention, but also of their gifts which many pressed upon His acceptance; though only so far as was necessary.   He showed His disciples
that though, as a rule of His Gospel, "they who preach the Gospel,
must live of the Gospel," they were not to enrich themselves by it;
much less were they to hold themselves justified in working miracles
in their own behalf, by the power with which they were endowed; for
many were willing to minister to them, many thus aspired to win the
blessing, "it is more blessed to give than to receive."   The rule is an
important one, and greatly productive of love and mutual goodwill
in the Christian community.

50. *Mary Magdalene.*—There is naturally much anxiety to inquire
into the history of this attached servant of our Lord; but directly we
leave the narrative of the Gospels, we fall into conjectures and debate.
Her very name is involved in uncertainty : the most natural explanation is that she was "Mary the Magdalene," *i.e.* "of Magdala," a
town or village of Galilee. · But some of the best MSS. do not give
the word "Magdala," but "Magada."   It is, however, likely that there
was such a place, and that it was a tower ("Migdol"), with a hamlet
round it; it has even been identified with the modern El-Migdel.
Another explanation is that the name was Megaddela, *i.e.* "the plaiter
of hair," as this fashion was then, it is said, adopted by women of no
character.   This derivation has its weight with those who identify Mary
with the "woman who was a sinner," in Luke vii. 37.   But the
majority of writers deny this identity altogether—it rests on no valid
evidence, and is not worth serious thought; it is merely perpetuated

and Salome the mother of Zebedee's children ; and many
other women which came up with Him unto Jerusalem.

His Side is pierced.

S. John xix. 31–37.

The Jews therefore, because it was the preparation,

by the creations of the painter and the sculptor. It appears to have
arisen from a misconception of the statement in Luke viii. 2, "out of
whom went seven devils," which shows that she was then the unhappy
victim of Satanic influence. But we should rather suppose her, from
this fact, to have been one of those instances of demoniacal possession,
so melancholy and so awful, which our Lord healed. Such persons
had generally a consciousness of thraldom ; and her deliverance from
this terrible bondage would attach her in deepest gratitude to our
Lord so long as she lived. She may have lived, during this time of
woe, in lonely misery in the watch-tower ("Migdol") spoken of; and
the name derived from it may have been retained (like "Simon the
leper") as a memorial at once of deliverance and gratitude. S. Jerome
attaches much weight to this derivation, as suggestive of the steadfast-
ness of her devotion to Christ; she stood like a tower, strong in faith.
Her personal wealth, and the association of her name with that of
women of repute (Luke viii. 2, 3), and the fact of her deriving her
name from her locality, and, indeed, the very nature of her awful
malady, are decidedly against the notion that she was "a sinner." We
find her name in repeated connection with those of our Lord's mother,
the mother of Zebedee's children, and the mother of James and Joses;
and we can well gather from this, that this wealthy and devoted
woman had much endeared herself, by acts of benevolence and charity,
to the community in which they were so deeply interested—to these
holy women : she by love and mercy, they by love and natural
relationship; all in the bonds of a common salvation, were united to
our Lord and His Apostles. There is one other version of her history,
which must be briefly noticed. Some writers have identified her with
Mary the sister of Lazarus; but there seems to be no real authority
for their doing so. It is, however, extraordinary that whilst, in many
points of excellence, devotion, and position, the two characters coincide,
there is no mention made of Mary of Bethany amongst the holy
women of the crucifixion and resurrection; this circumstance has
probably suggested the identification of these Marys. It is a pity that
so interesting a speculation is so devoid of foundation. (See also II. i.
34–39, and App. XIII.)

that the bodies should not remain upon the cross on the sabbath day, (for that sabbath day was an high day,) besought Pilate that their legs might be broken, and *that* they might be taken away. Then came the soldiers, and brake the legs of the first, and of the other which was crucified with Him. But when they came to Jesus, and saw that He was dead already, they brake not His legs:

51. *the preparation.*—(See **xxx.** *f.* 38.)

52. *remain.*—It was against the law (Deut. **xxi.** 23) that the bodies of those executed should remain all night unburied. Josephus declares that the Jews were most scrupulous in burying those who were crucified. The Roman punishment of crucifixion, however, included the leaving of the body until it was devoured by the fowls of the air. As soon as the Jews had discovered that our Lord was dead, or, perhaps, without waiting for that assurance, and certainly before the malefactors were dead, they went to the city to Pilate, and they scrupulously pleaded their law in order that the bodies might be buried. It would have been defilement if they had remained any night upon the cross; but much more when that night was the eve of the sabbath, and of one of such high solemnity as the sabbath within the feast of the Passover.

53. *an high day.*—"That sabbath was an high day, by reason that there was a concurrence of the Passover and the sabbath, both at once, in that one day." (*Bishop Hull.*)

54 *their legs.*—The Jews asked this as a means of hastening death in ordinary practice—so contemporary authors testify. Bishop Pearson has the following:—"Although, indeed, it must be confessed that the crucifragium and the crucifixion were two several punishments, and that ordinarily made the cross a lingering death; yet, because the Law of Moses did not suffer the body of a man to hang upon a tree in the night, therefore the Romans, so far to comply with the Jews, did break the legs of those they crucified in Judæa constantly; whereas, in other countries, they did it but occasionally." The shock might cause death to those already enfeebled; but in case it did not, they would receive a stroke upon the breast, which instantly did so. Pilate was not inclined to object to this request of the rulers; the sooner all signs of the execution that had given him so much trouble were removed, the sooner would the whole transaction be forgotten. The soldiers sent on this errand were different from those already mentioned as in charge of the execution; they were despatched on this particular service in compliance with the request of the rulers.

55. *the first.*—Probably, simply the first to whom they came—the nearest to the city.

56. *dead already.*—They saw at once, what their comrades, who had been all the while on the spot, knew well, that Christ was really dead;

but one of the soldiers with a spear pierced His side,
and forthwith came there out blood and water.   And he

otherwise, in obedience to their orders, they would have done the same
in His case, as in that of the malefactors.   But, lest He should be in a
trance only, one of these men pierced His heart with a wound that
must have been mortal.   Bishop Pearson says that the spear was
"directed by an inveterate malice;" and, in rage that their cruelty
should be prevented by His death, they endeavoured, "with foolish
revenge, to kill a dead man."   But we need scarcely think they
designed to offer this wanton indignity to the dead.   Had they done so,
the breaking of the legs would far more effectively have defaced the dead
body; but Pilate's sentiments were known, and would prevent such
outrage, which was also unlike the habits of Roman soldiers.   They
did not, therefore (so God's providence provided), break Christ's legs;
nor need we, with Bishop Pearson, Greswell, and others, suppose that
they wounded His side simply as an act of barbarity.   The orders
given to *make sure* would, in such a case, be peremptory.   Ford says:
" God would have none of His bones broken, or taken off from the
communion of His natural Body, to illustrate the indissoluble union
which was betwixt Him and His members."   The ancient writers
speak to the same effect, that thus is given to us a lesson against
schism, as dividing the Body of Christ.

57. *blood and water*.—This has been subjected to much medical
criticism, both in ancient and modern times; the evidence given is
conflicting, there being no possibility of any absolute decision.   But
this much appears to be generally agreed on, that the spear-point
reached the heart, or at least the *pericardium*; and that such a wound
must have proved mortal, had not Christ been already dead.   The
weight of opinion seems to lean to the impression that our Lord
literally gave His life's blood a ransom for the sins of the world; that
the intense mental anguish of the agony in the garden, and subsequently on the cross, resulted in rupture of the heart.   This, it is said,
would cause blood to escape into the pericardium; and the effect, on
the piercing of the pericardium after death, would be the flow of a
considerable quantity of clotted blood and watery fluid.   Greswell
thinks this "discharge of blood and water too great and extraordinary
to be accounted for on any natural principle; and, therefore, strictly
miraculous."   But what was the object of such a miracle? and what
authority is there for saying it was a "*great*" discharge?   S. John's
word, "*came* there out " (not flowed), is an extremely mild term in the
original.   If the above opinion is correct, the coincidence with Ps. lxix.
20, " Reproach hath broken my heart; and I am full of heaviness,"
etc., is striking.   If, however, the actual *cause* of death must remain a
question, the agreement of medical authority as to the positive *fact* of
death is of considerable importance.   But S. John, in narrating it, is

that saw *it* bare record, and his record is true: and he

apparently unconscious of the proof of death which he affords; for this was never seriously questioned in the days in which he lived. But he attaches a mysterious interest to the "blood and water," as typical of the two Sacraments. His Gospel (John vi. 33–63) speaks much of sacramental truth in spiritual language; and we find a very distinct allusion to the water and the blood in 1 John v. 6–8. It is evident that his mind was very strongly impressed with this subject. The ancient writers take, very strongly, the sacramental interpretation of his words; the tendency of the opinion is expressed and condensed in the following words of Hooker (v. 56, 7):—"The Church is in Christ, as Eve was in Adam; yea, by grace we are every one of us in Christ, and in His Church, as by nature we are in those, our first parents. God made Eve of the rib of Adam. And His Church He frameth out of the very flesh, the very wounded and bleeding side, of the Son of man. His body crucified, and His blood shed, for the life of the world, are the true elements of that heavenly being, which maketh us such as Himself is, of whom we come. For which cause, the words of Adam may be fitly the words of Christ concerning His Church, 'flesh of my flesh, and bone of my bones.'" The mixed chalice of water and wine in the Lord's Supper, was derived from this circumstance. Theophylact, in the eleventh century, says: "Shame upon them who mix not water with the wine in the holy mysteries; they seem as if they believed not that the water flowed from the side." In the fourth century we have the words of SS. Augustine and Chrysostom, which may favour the practice; the former says: "that blood was shed for the remission of sins, that waters tempers the cup of salvation;" the latter: "this being the source whence the holy mysteries are derived, when thou approachest the awful cup, approach it as if thou wert about to drink out of Christ's side." Bede argues that the water represents the people, and the mixture the union of Christ and His people; and that this is also shown in the mixture of the water with the flour whence the bread is made; and further, that in this Sacrament the death of Christ on behalf of His people, thus united to Him, is shown forth before God. This mystical and pious observance is not, however, clearly contemplated in our Lord's institution, nor is it evidently deduced from the passages before us. It is certainly safer not, in any way, to add to the simplicity of the elements as ordained by Christ, in a matter of such supreme moment as the Holy Sacrament; therefore, the Church of England, in not prescribing the admixture of water, without condemning an ancient practice, simply and safely went back to the original ordinance of Christ, and took that exactly as her standard; and decides that standard legal.

58. *bare record.*—This solemn attestation directs our attention to the great importance of the fact mentioned. We have the concurrence

knoweth that he saith true, that ye might believe. For these things were done, that the scripture should be fulfilled, **A bone of Him shall not be broken.** And another scripture saith, **They shall look on Him whom they pierced.**

of these witnesses given to us here; that of S. John as an eye-witness, and the coincidence, both of Scripture type and prophecy. The object of their witness is that we, of all ages, to the end of time, might believe the fact of Christ's death, its fulfilment of type and prophecy, and also the mystery of "eternal life, which God has given to us" (the Church of Christ) "in His Son." We may not fully comprehend this mystery now, as men of old understood not type and prophecy; but it is faithfully recorded, " that we might *believe.*"

59. *a bone.*—God had fore-ordained that there should be no mutilation of the form of Christ, this being no way necessary to the work of redemption, and also coutrary to the lessons of unity in His Body, the Church, founded upon it. (See note 56.) We see how wonderfully this was brought about, and yet how naturally, in the action of the soldiers. We see also the careful preservation of the typical lamb (Ex. xii. 46); the order for which is reiterated with a certain significance in Num. ix. 12. We find also, in Ps. xxxiv. 20, a distinct reference to this, with reference to God's preservation of the righteous in the path of obedience, which must have been striking to the mind of a Jew; but the type is fulfilled only in Christ.

60. *pierced.*—The exact words of the prophet are stronger than the rendering of the Evangelist : "They shall look on *Me* whom they have pierced; " *i.e.* He whom they pierced was God. This prophecy of Zech. xii. 10 refers to the time of the restoration of Israel, when God shall pour out upon them the spirit of reformation and grace, which may have had a partial fulfilment before the time of the Messiah, in their return to God, whose heart they had pierced with grief, for their waywardness and their sorrows. But no one can read the language of the prophet without seeing its fitness of application to the days of future glory, when "all Israel shall be saved :" then shall they own the Saviour, whom their fathers pierced ; and the prophecy is an assurance that, if they look in penitence, they shall be forgiven. But this prophecy must be read also in connection with that in Rev. i. 7, where "they which pierced Him," are ranked amongst those who "shall wail because of Him." We notice how entirely the personal act of the soldier, who caused this wound in the execution of his orders, is passed over, in its appropriation to those whose unbelief and rejection of Christ really compassed His death. The margin refers also to the piercing of Christ's hands and feet, and the staring crowd which gaped upon Him (Ps. xxii. 16).

Easter Eve.

XXXII. *CHRIST IS BURIED.*

S. Matt. xxvii. 57–61 ; S. Mark xv. 42–47 ; S. Luke xxiii. 50–56 ;
S. John xix. 38–42.

And now when the even was come, because it was the
preparation, that is, the day before the sabbath, there
came a rich man of Arimathea, named Joseph, an
honourable counsellor, which also waited for the kingdom
of God, who also himself was Jesus' disciple, but secretly
for fear of the Jews: *and he was* a good man, and a
just, (the same had not consented to the counsel and
deed of them ;) this *man* went in boldly unto Pilate,
and craved the body of Jesus. And Pilate marvelled if
He were already dead ; and calling *unto him* the centurion,

1. *the even.*—As the sabbath commenced at sunset, this must have
been quite late in the afternoon; for Christ was not yet dead at the
ninth hour, that is, three o'clock.

2. *the preparation.*—(See **xxx.** *f.* 38.) We have here the full designation of this day.

3. *a rich man.*—Thus was fulfilled (and the Evangelist intentionally
points it out) the prophecy of Is. liii. 9. This Joseph was of Arimathea,
generally supposed to be Ramathaim, the birthplace of Samuel (1 Sam.
i. 1, 19); he was a member of the Sanhedrim ; of repute for his personal
character, no less than for his wealth and official position. He was
one of those whose mind was bent upon the hope of Israel, the kingdom of the Messiah ; and he believed in his heart that Jesus was the
Christ. In this persuasion, either by his absence, or the refusal of his
vote (the phrase " had not consented " is a decided one, and suggests
a *veto*), he had taken no part in any of the councils held against
Christ's life and reputation, nor in His condemnation, thus dissenting
from " the counsel and deed " of Caiaphas and his colleagues. The
death of Christ, the touchstone of so many hearts, brought his belief
to a late crisis, and decided him in favour of Christ, though dead.
His former hesitation, and present decision, are suggested and contrasted in the words of S. Mark, " he went in *boldly* unto Pilate." An
early and well-known tradition states that Joseph afterwards went
and preached the Gospel of Christ in Britain.

4. *already dead.*—The order of narrative appears distinct, that
Joseph went after the departure of the soldiers, to whom Pilate had

he asked him whether He had been any while dead. And
when he knew it of the centurion, he gave the body to
Joseph.

And there came also Nicodemus, which at the first
came to Jesus by night, and brought a mixture of myrrh

given an order which must have fully accounted for death ; for the
order was to expedite the death of those on the cross, before the commencement of the sabbath ; it was not merely to break their legs,
which might have caused a speedy, but not immediate, death. It is
evident, therefore, that Joseph gave some information to Pilate, which
made him astonished at the fact of Christ being dead, without reference
to the act of the soldiers. He was not indisposed to grant the request
of Joseph, whose position entitled him to a courteous consideration ;
and Pilate was, probably, well pleased to find one, amongst the rulers,
who took his own view of Christ's innocence; and, further, the request
was an ordinary one on the part of the friends of those who had been
put to death. But he must require official proof of death; it would be
damaging to have the question raised afterwards, and the consequent
trouble which would ensue, if Christ was only in a swoon. He, therefore, sent for the officer in charge of the execution ; and, on his formal
report, granted the request of Joseph. The original word for "*gave*"
implies that he freely, and without demanding bribe or consideration,
gave over the body to Joseph.

5. *Nicodemus.*—This was another case of an imperfect faith being
brought to its happy decision by the cross of Christ. The story of
Nicodemus is one of great interest: it is related only by S. John
iii. 1–21, who there records the dawn of his faith ; in ch. vii. 50, 51,
he shows its progress ; here notes its development. His sincerity and
desire to learn is evident ; and Christ spoke to him at considerable
length, and addressed him as one who had both faith and earnestness.
It is said that he "came *at the first* by night ; but this does not forbid
—it rather suggests, the supposition that he had at other times also conversed with Christ ; and we see that his mind had been long directed
to the claims of Christ. He, too, could not have consented to the
malice of the majority of the rulers. He now, openly, and in the face
of day, joined Joseph of Arimathea, and brought a large quantity of
spice, for the embalmment of the body of Christ. We may suppose
that his faith must have been very much strengthened, if not absolutely
decided, by the recollection of Christ's words, significantly spoken to
him at that first interview : "As Moses lifted up the serpent in the
wilderness, even so must the Son of man be lifted up" (John iii.
14–16.) I. Williams remarks on the arrival of these two good men—at
first secretly, now openly and boldly, His disciples: "The Sun had
gone down to his rest ; and even now, at His setting, the stars begin
to come forth ; and one and two become visible."

and aloes, about an hundred pound *weight*. Then took they the body of Jesus down, and wound it in linen clothes with spices, as the manner of the Jews is to bury.

Now in the place where He was crucified there was a garden ; and in the garden a new sepulchre, which was hewn out of a rock, wherein was never man yet laid. There laid they Jesus therefore because of the Jews'

6. *an hundred pound.*—This is a very large quantity of spices ; the intention must have been entirely to cover over the body with these, until they had leisure, after the sabbath, more thoroughly to perform the rites of burial. Some writers also think that the intention was to burn some of these, as in the case of the Jewish kings. (See 2 Chron. xvi. 14, xxi. 29.)

7. *down.*—"The descent from the cross" has been ever a favourite subject with painters. It is, indeed, one full of painful interest, and suggestive of many thoughts. The process of death is always impressive ; but these men were taking down, from the "accursed tree," the lifeless form of that sacred Victim, whose life had been offered, and accepted, for the sins of the world. The atonement was complete ; and now, for a brief space, whilst the spirit, commended by Christ into the hands of the Father, was absent in the spirit world, the body of Christ, for this interval powerless and lifeless, rested in the guardianship of faithful men. We read of no wonders worked by the body of Christ, like those attributed to some of the mediæval saints, and true, of old, of Elisha's body (2 Kings xiii. 21); but the absence of such wonders, and this trust of Christ's sacred body (for whose preservation type and prophecy avouched God's will) to the reverential care of man, form subjects of deep and holy interest.

8. *a new sepulchre.*—(See i. 10.) It was fitting that the body, which might see no corruption, should rest in a tomb which had never known the presence of such taint ; for, though the human body and soul were now severed, by the act of death, neither was separated from the living and incorruptible Divinity, into which the manhood of Christ had been taken. (See xxxi. 37.) The fact of the tomb being so near, and its being new, and worthy as Christ's place of sepulture, by security and costliness, probably suggested its present use. And no doubt Joseph rejoiced that he had, unconsciously, prepared, beforehand, for so sacred a charge. We can, however, see the hand of God in this matter ; that He had pre-arranged, as He had also foreseen and foretold, what was now done. There is, perhaps, another reason for the mention of the sepulchre as "*new.*" Had it been previously occupied, it might have been disputed that it was not the body of Christ, but some other, which was removed. (See App. XV.)

preparation *day;* for the sepulchre was nigh at hand; and rolled a great stone to the door of the sepulchre, and departed.

And the women also, which came with Him from Galilee, Mary Magdalene, and Mary the mother of Joses, followed after, and beheld the sepulchre, and how His body was laid. And they returned, and prepared spices and ointments; and rested the sabbath day according to the commandment.

9. *a great stone.*—Some of the sepulchres, hewn in the rock, are fastened by a stone door, which revolves on a stone pivot; in other cases, like the present, the stone appears to have been a circular stone, like a mill wheel, which could be rolled along a socket grooved to admit it. In either case, the entrance stone could be fastened, and the fastening sealed. (See the type of the entombment of Christ, and the sealing of the stone, " that the purpose might not be changed concerning him," in Dan. vi. 16, 17.)

10. *the women.*—These left their station, at a distance from the cross (see xxxi. 48), and followed those whom they had seen remove their Lord from the cross, and bear His body away; they were witnesses of the entombment, and of the disposition of the body. They then hastened back to the city, and spent the short remaining space of the preparation day, in collecting all that was necessary for the embalming, after the Jewish custom. This service, they intended, should be completed after the sabbath. We cannot conjecture how far they were aware of what had been done by Joseph and Nicodemus. As these rulers had only, in this act, come forward boldly as Christ's disciples, they would not, perhaps, be acting in concert with the women, who might only know, in a general way, of their being friendly disposed. They saw what these men had done with the body of Christ, and marked the place where they laid it; probably they knew nothing of the spices, and the fine white linen, with which it was so thoughtfully and reverently covered. All was done quickly, and hurriedly, that had not been already prepared. In this case, their own preparation of aromatic spices was not to supplement what was done, but to make provision, which they supposed, in the hurry and excitement of the hour, could not have been thought of.

11. *rested.*—They kept the law of the sabbath, and this sabbath was a high solemnity. Christ rested this day, Williams notices, from the work of our redemption, as God had rested from the work of creation. It was, in reality, the last sabbath of the original prescription; the Lord's day at once superseded it. (See App. XX.) The notice of this *rest* is very significant. All was calm and quiet on the eve of the resurrection. The religion of the Jewish dispensation was no longer

His Sepulchre is sealed and watched.

S. Matt. xxvii. 62–66.

Now the next day, that followed the day of the preparation, the chief priests and Pharisees came together unto

that of the world; it was fulfilled, and had vanished away. The rise of the "Sun of Righteousness," the dawn of the new and last dispensation of God to man, would be inaugurated as Christ rose from the grave. All the agony and horror of death were past; the voice of opposition and derision was hushed. The dead Christ lay still and guarded in the rest of the grave; but the angels of heaven were gathering to proclaim the resurrection of the Lord, and His great triumph. Many hopes were seemingly crushed, and hearts were sorrowful, even unto death, that sabbath day; but the voice of the mourner did not break the sacred rest of that day of God. All troubles sank, hushed and subdued by the solemnity of the sabbath; but already the spirit world was rejoicing in the tidings the Saviour was giving of His victory. And but a few hours, and hope would rise in every heart on earth which owned Him as Lord; and the "Lord's day" would be a day of life to all—an earnest of that great doctrine which, henceforward, would be coupled with the Saviour's name, as the proclamation of the Gospel. "Jesus and the resurrection," would be the world's watchword from the morrow, to the end of time. Thus, unconscious of the joy and glory about to dawn for them (even as we, the watchers for the great day of the Lord's coming, and the final resurrection, are unconscious now of the full glory that shall be revealed), these faithful mourners "rested the sabbath day, according to the commandment."

12. *the next day.*—The phrase here is somewhat peculiar. We should have expected that the sabbath would have been mentioned, it being so high a festival. There must be some reason for so unusual a mode of expression. An ancient writer says, that the conduct of the rulers was so unworthy of the day, and their indignation was so great that two of their number should have given burial to Christ, that the Evangelist avoids naming it as the sabbath. This is not very clear. He may, however, design to point out, that, although the day of preparation was past, and, therefore, all but direct religious employment forbidden (the sabbath being now actually commenced), yet these men did not scruple to go to Pilate, the Gentile governor, to demand a guard. On the other hand, it has been said, by some writers, that they did not go to Pilate until the sabbath was past, that is, until the very eve of the resurrection; as it was not necessary to take precautions until the eve of the "third day." The former account would

Pilate, saying, Sir, we remember that that deceiver said,

place their interview with Pilate after six o'clock on Friday evening; the latter, after six o'clock on Saturday evening. They had evidently some fear of the stealing of the body of Christ by His friends, and of a consequent rumour that He was risen. But there was a deeper anxiety than this. We may safely assign to them a degree of fear, and uneasiness, lest the sign of Jonas should be made good in Him; and lest, as they knew His words implied, He should raise up the temple of His body on the third day, though they might not feel clear about the meaning of His own words, "I will rise again." Besides, had they left the body so long unguarded, they would have spread the report that the body of Christ was stolen before the guard was stationed, rather than (what they actually circulated) that it was stolen whilst the guard slept. If they really suspected the body might be stolen, they would not be likely to act on the presumption that there was no danger of such theft until the eve of the third day. It seems, therefore, probable that the Evangelist's somewhat circuitous phraseology is meant to direct our attention to the fact that the day of preparation was then over, and the sabbath commenced, before they thus went to Pilate; but that they went immediately after the preparation was past, and the sabbath begun; before nightfall; in fact, within an hour or two of death, in order that the sepulchre should not remain unwatched, even one night. It was a palpable infraction of the sabbath; but their anxiety would not postpone the matter. No doubt, some of them had beheld the act of Joseph and Nicodemus, and the gesture of the women who followed and remarked the place of burial, with suspicion of their design of returning to the sepulchre. To such watchers, the idea that Christ's friends wished to remove His body, would occur more naturally than that of their intention to complete the embalming. We may conjecture, therefore, that, whilst some went to Pilate, others remained on the watch; for it is unlikely that they left the sepulchre unwatched one single instant until the guard arrived. How little they thought that they were only rendering the fact of the resurrection an indisputable truth!

13. *we remember.*—Their memory was very accurate when prompted by their malice. If they here alluded to the charge their false witnesses had laid against Christ, of threatening to destroy the Temple (John ii. 19)—a saying of His which they comprehended sufficiently to see the necessity of representing His words, addressed to themselves, "Destroy (*ye*) this temple" (My body), as, "*I* will destroy this sacred building" (see xxx. c. 7), in this case—they must have remarked that the saying was verified as He had uttered it. The temple of His body had been destroyed by them; and there now remained the rest of the prophecy to be fulfilled: "In three days I will raise it up." But there were other, and far more explicit, declarations of our Lord, which,

while He was yet alive, After three days I will rise again.
Command therefore that the sepulchre be made sure
until the third day, lest His disciples come by night, and

though spoken to His disciples privately, had, no doubt, been widely
circulated. (See Matt. xvi. 21; Mark x. 32–34.) These words may
have suggested fears to their malice, at least as definitely as hopes to
the faith of the disciples.

14. *after three days.*—The expression is identical with that below:
"until the third day." The Jews reckoned any part of the day as
if one day; they therefore meant that one whole day, and the slightest
portions of the first and third days, might fulfil the prophecy. Hence
their anxiety to have the sepulchre guarded, and made sure, during
this interval.

15. *His disciples.*—They were in astonishing fear of these few
crushed and timid followers of our Lord. It was not very likely that,
after abandoning Him to His fate whilst still alive, they should now
take courage at once, and fight for an idle tale. Surely, these rulers
very much magnified the possible effect of such an imposture, were it
concerted and promulgated, in representing its consequences as *more
serious* than those which had resulted already from Christ's life, and
teaching, and miracles. Imposture of any kind would not cohere with
the past life of Christ. We cannot but see in this, their fear, another
proof that they sinned against light and knowledge, sufficient to
manifest to them the truth of Christ's claims; and that they had now
a strong conviction that Christ might rise from the dead, and that
they must prepare for such a contingency. There was evidently a
general, though undefined, feeling concerning the resurrection. Even
Herod thought that John was risen from the dead, when he heard of
the works of Christ; and the rulers knew more about this truth than
did Herod. Their plan, therefore, was such a one as might discredit
Him on His reappearance, did He rise again. They were ready at
once to disown Him as an impostor, put forth by the disciples, and,
therefore, not the real Christ who had died. His own words were
finding fulfilment: "Neither will they be persuaded, though one rose
from the dead." Thus they were not worthy of seeing Christ after
His resurrection; and He never publicly appeared, except to chosen
witnesses, worthy of such a grace. So this plan found no execution.
But we may suppose, also, that they had yet a further reason in
demanding a guard than merely the watching of the sepulchre: they
hoped that, did He rise, He might prove as vulnerable to the sword of
the guard as to the pains of the cross; they would not neglect a strict
charge to the guard to let none pass them. They did not think the
fact of the resurrection from the dead a security against death again;
for, whilst fully admitting the resurrection of Lazarus, they had taken
counsel to put him again to death (John xi. 47; xii. 9, 10).

steal Him away, and say unto the people, He is risen from the dead : so the last error shall be worse than the first.   Pilate said unto them, Ye have a watch : go your way, make *it* as sure as ye can.

16. *by night.*—Even this very night of the sabbath, quite as possibly as the following night.

17. *ye have.*—There was already a body of men, more or less at the disposal of the rulers, for the protection of the Temple during their festival. Pilate gives the necessary order that a guard for the sepulchre should be told off from this body ; the detachment would, according to custom, be sixty strong. Though he appears to give merely verbal directions, he doubtless issued a formal order. Some have thought that he referred to the guard already detached for service as the crucifixion, which is the less likely that it had already been long on duty. Some read, "Take ye a guard," as in grant of their request.

18. *as ye can.*—Gk. "as ye know."   There need be supposed no irony in this. Pilate desired them to take measures of security, and they well knew how best to do so ; he left the precautions to be detailed by themselves. They were interested in the matter, and professed to have fears, which he was not likely himself to share. He had had certain evidence of the death of Christ, and had no idea of His coming to life again. He complied, more courteously than they deserved of him, with this request of the Jews ; and, in leaving them at liberty to adopt measures which their superstitious fears dictated, he had done all that could be required of him ; and he had no wish to be further troubled in this matter. We cannot but notice how God's providence overruled that these men, who took such pains to prevent the resurrection of Christ, should give their energies to furnish the most convincing proof of that resurrection. The care they took to guard the sepulchre, made it impossible that a few timid and disheartened disciples, amongst whom the women were most prominent, should steal away His body ; whilst a very slight knowledge of the discipline of the Roman army, makes it as incredible that a guard should dare to sleep, as it was improbable, even to impossibility, that so large a body of soldiers should all sleep, at their post. And "there being a band of sixty soldiers placed as a watch to preserve the body from being stolen, 'tis not to be supposed that the disciples could beat this band ; and so there could be no ground of suspicion that our Lord was not truly risen." (*Whitby.*) (See II. i. 6 ; ii. 3.)

Thus Christ's body was committed to the devoted care of His followers ; His sepulchre to the watchful observation of His enemies. Over all, God's control is manifested in the ordering of every minute circumstance ; they combined to do exactly what "His hand and His counsel determined before to be done." Christ's body slept there within the tomb ; but "it was impossible that He should be holden

So they went, and made the sepulchre sure, sealing the stone, and setting a watch.

of it," because, though the spirit was dissevered from the body, that body was not, by death, severed from the Godhead into which it was taken. (See xxxi. 37.) At His will it had died the death of mortality; at His will it must revive in immortality—a spiritual body. (App. XIX.)

19. *watch.*—The Greek here is not " setting a watch," but " with the watch;" as if they would not trust to their doing this duty alone, but going with their officers to *affix their own seal* also.

END OF PART I.

PART II.

THE DESCENT INTO HELL.
THE RESURRECTION OF CHRIST.
THE FORTY DAYS.

The Descent into Hell.

" That Sabbath was an High Day."

THERE is a breathing of peace and repose, of which we become sensible, in reading the account of the eve of the last sabbath of the old dispensation. The contrast is striking between this interval of peace, and the previous scenes of malice and outrage : the shouts and screams of rejection and derision, the sounds of blows, and of preparation for death, and all the bustle and outrage which centred on the eminence of Calvary, where the crucified hung upon their crosses. The noise and business of the city, too, was stilled. The thousands of wayfarers and sacrificers, and the multitude of those passing and hurrying through the streets, noisy and excited in the performance of their various duties, had found their respective homes. The preparations of those faithful ones, who were anxious for the worthy discharge of the last rites of burial for their Lord, were cut short by the proclamation of the sabbath. The peaceful hour of twilight fell upon the world—that general summons to rest from the labours of the day, and to lay aside the burdens of duty.

All "rested the sabbath day according to the commandment ;" but none realized the fact that, though the commandment, given prior to the Jewish religion, that mankind should rest upon the sabbath day, remained eternal and general, for Jew and Gentile, for Christian and heathen alike—a rest typical of the rest of the grave, and of the sabbath of eternity—yet the seventh day of the Jewish religion, and of ancient dispensations, was now superseded; and "the Lord's day" was about to dawn upon the world. Henceforward the first day of the week" should be the day of rest until the end of time. This was, therefore, the last sabbath. The law, as delivered by Moses, had found its fulfilment; the day of the first covenant was to be known no more. Christ "had made the first old; and that which decayeth and waxeth old is ready to vanish away."

But there was nothing so still, and solemn, and peaceful as the repose of the dead. Two of those who had been crucified together, had entered the unseen world of the blessed dead; one of them, the Saviour of the world, in order that thus He might be "Lord both of the dead and of the living," and that, whether we live or die, we may be the Lord's. All three, who had lately suffered so much at the hands of men, rested in the death of the body. He who had been lately the object of so many interests, of so many hopes, and of such anxiety and dread, of so much hate and so much love, lay in His sepulchre in death. He rested that day from all the work of redemption which He had wrought. God surveyed the perfect work which the only begotten Son had finished in fullest obedience to His will; "and, behold, it was very good." Into these things "the angels desire to look." "That sabbath was an high day."

There was but one exception to this scene of outward peace and repose. There is no rest to the anxiety and foreboding of guilt; "there is no peace to the wicked;" and even now, upon the holy sabbath, a deputation of the chief priests and rulers might be seen waiting at the gate of the Gentile governor, arranging for a guard of soldiers to watch the sepulchre of the dead Christ. They feared He might, as He had declared, rise again, to their confusion; but they hoped He might again be slain by Roman swords, on His exit from the tomb, or that, by some craftily devised story, His reappearance might be discredited. These guardians of public religion did not scruple to break the law, and to pollute the rest of this last sabbath, in the furtherance of their iniquitous schemes.

But what of the dead Christ, whom they had succeeded in cutting off out of the land of the living, and whose body now lay in the silence and peace of the tomb, "with the rich in His death"? His murderers little knew the real issue of their deeds. His voice indeed was stilled upon earth, and His earthly ministry brought to a violent, though not untimely, close; but a fresh and wider scope was now given to His mission, and His work. It had ceased to do with men of the day and of that country, and with the limitations of time. "The middle wall of partition" between Jew and Gentile was thrown down; "the veil of the Temple was rent in twain from the top to the bottom," and its restrictions were abolished. The Gospel mission has advanced to include the generations of all mankind, of every people, and nation, and tongue; it is henceforward contemporaneous in effect with the duration of the human race—eternity past and future alone can bound it. "Put to death in the flesh, but quickened in spirit," into a more abundant and spiritual life, with extended powers, and influences, and vitality, Christ was set free from the restraints of the body, to range the vast confines of the spirit world. He had gone into the abode of departed spirits, and was there proclaiming the everlasting Gospel with which he was commissioned.

"He descended into hell!" Such is the creed of the universal Church. But between the fact and the meaning to be attached to it, there exist such varieties and difficulties of interpretation, that, as one writer declares, "the literature of this subject is a library."

The truth of this article of the common faith has been held and acknowledged from the beginning; but, as an article of the Creed, it is of less ancient definition than other articles concerning our Lord Jesus Christ. It is not perhaps found, expressed in so many words, until the close of the fourth century. Still the opinion of the earliest writers, though as varied as that of critics of modern date, as to the work of Christ in Hades, is quite unanimous as to the fact of the "descent into hell."

Upon a subject so restricted by the paucity and obscurity of direct revelation, and so perplexed by the differences of the opinion of all ages, it can scarcely be hoped that any new light can be thrown. It may be sufficient to lay before the reader some of the leading difficulties of the question, and the assertions and hints of Scripture upon which they are grounded. The interest of the work and occupation of Christ in the unseen world, into which all mankind have to enter, and which lies before us all, is infinite. But we shall find, in all that refers to it, that reticence and mystery which surrounds the whole subject of death, and of that world and its inhabitants which lie beyond the grave. Whilst, therefore, it is right to ponder all that is told us, we must be content with the general outline. With regard to this work of Christ, we must accept His assertion as a general one concerning the mysteries of His redemption: "What I do thou knowest not now, but thou shalt know hereafter."

I. It is evident that there is life, and locality beyond the grave, and an intelligence also of affairs of earth. It is not merely that the dead lie in their graves in the dust of the earth, awaiting the general resurrection, in a state of unconsciousness. It is the testimony of Scripture that all descend into hell, as Christ also descended. The word "hell," however, according to its current use, has a harshness to modern ears; since it has now come to signify only the world of future torment, "prepared for the devil and his angels," rather than, as at first and as in our Liturgy, simply the *unseen world*. It is an old Saxon word, meaning "covered" or "concealed," and is equivalent in its indefinite signification to the Greek

Hades (" unseen "), and to the Hebrew " Sheol," a *hollow* place, apparently, within the " lower part of the earth." All these terms are occasionally used in the restricted sense of the grave. Theologically speaking, they are not rightly used of the world of torment; their common, general, and extended reference is to the abode and society of the spirits of the departed; without reference, however, to the happiness or misery of their condition.

One of the earliest intimations which we have of there being locality and life beyond the grave, is in the instance of Samuel; for upon such expressions as that, for instance, of Jacob in Gen. xxxvii. 35 (" I will go down into the grave unto my son mourning "), we can only found theory, or seek support for it, in the light of after and clearer revelation. Samuel was permitted to come up from Hades (or " Sheol," as the Hebrew term is), at the call of the woman with a familiar spirit at Endor (1 Sam. xxviii. 7–25), to announce to Saul the fall of his throne and royal dynasty, and the defeat of Israel in the battle of the following day. He spoke to Saul with full apparent consciousness of the course of his life, and of the history of the kingdom in the interval of about four years, which had elapsed since his own death. We need not think his information on this subject necessarily of miraculous inspiration, for of the consciousness of beings of the spirit world of affairs of earth there seems to be little doubt. As their numbers are constantly recruited by those who pass " through the grave and gate of death " into their world from earth, they must receive constant intelligence of what is doing upon earth. Thus, also, the kings and " chief ones of the earth " address the King of Babylon, on his descent amongst them, as being fully familiar with his earthly career, and the terror of his name and deeds (Isa. xiv.). Thus, too, the rich man in our Lord's parable (or, more correctly, *narrative*) declares to Abraham the carelessness and irreligion of his five brethren's life upon earth, and the danger imminent over them. So also the departed are repre-

sented in Heb. xii. 1 as " a great cloud of witnesses " (*i.e.*
previous *martyrs*), cognizant of and deeply interested in,
though not (as angels) spectators of, the progress of those
running the race set before them towards the goal of
eternal life, and "fighting the good fight of faith," in
which they themselves had been more than conquerors
through Christ's grace. And, indeed, the whole of
Scripture, wherever there is allusion to the subject,
makes it evident that death is of the body alone; that
the soul is living and conscious, active in intelligence
and interest; that it has entered a world where there are
joys and sorrows, according to its condition of life,
and of future prospect; and various relationships, of
which, however, we know little at present for certain;
and longings and aspirations amongst those waiting, in
the imperfection of their present and intermediate state,
for their full reward. " For they without us shall not be
made perfect " (Heb. xi. 40); and they express before
God (whose presence they enjoy in a sense unknown
to us of earth, being " with Christ, which is far better "
than any condition of this life) their desire for the
great day of judgment, and for the beatitude of heaven
(Rev. vi. 9–11); and from whom they receive, as an
award in answer to their prayers, " white robes " and
the command to " rest yet for a little season."

This state, therefore, is intermediate between the life
of earth, and the life immortal and spiritual of the resurrection after the day of judgment. It is erroneous to
say of those who have left earth, that they have gone
to heaven or to hell (in the popular use of these terms),
as if the day of judgment were already passed, and the
sentences of eternity pronounced. Our Lord's own words
are sufficient to decide this point: "No man hath ascended
up to heaven, but He that came down from heaven, even
the Son of man which is in heaven " (John iii. 13).
Therefore, not even Enoch, who " was translated that he
should not see death," and "was not, for God took
him;" and not Elijah, for whom "there appeared a

chariot of fire and horses of fire," to conduct him from earth, and who "went up by a whirlwind into heaven," can have gone into heaven itself. They may be in the body among the disembodied tenants of the spirit world, pledges of the resurrection and immortality of the body, from whence Elijah came forth with Moses (who himself had seen death) to converse with Jesus upon the Mount of the Transfiguration. It is said that they " appeared in glory," a revelation of the altered condition of the inhabitants of the spirit world; and that they "spake of His decease which He should accomplish at Jerusalem "—a very significant evidence of the intelligence of beings of that world of the supreme affairs of earth.

There is also a similar consciousness of earthly affairs, in the division of that unseen world in which the souls of the wicked await the day of their doom. There is a remarkable scene (already referred to), which cannot be read without a thrill of awe (Isa. xiv. 9, 10), when the arrival of the proud King of Babylon makes all Hades to wonder. There we see the great ones of earth, still enthroned in eminence of woe, rise to meet the King of Babylon, as an unwelcomed and unhonoured intruder into their realms of mourning; upbraiding him, as with the mockery of fiendish voices, for his career of tyranny and wickedness, resembling and exceeding their own (*vv.* 10–20) : " Hell from beneath is moved for thee to meet thee at thy coming: it stirreth up the dead for thee, even all the chief ones " (marg. "great goats," cf. Matt. xxv. 33) " of the earth; it hath raised up from their thrones all the kingdoms of the nations." There is also a parallel catalogue of the nations " slain with the sword " of punishment for their pride and violence in Ezek. xxxii. 18–32, where the descent of the King of Egypt into their estate is spoken of, in an ode of lamentation of appalling grandeur.

In the New Testament, again, in the narrative of the rich man and Lazarus (Luke xvi. 19–31), we have the clearest revelation given to us of the locality and life of the spirits of the departed, in their intermediate state of being. Truth seems to be there distinctly and literally disclosed to us ; but still the whole revelation is pervaded by that intangible mystery, and subtle distance, which invariably veil the subject of the spirit world. There are represented to us two divisions of Hades, separated by an impassable gulf of partition, which is not, however, so wide as to preclude those on the other side from sight, speech, and hearing of each other. Here the souls of both good and bad are *in safe keeping* (or, as the A.V. of 1 Peter iii. 19 unfortunately expresses it, "*in prison* "). There is a material torment of fire in the place of the wicked; whilst the good are gathered into " Abraham's bosom," who is "the father of the faithful." Abraham speaks to Dives with a full information of the difference of life and position, and of religious character, upon earth between him and Lazarus; and we may surely gather that there is a difference of condition and of locality in the spirit world; though whether the possibility of seeing and hearing the sorrows of the lost is generally permitted to sadden the happiness of the good, or whether this feature is figurative in this special case, it is difficult to say, and impossible, perhaps, to decide. We notice, however, that Lazarus does not take part in the dialogue; and it would surely be a painful knowledge to the good, that any of those who on earth were bound up with them in ties of closest relationship and affection (the parent, for instance, with the child) were sorrowing in pain of torment and eternal separation, in the very sight of their own blessedness, upon the further side of the impassable gulf. Against this there is, however, the remark, " So that they which would pass from hence to you cannot," which may either suppose that they had a desire to pass over and comfort those of whose sorrows they were aware, or that, were they aware of them, and had they this desire, they could not exercise it. We may not, however, press too closely the words of this revelation; the very mention of material flame as tormenting immaterial and disembodied spirits, of the *tip of the finger* of Lazarus, and of the *tongue* of Dives, with reference to incorporeal spirits, is sufficient to warn us that the mysteries of the spirit world are veiled from us, and that they can only be made tangible to us on earth, by speaking of them under the figure of worldly and corporeal substances. It is enough if we can gather from the parable that there is life, intelligence, and locality, and differences of condition beyond the grave; and this is doubtless brought within our reach.

We have perhaps a further glimpse of the society of the blessed regions spoken of in this narrative in Matt. viii. 11: "Many shall come from the east and west, and shall *sit down with Abraham,* and Isaac, and Jacob in the kingdom of heaven;" and in a parallel passage in Luke there is the same power assigned to the lost of beholding the happiness of the righteous, with the same silence as to any similar power on the part of the saved of witnessing the sorrows of the lost: "There shall be weeping and gnashing of teeth when *ye shall see* Abraham, and Isaac, and Jacob, and all the prophets, in the kingdom of God, and you yourselves thrust out" (Luke xiii. 28). These passages would have a further and ampler fulfilment in the kingdom of heaven itself, as is the case with so many of our Lord's words of prophecy; not necessarily excluding, however, that of allusion to the conditions of the intermediate world.

II. But the great interest of the subject centres in our Lord: "He descended into hell." From His own promise to the penitent malefactor we know that He went into paradise. And some of the early writers entertained a peculiar view, grounded on this declaration: that this "paradise" was a place of happier circumstance and condition than the original Hades, in which the souls of the righteous had hitherto lived; and that after Christ's entrance into Hades, the souls of the righteous passed out with Him into "paradise;" and that in paradise they have ever since assembled,

" waiting for the adoption, to wit, the redemption of the body," on the morning of the resurrection. Works of early writers familiarize us with this theory. (See P. I. xxxi. 21.)

S. Paul seems to declare the fact of Christ's " descent into hell : " " Now that He ascended, what is it but that He also descended first into the lower parts of the earth ? " (*i.e.* perhaps we may explain, " places lower than the earth," Hades, a descent below the place of His earthly incarnation). " He that descended is the same also that ascended up far above all heavens, that He might fill all things " (Eph. iv. 9, 10) ; thus pointing to a certain fitness, if not necessity, that Christ should visit Hades also, in the course of His experience of human obligations and prospects. Thus did He become " in *all things* like unto His brethren." For it intimately concerned His work of redemption that His human soul should enter into the conditions common to man, and that " at the name of Jesus every knee should bow, of things in heaven, and things in earth, and things under the earth " (Phil. ii. 10).

But the chief information we have with regard to Christ's descent into the world of spirits, is gathered from a comparison of 1 Peter iii. 18–20, with the prophecy of David in Ps. xvi. 10, which S. Peter himself, in Acts ii. 31, expressly says concerns Christ—that David " seeing this before spake of the resurrection of Christ, that *His* soul was not *left in hell ;* " necessarily, therefore, it had descended into hell. S. Peter's words are distinct as to our Lord's occupation there, up to a certain point, after which they become involved in a cloud of mystery, which throws also the previous plain statement into obscurity. They clearly and explicitly declare that Christ, though put to death in the body, passed, in the increased vitality of spiritual life, into the world of spirits, and there made proclamation of His Gospel to the spirits of men there dwelling in God's safe keeping. The A. V. unfortunately so renders the passage that it supports the notion (perhaps as being that much held at the time of translation) that our Lord went into the lost world, to offer salvation to at least some of those who had perished in disobedience. The words of the A. V. are, "Being put to death in the flesh, but quickened by the Spirit: by which also He went and preached unto the spirits in prison : which sometime were disobedient," etc.   But the best writers seem nearly unanimous in rendering, "Being put to death in the flesh, but alive " (lit. "made alive ") "in spirit " (*i.e.* " in His human soul "); " in which also" (*i.e.* "whilst the body was lying in the grave") " He went and proclaimed the Gospel to the spirits in safe keeping; which were sometime disobedient," etc. (*i.e.* for instance, to such as were disobedient like those of the antediluvian world).   Here the following difficulties are offered by the A. V. In the first place, the preposition is not expressed, and therefore the rendering " *by* the Spirit " is not necessarily a translation of the original.   2. " By *the* Spirit " is equally open to question.   The article is not expressed in the best and oldest MSS.; it is found in some of more recent date, from whence perhaps it has passed into the A. V.   On these two points a closer and more accurate rendering would be, " in spirit," *i.e.* " in His spirit ; " the reference not being to the Holy Spirit, who indeed will " quicken *our* mortal bodies."   But He was not at this time commissioned to earth ; Christ had not passed yet into the heaven, and Christ was co-equal with God, and quickened His own Spirit. 3. The word " preached " somewhat conveys, or encourages the impression that Christ preached the gospel of repentance, accompanied with an offer of salvation, to those who had sinned (in which case He must have visited the abode of the lost); whereas the original word simply means to *proclaim* the Gospel, and is generally used in the sense of announcing its glad tidings " for a witness," as in Matt. xxiv. 14— a sense which would be entirely fulfilled, if we hold that our Lord went to paradise, the abode of the righteous, whose souls were there in the safe keeping of God (" kept by the power of God unto salvation ready to be revealed at the last time "), and there proclaimed to them the glad tidings, " It is finished,"—that redemption in hope of which they died, but of which they had so obscurely heard, and had so dimly seen. To these our Lord now became the herald of His own victory. 4. The A. V. term "in prison " (originally, simply safeguard, or safe keeping) attaches a penal significance to S. Peter's words which they need not necessarily bear.

But now follows the difficulty of the passage, the words of which are in themselves dark and mysterious, and which throw back mystery upon the preceding statement, otherwise so plain and distinct. It is said that the spirits to whom Christ " preached " were " sometime disobedient, when once " (the word " once " is not found in the best MSS.) " the longsuffering of God waited in the days of Noah, while the ark was a preparing." Upon this is founded the interpretation which the words of S. Peter may certainly bear, but which does not accord with the teaching of other passages—that He gave to souls which had been ranked amongst the lost, an offer of the gospel of salvation ; especially to those who perished in the Deluge. On the other hand, however, it is held by many writers, both ancient and modern, that all thus destroyed were not necessarily lost souls (the children, for instance, the ignorant who were not wilful sinners, and many who may have appealed for mercy) ; and that He announced to these (who are specially instanced by S. Peter as having perished under the most general and terrible overthrow which the world had ever seen, and of which God so far in mercy " repented," that He promised that He would never again so destroy the world) that they should not die eternally. And as He proclaimed to these, so He proclaimed to all others in the same safeguard of God, that His redemption was complete for them. And to how many such would the victory of Christ be grateful tidings ! How many there

are who die penitent for their sins, and for their neglect
of warnings and invitations of the Gospel; who die by
some terrible doom which, had they lived as faithful
to God's law, and to the natural laws of life, as they die
penitent for their folly, they had happily escaped! They
die in hope warranted by promises of Scripture, but not
with the calm assurance which blesses the departure
of those who have lived after Christ's example. To
myriads of these, the sufferers under the Deluge are a
type. And the proclamation of the Gospel to these
specially, tells us how often, in the judgments of His
providence, God remembers mercy; though their life's
work is destroyed, and ruin overtakes them in this world,
yet their souls are pardoned. Looking upon life as it is,
we are often sensible of the sad results of disobedience,
folly, youthful sins, in blighting fair prospects, talents,
and aspirations, and bringing lives that open with
every expectation of doing eminent service to God, to
an unhonoured and premature close. And, at the same
time, we frequently see this end accompanied by a deep
and humble penitence, which perhaps might not have
been the termination of a longer and more successful
career upon earth. Taking the precedent of S. Paul's
declaration in 1 Cor. v. 5, it seems to be often the mysterious way of Providence "to deliver such an one unto
Satan for the destruction of the flesh" (for it is through
his influence and agency that ruin overtakes men), "that
the spirit may be saved in the day of the Lord Jesus."
Surely to none more gratefully than to such as these,
would come the announcement, conveyed by Christ
Himself, of the completion of the redemption and victory.

There is another clue, which is important, to the
reason for S. Peter's particular mention of these of the
antediluvian world, which has thrown such an air of
mystery over the subject of Christ's presence and work in
Hades. It is this. He seems to be contrasting (*vv.* 20,
21) the restricted salvation offered in the Ark, with the
universal salvation offered through the water of baptism

into Christ's death and resurrection: "the like figure whereunto even baptism doth also now save us."

There is one other view of the passage which should be mentioned, as it receives the support of eminent writers of the Church of England—Bishops Pearson and Hall, and Archbishop Secker, and others—and follows also the opinion of some of the early writers: that our Lord preached, by His Spirit, in early times to the old world, as really as He did afterwards, when on earth, by word of mouth, and now also by His written word. Thus He preached to the antediluvian world, by the mouth of Noah. As a comment on this passage, this is true and fair; but it is surely not all that it conveys. For S. Peter is not speaking of the general influences of Christ's Spirit, but of what He did particularly, in the interval when, being dead and not yet risen in the flesh, but being alive in His spirit, He descended into the spirit world. The verbs of the passage are (as Dean Alford shows) all so closely linked together that it is impossible to avoid the difficulty, or to shun the conclusion that, in this interval, Christ made personal proclamation of the Gospel (with what intention and issue, however, is not stated) to these sufferers by the Deluge of old.

There is another passage a little later in the epistle (1 Peter iv. 6), which seems to refer to this same act of Christ, though it is more generally expressed; there being no special mention of any persons to whom the Gospel was preached, but simply stating that it was proclaimed "to the dead." The original word used here for preaching the Gospel is a less general term than that used above; it is frequently, though not exclusively, used of the offer of salvation: it may, however, simply bear the meaning of its announcement as glad tidings.

This subject is deeply interesting, but confessedly most difficult; nor does it appear possible to come to any certain conclusion concerning it. It may now be left to the meditation of the reader, after briefly summarizing the four principal opinions concerning the "descent into hell."

I. That our Lord descended into the abode of torment, and there—

(*a.*) Offered the Gospel to the acceptance of lost souls, specially to the disobedient of the era of the Deluge; a sense which the passage above quoted will undoubtedly bear, but which is opposed to the general doctrine of there being no further probation after death. And to this theory it may also be replied, that we need not necessarily conclude that it was to those who positively rejected salvation in the days of Noah, and died impenitent, that Christ offered pardon; but it may be rather to the many who must have earnestly called on Him for mercy at the last in the overthrow, which He would not now stay from working their temporal ruin; and that there is no intimation elsewhere in Scripture of any renewal of the offer of grace decisively rejected during life. It would therefore be unnecessary that our Lord should visit the abodes of the lost.

(*b.*) That He went there to triumph over Satan and his fallen hosts in those realms of woe, rescuing souls from their prison house; an opinion which is grounded on Eph. iv. 8, 9; Col. ii. 14, 15—passages which are very far from conclusive on this point—and which is contradictory to the constant representation of Scripture, which shows the fallen angels not yet remanded to the world "*prepared* for the devil and his angels" (but not yet tenanted by them), who, pending the doom of the day of judgment, are spirits and powers of the air, ranging earth in the execution of the evil influences at present permitted to them. In this case also there could be no object, or necessity, in Christ's visiting the place of torment. Such a theory might commend itself to those who hold the doctrine of a final universal salvation, on the one hand; and to those who hold that there is a purgatory, on the other. Accordingly, the mediæval painters represented Christ as passing out of the mouth of hell, triumphing over evil spirits, and rescuing the souls of men from their power, leading their captivity captive to His grace. The doctrines of final salvation of all souls, and of a purgatory, are, however, equally untenable within the terms of the Gospel as revealed in Holy Scripture; the latter being decidedly anti-scriptural.

II. That the "descent into hell" is simply that into the grave; which, in fact, supposes Hades to be a condition, rather than a locality, of the departed. To which it need only be replied that, in this interpretation, the two articles of the Creed, "He was buried" and "He descended into hell," would be merely two forms of assertion of one single truth, instead of (as the Church Catholic holds them) separate declarations of two distinct experiences of our Redeemer.

III. That Christ went into a general place of the abode of the souls of the dead, from whence He drew forth the faithful with Him to paradise, leaving the bad behind. This again is familiar to us in the paintings of mediæval artists, and might coincide with the doctrine of a purgatory; but it cannot be said that, according to Scripture, either there is one general place for the reception of all souls, or that the souls of the faithful dead were ever condemned to any association after death with those of the wicked, any more than they are to association with evil spirits.

IV. That Christ descended into "paradise" (Luke xxiii. 43), the blest abode of those reserved in God's safe keeping to eternal life, and there assured them of the completion of the salvation of which many of them had died in hope, though beholding it afar off, dimly as through a glass; and of which all were, doubtless, resting there in hope. This view has been advocated at length above.

The opinions of the early writers upon this subject are quoted at length, or cited and referred to, in Bishop Pearson on the Creed, art. v., and Bishop Harold Browne on the Thirty-nine Articles, and many other writers upon this subject. They must, however, as these writers observe, be read with the recollection that, in many instances, their primary and manifest intention was not so much to offer decision upon the occupation of Christ during His "descent into hell," as to oppose Arian and Apollinarian heresies, which denied the existence of Christ's natural human soul; to whom, therefore, the fact of the occupation of that soul, when severed from the body by death, became an argument of extreme importance. As has been already observed, whilst they differ as to the nature of this occupation, and as to the locality of His descent, they are unanimous as to the actual descent into Hades, in the disembodied, but living spirit of His humanity. In the same way the writings of many authors of more modern date, are directed either to the support or refutation of the doctrine of purgatory, or to the support of some theory of universal salvation. In like manner, again, there is a common consent to the facts of the "descent into hell."

Thus, veiled as the subject is with the shadows which rest upon the unseen world, which we cannot now penetrate, and guarded by the reticence of Scripture, which upon this subject is invariable, we may at least gather that there is life, intelligence, and locality beyond the grave; and that Christ has gone before, in the exercise of His commission of salvation, whither it is appointed to all to follow Him. His steps have illumed the dark valley of death, which all must traverse. There can be no more comforting reflection, when we stand on the threshold of that world into which all must pass, than that, if we die in His faith, we shall find there the traces of Christ's presence, and the proclamation of His gospel of salvation; and that the assurance is literally true— "Though I walk through the valley of the shadow of death, I will fear no evil; for Thou art with me:" "if I make my bed in hell" (lit. "if I should make Hades my resting-place"), "behold, Thou art there!"

The Resurrection of Christ.

THE records of the forty days which our Lord spent on earth after His resurrection, are silent about the great act of resurrection itself. It is distinctly shown that Christ rose from the dead identical, in body and spirit, with the Christ who had died; that the spirit, which had descended into hell, returned from its mission to the spirit world, to the body lying in the sepulchre; and that then, in the divine nature of Christ (from which neither living soul nor dead body had been severed), body and soul were reunited in everlasting union; and the dead Christ arose from the sleep of death. So much of this as could not come within the range of human perception is to be gathered from the revelation of Scripture. But as regards the identity of the risen Christ with the Christ crucified, we have the credible statement of many witnesses, never shaken in the age of their testimony. They with one mouth declare that He was the same; and that the same spiritual work and the same merciful character which was His from the first, was His after the resurrection. There is shown in their statements a certain mystery and awe of His presence after the resurrection, which is credible of a spiritual body, and which never could have been represented from the imagination of man; but yet all statements are consistent with the great truth of Christ's resurrection, with the voice of prophecy, and with His own declarations.

He was the "Christ that died; yea, rather, that was risen again." But though identically the Christ that was crucified, bearing still the open wounds of His crucifixion (John xx. 27), there was a wondrous change passed over Him; He was "raised a spiritual body." But He was not only this; "the last Adam was made a quickening spirit," and therefore, as He declares, "the Son quickeneth whom He will" (John v. 21). It is His to breathe into whom He will, the breath of that spiritual life which can never die. *When* this life-giving power was made part of His commission concerning us, is a question upon which there are many opinions. Some say that it was from the first, as His words seem really to declare, and as the powers of His ministry upon earth would strongly argue; others, that it was at the resurrection; others, at the ascension into heaven. This is, however, a question which concerns us little.

But the body of His resurrection was a changed body, endowed with various powers which natural bodies do not possess. It was a "body of glory" (Phil. iii. 21, *orig.*); but its glory was not generally shown to men before His ascension, as S. John beheld it in heaven (Rev. i. 13–16). That glory was veiled, as may have been necessary to mortal men. But it possessed also powers of passing, apparently with great rapidity, from place to place; of being present, without there being sign or sound of arrival; of becoming suddenly visible in the midst of those who were sitting with closed doors, without there being any apparent way or means of access; of withholding and permitting recognition at will. And yet such attributes do not seem to be simply those of Christ's Divinity (though, of course, they might have been divinely manifested), but rather to belong to the body of the resurrection. (See II. iv. 3.) The narrative of the Evangelists does not seem to carry any expression of miraculous agency in these instances. There may be also another property of the body of the resurrection, which is referred to in the notes (see II. iv. 7), namely, its bloodless character. It is noticeable that the "flesh and bones" of the body of the resurrection are spoken of, but never is the phrase "flesh and blood" used, nor *blood* spoken of in connection with it. S. Paul's words in 1 Cor. xv. 50 seem expressly to deny the connection. This has been much dwelt on by modern writers; and though it may not be pressed too far, both because it is unimportant to us now, and because there is no express declaration of Scripture in its favour, yet it may be thought to be inferred, with reasonable probability, from the peculiar terms in which the body of the resurrection is spoken of. It seems also probable that "the blood, which is the life thereof," with regard to the mortal and corruptible body, the arrest of whose circulation in that body is death, should be wanting in "that body which shall be," which is endued with a new and spiritual principle of vitality, a "more abundant" life, communicated to it by Christ. The question must remain unsettled until we rise in this "newness of life," and know the mysteries of the spiritual body; but it is now surely a legitimate subject for reverent speculation.

In His risen humanity Christ now arose with a spiritual body. But though the indisputable fact of the resurrection is declared, and rests upon evidence more carefully and distinctly set forth than perhaps any other single fact of history, there were no witnesses of the act of resurrection itself. We know that it was on the morning of the third day, and that, in the ways of Jewish speaking and reckoning, He had lain in the grave portions of the "three days and three nights" which constitute days of solar ruling; that is, that on the evening of the first day He was placed in the grave, where He lay throughout the second day, and rose again early upon the third day, before day had broken, but after its hours had begun their reckoning, according to the Jewish computation.

Very early He rose. The guard was at the sepulchre, but not all sleeping, we may be sure; but yet there were

no spectators of the mightiest of all the miracles of
Christ, unless there were angel witnesses. None, therefore, saw Christ come forth from the tomb. It may be
that as He passed unnoticed into the midst of His
disciples (John xx. 19), so He passed forth into the
world, through the midst of the guard, without regard
to the closed sepulchre, and withholding recognition
of Himself at will. He rose from the dead; but as
there were no human witnesses of this act of power,
so upon this mystery of His resurrection we may not
too curiously gaze or speculate. But the powers of
nature, which had shuddered when He died upon the
cross, hailed the resurrection. "There was a great
earthquake," and then, in the brightness of celestial
glory, the angel of God became visible (Matt. xxviii. 2);
others of these glorious beings (cf. Mark xvi. 5; Luke
xxiv. 4, 12, 23; John xx. 1, 5–7, 12) kept revealing and
withdrawing themselves from human gaze, as if the
place of Christ's burial was thronged with visitants of
heaven. Terror seized upon the guard; and though all
could not, as the rulers lied, have slept (Matt. xxviii.
12, 13)—an impossibility in the case of sixty Roman
soldiers—they sunk as dead men in the presence of the
angel. They must have had one glimpse of the open
sepulchre, from which the angel rolled away the mighty
stone, and sat upon it, forbidding its replacement by act
or lie of man; and, behold, the sepulchre was empty!
The Evangelist who tells the falsehood of the rulers, tells
also the true story (which the guard must themselves
have declared, to them and to others, whence he derived
it) of the great earthquake; of the descent of the dread
angel; of his rolling back the stone, and sitting upon it;
of the empty sepulchre, and then that they knew no
more (Matt. xxviii. 2–4, 11–15).

Of the fact of the resurrection of Christ there can be
no doubt possible, to a fair exercise of the reason which
God has given to man; there is none open to that faith
which would " know Christ and the power of His resur-

rection." It is not necessary here to dwell upon the proofs on which it rests as truth, upon which so much has been written in all ages. As the great fact in which mankind are more deeply concerned than in any other, it has been examined with a scrutiny which must have detected and exposed any valid flaw in evidence—a scrutiny both on the part of those who have endeavoured to deny and overthrow it, and also on the part of those who have been conscious, that upon it rested all their hopes of immortality and happiness. We may feel assurance of it, since the eye of an enemy has not succeeded in detecting failure. But much more keen, even than that of an enemy, is the eye of love and hope; and this, too, has been satisfied of the truth.

It may suffice here to quote the words in which Bishop Andrewes has admirably expressed the results of different modes of examination and evidence: "The resurrection became credible at first by the certainty of them that saw it (*i.e.* the risen Christ after His resurrection); then by the constancy of them that died for confession of it; and to us now the multitude of them that have and do believe it maketh it credible. For if it is not credible, how is it credible that the world could believe it? the world, I say, being neither enjoined by authority, nor forced by fear, nor inveigled by allurement; but brought about by persons, by means less credible than the story itself. Gamaliel said, 'If it be of God, it will prevail.' That which all the powers of the earth fought, but could not prevail against, was from heaven certainly."

The Forty Days.

———

THERE are certain difficulties with regard to the exact order of events in which the witnesses of the resurrection come before us, which are remarked in the notes, but which require a passing notice here. It is extraordinary how distinct and connected a narrative we gather, in spite of these difficulties, from the combined accounts of the Evangelists. Indeed, the difficulties of the order are of inferior importance; they are sufficient to exercise the ingenuity of the critic and the commentator, but altogether insufficient to raise, or ground, any reasonable doubt as to the credibility of the great fact. Such questions, for instance, may be cited, as whether the guard lay long entranced, or at once recovered themselves and fled; whether the women, on their arrival at the sepulchre, found the guard lying in their death-like swoon, and then looked up and saw the angel and the open sepulchre—as some have argued from the angel's words in Matt. xxviii. 5, "Fear not *ye*" (see II. i. 15)—or whether the guard had fled before the arrival of the women; whether there were two parties of women, or one only, and whether that one returned to the sepulchre after seeing the Apostles, and before Christ met them,—questions which have been most hotly disputed; whether Mary Magdalene delivered her story alone to the Apostles, or had overtaken the other women, and went with them to the presence of the Apostles

(cf. Luke xxiv. 10, 11; Mark xvi. 9–11; John xx. 18);
whether the report of the women was given before the
disciples to whom Christ manifested Himself at Emmaus, or they heard it from others, or had not heard
the additional report of Peter and ⊦John before they
set out for Emmaus. These, and many other similar
points, are of great interest; but not one of them
can be rightly said to pass out of the limits of theory,
criticism, and inquiry, into those which include doubts
of historic accuracy and truth; doubts on which argument might rest, which could shake the credit of
the great fact itself, and render our faith vain. (See
1 Cor. xv. 12–20.)

Without, therefore, discussing these (most⋅ of them
being mentioned in the notes), we may proceed to show
the order of events, as it may with fair probability be
harmonized from the Evangelists and inspired records.
As so many points of such a harmony are matters of
criticism far beyond the scope and limits of the present
treatise, it may suffice to say that it has been constructed
after careful consideration of the arguments of all avail-
able authorities upon this subject.

I.* Very early in the morning, when the sabbath was
over, but in the darkness which soon gave place to the
signs of the dawn of day, a company of women (including
those who noted the position of the sepulchre and the
burial of Christ, and who had made that preparation of
spices which the sabbath interrupted) set out from the
city, bearing what they had prepared for the burial rites
of Christ. They may have set out, probably, from the
house of Salome, the mother of John, where Mary, the
mother of Jesus, was now staying. Mary was not herself, however, one of this party of mourners; not merely
because she was overborne by too much sorrow, but
perhaps rather because in her heart (so observant and

---

* The numbers of these sections are those of the order of times of
Christ's appearance.

meditative of all that He had spoken, and of all that concerned Him), there were the dawnings of belief in His resurrection. If she thus waited for the accomplishment of "those things which were told her of the Lord," there was a readiness for higher things than those which merely concerned the rites of burial: she who looked for a resurrection, could not be wholly absorbed in such last rites of sorrow.

(*a.*) As they hurried forward, they must have felt with alarm the shock of the earthquake: but theirs was an errand which was too urgent for such terrors of nature to stay them. As they advance, they remember the ponderous stone which sealed the cave's mouth, and converse amongst themselves about the prospect of finding any to remove it. As they draw nearer they see, in the still obscure twilight of dawn, that the stone is rolled away, and that the sepulchre is empty.

(*b.*) At once Mary Magdalene, without staying to satisfy curiosity, or to inquire further, runs back to the Apostles with these startling tidings.

(*c.*) The other women reach the sepulchre; and, behold, it is empty! And as they are in perplexity about the removal of Christ, they become conscious of the presence of an angel, who calms their fears, asserts the resurrection of Christ, and charges them with a message to the disciples; mentioning specially Peter, the sorrowing and penitent Apostle, over whose restoration there was joy amongst them. The women then return towards Jerusalem, in much awe, but in true faith and hope. "He that believeth shall not make haste" (Isa. xxviii. 16); and they seem to have gone homewards in the trust of sure faith, rather than in the hurry of terror or doubt; conversing, as they went, about the great announcement with which they were charged.

(*d.*) Mary Magdalene, in the mean while, having speedily reached the city, delivered her tidings to the Apostles, expressing her own suspicion of the removal of the body by enemies—an impression apparently prominent in her mind (John xx. 2, 13), although she appears also to be pondering the hope of the resurrection.

(*e*.) On hearing this, John the beloved disciple, and Peter the earnest and zealous, now also so sorrowful and hopeful, run to the sepulchre, eager to find out by what means, or by whom, the body has been removed; surely not altogether without hope that He was risen. They take a different, probably a shorter, path than that by which the women are leisurely returning, and do not meet them. John, in the strength of his youth, arrives first. He sees the sepulchre empty; and, stooping down reverently and lovingly, to see fully into the interior, within the low aperture, he notes the orderly position of the grave-clothes, so suggestive of quiet and of hope; but he sees no angel, nor any other to tell him of what had happened. The women had gone away, leaving, no doubt, their spices behind them; signs of the occupation and flight of the guard may have been visible around, but they had gone; still John entered not into the sepulchre. He meditated, and held high argument in his mind.

Whilst he is thinking of what he has seen, Peter reaches the spot, and enters the open sepulchre. He too remarks the singular order of all things within. Christ is gone, but there are left behind all the wrappings of the dead, separately and carefully folded; particularly so that which had been about Christ's head, which, had the rest been abandoned, certainly would not have been taken off by those hurriedly removing the body. All is entirely irreconcilable with the supposition that it has been stolen away by enemies. Peter wonders very greatly, and departs in deep meditation. He is not, in the consciousness of his late denial, so quick to entertain hope and faith as John; but we may well believe that faith had dawned in his heart, and a readiness to cherish the tokens of approaching blessings.

John then enters the sepulchre; and the sight of what

is left there, and the quiet and order of the sepulchre, are enough to convince his faith that Christ had fulfilled His promise, and was indeed risen ; and he first believes the truth of the resurrection. " Blessed are they that have not seen and yet have believed ! " His faith is not forgotten ; it is destined to be rewarded by the apocalypse of Christ ascended, enthroned, and adored in heaven.

The two Apostles seem to have returned to Jerusalem together ; and how much the worthiness of Peter to receive the personal revelation presently made to him, first of the Apostles, was owing to the inspiration of John's faith, accredited by the message of the angel and the tidings of the women, we can only conjecture.

(*f.*) Mary Magdalene has followed Peter and John by the path which they had taken. They most probably, on their return, took the more usual road, by which the women were now well advanced towards the city. She did not therefore meet them again ; nor did she pass them, if she rejoined the women on her own return. There may have been many divergencies from a main road leading to so populous a city ; and the place of the Apostles' assembly may have been in a different direction within the city from that leading towards the house of Salome, where perhaps the women met before going to the Apostles, and where Mary Magdalene may have rejoined them, if indeed she did not overtake them on the road.

She now reaches the sepulchre alone. She stands there weeping bitterly ; but perhaps some recollection of Christ's words, and the desire to note every particular sign of His removal, rouse her from inactive sorrow, and she stoops down to examine the interior of the tomb. And now she beholds two angels in white sitting, "the one at the head, and the other at the feet, where the body of Jesus had lain." They commiserate her sadness, and ask why she thus weeps. Why should she weep ? is she not bewailing an unreal sorrow ? She is too deeply absorbed in mind to feel either fear or wonder, though those who address her are visibly not of earth (elsewhere they are spoken of as "men," here as "angels"). (Cf. Mark xvi. 5; Luke xxiv. 4; John xx. 12.) She answers that those who brought her Lord to His death have continued their malice to the grave; they have removed the body, and she has now lost even the consolation of mourning over it.

As she speaks there are steps behind her; or, it may be, she sees unutterable reverence in the faces of those she is addressing, as they look out beyond the opening. She turns round; and there is One standing before her whom she knows not. He speaks, as the angels had spoken, to her sorrow and anxiety. She takes Him for the man into whose charge Joseph has placed the garden and the sepulchre. A flush of hope rises in her heart, that he may have removed the body; or at least can tell whither it has been taken from his charge, and by whom.

Our Lord answers but one word, "Mary!" and at once she recognizes and adores Him, who now has manifested Himself to her first of all His followers; and she acknowledges Him to be the Lord. Her first and natural impulse is to cling to Him who has returned to her from the grave; but He stays this gesture. It is neither the time nor the place for such embrace. There are others on their way, to whom He must manifest Himself before they reach the city. Other opportunity will be given to Mary's faith before He ascends to the Father; and she must now also know Him in the power and majesty of His Divinity, rather than as the Teacher and Friend of earth. He announces to her His approaching ascension, and sends her to His brethren with these tidings, expressed in words of most gracious assurance.

Mary Magdalene returns with this message to the Apostles. Whether she arrives alone, or, hurrying in her joyousness, overtakes the women as they enter the city, is one of those slight difficulties above spoken of. Seemingly she rejoins them, after they too have seen the Lord, either as they reach the city, or before they go to the Apostles with their tidings.

II. But there is One before her on the road, who over-takes the company of faithful women, her associates, and comes forward to meet them. They are permitted at once to recognize Him; and they acknowledge and worship the risen Lord. By them also He sends a message to His disciples, "His brethren," recalling to them His promise of general meeting in Galilee. He desires to prepare their faith to receive the revelation presently to be granted to them, and to receive it upon mature and full conviction, rather than in the flush of enthusiasm. They must teach others, who would not be eye-witnesses, to believe, upon their testimony, the fact of the resurrection; they must therefore themselves also first learn to believe, on the testimony of others.

But the circumstantial story of Mary Magdalene, and the joint testimony of the other women, seem to them as "idle tales;" and they believe them not.

III. The day passes in expectation and hope; and towards the evening hour, and at a distance from the busy city, again Christ shows Himself to His disciples. Again, as in Mary's case, it is sorrow and anxiety which claim His gracious sympathy. Two disciples were journeying towards Emmaus, a village about eight miles distant from Jerusalem. The name of one of them, Cleopas, is recorded; that of the other, the subject of many surmises, is unknown. They were talking earnestly and sadly together as they journeyed. A stranger joined them, unnoticed in their preoccupation, from the direction of Jerusalem, and kindly asks the reason of their unusual talk and sadness. They know Him not; and (forgetting that all are not equally of their way of thinking, and with some incaution in their defence of a cause now everywhere spoken against, to a stranger of however friendly address) they reply to His question with a naive expression of astonishment, that He must indeed be of strange and solitary habits in Jerusalem, not to know the great event of the day. By other questions He draws them on to show their hopes and fears, the tidings of the women, and the hesitation of the Apostles to admit more than was vouched for by Peter and John. He then drew their attention to the same subject through the aspect of type, and psalm, and prophecy. As He does this, with a power which none but Christ could have put forth, their hearts burn with a consciousness that He was no uninterested stranger, no ordinary teacher, who conversed with them. It was now evening; and they pressed Him to enter into the house, and to receive their hospitality. His face was as though He would pass onward, and away from them; but their earnestness and entreaty constrain Him (such is ever the result of man's earnest prayers upon the Son of man); and then, as they sit at meat (where He assumes the action of the host), in the eucharistic act of " the breaking of the bread," He manifested Himself to them. And so He vanished out of their sight. Although it was now nightfall, and eight long miles lay before them, they hurry back to Jerusalem with their glad tidings to the Apostles.

IV. Whilst they were on their way to Emmaus, or perhaps upon the return journey (for the manner in which the Apostles addressed them on their arrival, seems to mark facts which had recently occurred), Christ now showed Himself for the first time to one of His Apostles. To Peter, the Apostle who had thrice denied Him, and who was now full of penitence, who had run to the sepulchre to have the first assurance of the resurrection, and had left it pondering deeply, half despondent, half hopeful, Christ granted this grace of His presence. The particulars of this greeting we know not—the Evangelists only incidentally allude to the fact; long years afterwards, we learn the order in which this manifestation occurred, from the pen of S. Paul. The restoration of the fallen Apostle was with Christ alone. We cannot say what revelation of Himself Christ now made, or how, or when; but He certainly now convinced Peter, accepted his faith and repentance, and gave absolution for his sin, his great sin. Christ did not at this time formally renew His commission of Apostleship, nor yet his primacy among the Apostles—that was the grace of a later day (John xxi.); but He evidently now sent him forward on that special mission which He had announced before the betrayal: "When thou art converted, strengthen thy brethren." Except John only, these were slower to believe than Peter; but the result of His testimony to them was the removal of their doubts, and their conviction of the fact that Christ was indeed risen from the dead.

We see this in their reception of the two disciples, who came in with such joyful haste from Emmaus. When they were admitted to the room where the Apostles were sitting with closed doors, they found a joyousness amongst them, very different from the depression in which they had left them. At once the narrative of their experience is prevented, by the glad tidings of great joy which the Apostles had to communicate : "The Lord *is* risen indeed, and hath appeared unto Simon!" Now at last the risen Saviour had declared Himself to one of their own number, who were appointed to receive and to promulgate His truth. They had waited for such proof, and were now convinced. But when the disciples proceed in turn to tell this marvellous story (and how circumstantially they did tell it, we may gather from the record of S. Luke), the Apostles again relapse into their former reserve and caution. The truth was too important to be received with ecstasy of joy; they are not fully convinced; and to themselves, all of them, must Christ appear as He had promised—He must be again in the midst of them, as He had so often been, and so lately at the Last Supper, ere they can formally accord their entire acceptance of the blessed fact. Till then, though they now no longer hold them as "idle tales," they postpone their full credence. Slow as they were to believe, weak and blameworthy as was their faith, inferior to that of many others who believed on their word, surely we of later and sceptical days have to praise God, "who, for the more confirmation of the faith, did suffer His holy Apostles to be doubtful in His Son's resurrection," and who turned their caution and hesitation into the strengthening of the faith of all after ages; who accept the truth, as one carefully and thoroughly weighed—a truth winning conviction against doubt and hesitation, triumphing over infirmity and scrutiny; set forth and revealed, in its brightness and certainty, by investigation, not as the enthusiastic impression of those who wished to believe it, against any force of incredibility or difficulty.

V. There was yet another manifestation of Christ made on this day of the resurrection. It is evident that the testimony of Peter, and that of the two disciples from Emmaus, had roused faith sufficient for the reception of the truth; and therefore faith sufficient for the manifestation of Christ. And so, as the two disciples finished their story, Christ Himself stood there in the presence of them all. They were sitting at meat (Mark xvi. 14) as He joined them; they were therefore reclining in the usual Eastern way. None was at the door, which they could all see was fast and secure; but yet Christ stood there, standing alone where all reclined; and they at once recognized Him. He greeted them with His salutation of peace, so different from that "which the world giveth," and so remarkably His custom after His resurrection. He read every heart, and the awe and fear that had fallen upon them. They thought that He was a spirit—a supposition dangerous in tendency, as containing the germ of deadly heresy. But when He showed them His hands and His feet, and His side, pierced and wounded; bidding them satisfy their minds by touching, and handling the substance of His body; declaring that the flesh and bones which, palpably to their senses, formed His body, were totally different from the incorporeal essence of a spirit's form; then their faith revived. They discerned, indeed, that the spiritual body of the resurrection had powers and properties with which they had not before been acquainted; but yet Christ stood there in their presence, risen, in the very body which had lately been crucified. Still the fact was all too joyous; its very gladness suggested doubt. The experience and maturity of man's reason could not be entirely convinced by the enthusiasm of hope. It was, to speak reverently in common parlance, "too good to be true" tidings. But now another proof is given them of the material and bodily presence of Christ: He took of the food from their table, and did eat it before them. Then "they saw the Lord" in the full truth of His resurrection. The great doctrine was established in the person of the risen Christ; and He was now no more to them simply the Master, or Teacher, but emphatically "the Lord."

He then reproved them for their slowness to admit the testimony of others—a reproof which must often have recurred to their mind, perhaps with a softening influence, when they, in their turn, experienced the reluctance of those to whom they preached "Jesus and the Resurrection," to accept their testimony as witnesses of a new and strange fact.

And here follows a charge which claims our careful and devout attention. There was sorrow and penitence mixed with their faith, as Christ now reproves their unbelief. Were they worthy to bear the high commission to which they aspire? Again the blessing is spoken, "Peace be unto you!" and then the charge, "As My Father hath sent Me, even so send I you." The mantle of His mission from heaven falls upon them from His ascension; a wider and ampler commission, as regards its locality, and as directly accredited as His, would now be theirs, who were henceforth to witness for the acknowledgment of the world, that "they had been with Jesus" (Acts iv. 13). And then the Son of God, who had formed the heaven and the earth by the breath of His mouth (Ps. xxxiii. 6); who had, again, "breathed into man's nostrils the breath of life, and he became a living soul" (Gen. ii. 7. Cf. John i. 3; Col. i. 16); as a "quickening spirit," now breathed upon them the inspiration of His spiritual life—breathed upon them the Spirit of life and truth, and gave them power, in His behalf, to pronounce authoritatively His absolution of sin, or to bind upon the impenitent those chains which would lay them before Him, at the last, captives of His wrath. He had before given them authority of binding the rules of His Gospel, and of loosing the restrictions of other dispensations of religion, within the community of His Church. He now gives them, with this inspiration of spiritual life, a charge for individual members of that Church, retaining and reserving, through their ministration of it, His " power on earth to forgive sins; " and a charge reaching within the very sanctuary of the spiritual world, " Receive ye the Holy Ghost : whose soever sins ye remit, they are remitted unto them ; and whose soever sins ye retain, they are retained."

VI. But one was absent when this commission was given; how nearly shut out from work, and mercy, and hope by his despondent incredulity, who shall say? When the Apostles told Thomas of the manifestation and assurance they had received, he would not accept their witness. They had handled the risen Word of life; but Thomas must do more. The most material evidence possible, would alone satisfy the cravings of his mind. He did desire to believe—he was no sceptic, looking for grounds of doubts ; but he could only believe on evidence greater far than that demanded by any other. He required to put his finger into the print of the nails, and to thrust his hand into Christ's wounded side ; and then he would rejoice to believe.

A week passed; and again, upon the second Lord's day, the disciples were assembled as before. A week's meditation and prayer had worked in the mind of

Thomas the dawnings of belief; and he was now present, as of old, amongst his brother Apostles. The doors were closed and barred as before, yet Jesus stood suddenly in the midst of them, and was at once recognized by them all. He hailed them with the same salutation of "Peace." Though absent, He had been spiritually present, when Thomas had refused credence, and made his demand of material and tangible evidence; and at once the Lord offers to him the exact proof which he had required. It was accepted (see notes II. v. 1–10); and now Thomas owns Christ even more unreservedly than the most faithful, "My Lord and my God." Christ's reply to him is in remarkable words; they contain a blessing for all ages, truly and specially valuable in days of scepticism, which demand proof and demonstration of truth, as material as that demanded by Thomas: "Thomas, because thou hast seen Me, thou hast believed: blessed are they that have not seen, and yet have believed!"

VII. Christ had thus shown Himself to all His chosen Apostles; and now weeks seem to have passed without any further manifestation of His presence, and it was drawing towards the close of His stay upon earth. The Apostles knew that they should see Him again; and they hasted to fulfil His charge that they should assemble, with the body of disciples (for so, probably, we may understand His command), to meet Him in Galilee. There was time and earnest work needed in preparation for this. They had been themselves slow to believe, and we may be sure that, if such was their charge, it required patience and labour to draw together "above five hundred brethren at once" (1 Cor. xv. 6), so qualified in assurance of faith and hope, that our Lord could manifest Himself to them.

But at length this work was accomplished; and, in fulfilment of the Lord's command, they were now again in Galilee. Whether memories of their ancient calling, or more probably some actual need, suggested the resolve, we know not; but Peter said to six of the disciples who were with him, "I go a fishing!" They acquiesced; and they spent, as once of old (Luke v. 4–11), a night in unsuccessful toil, disheartened and wearied. Towards morning a stranger hailed them from the shore, and asked kindly of their success. He then bade them cast upon the right side of the ship; and at once they drew in a multitude of fishes, all large and good, numbered, but representing an indefinite number (see notes II. vi. 9, 17); and, unlike the former instance, their net did not break.

The allegorical significance of this miracle is very remarkable, and is fully dwelt on in the notes; in it lay the assurance of fulfilment of Christ's promise, "From henceforth ye shall catch men." John, prompt to believe, and quickened in loving sympathy, said, "It is the Lord!" At once Peter girded himself; and then, as before (Matt. xiv. 28, 29), threw himself into the sea, and first reached Jesus. The others came more slowly, neither quitting the instruments, nor abandoning the fruits, of their labour. They too reach Christ. And thus both ardent zeal, and patient labour, come into the presence of the Lord.

There was, upon the shore, a fire, and food; and once again they eat, in His presence, of His bounty; and He serves them, as He will serve His guests at the Supper of the Lamb in heaven (Luke xii. 37).

This was the third time that Jesus showed Himself to His disciples collectively, and in numbers, after His resurrection; and this third time is a revelation of Himself in mystery, unlike all other occasions, and surcharged with wonders of instruction.

And now follows a simpler and touching episode, in which Peter is at once reproved for his denial, and reinstated in the privileges of his Apostleship. Thrice, as he had thrice denied, our Lord asked the question of him who had professed that, though his fellow-Apostles should all of them forsake Christ, yet never to the death would he: "Simon, son of Jonas, lovest thou Me more than these" thy brethren do? Peter does not now profess a greater devotion than they; but he humbly and fervently declares his own love to Christ. "Feed thou My lambs, My sheep!" And then our Lord foretold his future faithfulness unto that very death of the cross in which he had once abandoned his Lord. Peter was now absolved, restored, and blessed.

Seeing his beloved fellow-Apostle, John, following and wistfully looking towards them, Peter asks to know his destiny also—his career, and its close. Christ represses curiosity, but says, "He will tarry till I come." The disciples thought at first that this meant that he should not see death; but John lived to see the destruction of Jerusalem, and, having survived all the Apostles, died at last in peace.

VIII. The Apostles were now all assembled in Galilee, and upwards of five hundred brethren gathered to them upon a mountain level in that district, which had been specified by Christ. And there He came forward to greet them. Those near, as He approached them, at once recognized and worshipped Him; some of the more remote, or more difficult of conviction, at first doubted or hesitated, but were also speedily convinced of His identity, and of His resurrection.

This was the most formal of all occasions of Christ's appearing, after He was risen. It was the solemn assurance given to the assembled Church; and Galilee, the scene of so many of His mightiest works, and of so much of His public teaching, was fitly the scene of this gathering.

The Apostles were now, in the presence of all, designated as the chosen leaders of the Christian community. They were publicly commissioned to extend the Gospel beyond the limited confines of Judæa, to the very ends of the earth; "to make disciples of all nations," baptizing their converts in the Name of the Father, and of the Son, and of the Holy Ghost, the coequal and triune God;

delivering faithfully all the doctrines of the Gospel; and in the reception or rejection of their witness in His Name, was placed the inheritance of salvation, or its loss. To them also Christ now confirmed the gift of miraculous powers; and gave finally to them, and to those who followed them in the succession of their apostolic office, specially; and to the Church, at large and individually, the assurance of His continual presence and support, through all the ages of this the last dispensation of religion, until the end of the world.

IX. There is one other appearance to an individual Apostle recorded, which is mentioned by S. Paul (1 Cor. xv. 7), but of which we have no particulars; it was therefore, like that to S. Peter, a personal privilege. It occurred subsequent to the general gathering in Galilee; but whether it took place in Galilee, or in Judea, is not stated. S. Paul says that "after that" gathering, Christ "was seen of James." There was evidently a special object for this visit; and it was one known amongst the Apostles, but not apparently of particular moment to the Church at large. Some writers, ancient and modern, have supposed that, as S. James is presently placed in the position of president of the apostolic college (Acts xii. 17, xv. 13–21. See also Gal. ii. 9; Acts xxi. 18), a position with which the prominence of Peter's ministry does not apparently interfere, the purpose of this special appearance of Christ was to confer upon him that distinction and office, which we might have supposed would else have fallen to Peter, and to define the duties and responsibilities it would entail upon him as first Bishop of Jerusalem.

X. The time was at length come for Christ to depart unto the Father; and, on the day of the ascension, we find the Apostles once more gathered together at Jerusalem; and Christ is personally present amongst them all for the last time (1 Cor. xv. 7). He gave them a solemn and farewell charge, declaring once more the fulfilment of the voice of Scripture prophecy in the events of His earthly career. He then gave them a special gift of spiritual understanding, " that they might understand the Scriptures ; " appointing them witnesses on His behalf to the world, of the truth of His word and of His Gospel. He further promised to them the gift of the Holy Spirit, of whom He had spoken so much before; and bade them await, in the city of Jerusalem, this signal manifestation of power and glory, to be accorded to them within a few days of His own departure from amongst them.

It seems strange, and out of place, that they should still inquire if now the kingdom should at last be restored to Israel. But Christ's reply was to the effect that the Holy Spirit would give them satisfaction and information concerning this great object of their anxiety.

He then took them forth from the city, for the last time, through scenes so often memorably traversed together with Him, and so lately, in deep sorrow, over the Mount of Olives, towards Bethany ; and then, as He was conversing with them, He rose up slowly from amongst them, towards heaven. There was no abrupt and sudden vanishing ; they all distinctly saw Him ascend, just as He had foretold to them, His voice still uttering words of blessing, and His hands, so long as they could see Him, lifted up in the gesture of benediction. And then He passed within the curtain of a bright cloud of heavenly glory, which veiled Him from their ardent gaze.

As they continued looking earnestly upwards, two angels stood amongst them, with Christ's message of peace, and with the promise of His coming again.

The Apostles returned to Jerusalem, now indeed deprived of their Lord's visible presence ; but possessed of a new and spiritual joy, in the assurance of His truth and Divinity.

For some time they continued in devotion to the services of the Jewish sanctuary ; but presently the time came, after the gift of the Holy Spirit was conferred upon them, when neither at Jerusalem, nor in any restricted locality, could the worship of the Christian Church be centred—when their labours must be extended to the full expanse of their catholic commission. And then they went forth into the wide world, and preached the everlasting Gospel; the Lord working with them, and accrediting their labours in His cause with the manifestations of His spiritual presence, and confirming the word spoken by their mouths, with signs of His Divine approval, which all the malice and wisdom of their associated adversaries could neither gainsay nor resist.

Note.—The authenticity of Mark xvi. 9–20 is assumed in this narrative and in the notes. To enter into the controversy on this question is foreign to the scope of this work. The author may, however, state that his own conviction is that the disputed verses are authentic, and that they form an integral, as well as a highly important, portion of the Gospel as given by S. Mark. For one of the latest and clearest discussions of this subject, the reader may be referred to the short treatise, and its references, at the close of the "Speaker's Commentary."

I. *THE RESURRECTION.*

The Women set out to the Sepulchre.

S. Matt. xxviii. 1 ; S. Mark xvi. 1 ; S. Luke xxiv. 1 ; S. John xx. 1.

In the end of the sabbath, when it was yet dark, as it began to dawn towards the first *day* of the week, came Mary Magdalene, and Mary the *mother* of James, and Salome, and certain others with them to see the sepulchre;

1. *in the end*, etc.—The apparent discrepancy in the accounts of the Evangelists has raised a great many questions, which have exercised the ingenuity of commentators ; but the simplest explanation seems to be this, that very early, before the faintest indication of dawn, the women of Galilee here mentioned, set forth from the city to visit the sepulchre; and that, before they reached it, the day began to dawn over the darkness. If they came from different parts of the city, or from its suburbs, some time would be spent in assembling together at the place, whence they started for the sepulchre. It was, therefore, "about the rising of the sun," which asserts itself long before it becomes actually visible; for, even now, it was still somewhat dark, and they could not see clearly, until they arrived close to the sepulchre. This is intelligible to those who are familiar with the changes, towards day, in Eastern lands. The actual twilight of dawn is short, but there is a considerable interval between the moment when the first rising of light appears, and the dawn of day ; there is a long contest between the light and darkness, before the light prevails.

2. *the first day of the week.*—(See App. XX.) Besser points out that Christ rose on the first day of the week, on which God had commenced creation with the fiat, "Let there be light." Christ Himself is "the Light of the world." The three days, which intervened between the death of Christ and His resurrection, are reckoned inclusively, after the Jewish fashion ; the extremest portion of a day reckoning for that day. Thus, Christ was in the grave on the evening before the sabbath, on the whole of the sabbath day ; and, at some early time of the first day of the week (after the reckoning of its hours by the Jewish system had commenced, but how long before the actual dawn of day, is not told us), He rose from the grave, and came forth, in His own power, and unseen by mortal eye, into the world. The commonly received idea is, that our Lord arose almost immediately after midnight.

3. *Salome.*—She was the mother of John, the beloved disciple, in

bringing the spices which they had prepared, that they might come and anoint Him.

Descent of the Angel. The Earthquake. Terror (and Departure?)
of the Guard.

S. Matt. xxviii. 2-4.

And, behold, there was a great earthquake; for the angel of the Lord descended from heaven, and came and

whose care was our Lord's mother. As she was of the party, it is likely that the women set out together from the house where Salome lived. If so, it is specially "worthy of remark that, as Mary, the mother of Jesus, was not of the number of these women who went to the grave, we may venture to say *she* sought *not* 'the living among the dead.'" (*Besser.*) Amongst the many difficulties, which present themselves in the attempt to harmonize the occurrences of this section, is that concerning the names and number of the women. Some early writers contend that there were two distinct parties of women, one of which set forth from the house of Salome, and another from that of Joanna, who, being the wife of Chusa, Herod's steward, would be living at the distance of Herod's palace, with the width of the city between them; and suppose that this last party was the one to which Christ appeared personally, and that they did not return until the two disciples, who went to Emmaus, had departed; who do not appear to have heard of the fact, that Christ had shown himself personally. (See notes 15, 43, 45; and iii. 12.) It is, perhaps, a little unnecessary to construct so elaborate, though plausible, a theory, which is here stated as a type of many others; for it is impossible to reconcile all the minor difficulties of the subject. Indeed, we might easily dispose of the whole theory, by supposing that Joanna was, at this crisis, at the house of Salome, and thence set out with the other women. We must at once assume that these minor difficulties cannot be solved, without our being in possession of far more minute particulars, than we have in the brief record of the Evangelists. It must suffice to construct a narrative out of these records, the main features of which shall be in harmony.

4. *the spices.*—(See I. xxxi. 10.) Their first object was, to see if the sepulchre remained as they had left it; and then, if practicable, and if they could gain entrance into the tomb, which was closed with so heavy a stone, to finish the embalming of the body, which they had left incomplete, in order to keep the ordinance of the sabbath.

5. *and, behold.*—The introduction of this suggests the occurrence of the earthquake, whilst the women were on their way. They must

rolled back the stone from the door, and sat upon it. His countenance was like lightning, and his raiment white as snow: and for fear of him the keepers did shake, and became as dead *men*.

have felt it with considerable alarm; but that they connected it, at the moment, with our Lord, it is difficult to suppose. It must, however, have struck terror into the heart of the guard at the sepulchre, as it occurred in connection with the descent of the angel. Some writers suppose that the angel was not visible to the guard; but that the brightness of his appearance, and the terrors of the earthquake, prostrated them, as was the case with those who journeyed with Saul of Tarsus (Acts ix. 7). (See also Dan. x. 7; Ps. cxiv. 4–7.) But the narrative distinctly states, that it was "for fear of him," not through an indefinite awe, that the keepers sank down as dead. "The earth quakes, the angel appears, that it may be plainly seen that the Divine Person now rising, had the command both of earth and heaven." (*Bishop Hall.*) (See I. i. 30, xxxi. 29, 41.)

6. *rolled back.*—This specifies one reason for his appearance; he came to roll back the stone, and to open the sepulchre for the disciples. It is likely that the soldiers saw that the sepulchre was empty. The narrative is so graphic, that we shall best gather what happened from the exact order of the words. The earthquake roused the guard, not all from sleep, for they could not all have been sleeping (see I. xxxii. 18); and, as they experienced that peculiar awe which an earthquake always produces, they beheld the angel, terrible in the bright light which clothed him, and they saw him roll back the mighty stone, and sit upon it; thus forbidding that the tomb of Christ should ever again be closed. Who else but they could have narrated these facts? It is more natural to suppose we have their narration, than the revelation of inspiration, in this case. One glimpse of the empty sepulchre may have been possible to them; and they saw it tenantless, and saw no more. How long they lay in this trance, we know not; but, probably, in a short time they came to themselves, and, seeing the angel no longer, they arose and hurried in terror to the city, to give their report to the rulers, which then at once accounted for the removal of the stone, which could not, therefore, be attributed to the disciples, or to the earthquake; and they distinctly affirmed that Christ's body was no longer within the tomb.

We cannot connect the earthquake, or the descent of the angel, with the great act of the resurrection itself. There is nothing told us of the moment when the spirit of Christ came back from Hades, to reanimate His body, and He arose from the dead, the first to rise of them that slept. It concerns us to know the fact of His resurrection, but not the time and details of the mystery, which, in ourselves, we shall all soon realize. Tradition, with the assent of some of the early writers,

The Arrival of the Women.

S. Mark xvi. 2-4 ; S. Luke xxiv. 1, 2 ; S. John xx. 1.

And very early in the morning, the first *day* of the week, they [*the women*] came unto the sepulchre at the rising of the sun. And they said among themselves, Who shall roll us away the stone from the door of the

states our Lord rose at midnight. We need not look too curiously into the secrets of the sepulchre, before God opened it to man by the ministry of the angel; but this we believe, that Christ, in His own power, did (as Bishop Pearson expresses it) " revive and raise Himself, by reuniting the same soul which was separated, to the same body which was buried, and so rose the same man " from the grave; unbeheld, unless by angel witnesses. (See App. XIX.; I. xxxi. 36; Essay, " The Resurrection of Christ.") And, as He passed through the closed room into the presence of His disciples (John xx. 19), so did He pass from the closed tomb into the outer world. The angel did not come down to open the tomb for His exit; but to open it to the disciples, and to give them knowledge of the resurrection—to rouse in them that faith to which Christ might reveal Himself personally.

7. *very early.*—(See note 1.) The twilight of the morning was now giving place to the break of day; so much of the day's dawning had intervened, since they set out, in the darkness, from the city.

8. *they came.*—" Verily, there will appear more love and labour in these women, than in men, even the Apostles themselves. The Apostles, they sat mured up, all 'the doors fast' about them; sought Him not, went not to the sepulchre; neither Peter that loved Him, nor John whom He loved, till these women brought them word. But these women, we see, were last at His Passion, and first at His resurrection, stayed the longest at that, came soonest to this, even in this respect to be respected." (*Bishop Andrewes.*)

9. *who shall roll.*—It is evident that the women knew nothing of the placing of the guard, and sealing the stone. They had left the sepulchre, on the evening of the entombment, before the rulers had obtained the guard; and it is interesting to notice the entire obedience with which they had observed the sabbath. The rulers had transgressed the ordinance of the day, in order to complete the precautions suggested by their unholy fears. But these, most deeply concerned in the dead Christ, so far from conspiring to steal away His body for purposes of imposture, as the rulers feigned, were so reverently observing the holy day, desecrated by themselves, that they refrained even from going near the tomb in which all their hopes lay buried, and did not hear of the soldier guard there stationed. Their obedience to the

sepulchre? And when they looked, they saw that the stone was rolled away : for it was very great.

Mary Magdalene runs back to tell Peter and John.

S. John xx. 1, 2.

Mary Magdalene seeth the stone taken away from the sepulchre. Then she runneth, and cometh to Simon Peter, and to the other disciple, whom Jesus loved.

ordinance of God won, as usual, its blessing; they thus knew no fear to detain them from their present errand; and they were speedily rewarded by the vision of holy angels, the tidings of the resurrection, and the personal greeting of the risen Saviour.

10. *when they looked.*—They did not yet see the angels. There was light enough, as they came near, to see the open mouth of the sepulchre, and that the stone was gone from the entrance; and they wondered what strong force had removed it, "for it was very great."

11. *then she runneth.*—Mary Magdalene may have hurried on, a little in advance of the other women. As soon as she saw that the stone was gone, she seems to have examined no further; but to have run back immediately with the tidings, that instant measures might be taken in the matter. She did not stay to ascertain more than the fact of the removal of the stone; she could not lose time, when charged with tidings of such importance. She may have glanced through the opening, and, in the dim light, satisfied herself, without going nearer, that the body of Christ was not where she had seen it laid. She ran to two of the disciples, who had been latterly much together (see John xiii. 24, xviii. 15, 16), and were strongly attached; they had together been favoured witnesses of our Lord's mightiest works, and of His glory, and of His agony. Mary had probably left them together at the house from which she had set out to go to the sepulchre. These were Peter, the most ardent, and now the most sorrowful, of the Apostles, and John, "the disciple whom Jesus loved," the most loving of the twelve. She speaks with the indefiniteness of haste and consternation, "*They* have taken away the Lord out of the sepulchre, and we know not (we saw nothing to guide our conjecture) where they have laid Him." She seems to suppose that, possibly, Joseph and Nicodemus had transferred the body to some other sepulchre; she does not seem to fear that the rulers had interfered further concerning Him. The guard had evidently got clear of the sepulchre, and out of sight, before her arrival there; and perhaps she did not go near enough, or look close enough, to observe traces of their occupation. But we can

The Women enter the Sepulchre, and see the Angel. They return.

S. Matt. xxviii. 5–8 ; S. Mark xvi. 5–8 ; S. Luke xxiv. 4–9.

And they [*the other women*] entered into the sepulchre, and found not the body of the Lord Jesus. And it came to pass, as they were much perplexed thereabout, behold, they saw a young man sitting on the right side, clothed

scarcely err in supposing that Mary's faith entertained hopes, not clear and defined perhaps, but sufficient to send Peter and John in haste to the sepulchre. They did not know the meaning of His rising again, but these tidings excited some faint hope; their haste seems rather the speed of anticipation, than that of fear or anxiety.

12. *entered.*—The narrative is now resumed, which was broken off when Mary Magdalene left her companions, to carry news of the open sepulchre to Peter and John; to relate, also, *their* visit and return, and the revelation of Christ to Mary Magdalene. These women must have arrived at the sepulchre, whilst Mary was gone on her errand; they probably spent some time there (note 13), and left it very shortly before the arrival of the two disciples, and by a somewhat different road, for they could not have met each other on the way. Whilst they are on their way to the city, Peter and John see and leave the sepulchre, Jesus appears to Mary Magdalene, and then to themselves also, before they reach their home. Our Lord now receives a title not given before His resurrection. It is said, "they found not the body of the *Lord Jesus;*" He is now to us the " Lord Jesus Christ."

13. *much perplexed.*—They had entered the sepulchre, and the removal of the body troubled and astonished them. There were no signs of forcible entry, or of the carrying off of Christ's body, in order to conceal it. All that met the eye suggested very different conclusions. How long they may have spent in discussion of the extraordinary circumstances of the case, we can only conjecture, by comparison of the time when Christ appeared to them, on their return to the city, with the events which must have intervened.

14. *behold, they saw.*—The words suggest that they became suddenly conscious of the presence of a being whom they had not previously seen, but who now became visible to them, sitting within the tomb. The account in S. Luke states that "two men stood by them in shining garments " (Gk. " that flashed light "). It appears that one spoke to them, as mentioned by S. Mark. Just in the same way, S. Mark mentions Bartimæus only, instead of the " two blind men " spoken of by SS. Matthew and Luke. We need not, therefore, consider this an argument in favour of there being two parties of women, visiting the sepulchre separately, at different times (note 3). Again, S. Luke

in a long white garment; and they were affrighted. And as they were afraid, and bowed down *their* faces to the earth, the angel answered and said unto the women, Fear not ye: for I know that ye seek Jesus of

states that "two men *stood* by them in shining garments," whilst S. Mark says, "they saw a young man sitting on the right side, clothed in a long white garment." The discrepancy is only apparent, and may thus be reconciled: At first they saw the two standing, and, in fear, "they bowed down their faces to the earth;" when they looked up again, one had withdrawn, and one was sitting, calmly and quietly, at the right side of the sepulchre, who now addressed them. (See note 33.) The frequent evidence of Scripture is, that these bright ministers of heaven are constantly about the people of God; and that, at God's will, they have become visible to man. (See notable instances in 2 Kings vi. 14–17, and Luke ii. 8–14.) It is quite evident that the angel thus showed himself in the present instance. The women were within the tomb; they had leisure to note all that met the eye, and were in troubled conversation concerning the removal of the body of their Lord; and "they were affrighted" at the sudden appearance of so unearthly a being. The thought that the angels of God are present on very frequent occasions, listening, unseen, to the converse of those of earth, is very suggestive of the great duty of watchfulness over ourselves, and should be an incentive to devotion, and exertion in the way of holiness. See, in 1 Cor. xi. 10, a remarkable reference to their presence; it is interpreted of public worship.

15. *fear not ye.*—The sequence of words in the original is exactly rendered here; the emphasis rests on "*ye*," and there is a connection, in the narrative of S. Matthew, between the impression produced upon the guard, and that upon these women. The former had no reason for anything but fear; the women, only for reverence and joy. Greswell, and others, think that the guard was still there, prostrate with fear, and that the women were terrified at the sight of them. It is, however, likely that any such terror would have prevented their even approaching the sepulchre, round which men were lying, much more entering in; and, until they had entered, they did not see the angel. The guard had probably gone from the precincts of the sepulchre, as Theophylact, and the majority of writers, suppose; and, therefore, were not seen by the women. The emphasis of the angel's words must, therefore, signify, "Whatever cause others, enemies, may have for fear, from the angels of Christ's kingdom, 'fear not ye' who are of His friends." The greeting, in these terms, is a special and personal welcome, and a recognition of these faithful followers of Christ, and of their errand.

16. *Jesus of Nazareth*, etc.—Gk. "the Nazarene, the crucified"—

Nazareth, which was crucified. Why seek ye the living among the dead? He is not here: for He is risen, as He said. Come, see the place where the Lord lay. And go quickly, and tell His disciples and Peter that He is

echoes, with a very different accent, of the derision of the multitudes which had done Him to death. These words give point to the accent of the angel's address, remarked in note 15.

17. *the living.*—Gk. "the living one" (sing.) "amongst those dead" (plur.). "Death hath no more dominion over Him;" He hath "life in Himself." Dr. Plumptre gives the following note: "It is in vain that we seek 'Him that liveth,' in dead works, dead formulæ, dead or dying institutions. The eternal life that is in Christ, is not to be found by looking into the grave of the past in the world's history, or in those of our individual life. In both cases it is better to rise, as on the 'stepping stones of our dead selves,' to higher things."

18. *the place.*—They had already been looking on the empty tomb; it is now, to them, no more than the place where the risen Lord had lain. The order and arrangement visible in all around argue, not the removal of the dead, but that One who is living has gone out. (See note 13.)

19. *and Peter.*—(See I. xxvii. 10.) This special message to Peter is generally supposed to have conveyed the merciful Saviour's special greeting to that disciple who had denied Him, the last glance from whose eye had sent him forth in such deep humiliation and penitence. A personal message of forgiveness, and love, is now, therefore, sent to Peter by the mouth of His angel. But Peter himself must have arrived at the sepulchre almost immediately after these women had gone quickly on their errand to the disciples; and he had not faith, or, in his sorrow and humiliation, dared not hope, that the Lord was risen. No vision of angels, or of the Saviour, was yet accorded to Him; but yet the first thing he hears, on his return, is the account of the women, who had seen angels where he had not seen them, and had met Jesus Himself, perhaps upon the very road he had traversed. We cannot doubt that the special message to himself, as a token of love and mercy, roused that faith in him, which, later in this eventful day, was rewarded by a separate and personal revelation of Christ. Peter was the first to see Him, of all the Apostles. (See Peter's own thanksgiving for this mercy in 1 Pet. i. 3.) The early writers, generally, speak of the announcement of the resurrection to men by woman, in reference to the Fall through her transgression; that she might not for ever bear the blame of the Fall, it is committed to her to bear the glad tidings of its reversion. Ælfric, the Saxon homilist, says, "Death and perdition befell us through a woman, and afterwards life and salvation came to us through a woman." (See note 39.)

risen from the dead; and, behold, He goeth before you into Galilee; there shall ye see Him: lo, I have told you. Remember how He spake unto you when He was yet

20. *into Galilee.*—(See I. xxvii. 6.) This was the scene of our Lord's meeting with the great concourse of His disciples; it had been the country where He was best known, and perhaps best appreciated, "wherein most of His mighty works were done," and where many of the chief events of His ministry had transpired. There was a ready faith amongst the rough-spoken, but warm-hearted, natives of Galilee, which drew forth the exercise of His miraculous power, but which was less apparent amongst the dwellers near Jerusalem. Many of our Lord's Apostles were of this northern district, amongst whom Peter was thought worthy to be foremost; but when he came within the circle of servants, round the fire in the courtyard of the high priest's palace, he had to bear their contempt, because of his provincial accent, as they turned round on him with the taunt, "Thou art a Galilæan; thy speech bewrayeth thee!" (See I. xxx. c. 27.) The state of public feeling in Jerusalem also rendered Galilee far safer, and more suitable, for so large a gathering of disciples. The message now given to the disciples, may refer to some former conversation, when the precise spot, and other details, may have been communicated; unless we suppose these more precise directions were given after His resurrection. It has been remarked that, notwithstanding our Lord's injunction to go into Galilee, He showed Himself chiefly, so far as we have record, in Jerusalem. But this general direction would not interfere with His private manifestations to His chosen Apostles, nor does it indicate, as some have ventured to affirm, any change of purpose. It would, on the contrary, seem almost necessary that these Apostles, on whom must devolve the arrangements for gathering the body of the disciples, but who themselves so little realized the full truth, should have personal evidence to themselves of the resurrection, apart from the many reasons for Christ's meeting them separately from the body of Christians, to whom they must minister in His stead.

21. *shall ye see Him.*—It is likely that, though part of a message to the disciples, the pronoun "*ye*" has a personal application to the women, who bore the message; they also were to be present, when Christ appeared to the disciples in Galilee. So the meaning of the word "*ye*" here is the disciples generally.

22. *remember.*—In no way could the angel more practically recall the women, and those to whom they gave in their account, from any separation of these events of the resurrection from the other events of the life of Christ (as might have ensued from so many marvellous experiences, and after these visions of angels), than by pointing out their exact sequence on what had preceded; and their fulfilment, and no more than this, of what Christ had before told them should happen.

in Galilee, saying, The Son of Man must be delivered into the hands of sinful men, and be crucified, and the third day rise again.

And they remembered His words, and they went out quickly, and fled from the sepulchre with fear and great joy; for they trembled and were amazed: neither said they anything to any *man;* for they were afraid: and did run to bring His disciples word.

By another Road, Peter and John arrive at the Sepulchre: Mary Magdalene following them.

S. Luke xxiv. 12; S. John xx. 1-11.

Mary Magdalene cometh to Simon Peter, and to the disciple whom Jesus loved, and saith unto them, They have taken away the Lord out of the sepulchre, and we know not where they have laid Him.

Peter therefore went forth, and that other disciple, and came to the sepulchre. So they ran both together: and the other disciple did outrun Peter, and came first to the sepulchre. And he stooping down, *and looking in,* saw

It was when "they remembered His words," that they recovered themselves, and addressed them to their mission.

23. *fear and great joy.*—Fear, or, rather, awe and reverence, for the mysteries revealed to them; and great joy, far outweighing the fear, for the tidings which their faithful hearts received and acknowledged. Fear and joy are often mentioned together in Holy Scripture; reverence naturally accompanies holy joy. (See Ps. ii. 11.)

24. *neither said they,* etc.—That is, they spoke to no one by the way; they said not a single word about these matters, until they delivered their wonderful tidings to the Apostles.

25. *did outrun.*—Many writers explain that the youth and strength of S. John gave him the advantage over the more aged Apostle; but, had there been anything to venture, which could rouse the zeal of Peter, he would not have been found behind. It seems likely that the strong attachment, and the faith which had not faltered, gave speed to the one; whilst the consciousness of his base denial, though so bitterly repented of, stayed the feet of the other. He still "thought thereon," as he ran to the place where he might, perhaps, even see the risen Saviour, true to His word of resurrection, as to that of death.

26. *stooping down.*—This act of stooping down is thrice noticed

the linen clothes lying; yet went he not in. Then cometh Simon Peter following him, and went into the sepulchre, and seeth the linen clothes lie, and the napkin, that was about His head, not lying with the linen clothes,

(Luke xxiv. 12; John xx. 5, 11); it shows the narrowness of the entrance to the sepulchre. The gesture, however, suggests deep reverence, rather than curiosity, or, perhaps, than even the natural act which the size of the opening might necessitate. He saw the linen clothes lying there; but, though he had come in such haste to the sepulchre, he was reluctant to enter, and search for further signs of his Lord's removal. We can scarcely think he feared any shock to his faith (as some have supposed); but John knew enough of his Lord's mind, to make him hesitate to examine closely and curiously, where he had, at least, an undefined consciousness that his faith was on trial. The demand of Thomas could never have come from the heart of John; nor had he any of that spirit in which the sons of the prophets, against Elisha's remonstrances, prosecuted, for three days, the search for traces of the translation of Elijah.

27. *then cometh.*—It did not occur to Peter to stay, as S. John had done; his pressing forward to where his Lord had lain, was equally characteristic of this disciple. Full of earnest and stirring thoughts, he went directly to the tomb; and he saw the garments of the dead Christ laid in order within, that which had bound His head (which those removing the body would never have torn from the lacerated brow) lying separate by itself. The sight of the deserted tomb was very suggestive of thought to Peter; but, apparently without noticing his fellow-disciple, he went out again, wondering what explanation he would presently hear, and what would result from these extraordinary circumstances. But it does not appear that even the prompt and ardent Peter perceived any fulfilment of Christ's promise of the resurrection.

28. *the linen clothes.*—S. Gregory notices the orderly arrangement of the clothes, and the fact of the napkin placed and folded separately, as a conclusive argument against the stealing of Christ's body. Such a theft must have been characterized by hurry and terror; for the time was short, and fear of the *sleeping* guards imminent. S. Chrysostom also gives the following explanation of this arrangement of the grave-clothes: "This was a token of the resurrection: for if they had carried away the body, they would not have stripped it; nor, if they had stolen it, would they have been careful to roll up the napkin, and put it aside by itself. Therefore John previously stated that Christ was buried with myrrh, which cause the linen clothes to adhere closely to the body, that you may not be deceived by those who said He was stolen away; for what thief would be at so great pains about a superfluous matter?" The following description of the

but wrapped together in a place by itself. And [*he*] departed, wondering in himself at that which was come to pass.

Then went in also that other disciple, which came first to the sepulchre, and he saw, and believed. For as yet

sepulchre is interesting for its antiquity : "It is said that the sepulchre of the Lord is a round cell, hewn out of the rock which was round it, so high that a man, standing upright, could scarcely touch the roof with his outstretched hand ; and it has an entrance to the east, to which the great stone was rolled, and placed upon it. In the northern part of it is the tomb itself, that is, the place where our Lord's body lay, made of the same rock, seven feet in length, raised three palms higher than the floor. It is not open from above, but on the south side, the whole of which is open, and through which the body was brought in. The colour of the sepulchre, and of the recess, is said to be mixed white and red." (*Bede.*) Dr. Pusey quotes a passage from the same early English writer, as explanatory of the then very ancient custom of using a linen "*corporal*" in the celebration of the Holy Communion: "According to the spiritual meaning, we may think that the body of the Lord is not to be enveloped in gold, or gems, or silk, but in pure linen ; although it signifies this too, that *he* enwraps Jesus in pure fine linen, who receives Him in a pure heart. Hence it has been the custom of the Church, that the sacrifice of the altar should not be celebrated on silk, or on dyed cloth, but in linen from the earth, as the body of the Lord was buried in a pure linen cloth."

29. *lying.*—*i.e.* laid straight and orderly, but without the body which they had enfolded.

30. *saw, and believed.*—Some of the early writers, with S. Augustine, explain that John now believed that Mary had spoken the truth concerning the removal of the body. Others of them say that John believed, on this evidence, Christ's words concerning His resurrection ; and that Peter did not believe. Hence one reason for the special message to Him by the women—a message which must have made a deep impression on the mind of Peter, when he received it on his return from this visit to the sepulchre, and considered it in connection with the hesitation and sorrow which distracted his mind. If we take the natural impression which S. John's words convey, remembering how modestly he speaks always of himself, it seems natural to coincide with the latter interpretation, that John did now believe that Jesus was risen. The difficulty of the following verse is not an insuperable one. John believed the *fact*, as stated by our Lord, that He would rise from the dead on the third day ; but the fulfilment of Scripture, and all that this doctrine included, and its central position in the plan of the Gospel, he did not as yet understand. Thus, we ourselves believe,

they knew not the scripture, that He must rise again from the dead. Then the disciples went away again unto their own home.

Mary Magdalene remains at the Sepulchre: Christ appears first to her.

S. Mark xvi. 9–11 ; S. John xx. 11–18.

But Mary stood at the sepulchre weeping; and as she wept, she stooped down, *and looked* into the sepulchre, and

on the evidence of God's word, the mysteries of the unseen world, and the great doctrine concerning the holy Trinity; but we "know not the Scriptures," as yet, concerning these truths in all their significance —we see them "as through a glass darkly." This faith of John's was present to our Lord's mind, and to the thoughts of the disciples, quite as much as any reference to the faith of future ages, when He pronounced the blessing on those who believed, without the assurance of sight, the truth of the resurrection : "Blessed are they that have not seen, and yet have believed."

31. *went away.*—No further proof was, at present, given to them; no vision of angels, no revelation of Christ Himself. But to Peter, later in the same day, Christ did reveal Himself personally—"He was seen of Cephas" (see iii. 25); and the words with which the Apostles received the two from Emmaus were, "The Lord is risen indeed, and hath appeared to Simon." The Apostles do not seem to have embraced the truth fully, until one of their own number, who were Christ's chosen witnesses, had been favoured with the revelation granted to the women. To Peter, the first in zeal, and the deepest in penitence, and now also in humility, Christ had first shown Himself. But we may feel some surprise that John, who loved Him so deeply, and was Himself "the beloved disciple," to whom was entrusted the guardianship of our Lord's mother, was not distinguished now by any special and personal revelation of his Lord. Perhaps John needed it not; he believed already, and was well content to wait his Lord's time. And thus he was already in training to receive that fuller and grander revelation of Christ, than was granted to any other mortal upon earth, which was given to him upon another Lord's day, in the Spirit; when he beheld the glories of heaven, and Christ the King, the Son of God, in His majesty (Rev. i.).

32. *Mary stood*, etc.—Mary Magdalene had therefore followed the disciples, and returned to the sepulchre. The other women appeared to have left it, but this could only have been immediately before the

seeth two angels in white sitting, the one at the head, and the other at the feet, where the body of Jesus had lain. And they say unto her, Woman, why weepest thou? She saith unto them, Because they have taken away my Lord, and I know not where they have laid Him.

And when she had thus said, she turned herself back,

arrival of the two Apostles; and they could not have met upon the way.

33. *two angels.*—There were, we know not how many angels, about the tomb of Christ. One showed himself to the guard, in aspect of terror and power; he sat upon the stone of entrance, barring the way to those who were not permitted to search into its mysteries. Here two angels are sitting where the head and the feet of Jesus had been. We read, also, that two angels are seen by some of the women; but that one addressed to them words of consolation and promise. (See note 14.) They come and go upon errands of the Saviour's kingdom; they withdraw and present themselves, according as they are commissioned by Him; and we gain glimpses of the bright and glorious beings, which are always surrounding us, ministering to us (unseen, but with the truest sympathy) the administrations of our Lord's service; and they reflect, to the beholders, the light which proceeds from God's presence. Some of the early writers notice them, as representative of the two testaments, which bore witness to Christ's incarnation, death, and resurrection. Bishop Andrewes (quoted by I. Williams) notices how they were present where the body of Jesus had lain, as the Ark, in which the presence of God was shadowed, lay between the two cherubim of mercy.

34. *woman,* etc.—The sorrow of Mary Magdalene impressed itself upon them; they saw how deeply she bewailed her loss, and how little she knew of the real truth—how there was cause for deeper joy, than she could experience sorrow. It must have been evident to her, that they were not beings such as she was accustomed to look upon; but, absorbed in the selfishness of her sorrow, she does not appear to have been greatly struck, even by a vision so extraordinary. Her reply to their questions shows more thought of the supposed removal of the dead Christ, than faith in the promise of His resurrection. It seems strange that she, who had fled to give tidings to the disciples, should now return, and that only to weep.

35. *turned herself.*—It is less likely that, as has been thought, Mary should have turned away from the angels, in the absorption of her grief, than that (as some of the early writers supposed) our Lord now approached; and that, at His coming, the angels rose, or so looked towards Him, as to arrest the attention of Mary, who turned herself round from them. He addressed her in the terms in which the angels

and saw Jesus standing, and knew not that it was Jesus. Jesus saith unto her, Woman, why weepest thou? whom seekest thou? She, supposing Him to be the gardener, saith unto Him, Sir, if Thou have borne Him

had spoken; but she neither recognizes His voice, nor person. It is a strange peculiarity of the body of the resurrection, that, though the same body, it is so changed and spiritualized, that it possesses new powers and faculties. Christ disguised or revealed Himself at will; He was unknown to Mary Magdalene, to the disciples going to Emmaus, to the disciples fishing in the Galilæan lake, until, in some familiar action, He manifested Himself to those, who then at once recognized and adored Him. Again, no bars, which prevent the progress of natural bodies, hindered His entrance or exit. He left the tomb, but none saw Him pass, and His passage left no trace; He came to the eleven disciples, without opening the fastenings which so jealously closed their doors, "for fear of the Jews." He came without being noticed, or His approach heard. He does not, any more than before His death, appear to have been at once in more places than one—for that is not a condition possible to created body, but only to the omnipresence of the Deity—but time and space appear to be as nothing to Him. He was present with Mary at the tomb; and, it would seem, immediately on leaving her, with the other women, who were now approaching the city. He assumed, also, various powers, or likenesses. He was to Mary, as the gardener; to the other women, as Himself at once; "in another form." He appeared to those at Emmaus. And there is, further, the power to convey instantaneous and full recognition, by a word, as to Mary, or in an action, as to the disciples at Emmaus, and to those who had been fishing on the Lake of Galilee; and this, evidently, quite different from the way in which, to ourselves, some casual accent of the voice, or a gesture, may recall features once known and forgotten. We must remember that the excellencies, and powers, of the body of the resurrection, were not fully perceptible to those bound by the fetters of mortality. We know little of "that body that shall be," or of "the glory which shall be revealed in us;" but these glimpses of the activities, and powers, of the body of the risen Saviour (and they are but the faintest glimpses), reveal a condition of being immeasurably superior to that which is ours now. (See iii. 5; iv. 3.)

36. *the gardener.*—Not Joseph, the owner of the garden, but him under whose care it was. The word "*gardener*" may mislead an English reader, who is unacquainted with Eastern customs; the man was rather a keeper of the ground, than one employed in cultivating it. Christ seemed to Mary, either from His habit, or to her fancy, as being in charge of the place. She at once applies to Him for informa-

hence, tell me where Thou hast laid Him, and I will take Him away. Jesus saith unto her, Mary! She turned herself, and saith unto Him, Rabboni; which is to say, Master. Jesus saith unto her, Touch Me not;

tion about the removal of the body; but, as she has invested Him with a supposed character, so she concludes He will at once conjecture whom she is seeking, and her own right in the dead. To her devout and faithful heart, there is but one " *Him.*" Many words could not more fully pourtray the hastiness, and inconclusiveness, of one entirely absorbed in her own sorrows.

37. *Mary.*—This is one of the most touching and beautiful incidents in Holy Scripture. Description can do it faint justice; and he who reads it to others, must feel how inadequately he can render accent or gesture, which he knows must have thrown life into this our Lord's single word, "Mary." How many memories of past years must have flashed across her mind! One of the Evangelists, in speaking of this revelation of Christ to Mary, adds, " out of whom went seven devils;" and this recollection is not needed to identify her, but to point out how, to her penitence and love, Christ now showed Himself, first of all His followers, crowning the deliverance of her past life with the earnest of the resurrection. Who can follow a glance of the mind? Yet, surely the past and future blessings called her at once from the very depths of despair; sorrow and mourning fled away before the light of Christ's presence. She at once knew Him as her Lord, and confessed Him.

38. *touch Me not.*—This is an injunction difficult to understand. To Mary, doubtless, our Lord's voice and gesture conveyed the meaning, which (like the rendering of His mention of her name) we cannot exactly realize. Scarcely any two of the early or later writers agree in interpretation. But there appear to be two or three main ideas, which sum up the opinions which they have very variedly expressed. (i.) Our Lord, who is just leaving her, to show Himself to the other women, who were already approaching the city, on their return from the sepulchre, says, " Detain Me not; cling to Me not now" (as the original implies). "You will have other opportunities of seeing and conversing with Me, for I am not immediately about to ascend to My Father." (ii.) Our Lord restrains Mary from such familiar embrace, as she now proffered, not understanding the great difference and dignity which belongs to the body of the resurrection, impressing her, therefore, with right perception of the reverence due to a spiritual body; and pointing her to that future state, and to the kingdom of His Father, whither presently, but not immediately, He was going, where all who are " risen with Him, shall have the fruition of His glorious Godhead." The want of intelligence of this spiritual condition, would be a bar to real and true association with Christ; and it would never be perceived

for I am not yet ascended to My Father: but go to My brethren, and say unto them, I ascend unto My Father, and your Father; and *to* My God, and your God.

by those who thought of Christ as merely human; therefore, "though we have known Christ after the flesh, yet henceforth know we Him no more." Perhaps the words of our Lord conveyed something of both these meanings to Mary—the intimation that the relationships of earth were spiritualized, and exalted, by the resurrection, which brings humanity into the presence of God; and that, therefore, she must rise to higher conceptions of the intercourse of those risen from the dead; but that this would not be her last, and only, sight of her Lord upon earth. The change would not come like a sudden shock and repulse; there would be other opportunities of learning what He declared now; for, though He was about to ascend to God, He would not so immediately leave the earth, as to see her no more. Bishop Hall takes this view: "There may be a kind of carnality in spiritual actions. Thou that livedst here in this shape, that colour, this stature, that habit, I should be glad to know; nothing that concerns Thee can be unuseful. Could I say, Here Thou satst, here Thou layst, here and thus Thou wert crucified, here buried, here settedst Thy last foot; I should, with much contentment, see and recount these memorials of Thy presence; but if I shall so fasten my thoughts upon these, as not to look higher, to the spiritual part of Thine achievement, to the power and issue of Thy resurrection, I am never the better."

39. *go to My brethren.*—(See Rom. viii. 29; Heb. ii. 11.) Mary Magdalene would thus ever be known, amongst the disciples, as the first messenger of the resurrection, on the part of Christ Himself; and by her mouth was conveyed to them that name, "brethren," now first used by our Lord, and expressive of a more intimate relationship than any used before; and also indicative of His still being the Son of man, though the risen Lord. Hilary says, "Since death began from the female sex, to her first is given the seeing and announcing of the glory of the resurrection;" and, "as Eve brought the message of death, so did woman the tidings of resurrection." An English writer calls her "an apostle to the Apostles." (See note 19.)

40. *My Father, and your Father,* etc.—Our Lord expresses a mutual relationship between Himself and His people, but not an identical one. God is our Father and our God, as He is "the God and Father of our Lord Jesus Christ;" but Christ is the only begotten and Divine Son of the Father, "equal to the Father as touching His Godhead;" whilst we, whom He is not ashamed to call brethren, are the adopted "children of God, through faith in Jesus Christ." God is also our God, as He created, redeemed, and sanctifies us; He is the God of Christ, in that relationship in which Christ is "inferior to the Father, as touching His manhood." Christ could not, therefore, in speaking to us of His, and

Mary Magdalene came and told the disciples, as they mourned and wept, that she had seen the Lord, and *that* He had spoken these things unto her. And they, when they had heard that He was alive, and had been seen of her, believed not.

our, relationship to God the Father, say, "*our*" Father, and "*our*" God; but "My Father, and your Father; My God, and your God." S. Augustine explains, briefly: "Mine by nature, yours by grace." Bishop Andrewes also defines, very clearly: "His Father is our Father, by His means; our God is His God, by ours. Him that was our God, we make to be His God, that Him that was His Father He may make to be our Father. God is His Father in His estate of immortal life; ours, in our estate of this mortal life. His by nature, by very generation; ours by grace, by mere adoption. Our God by nature, His no otherwise than as He took upon Him our nature." There is here a very remarkable instance of what is an invariable rule, in the original Greek, when Christ speaks of God as Father. When speaking of God as *His* Father, He always prefixes the article; but when He speaks of Him as "our," or "your" Father, the article is not prefixed. There is great subtilty of expression, often quite untranslatable, in the insertion, or omission, of the Greek article.

41. *as they mourned.*—The interval of the sabbath was passed, with its special duties, and its restraints of sorrow; and now the days of the world's life were beginning again for them, and they felt the full force of their loss. They did not yet know "the Lord's day," and its associations of great joy. Christ's message, by Mary, came to them (as He loves to send His messages of love and happiness) in the hour of depression and sorrow; "your sorrow shall be turned into joy."

42. *believed not.*—"Slow of heart to believe," is the characteristic of all the disciples, unless we may except S. John. It is only natural that this should be the case, as their conception of Christ's mission, and kingdom, has been so uniformly earthly and temporal. It was, however, sad that they refused direct testimony from one, who could neither be mistaken, nor convey an intentional untruth to them; they believe neither the vision of angels, nor the message of Christ Himself. If we understand this unbelief in its higher and spiritual sense, it represents the slowness of the heart to receive, as its *own* interest, that sure doctrine of Scripture, which, on the evidence of Scripture, men do not deny nor doubt; but which they must be taught of God to realize, as the tidings of their personal salvation. It matters little to them, that Christ is seen and acknowledged by the faith of others, until His Spirit reveals the truth to themselves. It is, however, dangerous to refuse to hear, even when we do not fully realize what we hear; for, ultimately, "*faith* cometh by hearing."

Christ appears to the other Women on their way to the City.

S. Matt. xxviii. 9, 10.

And as they [*the other women*] went to tell His disciples, behold, Jesus met them, saying, All hail. And they came and held Him by the feet, and worshipped

43. *to tell His disciples.*—Greswell has adopted the opinion, that there were two parties of women, quite distinct. He lays great stress on the omission of the words of S. Matthew, "as they went to tell the disciples." It is quite possible that these words, which are omitted in many old MSS., are spurious; but their omission would scarcely give the support he claims from it, to the theory he advances, that our Lord's appearance to the women did not take place till after the eighth day from the resurrection—in fact, that Christ did not show Himself to either of the parties he mentions, on the day of the resurrection; but to some of the same women, on a later occasion. The difficulty, with him, is the message to assemble in Galilee; and he says we may take it for granted, that they set out as soon as they were commanded— "they could not have received the message on one day, and obeyed it only a week afterwards." The narrative of the Evangelists, however, seems certainly to justify the usual opinion, that Christ did appear to the women (*one party*, even if they started from different parts of the city) on the morning of the resurrection, and they then received Christ's message concerning the meeting in Galilee. The disciples, as they did not believe the women, would not expedite their arraugements for this gathering; which must have required so much preparation, that they may well have allowed a longer interval than eight days to elapse, before they set out for the appointed place. The words of S. Luke (xxiv. 9–12) seem especially conclusive against this theory. In the first place, it is not likely they would have been visiting the sepulchre, as there stated, eight days after the resurrection; and S. Luke certainly connects the visit, and the delivery of the tidings, too closely to admit an interval. (See note 3.)

44. *held Him.*—Christ, who had left Mary Magdalene, now presents Himself to these women, on their way to the city, and, with words of greeting, manifests Himself at once to them; and they now receive this, as the reward of faith. We notice that our Lord allows, in these women, the embrace which He had discouraged in Mary Magdalene. They were still alarmed; and He gave them—as, subsequently, to the disciples (Luke xxiv. 39), and to Thomas (John xx. 27)—this substantial evidence of His corporeity, to assure them, after their converse with the angel spirits of heaven. The message repeated by Christ is that already given by the angels, for the general gathering of the

Him. Then said Jesus unto them, Be not afraid : go tell My brethren that they go into Galilee, and there shall they see Me.

The Women (Mary Magdalene included) bring their Tidings to the Apostles.

S. Matt. xxviii. 8 ; S. Mark xvi. 10, 11 ; S. Luke xxiv. 9–11 ;
S. John xx. 18.

And [*they*] returned from the sepulchre, and told all these things unto the eleven, and to all the rest.

disciples in Galilee. Their gesture is at once expressive of devotion and adoration, not of mere earthly affection.

45. *they returned.*—The names of all who had been to the sepulchre, are here gathered together ; and others are mentioned as having been present, though previously unnamed. Some writers reconcile an apparent difficulty in the grouping of all these, by supposing that Mary Magdalene, hurrying from the sepulchre, joined the rest before they reached the Apostles—a supposition very probable. But others argue that Mary Magdalene, charged with her special message, and the other women, with their more general tidings, came separately to the Apostles ; and their embassies are here mentioned together, to show what evidence of the resurrection was given to the Apostles, early in the day (that of Mary Magdalene being delivered, perhaps, at an earlier hour than the other women took courage to deliver theirs), and how it was received by them. There is another theory, which may be mentioned here,—that the women (not including Mary Magdalene), after delivering to the Apostles the message of the angel, returned to the sepulchre, and, on their way back, were met by our Lord ; and that, before their return the second time, after seeing Christ, the two disciples had left the Apostles, on their walk to Emmaus. But, however little value may be attached to the words of the present text, "As they went to tell His disciples," they doubtless represent, at the least, the *tradition* of the time of Christ's meeting the women ; and this theory, of the second visit to the sepulchre, has simply the merit of an ingenious mode of reconciling some difficulties, the real clue to which has been lost.

The visit of these women to the sepulchre, with the intention of embalming our Lord, was the original visit from which these various incidents diverged,—the return of Mary Magdalene ; the visit of Peter and John ; and the appearing of the angels, and then of our Lord Himself, to Mary ; and lastly, also, the same revelations to the other women. These events of the early morning of the resurrection, form themselves into a distinct group.

It was Mary Magdalene, and Joanna, and Mary *the mother* of James, and other *women that were* with them, which told these things unto the apostles. And their words seemed to them as idle tales, and they believed them not.

II. *REPORT OF THE GUARD.*

S. Matt. xxviii. 11-15.

Now when they were going, behold, some of the watch

46. *to all the rest.*—As distinct from the eleven; to those believers gathered together with them, and to all others friendly to His cause in Jerusalem. (See iii. 23.)

47. *idle tales.*—As unfounded in reality, and arising from the excitement and imagination of the women. They must, however, have understood that the sepulchre was deserted; but they declined to entertain further evidence, in the blindness of their present state of sorrow and despondency. Their unbelief was not that of scepticism, but of slowness to throw off preconceived errors, and to admit the light of truth. We may suppose that this partly wore away, as the day progressed, and as they continued to talk and meditate upon the wonderful tidings brought to them. It is evident that Peter's testimony made some impression on their unbelief; for, though they still believed not the disciples, who came from Emmaus, their incredulity was giving way before the multiplication of evidence. However sad was their want of faith, we cannot but admit the value of their caution and slowness, as tending, in no slight degree, to satisfy and convince the minds of men in after ages. Particularly is this the case with regard to the incredulity of Thomas. There can be no doubt as to the truth itself; if the Apostles had been over-credulous, the world would never have been persuaded, without full assurance of facts. The Apostles " were incapable of falsehood; and, even if it had not been so, a conscious falsehood could never have had power to convince the disbelief, and regenerate the morality, of the world." (*Farrar.*) There was a keen sifting of all evidence, by those attached to ancient systems of religion, and by antagonistic philosophy. The historical truth of the resurrection, could scarcely have rested satisfactorily on the ready faith, and unhesitating conviction, of the women. It was, doubtless, because Christ had appeared to none of themselves, the chosen Apostles, that they distrusted the evidence of others. (See iii. 35.)

1. *were going.*—Whilst the women were on their way to the city, to give their account to the Apostles, some of the guard were engaged in

came into the city, and shewed unto the chief priests all
the things that were done. And when they were assembled with the elders, and had taken counsel, they
gave large money unto the soldiers, saying, Say ye, His

reporting the great fact of the resurrection, from very different motives,
to an audience interested from an entirely different point of view. It
is said that " some of the watch " only, went on this errand ; and,
though it is, of course, possible that they were told off to give an official
report, or went as a deputation from the rest, it may be that others
were being drawn to better thoughts, by the evidence of the resurrection which they had received. Corn. à Lapide suggests that the
soldiers lay hid in terror, and that, whilst concealed, they heard and
saw all that transpired at the sepulchre ; and that, when the women
were gone away, they came forth, and went on their errand. Rosen-
müller also says that the present is here used for the past tense—
" when they were going," for " when they had gone "—thus implying
that the departure of the soldiers was subsequent to that of the women.
But, though the present tense may be so used, it is better to understand
it in the usual way here ; the statement of S. Matthew does not necessarily mean, that they started after the women had left the sepulchre,
but merely that these two, so different, embassies were fulfilling their
errand simultaneously. We may be sure that they were *not* privileged
to see the risen Saviour ; and it is more natural to think that, if they
had the power to get up and hide themselves, the same impulse would
prompt them to flee at once to the city. How so large a body could
hide themselves, is not apparent ; and they certainly could not hide
themselves from the angel guard, who were now in possession of the
sepulchre. It may seem difficult to think that a body of Roman
soldiers would flee from their post of duty ; but, as the sepulchre was
empty, their duty was discharged ; and we know that the bravest men
may be entirely overcome by supernatural terror. Their flight means,
that they went, as fast as possible, to give their report.

2. *assembled.*—This may not have been a full assembly of the
Sanhedrim, for there were some of the rulers, " who had not consented
to the deed " of those who plotted against Christ ; and the circumstances
of His death had made a strong impression upon others. But it was
no informal meeting ; it was, in fact, one of that series of councils, held
by the rulers against Christ, and continued by them against His
Apostles. S. Jerome says that the " large money " now offered to the
soldiers for their false statement, as also that given by the rulers to
Judas, was taken from the treasury of God, and so diverted from its
legitimate purpose, for use against His cause.

3. *say ye.*—Anything more palpably false, and improbable, could
scarcely have been invented ; and it shows how difficult it was to put
aside the truth in this matter. The story was hardly worth the

disciples came by night, and stole Him *away* while we slept. And if this come to the governor's ears, we will persuade him, and secure you.

So they took the money, and did as they were taught: and this saying is commonly reported among the Jews until this day.

trouble and sin, which it entailed on its contrivers and propagators. They did, however, well know how easily excited, and readily duped, were the Jewish people; and their lie was commonly current amongst the ignorant, so late as the date of the publication of S. Matthew's Gospel. But it has never obtained credit with the world; the story was too clumsy and improbable. If these soldiers of the guard can be believed *all* to have slept at the same time—a matter incredible of Roman soldiers, and entailing certain death (Acts xii. 19, xvi. 27)—how could they know that the disciples came to steal away the body? But that sixty men should sleep at once, on guard, would be a miracle in itself, sufficient to imply Divine interference in the case. (See i. 6, and I. xxxii. 18.)

4. *if this come.*—*i.e.* by process of public rumour; for it was evidently intended there should be no official report made to the governor. But it would appear, from the testimony of early writers, that Pilate, in his account of the circumstances of the crucifixion of Christ, sent to the Roman emperor, expressly mentioned the well-supported rumours of the resurrection. And Corn. à Lapide quotes from Hegesippus (who takes his information from the "Acta Pilati"), that Pilate obtained from the soldiers the full account of this story, and of the bribery of some of their number, by the Jewish rulers; and makes use of it, as an evidence of the scanty credit that can be given to any statement advanced by them. That the true story of the resurrection, as declared by the Apostles, had also gone abroad, and was credited, we have the evidence of Josephus, whose short but interesting paragraph relating to Christ, and the Christians ("Antiq." xviii. 3, 3), may here be quoted, though its authenticity has been questioned: "Now, there was about this time Jesus, a wise man, if it be lawful to call Him a *man*, for He was a doer of wonderful works—a Teacher of such men as receive the truth with pleasure. He drew over to Him both many of the Jews, and many of the Gentiles. He was [the] Christ; and when Pilate, at the suggestion of the principal men amongst us, had condemned Him to the cross, those that loved Him at the first did not forsake Him, for He appeared to them alive again the third day, as the divine prophets had foretold these and ten thousand other wonderful things concerning Him; and the tribe of Christians, so named from Him, are not extinct at this day." (See App. III.)

5. *this saying.*—As the rulers desired to deceive, and as the people

III. *CHRIST APPEARS TO THE DISCIPLES THAT WENT TO EMMAUS.*

S. Mark xvi. 12, 13 ; S. Luke xxiv. 13-35.

After that He appeared in another form unto two of them, as they walked, and went into the country that same day to a village called Emmaus, which was from Jerusalem *about* threescore furlongs.

were not careful to discern truth, this perversion of the fact sufficed them ; and there was no other sign of the miracle granted to them, than this, which they had despised. Olshausen points out that the resurrection was the especial sign given by God to the Jewish people. Christ clearly said that the sign of the prophet Jonas, and its fulfilment in Himself, should be the one sign peculiarly addressed to them (S. Matt. xii. 39, 40, xvi. 4). Ample evidence of its truth was given; and, wherever the preachers of " Jesus and the resurrection " encountered Jews, they brought this forward, but manifested it in vain. Christ could not personally manifest Himself to them, because they were, through unbelief, unfitted to behold Him. Those who wilfully blinded, and fettered, themselves with the prejudices and vices of the natural body, could not discern, and grasp, the truth of the spiritual body. Had Christ shown Himself to them in their unbelief, His so doing would not have served to convince them (Luke xvi. 31). "One risen from the dead," would preach in vain ; and this would only enhance the condemnation of those, who received neither the testimony of Scripture, nor of eye-witnesses. There is substantially the same evidence still submitted to this fallen and incredulous, but isolated, people ; isolated, that they may be reserved for future mercy. (See I. xviii. 69, 93.) It is urged upon them, by the belief of so many nations of the world, and by the light and blessings which have ever attended its reception and progress. But they still turn away from it, and no other sign is granted. But, surely, that specially offered to them, must be wisely ordained, as the truth most suitable to them ; and one day this truth will be vindicated.

1. *another form.*—See note 5, and i. 35; iv. 3.
2. *Emmaus.*—The name is supposed to have reference to some hot springs, which were there; but the site, which has been the subject of much dispute, has not yet been satisfactorily identified. Its distance from Jerusalem was rather more than two hours' walk—seven miles and a half.

And they talked together of all these things which had happened. And it came to pass, that, while they communed *together* and reasoned, Jesus Himself drew near, and went with them. But their eyes were holden that they should not know Him.

And He said unto them, What manner of communications *are* these that ye have one to another, as ye walk, and are sad? And the one of them,

3. *they talked.*—(See Mal. iii. 16.) The claims, Passion, and crucifixion of Christ, with the hope of the resurrection—all these were the subject of their talk. This is a noticeable feature in the narrative; all that followed was the consequence of this conversation, for it was in their anxiety and earnestness in this, that Christ came near to comfort them. The inference is certain, that Christ will be present in spirit, and inspire the thoughts of those who thus converse earnestly, though in perplexity, concerning the truths of His religion, as these disciples "communed together, and reasoned" in their sadness; itself another powerful appeal to the Saviour's regard.

4. *drew near.*—He overtook them, coming, like themselves, from the direction of Jerusalem; so they address Him as one from Jerusalem, though, apparently, not conversant with what, to them, was the great topic of the day there.

5. *their eyes.*—S. Mark says that Christ appeared to these disciples "in another form." We conclude, therefore, that, not only was Christ, to the outward eye, different in appearance, but that there was also the putting forth of power, which prevented recognition on their part. Ebrard says, "The body of the resurrection becomes an expression of the spiritual being;" so that Christ's disguise of Himself, or appearance in any strange and unrecognizable form, is not an actual change of outward form, or the wearing of external disguise, but something intermediate between appearing and vanishing. "The will of the soul *subjects* the body to itself, gives to the expression of the form as much, or as little, as it will, and can weaken or withdraw the characterizing expression, even to becoming invisible. A relative degree of this vanishing is that general, indefinite form, without personal recognizability, which the Lord assumed." (*Stier.*) Such a body would be, in every sense, a *body*—no phantom. We cannot, indeed, know now how the body of corruption dominates over the spiritual being, and subdues it, or clogs it; but we know that Christ's spiritual body was endowed with marvellous powers, without losing, in any degree, its actual bodily reality, and substance. (See i. 35; iv. 3.)

6. *are sad.*—Gk. "of a sad countenance." Our Lork marked the expression of their countenance, as well as their words, as He now joined Himself to their company; but He could not manifest Himself

whose name was Cleopas, answering said unto Him, Art Thou only a stranger in Jerusalem, and hast not known the things which are come to pass there in

to them, till faith was kindled in their hearts. From the phrase preceding, "making communication one to another, and reasoning," it is likely that they were in argument and debate together, a step in process towards conviction of truth.

7. *Cleopas.*—This name is, in derivation, different from that noticed in I. xxxi. 24. It is a contracted form of "Cleopatros." It is unlikely, therefore, that this man was (as Hammond, Elsley, and some others declare) the husband of Mary. Tradition makes him one of the seventy, a resident of the village of Emmaus, and subsequently a martyr in the cause of Christ, for his testimony to the resurrection. Who the other disciple was, is not known; but there have been many conjectures, from the age of Origen to our own times. Amongst the most strongly urged, are James, Peter, and Nathanael. Peter seems out of the question, as he had his separate manifestation later, either shortly before, or after, this meeting of Christ with the two disciples, and on the same evening. Besides, if Peter was one of these two, the Apostles could not possibly have greeted them with the words, "The Lord is risen indeed, and hath appeared to Simon." As these two disciples went specially to give in their report to the Apostles (Luke xxiv. 33), it is most improbable that either of themselves was of that body. (See note 23.) Others have supposed that S. Luke himself was one of them; but he speaks of himself as distinguished from those who were eye-witnesses (Luke i. 2). Stier quotes a quaint remark of a preacher, very much more to the point than the rehearsal of these speculations: "The learned cannot come to any agreement who the other was; and I will give you this good counsel, Let each of you take his place."

8. *a stranger.*—A temporary, a solitary sojourner, not familiar with the local affairs. Such a stranger might be a foreigner, or, at least, a Hellenist, or one of the Greeks (I. xvi. 1). The tenor of the information given by the disciples, and especially the words "*our* rulers," seem to indicate that they did not think Him a Jew. Persecution had not yet taught reserve and caution to the disciples, or they might have been less frank with a stranger. Archbishop Trench, and others, instead of laying the stress on the word "only" (which is really an adjective), lay it on the verb, and give the literal rendering of the words: "Dost thou lodge alone at Jerusalem," *i.e.* apart from social intercourse, and so ignorant of the common talk and topics of the day. The question is thus equivalent to asking, "Art thou the only one, of the many thousand strangers at Jerusalem at this feast, who is ignorant of what is in every one's mouth, as the topic of the day?"

these days? And He said unto them, What things? And they said unto Him, Concerning Jesus of Nazareth, which was a prophet mighty in deed and word before God and all the people: and how the chief priests and our rulers delivered Him to be condemned to death, and have crucified Him. But we trusted that it had been He which should have redeemed Israel: and beside all this, to-day is the third day since these things were done. Yea, and certain women also of our company made us astonished, which were early at the sepulchre;

9. *what things.*—A natural question from a "stranger," to whom "*the* things," so expressly important to the disciples, might be, at least, trivial in comparison with the interests of the great festival, which had drawn so many foreigners to Jerusalem. The crucifixion of Christ would seem, to such a one, of little general interest. He might be supposed to know as little about Christ, who was put to death, on the representation of the Jews that He aspired to royalty; as about Barabbas, who had been a leader of revolution, with the same object, and was released on their petition.

10. *a prophet.*—They had not lost faith in what Jesus Christ had been; they thought Him true before God and man; and so many of the prophets had been slain by the Jews, that the mere fact of His death did not discredit His character as a prophet. But they give Him this title, as the lowest which might be accorded to Him. He had higher claims, and, in this capacity, had disappointed certain hopes of theirs. "*We*" (His followers) "were hoping" that He was far more than a prophet, namely, *the* Prophet (Deut. xviii. 15), the Messiah, the Son of David, the King and Redeemer of Israel. His word was pledged to the fact of His being the Messiah of God; and they could not, at present, reconcile this claim with His death. The third day was passing to its close, without signs of His promised return; though angels had declared Him alive, and He had actually been seen as risen, if the account of women of their company, not accepted authoritatively by the Apostles, might be believed. It was to their faith, though weak, and to their earnest longing, that Christ now revealed Himself. The contrast between the unbelief of the people generally, and theirs, is very marked: they were arguing ground for faith; Israel was unwilling to know the truth, lest they should be convinced by it; and so they were blinded, and continue blinded, to the revelation of Christ.

11. *redeemed.*—The same word is used in Luke i. 68, ii. 38, where, from the context, we see that both spiritual and political deliverance is meant; as is the case also here.

and when they found not His body, they came, saying, that they had also seen a vision of angels, which said that He was alive. And certain of them which were with us went to the sepulchre, and found *it* even so as the women had said: but Him they saw not.

Then said He unto them, O fools, and slow of heart to believe all that the prophets have spoken: ought not Christ to have suffered these things, and to enter into

12. *a vision of angels.*—Hence some have supported the theory, that there were two embassies of women to the sepulchre (see i. 3, 43); and that the one here referred to, had not seen Jesus. But this is not conclusive. They may have hesitated to say to a stranger that Jesus was risen, and it was the very fact of which they were not themselves absolutely assured. The words below, " Him they saw not," which refer to the visit of Peter and John to the sepulchre, may imply that the woman had asserted that they had seen Christ, and that it was, therefore, a special disappointment that Peter and John had not been similarly favoured. It is difficult to think that these disciples had left the city *before* the arrival of Mary Magdalene, and the other women; for they set out when the day was well advanced, and they own to having heard part of the tidings from them; and their having heard part, must imply that the most important part had been told them.

13. *O fools*, etc.—Dull, both as to the intellectual appreciation of what is written, and also with regard to faith; slow of head to understand, and of heart to entertain belief; therefore entirely dull. The disciples are not here blamed, because they did not believe the testimony of angels, or even of those who asserted that they had seen Jesus; but for not receiving the " more sure word of prophecy; " just as our Lord says, " Had ye believed Moses, ye would have believed Me: for he wrote of Me. But if ye believe not his writings " (Scripture), " how shall ye believe My words?" (John v. 47). The evidence, therefore, of Holy Scripture, is supreme and final, with regard to Christ; for, if this is Christ's own testimony concerning the Scriptures of the O. T., what may we not assume of those of His own revelation, written under the special dispensation of the Holy Spirit? It is not, however, the interpretation of contested passages, which may be disputed with all the subtleties of the schoolmen; our Lord here speaks of the general testimony of Scripture. " All that the prophets have spoken," is the concurrent witness of the voice of prophecy. (See I. xvii. 18.)

14. *Christ.*—Gk. " *the* Christ; " the Messiah promised to the fathers, and the great subject of type and prophecy, to whose revelation it was the purpose of the law to lead mankind for instruction. Had not Jesus thus fulfilled the anticipation of Scripture? Ought not the Christ therein spoken of, to have been been, as Jesus had been, a

His glory ?   And beginning at Moses and all the prophets, He expounded to them in all the scriptures the
things concerning Himself.

And they drew nigh unto the village, whither they went :
and He made as though He would have gone further.
But they constrained Him, saying, Abide with us : for it

suffering Messiah, not a temporal sovereign ; and to enter upon the
glory of the resurrection, and victory, through the grave and gate of
death ?

15. *in all the Scriptures.*—Not every Scripture, but (see note 13) a
brief and lucid summary of the consentient voice of Scripture ;
showing that its testimony is throughout conclusive to His truth.
The Scriptures were familiar to them from childhood ; and now, as in
memory they follow our Lord's words, familiar passages become invested with a new and real light, under His interpretation.   We may
see an illustration here of the importance of familiar acquaintance
with the text of Holy Scripture ; for in time of sickness and distress,
in the moment of exigence, or of argument, the light of the Spirit's
teaching can glance over things known, but not fully realized ; whilst,
to those who know them not, and have not, in time of need, the power
to turn to them, no such illumination can be possible.

16. *Himself.*—See John v. 39–46.

17. *He made.*—Gk. "He was making." (See Mark vi. 48.)   A great
deal of criticism has been expended on this phrase, which some have
thought to imply that Christ made a feint, or pretence, of doing what
He had really no intention of carrying out ; that He, therefore, here
acted a part, and so justifies artifices which may lead to good results,
which are expedient, but are slightly divergent from the exact line of
truth.   But this is a misapprehension of the character of Him who is
"the Truth ;" it is impossible for Him thus to *act.* (See I. xi. 16.)
Had the disciples not constrained Him to stay, and had not their
desire been to learn from Him, this gesture, which was designed to
draw forth their request, would have been completed, and Christ
would have been near them, without their then noticing His presence ;
the revelation, now within their reach, would have been deferred.   There
may have been instances where Christ desired to manifest Himself,
but did not, from some such cause, after His resurrection.   It is sometimes the case, that men notice, and rightly value, their blessings at
the moment they seem about to be withdrawn ; the prospect of losing
them makes us urgent to retain them.   It is so with means of grace ;
the fear of their withdrawal sometimes opens our eyes to their great
importance to us.

18. *abide with us.*—In the exercise of that virtue so highly esteemed
in Eastern lands, and by which, in Israel, "some had entertained

is toward evening, and the day is far spent. And He
went in to tarry with them. And it came to pass, as
He sat at meat with them, He took bread, and blessed

angels unawares," they press the stranger to enter their home, urging
the lateness of the hour—a fact which they themselves entirely for-
got, when, shortly after, they hurried the long distance of return to
Jerusalem, to carry their tidings of great gladness to the Lord's
Apostles.

19. *took bread.*—Dropping the attitude of a guest, and assuming
the functions of the master of the house (in itself a significant act),
He proceeds to distribute, in an impressive and unusual manner, a
portion of the food which is set before them; not, apparently, at first,
but whilst they were still seated at the table. "As He sat at meat
with them," is a phrase very parallel with the "as they were eating" of
SS. Matthew (xxvi. 26) and Mark (xiv. 22). The Romish Church finds,
in the mention solely of "*bread*," support for their administration of
the Holy Communion in one kind only; and explains the injunction
at the institution of the Eucharist, "drink ye all of it," to apply to
the Apostles, and their successors in the ministry, not to the laity of
the Church. Perhaps a horror of this grave abuse, led some of the
writers of the Reformation era to the opposite length, of denying that
there is any sacramental meaning in our Lord's act, in this instance—
an opinion which has certainly the support of several eminent names
amongst modern scholars. Others argue that, though it seems impossible for these disciples to recognize a sacramental act, in that
which they had not before witnessed—for they were not themselves
present at the institution of the Lord's Supper, and there had been
since no celebration of it amongst the Apostles—they did recognize a
familiar gesture in "the breaking of the bread." The interpretation of
the ancient writers, however, gives strong support to the more general
opinion, that this was a sacramental act. A comparison of Luke
xxiv. 30, with xxii. 19, shows, we must think, more than an accidental
coincidence of expression. We need not assume that these disciples
knew nothing of the Lord's Supper, because they were not present at
its institution; for the events of the last week must have been told
by the Apostles, who must have been closely questioned upon all that
preceded the crucifixion, in order that our Lord's last words and
promises might be treasured, and observed, by the disciples. And
prominent amongst all such topics of conversation, must have
been this of the Eucharist. We may as fairly assume that these
disciples were aware of what had been done, as that they did not
know. Doubtless, they then saw (as has been beautifully supposed)
the marks of the nails, and also recognized our Lord's familiar
way of breaking the bread (see notes 20, 27); but as we simply
read the passage, the natural inference is, that recognition was per-

it, and brake, and gave to them. And their eyes were opened, and they knew Him; and He vanished out of their sight. And they said one to another, Did not our heart burn within us, while He talked with us by the way, and while He opened to us the scriptures?

And they rose up the same hour, and returned to Jeru-

mitted in this solemn and Eucharistic mode of "*the* breaking of *the* bread" (Luke xxiv. 35; Acts ii. 42, xx. 7, Gk.). Wherever the "*stigmata*" are offered, as a means of recognition, their being so is specially stated.

20. *their eyes were opened.*—Whether we admit the giving of the bread, as a sacramental *act*, or merely as invested with a sacramental character, the truth here suggested is distinct and forcible: that Christ is known to His people in their observance of the Sacrament which He instituted. "The eyes of those who receive the sacred bread are opened, that they should know Christ." (*Theophylact.*) It is a strong argument for obedience to this command, and for the efficacy of thus "showing forth the Lord's death till He come," that Christ had walked and conversed with these disciples, and had even interpreted to them the Scriptures, as only He could do; but, though they were conscious of an extraordinary influence, they did not see in Him the Christ, until He was known of them in "the breaking of the bread." And, no doubt, many earnest persons who read God's word, and pray to Him regularly, and attend the stated services of His House, but hesitate about the full act of communion with Him in the Lord's Supper, would often find that, though their heart had burnt within them, as they observed other means of Christ's grace, their eyes were opened to a special perception of Christ, in their obedience to His dying command. There is a secret unbelief, which prevents many persons from fulfilling this command; and faith is essential to our seeing Him—unbelief is an insuperable bar.

21. *He vanished.*—The original expresses His sudden and instantaneous withdrawal from perception; and that He left them, not merely that He became invisible to them.

22. *our hearts burn.*—If these disciples had listened before to Jesus, during His past ministry—as they must have done, if the very probable tradition is correct, that both were of the seventy—we may suppose they discerned many a reference to past discourses latent in His present words. They had not, however, full faith at the time He spoke to them. It matters little our seeing Christ until we fully believe; therefore, belief is superior to sight, as regards our present condition. But faith on earth will inevitably lead to sight in heaven; those "who know Christ now by faith, shall, after this life, have the fruition of His glorious Godhead." (*See Collect for the Epiphany.*)

salem, and found the eleven gathered together, and them that were with them, saying, The Lord is risen indeed, and hath appeared to Simon.   And they told them what things *were done* in the way, and how He was known

23. *the eleven.*—"The twelve" (as in John xx. 24, and 1 Cor. xv. 5, of this very instance, and elsewhere), and here "the eleven," as marking the loss of Judas, are phrases used to designate the Apostles specially. On the present occasion, there were only *ten* present, as "Thomas was not with them."   This expression is certainly against the supposition that either of these disciples was an Apostle.   (See note 7).   In Acts i. 13, 14, there is an enumeration of the eleven, "and them that were with them," where there appears to be an inner circle around the Apostles, but considerably expanded, in *v.* 15, to include the Christians generally in Jerusalem, who numbered about "an hundred and twenty."

24. *the Lord is risen.*—We must read this joyous declaration of faith with S. Mark's words (xvi. 13), "Neither believed they them;" each must modify the other.   John believed, and Peter must now have believed, perhaps others also; but they did not all believe even the evidence of Peter, and of the two from Emmaus—they waited for a personal manifestation of Christ to themselves.

25. *to Simon.*—(See i. 27, 31.)   This was, we may suppose, the fourth appearance of Christ on this day; and, no doubt, Peter's faith had risen to that power which enabled him to apprehend the personal presence, and revelation, of Christ.   This appearance of Christ is mentioned as the first on the list of S. Paul (1 Cor. xv. 3–8), but he is apparently recording those revelations which were granted to Apostles, or when Apostles were present.   The Apostles, with the exception of John, and perhaps of Peter, did not believe, until Christ was manifested to themselves.   They did not think that His personal manifestation to the women, and to other disciples, warranted their embracing the faith, until He, who had specially distinguished them, by making them His companions in preaching the Gospel, had appeared to themselves officially.   They ought to have been the quickest in faith, but they were indeed "slow to believe."

26. *what things.*—A review of this most touching and interesting narrative, renders prominent many points, as either conditions of the spiritual revelation of Christ to ourselves, or as being inducements to our loving Lord, to favour us with His presence.   Some of these may be briefly given :—(i.) Meditation, or conversation, on subjects connected with Christ, bring Him closely near us.   (ii.) Our sadness exercises a constraint upon the merciful Son of man.   (iii.) The desire to believe induces Him to draw us forth from the difficulties which surround the faith; or with which our peculiar bent of mind, and disposition, obscure it to our perception.   (iv.) The association of Christians for any religious purpose, guarantees the presence of Christ, in fulfilment of

of them in breaking of bread. Neither believed they
them.

His promise, " Where two or three are gathered in My Name, there am
I in the midst of them; " " I am with you always, even unto the end
of the world." (See also Mal. iii. 16, 17.) (v.) Our thoughtful and
prayerful study of Holy Scripture in private, draws Christ near us, to
open our eyes to understand the Scriptures. (vi.) Exhortation and
prayer, the public teaching of God's word, are remarkable means of
grace; Christ is present whilst His ministers are teaching to us the
interpretation of His will. (vii.) Eminent amongst all means of grace,
and, as it were, the crowning act, in which His presence, felt before,
is distinctly realized, is " the breaking of the bread," which He has
instituted. (viii.) We may add that this narrative offers a most
gracious and peculiar welcome, to those who are walking with Christ in
the evening of life; and who earnestly constrain Him to be their
indwelling guest, and to tarry with them, because they know that, with
themselves, " it is towards evening, and the day is far spent."

27. *breaking of bread.*—Gk. " *the* breaking of *the* bread." The
phrase is one used to signify the celebration of the Lord's Supper, in
Acts ii. 42, xx. 7, and has, therefore, a technical sense. There is
some difficulty and obscurity in interpreting it of this Sacrament, in
the present instance, chiefly for the reasons stated in note 19; but
they are not insuperable difficulties, and they are less than the difficulty of thinking that S. Luke (who uses the same words, in which
he had before described the institution of the Lord's Supper, to express
" the breaking of the bread " on this occasion, and here again employs
the exact phrase which he uses technically in the Acts, to express the
Lord's Supper) meant nothing more than an ordinary act of distribu-
tion of food, with, it may be, some familiar gesture. It is probable
that, had not the Church of Rome attached to the passage an argument for communicating under one kind, the decision in favour of
this being a sacramental act, would have been more unanimous. But,
surely, that argument is of little weight. We might as well say that
the Lord's Supper, being called " the giving of thanks," was simply a
thanksgiving; as that, because it is called "the breaking of the *bread*,"
it is signified that the giving of the cup is excluded.

28. *neither believed.*—(See note 25.) It seems strange that, after
they had, at least in part, admitted the Lord's resurrection, on the
evidence of Simon, they should reject the same truth by the mouth of
these two witnesses. We may suppose a natural reluctance, in the
Apostles, to receive testimony not granted to themselves, the chosen
witnesses of the truth. They were conscious of the supreme importance
of the doctrine, and of their being fully convinced, before they proclaimed it. Their caution is of the utmost value to the world. At
the same time, we must admit that they were " slow of heart to

IV. *CHRIST APPEARS TO THE APOSTLES.*
THOMAS ABSENT.

S. Mark xvi. 14 ; S. Luke xxiv. 36–43 ; S. John xx. 19–23.

And as they thus spake, the same day at evening, being the first *day* of the week, when the doors were shut where the disciples were assembled for fear of the Jews, came Jesus and stood in the midst, as they sat at meat ; and saith unto them, Peace be unto you.

believe." But, perhaps, there is a difference here, and above, in their unbelief. They treat the tidings no more as "idle tales;" the manifestation of Christ to them *all*, shows that they had faith, else He would not, or could not, have come amongst them.

1 *thus spake.*—Whilst the disciples were telling their glad tidings, and the hearts of the Apostles burned to hear this confirmation of previous intelligence of their Lord's resurrection, and in answer and satisfaction of all the doubts which they had (so unworthily of themselves, so happily for the faith of others) entertained, our Lord revealed Himself to them, in their full conclave.

2. *the doors being shut.*—S. John's description is very minute and graphic. The hour; the company of faithful disciples; their reasonable apprehensions, and precautions against the enemies who had destroyed their Lord, and were hostile against themselves; the suddenness of the Lord's arrival ; the awe and mystery which surround His person ;—all are distinctly impressed upon the reader.

3. *stood in the midst.*—Some have thought to vindicate the truth of the corporeity of our Lord, by explaining *how* He entered the room, knocking at the door, or entering by the window. But the natural and plain meaning of the words is, that, although the doors were fast (and no allusion is made to windows, which, in the East, are generally too small, and too well barred, for entrance), Jesus came suddenly, without announcement, or warning, and became visible in the midst of them ; not in the act of entering the room. It may be difficult to understand *how* this could be; but it is, at least, a rash venture to decide what are the limitations of power to a spiritual body. S. Augustine remarks, that those who object in this instance, must explain how our Lord could walk upon the sea, contrary to the laws which influence natural bodies. The question is a fair one, in the view that Christ, being without sin, was not subject to the law of death, even before He died by permission of His own will ; and that, therefore, He may have possessed bodily powers, forfeited in Adam's fall, but restored in the

But they were terrified and affrighted, and supposed that they had seen a spirit. And He said unto them, Why are ye troubled? and why do thoughts arise in your hearts? Behold My hands and My feet, that it is I Myself: handle Me, and see; for a spirit hath not flesh

resurrection. But this power of walking on the waters is, more probably, due to His Divinity; whereas, here, it is very possible that He only exercised one of the ordinary powers of a spiritual body, at present unascertained by us. For we see one limitation, which His Divine power does not supersede—He was not in bodily presence in more places than one, at the same time; we conclude, therefore, He is exercising here, also, the powers of His body of the resurrection. He seems also to be unrestrained by the difficulties of time, or space, or material bars. (See 35, iii. 5.) Stier observes here, " Doors hinder Him not like closed hearts."

4. *as they sat at meat.*—The fashion of reclining, amongst the Jews, gives great significance to these words. As they were all reclining at table, it was easy to see that none opened the door to our Lord; and that the door had not been opened at all, to admit Him.

5. *peace.*—Our Lord promised, " In Me ye shall have peace. Peace I leave with you, My peace I give unto you " (John xiv. 27). He now solemnly renews this blessing. We may suppose how grateful to them were His first words; for their last act, when before He stood amongst them, was to forsake Him, and flee. His peace not only spoke forgiveness of this wrong, and of their unbelief; but it was the imparting to their spirit of that peace of God, which possessed His own spirit. This, which was His commission to the seventy, He gives as His example of blessing.

6. *a spirit.*—A disembodied spirit. It is not stated that " He appeared in another form," in this instance. Most probably, they saw Him as Himself; but they were astonished, and terrified, by His unexpected and sudden presence. In their fear, we have an additional argument for the belief that He did not knock, or enter any open door (note 3). They experienced somewhat of this terror before, when they saw Him walking on the sea (Matt. xiv. 26). The remedy against this terror, would have been belief in the tidings brought to them, and watchfulness; for, as Christ vanished from the sight of the disciples at Emmaus, so did He manifest Himself now to the Apostles at Jerusalem. Any thought of dread and terror, connected with the advent and manifestation of the Saviour, is sad and painful; it must ever be occasioned by unbelief of heart or life.

7. *thoughts.*—The original implies argument and disputation; the confliction of faith with belief, in the heart.

8. *flesh and bones.*—Mr. Westcott has the following remark, which

and bones, as ye see Me have.   And when He had thus
spoken, He shewed them *His* hands, and *His* feet, and

expresses the opinion of other writers: " It is not, I believe, a mere
fancy, to see a typical indication of this change in the words used by
our Lord Himself of His glorified body (Luke xxiv. 39; cf. Eph. v. 30)."
The significant variation from the common formula, " flesh and blood,"
must have been at once intelligible to Jews, accustomed to the provisions of the Jewish ritual; and nothing could have impressed upon
them, more forcibly, the transformation of Christ's body, than the
verbal omission of the element of blood, which was for them the seat of
corruptible life.   (See Gen. ix. 4 ; Lev. xvii. 11, 14: " The life of all
flesh is the blood thereof," *i.e.* the *animal* life.)   Alford, who advocates
this view, points out, in the instance of the revelation given to Thomas,
that Christ's wounds were open, not merely scars ; and adds, " this
would itself show that the resurrection body was *bloodless.*"   It is
curious, in illustration, to notice how Homer (Iliad, v. 340) couples
bloodlessness with immortality, in the nature of the gods :—

> " They eat no bread, they drink no ruddy wine,
>   And bloodless thence, and deathless, they become."

It is remarkable (though the argument may not be pressed too far)
that, in speaking of Christ's body, we read of God's care for the flesh
and the bones, but not of the blood: " My flesh shall rest in hope "
(Ps. xvi. 9); " He keepeth all His bones, not one of them is broken "
(Ps. xxxiv. 20. cf. Acts ii. 31 ; John xix. 36); " His blood was poured
out an offering for our sins." (See v. 6.)   Of His Church, it is said,
We are members of His body, of His flesh, and of His bones " (Eph.
v. 30).

9. *He shewed.*—He retained these " stigmata," the marks of His
death, and they became visible at His will, for the establishment of
the faith of those, who doubted the fact of His personal identity.   It
has been noticed that there are two principal objects, which Christ
made prominent, in this revelation of Himself to His Apostles: the
establishment of their faith, and their commission to evangelize the
world in His Name.   And He gave them now a threefold evidence
of His resurrection : the evidence of sight of His wounds, of touch, and
also, " He did eat before them."   " His eating was from power, not
from necessity.   In one way does the thirsty earth, in another the
burning sun, absorb the water; the one from power, the other from
necessity." (*Bede.*)   It was impossible to doubt the evidence thus
offered to them.   Angels, who appeared in bodily form, had, indeed,
given two such instances of corporeity.   It is not distinctly asserted,
but the context, and the customs of the country, made it clear that
Abraham, and Lot, both washed the feet of angel guests; and it is
especially declared that " they did eat " (Gen. xviii. 2–8, xix. 1–3).

His side.   And while they yet believed not for joy, and wondered, He said unto them, Have ye here any meat? And they gave Him a piece of broiled fish, and of an honey-comb.   And He took *it*, and did eat before them. Then were the disciples glad, when they saw the Lord. And [He] upbraided them with their unbelief and hard-

But, whilst our Lord offer these two signs of His bodily reality, He desires them to *handle* Him, for the special purpose of conviction. He also shows " the wounds which He had received in the house of His friends " (Zech. xiii. 6) ; and He expressly offered these, as evidence of the great fact of the resurrection, which He declared.   It was impossible that He could deceive, or that God would permit any spirit of lying to deceive mankind in His Name.   Therefore the disciples, in this instance, embraced the truth, which was manifested, on other occasions, with other and additional proofs.   It is often, and most truly declared, that there is no fact of history, which rests on so firm a foundation, as the historical fact of the resurrection of Christ.

10. *for joy.*—We must give this explanation of the doubts of the Apostles its full value.   They did not disbelieve, because they were indifferent, or hostile, to the truth of the resurrection ; or because they did not wish to believe.   This contrast with the unbelief of the Jews, and of heathen opponents, must be carefully marked.   They could not at once trust that, which was the most joyful and happy news to them, that God could send them.   How often, to use a trivial comparison, we hesitate to admit the truth of something we hear, because " it is too good to be true."   This was not the only source of the disciples' unbelief, but it was one prominent feature.

11. *then.*—All doubt, hesitation, and fear now melted away in the great joy which fell upon them, when their hearts recognized their Lord, and they received His blessing of peace.   Thus was realized the promise of John xvi. 22.   How " glad " shall His disciples be, on the day of their resurrection, when " they see the Lord as He is."

12. *upbraided.*—It was unfitting that a matter of so much moment, to themselves, and to their Lord's cause, as their temporary unbelief in the great doctrine of the Gospel, should be passed over in that gentle and kindly manner, in which our Lord spared them one word of reproach for their desertion of Himself, and for their misapprehension of His spiritual kingdom ; since, from their prejudices in favour of a temporal kingdom, so many difficulties had resulted.   Christ's providence did, indeed, overrule the doubts and difficulties on the part of the disciples, which they have so candidly recorded, to the establishment of the faith of future ages ; but that does not make their personal error venial.   Those who misapprehend Christ, are likely to desert His cause in the day of trial ; and the same will also want faith to

ness of heart, because they believed not them which had
seen Him after He was risen.

Then said Jesus to them again, Peace *be* unto you: as
My Father hath sent Me, even so send I you. And

realize His spiritual presence. The point of His reproof is, that they
did not receive oral testimony to the resurrection—the very evidence
which they, on His behalf, must offer to the world, as they preached
the Gospel; and the rejection of which oral testimony would be, to
their hearers, and to all after ages, destruction. They hesitated as
to the historical proof of Christ's resurrection, on which really depends
the belief of the world. But we cannot sufficiently admire, and value,
the candour which published to the world their errors of unbelief;
and the satisfaction which they afford to the doubts of other ages,
which could not have been equally met, had all but the *belief* of the
Apostles been concealed from us.

13. *again.*—This was no mere repetition. There was need of Christ's
peace, to reassure the doubts and fears of the Apostles. This, however, is a formal and official blessing. The peace of Christ was to be
theirs, in their warfare against sin, and in their efforts for the propagation of the Gospel. Strife from without, from those who opposed, and
disquiet, where the Gospel separated a man from those of his own
household, must reign around them, as the truth, in their mouth,
fronted the errors of the world. But, in themselves, they should have
peace; thorough conviction of the truth and right of the cause they
advocated, should be theirs. And they should also bring peace, the
peace which Christ gave to them so freely, to give freely to others.
This was a commission parallel to that given before, in Matt. xviii. 18,
but of far higher consequence, and with ampler powers.

14. *even so.*—With the same commission to evangelize the world;
with the same Gospel to deliver to men; with the same promise of
support, and assurance of victory; with the same testimony to their
word, namely, prophecy, and the Spirit. They are entrusted, in Christ's
stead, with God's embassy of mercy to the world—an offer of grace,
and a dispensation of religion, which are final, and which shall not be
superseded until He come. And thus, as the Father sent Christ into
the world, so did Christ send the Apostles; to proclaim salvation, in
His Name, and in that of the Father, as He proclaimed it in the
Father's Name.

15. *breathed on them.*—To see the full meaning of this solemn act,
we must look back to Gen. ii. 7, where God breathed the breath of life
into Adam, of the first creation, "and man became a living soul." The
life thus given was that immortal and spiritual life, which is distinguished from the animal life common to all the animal creation,
"which is the blood thereof" (Gen. ix. 4). Job acknowledges this
(xxxiii. 4): "The Spirit of God hath made me, and the breath of the

when He had said this, He breathed on *them*, and saith
unto them, Receive ye the Holy Ghost : whose soever sins

Almighty hath given me life." But the resurrection of Christ, introduced a new and "more abundant life" into the world, the life which
He inspires; and into this we "must be born again." With regard
to this life, Christ, "the last Adam, was made a quickening Spirit;"
it is His to communicate it to His people—"He quickeneth whom He
will" (John v. 21). There is a passage in Ezekiel (xxxvii. 9, 10), where
the multitude of the converts to the life of the resurrection is typified;
and where the prophet is commissioned to invoke the breath of the
Lord, to animate the dead with a new life. The ministration of that
Spirit is in the commission of the prophet. The shadows and types
of the O. T. are vastly inferior to the realities of the Gospel; we may
feel sure, therefore, that there is, in the inspiration of Christ now
given, a greater power than in either of these cases, as He breathes
the life of the resurrection into the Apostles, and places its communication to the world within the terms of their commission. We must
extend this trust beyond them, to the end of time; according to the
terms of His promise, "Lo, I am with you always, even to the end
of the world."

16. *receive ye.*—This was, like the promise of the Comforter, a gift
not fully realized until the day of Pentecost. Christ, however, bestows
the gift now, and He connects it with Himself; for the dispensation of
the Spirit is no new dispensation, but the completion of Christ's
mission. For, as in John xv. 26, Christ declares that He will send
the Holy Spirit, "which proceedeth from the Father;" it is clear,
also, from this passage, as from others, that He proceedeth from the
Son. His procession from the Father and the Son is, to give a single
proof, so placed in a distinct light, in John xv. 26. xiv. 26. But that
"no final gifts of Apostleship were now conferred, is plain by the
absence of Thomas; who, in that case, would be no Apostle in the
same sense in which the rest were." (*Alford.*) The absence of
Thomas may also show, that all future ministers of Christ's Church, in
succession to the Apostles, are partakers of this breathing of the new
life, and the commission connected with it, and of this eminent gift
of the Holy Ghost—the Apostles, in their special and apostolic degree;
their successors in the ministry of Christ's word and Sacraments, in
their general and ministerial degree.

17. *whose soever sins.*—(See App. XIV.). A commission in terms
resembling this, was given originally to S. Peter (Matt. xvi. 19), intended, perhaps primarily (the neuter pronoun being used both in
Matt. xvi. 19, xviii. 18) to refer to the enactment, or abrogation, of
ordinances of the Church; and certainly, also, to admit into, or repel
from, Church communion, with the power of the keys of Christ; and
then, afterwards, to the Apostles generally, with regard to trespasses

ye remit, they are remitted unto them ; and whose soever
sins ye retain, they are retained.

between brother and brother, and in general discipline. We gather,
therefore, that the power, then promised, was now substantially given
to the Apostles, to decree or abolish, in all matters essential to the
government of the Church of Christ ; and also to decide, in all cases
of dispute within the Church, in matters of wrong or error. Decisions
given in such cases should be ratified in heaven. We are taking the
lowest view of these passages, which are not now under review ; they
admit of far higher interpretation. There is usually claimed for them,
and fairly, the sense of pronouncing authoritative decision in the
Name of Christ. But, looking on the occasion when the present
commission was spoken, and the plainness of language which the
risen Lord now uses, and the solemn manner in which He was confirming this apostolic and ministerial commission, we cannot be
justified in assigning anything less than the most literal force, to these
words now spoken by our Lord. As the Father sent Jesus Christ
into the world, to preach the forgiveness of sins ; so did He send the
Apostles into the world, to proclaim, in His Name, remission of sins ;
and to pronounce authoritatively, in the Name of Christ, the absolution and remission of the sins of the penitent, within the terms of
the Gospel proclamation. This is not a personal act ; it is the official
declaration, with authority, of the act of Christ. There are three
occasions, recognized in the services of our Church when this is emphatically exercised : (i.) In the office of " Baptism for the remission
of sins ;" (ii.) in the Holy Communion, where there is remembrance
made of that sacrifice once offered " for many, for the remission of sins ; "
(iii.) in the Visitation of the Sick, where, " if he humbly and heartily
desire it," provision is made for the authoritative absolution of sins, in
the Name of Christ. The powers are recognized, and are conveyed and
received, so far as our Church is concerned, in the office for the ordination of priests, where they are bestowed exactly in the words of Christ,
recorded in this passage of S. John. The voice of the ancient writers
may be expressed in the words of S. Chrysostom (quoted by Bishop
Wordsworth, " *Theoph. Angl.*") : " Heaven waits to expect the priest's
sentence here on earth ; and what the servant rightly binds or looses on
earth, that the Lord confirms in heaven." The whole point lies in the
word " *rightly,*" for such an authoritative declaration must be within
the terms and conditions of the Divine will ; then " He pardoneth and
absolveth all them that truly repent, and unfeignedly believe His holy
Gospel." Such censures of the Church as one prelate, or one sect, has
launched against another, are merely human curses, not within the
commission given by Christ ; not, therefore, confirmed and valid through
Him. The caution, however, of Erasmus (quoted by Hengestenburg),
is a just one : " Hold your authority, but take care that it has the

Incredulity of Thomas.

S. John xx. 24, 25.

But Thomas, one of the twelve, called Didymus, was

Spirit, through whom Christ gave the authority." Volumes have been written against the strict interpretation of our Lord's words; but they are generally protests against usurpations, and perversions of the truth, carried to the opposite excess, in the zeal of party spirit; they do not disprove their literal force, or truth. It is a sad reflection, that this must be noticed amongst the passages on which the Church of Rome has brought such discredit, by the pretensions and usurpations founded upon it, that a large portion of Christian people welcome any explanation which may lessen the value of the words; until at last, to them, they are meaningless, or confined only to the Apostles themselves. Our Church must, however, maintain the true doctrine upon this important question, both against those who found extravagant pretensions and fancies upon it, and against those, equally, whose timid or sectarian policy inclines them to explain away, weaken, and negative the truth. However, as Dr. Comber remarks, "absolution was instituted by Jesus, and if it has been corrupted by men, we will cast away the corruptions, not the ordinance itself."

18. *Thomas.*—This incident in the life of Thomas is full of interest, both as it regards the picture it presents of his own mind, as a type of many others; and also as it gives the strongest and most material proof of the resurrection. The character of this Apostle was a strongly marked one. There are three instances in which he is particularly mentioned, and these show a man despondent, and firm in the gloomy view he adopts. They show one whose views of religion were decidedly not of a high spiritual order, but, as several writers note, somewhat inclined to rationalize. If such a man grasped the truth, which he was so slow to admit, he would be firm and unshaken in his convictions, as he was devoted in his love of his Lord. The three occasions alluded to are :—(i.) When our Lord proposed to go into Judæa, to raise Lazarus from the dead, Thomas could see no other termination of such a journey than death; but, without hesitation, he expressed his adherence to Christ, even to death: "Let us also go, that we may die with Him" (S. John xi. 16). (ii.) When our Lord was speaking of His departure, saying, "Whither I go ye know, and the way ye know," Thomas at once involves the whole question in characteristic gloom and despondency: "Lord, we know not whither Thou goest, and how can we know the way?" (S. John xiv. 5). (iii.) This present occasion. Such a character would find great difficulties, but not insuperable, in a religion of faith; and, when they were surmounted, his whole heart would be won. For he did not strive not to believe; he was slow to

not with them when Jesus came. The other disciples therefore said unto him, We have seen the Lord. But he said unto them, Except I shall see in His hands the

discern the bright side of faith, which he would, however, fain have perceived. We can suppose how tender Thomas must afterwards have been, as he taught the truth to others, in whom he discerned the same difficulties which he had experienced in his own mind.

19. *Didymus.*—Thomas is the Hebrew equivalent of the Greek name, which signifies "the twin." There are several legends concerning the origin of the name, which are not trustworthy. Several modern writers have supposed that our Lord gave him the name, as being of double mind, at once believing and unbelieving—a dangerous frame of mind; and we may see, in his case, how it may cut a man off from the privileges accorded to others. But we may not certainly conclude the derivation to be the correct one.

20. *not with them.*—Some writers have taken this for granted, as accidental; as if Thomas was engaged on some business connected with the eleven, or of his own. But others think that Thomas was of his own will absent; that he had given up hope, and was now indulging only deep, and gloomy, sorrow for the loss of his Lord. This appears to be the more probable opinion. Considering the lateness of the hour, the fact of all being assembled at their evening meal, and the news of Christ which had come from time to time; the hope that must have rested on them, that Christ would yet reveal Himself to His chosen Apostles; remembering also the general despondency of Thomas's character, and his slowness to see any brighter side of the troubles before him,—it seems most likely that he felt the difficulty that a body, so terribly and mortally wounded, should revive; and was, therefore, not with the rest, who were discussing the tidings of the resurrection.

21. *except I shall see.*—Thomas does not ridicule the notion of the resurrection, or simply declare his disbelief. He says he must have a fuller, and more material, evidence than the word, or belief, of any other man, before he can adhere to their faith. No doubt, the Apostles did not merely say, "We have *seen* the Lord;" but mentioned, also, the proofs of touch He had granted, the sight of His wounds, and the evidence of His eating before them. And now Thomas demands for himself this same evidence, and in a fuller degree. Corn. à Lapide notices the following sins in his case: incredulity, pertinacity, pride, irreverence, presumption, obstinacy, in remaining for eight days in his incredulity. He is a severe critic.

22. *I will not believe.*—These are terrible words, when uttered by man, of an accredited revelation of God. In the case of Thomas, Christ mercifully forgave the sin, for He read the heart of the erring Apostle. But no man may presume upon such mercy. In the first place, the doubt of Thomas, and the evidence accorded to him, and

print of the nails, and put my finger into the print of the nails, and thrust my hand into His side, I will not believe.

The Second Lord's Day.

V. *CHRIST APPEARS TO THE APOSTLES. THOMAS PRESENT.*

S. John xx. 26–31.

After eight days again His disciples were within, and Thomas with them: *then* came Jesus, the doors being

the history of his conviction, dispose of the right of any to doubt upon grounds such as his. Men are sometimes inclined to plume themselves on their " honest doubts," as being indicative of a candid, inquiring, and independent mind. No doubts are "*honest*," which have not come in contact with the evidence of God's word, which have not been earnestly prayed against, and which are not the doubts of one thoroughly desirous to believe. All doubt is not of faith, and is dangerous to the life of the soul; for " by faith we are saved."

1. *after eight days.*—On the following Lord's day; the eighth day after the previous manifestations, reckoning, in the Jewish fashion, inclusively. Time was thus given to satisfy Thomas's doubts. It is evident that our Lord places the highest honour upon this day. On this day, also, He appeared to S. John in Patmos (Rev. i. 10).

2. *Thomas with them.*—(See iv. 19.) Perhaps we may see, in his presence on this occasion, the effect of the announcement of the disciples, and of their evident and firm belief in the truth of the resurrection. To one in heart devoted to Christ, and willing to believe, such strong testimony, of such reliable and circumstantial witnesses, must have had weight.

3. *the doors.*—(See iv. 2, 3.) This is even a plainer statement than before, that, though the doors were shut, and no man opened them, yet Jesus became visible in the room, in the midst of the Apostles. We see also, in the absence of any evidence to the contrary, notification of this being the same place of meeting, as that in which Christ before appeared to the ten. The opinion of Olhausen and others, that this appearance of Christ took place in Galilee, quite wants foundation. A beautiful application of this manifestation of Christ, has been made with reference to those who are dying, to whom unconsciousness may shut the doors of access to man's ministration, but to whose spirit Christ can say, Peace.

shut, and stood in the midst, and said, Peace *be* unto you. Then saith He to Thomas, Reach hither thy finger, and behold My hands; and reach hither thy hand, and

4. *peace.*—(See iv. 5.) Christ here solemnly repeats the blessing He had before pronounced, and so seals the share of Thomas in the other privileges of the Apostles of Christ. He comes, as before, to the Apostles, on the Lord's day; offering the same, and fuller, evidence to Thomas, and the same greeting of supreme " peace."

5. *reach hither.*—Our Lord shows His cognizance of human thoughts and words, as before His Passion—a sign of Divinity, which commended itself to Thomas, who was indeed ready to believe, when the proofs were accorded to him, which his slow faith and proneness to reason demanded. Many modern critics think that Thomas now believed, without taking advantage of this permission to receive the full proofs he had demanded; and argue that the words, " because thou hast *seen*, thou hast believed," show that Thomas was satisfied with the sight only. This may be; but on what the notion is grounded, unless on some sentimental tenderness for Thomas, it is difficult to say. The natural impression conveyed by the words, is that he accepted the full proof offered by our Lord, and availed himself sufficiently of it, to convince himself thoroughly of the corporeity of Christ. Little is gained for Thomas, by explaining that his faith now dispensed with the tokens which he had demanded, and for which Christ expressly now appeared, in order that He might grant them to him. But it does weaken the support given to the faith, and the satisfaction afforded to the doubts, of others of a later age, to say that Thomas did not now require, and therefore dispensed with, these proofs. The fact that, on a previous occasion, the Lord had shown to the rest His wounded hands, and feet, and side, and had bidden them " handle and see," etc., may, perhaps, when taken in connection with the conduct of Thomas, argue that *they* had not taken advantage of this offered proof, though it seems pretty certain they did take advantage of it; but if so, this would also make it almost a certainty, that Thomas proposed to do what they had not done, and actually did so. But why should we suppose that our Lord offered proofs, which were not taken? or, that He would allow the Apostles to be satisfied with less than He thought fit to grant, more especially in Thomas's case? Stier and Maldonatus quote a forcible remark of Gregory the Great, on the value to the world of this evidence in the case of Thomas: "Supreme mercy so wonderfully ordered it, that that doubting disciple, when he touched the wounds of his Master's body, healed in us the wounds of unbelief; for the incredulity of Thomas has been more profitable to our faith, than the faith of the believing disciples; because, whilst he is won to faith by the evidence of touch, our mind, putting aside all doubt, is established on that of faith." There is an almost unanimous consent of the early writers,

thrust *it* into My side : and be not faithless, but believing.　And Thomas answered and said unto Him, My
Lord, and my God.　Jesus saith unto him, Thomas,

Greek and Latin, to the belief that Thomas did actually avail himself
of the permission to touch Christ, as he had required.

6. *into My side.*—These still open wounds afford an argument for
the theory, noticed in iv. 8, that the body of the resurrection was a
bloodless body ; were it not so, it seems natural that the wounds would
speedily have drained it of the principle of life, though it could not
again encounter death.

7. *be not.*—Gk. "become not unbelieving, but believing." The
word "*become*" seems to point out the force of habit, in matters of
faith, which is a consideration of great importance.　It is ever more
difficult, or easy, to place faith in matters of revelation, according as
we habitually set ourselves to doubt, or to believe.　The Holy Spirit
does not force us ; but He is a ready and constant guest, with those
who yield themselves to His influence ; and, as "no man can say that
Jesus is the Lord, but by the Holy Ghost" (1 Cor. xii. 3), His aid is an
absolute necessity to faith.　Hence to two men, of equally powerful
intellect, and of equal information, there is a great difference in their
disposition and power to believe the truth.　It is not merely that one
is credulous, the other rationalistic ; they are forming *habits* of faith, or
unbelief.　Faith is eminently the gift of God ; but it is one of the
most improvable of His good gifts, and, at the same time, one whose
neglect of cultivation is the most dangerous to us.　Belief becomes
truly difficult to those who accustom themselves to doubt.　They are
aware of the difficulty they find, in believing matters within the province of faith ; but they do not see the force which habits of unbelief
exercise upon them, but rather suppose themselves to be possessed of
a liberal and inquiring mind.　It is not always that they become subjects of the love which saved Thomas ; because they have not always,
what he had, a true love for Christ, and a genuine desire to believe
what they now doubt.

8. *my Lord, and my God.*—Thomas, whose incredulity had been
beyond that of all other friends of Christ, now gives the most unqualified confession of faith which had been given, since the resurrection, and the most intelligent professed, on any occasion, by any
Apostle.　He gives in his personal adherence to Christ, as the Messiah
—as the Messiah and Lord he had followed before His crucifixion ; and
he owns also His Divinity.　Thus, he acknowledges the personal
identity of that risen Saviour, and that Godhead, which had raised
Himself from the grave, and which could, therefore, raise all others
from the dead.　Such words, from the heart of one like Thomas, are
deliberate and emphatic in the highest degree.　They spring from full
conviction, not from the ardour of faith.　They are the words of one

because thou hast seen Me, thou hast believed: blessed *are* they that have not seen, and *yet* have believed.

And many other signs truly did Jesus in the presence

who had perfectly satisfied every doubt, and was thoroughly convinced of the truth. The importance of this declaration is evident, from the attempts which have been made to set it aside. Those who have held Arian and Socinian views, have seen that their views could not stand, if they were to admit the literal truth of this confession; they, therefore, have explained it as an exclamation of surprise and joy. But it is impossible that, under such circumstances, a man like Thomas should use, as an exclamation, these remarkable and forcible words of confession; nor would any Jew, brought up from infancy in the strictest reverence for the Name of God, at such a moment, and in such a presence, profane it. To strengthen their view, the Socinians expunge the words "*unto Him*," leaving the passage, "And Thomas answered and said, My Lord, and my God." But these words, "*unto Him*," which entirely remove the possibility of its being an exclamation, by giving personal application to Christ of the confession, are found in all the best MSS. Christ also accepts the declaration made by Thomas, and addresses him upon it, which would be impossible, were it only a meaningless exclamation. Maldonatus, quoting the opinion of several early writers, points out the emphatic use of the Greek article, both before the words "*Lord*" and "*God*," which, he says, is never so used, but to designate the true God; so assigning to the declaration of Thomas the most decided and deliberate meaning.

9. *blessed.*—The resolution of Thomas's doubts, had established the identity, and corporeity, of Christ, on a firmer foundation than the faith of all others had done. But he further draws forth this last blessing of our Lord, for the consolation of all who, in after ages, have become obedient to the faith. It is a gracious rendering of the incredulity of Thomas, which has turned it into a blessing to the world at large. Such are ever the mercies of Christ; His love turns evil into blessing. This blessing itself could not apply to any who had believed on the evidence of sight, or touch, as had all the Apostles, except S. John, whose belief, we may suppose, was in the Saviour's mind, when He spoke these words. (See i. 30.) It has, therefore, been given, as the special blessing of those who have believed on the evidence of the apostolic preaching, or writing (see 1 Pet. i. 3, 8).

10. *many other signs.*—Some of the early writers refer these words to the miracles of the Gospel, as a kind of summary of what has been recorded; others, with S. Chrysostom, to the manifestation of Christ, after His resurrection. The original word for "*signs*," is used to express miracles in S. John's Gospel, but not exclusively of other significations; whilst the position of this summary, following closely on the narrative of the resurrection, and especially on the confession of

of His disciples, which are not written in this book : but these are written, that ye might believe that Jesus is the Christ, the Son of God ; and that believing ye might have life through His Name.

During the Forty Days.

VI. *CHRIST APPEARS TO SEVEN DISCIPLES AT THE SEA OF TIBERIAS.*

S. John xxi. 1–24.

After these things Jesus shewed Himself to the dis-

Thomas, and the blessing just spoken, argues that it has, at least, a primary reference to the signs of the truth of the resurrection. There is also a second conclusion of the whole Gospel, in somewhat similar terms, which points the former summary, as having a less general object. Whilst, therefore, we need not exclude an application of these, to the series of great miracles recorded by S. John, which is terminated, as a climax, in the greatest of them all, the resurrection of Christ ; we should consider them as most especially, and distinctly, referring to those signs and proofs which S. John has selected, out of many others alluded to in Acts i. 3, as being most conclusive with regard to the faith of after ages.

11. *that ye.*—We of later days, and of the Gentile world, have this as our portion of the evidence of Christ's resurrection. We have not been forgotten, nor are we specially favoured, whilst personal revelations of Christ were granted to those of the apostolic age. We have the advantage of a selection, made under the inspiration of God's Spirit, of those appearances of Christ, which may meet the demands of all who come to the Gospel, with the same desire to find the truth ; all, therefore, of merely individual application, or which come under other heads, are omitted. And we have also our special blessing, which exalts the belief of pure and simple faith, above that grounded on the material evidence of sight and touch.

1. *after these things.*—Some writers call this chapter an appendix to the Gospel of S. John, which, they declare, ends with the last verse of the preceding chapter. Others go further, and question the genuineness of the chapter. The latter objection has been decisively refuted, by the enumeration of the many phrases and words peculiar to S. John, which the chapter contains ; *v.* 24 seems to contain direct evidence of genuineness. There is, doubtless, a separation between this and the preceding chapter ; but only such as may be accounted for by the

ciples at the sea of Tiberias; and on this wise shewed He *Himself*.

There were together Simon Peter, and Thomas called Didymus, and Nathanael of Cana in Galilee, and the *sons* of Zebedee, and two other of His disciples.   Simon Peter saith unto them, I go a fishing.   They say unto

peculiar object of chapter xxi. S. John has given various instances of Christ's appearance in Jerusalem, by which He established the fact of the resurrection.   He then sums up by saying, that he has given, in summary, a selection of proofs of the resurrection, in continuation of the great miracles recorded in his Gospel; they form an hármonious series.   He so draws a line, which gives a special and detached character to the chapter which follows.   Its contents justify this separation. It gives to us one more appearance of Christ, under circumstances distinct from any of the former.   He symbolizes the work of the Church in time, until it is gathered to Himself upon the eternal shore, and summoned to the Supper of God in heaven.   There is drawn the future career of the two Apostles, whose characters are typical, severally, of two prominent classes of Christ's agents in the world.   This chapter, full of mystery, is then gathered to the rest of the Gospel; and the whole is with the emphatic and figurative assertion, that so many were the actions of Christ's life, that were they all recorded, the very world could not contain the books that should be written.

2. *at the sea.*—They had now gone into Galilee, in accordance with Christ's command, and were waiting the fulfilment of the *promise* of His appearing.   How long an interval there may have been, between His last appearance and this, it is difficult to say; but it is likely that it was now towards the close of the Forty Days, when the minds of the disciples were become settled in the faith of the resurrection.

3. *two other.*—These are generally conjectured to have been Andrew and Philip.   Hengestenberg gives thus the grounds for this opinion: "When Peter went a fishing, his brother Andrew would needs accompany him (cf. Matt. iv. 18; Mark i. 29; Luke vi. 14; John vi. 8). And where Andrew was, we should expect to find Philip (cf. John i. 44, xii. 22; Mark iii. 18).   The latter we might expect with all the more confidence, as he was connected with Nathanael, or Bartholomew, by a very close bond (cf. John i. 45, 46; Matt. x. 3; Luke vi. 14)." They are all called disciples, in every instance in this passage, but the whole purport of the chapter shows they must have all been Apostles, the two unnamed as well as those named.   We never meet with the word "apostle," but always "disciple," in S. John's Gospel. The mention of Cana in Galilee here, seems designedly to take the mind back from this last, to "the first miracle that Jesus wrought."

4. *I go a fishing.*—Peter is foremost, as usual, in decision.   It had

him, We also go with thee. They went forth, and entered into a ship immediately; and that night they caught nothing. But when the morning was now come, Jesus stood on the shore: but the disciples knew not

become necessary now to provide for themselves, until the Lord came and gave the direction what to do. He had already told them that they would have need of purse, and scrip, and even of the sword. They must, therefore, return to their worldly calling for the present, and lead lives energetic in action, for their support, and holy in meditation, with regard to their future office. The other Apostles recognize the necessity and propriety of the proposal, and at once join with Peter.

5. *that night.*—We now enter upon the circumstances of this, our Lord's last miracle, which, in many respects, resembles that with which the acquaintance of these fishermen-Apostles with our Lord, was inaugurated (Matt. iv. 18–22; Luke v. 1–11). This is one of those instances of former truths, parables, and miracles of our Lord's earlier ministry being renewed, and pointed afresh, and set with extended meaning, during the last days of His life on earth (I. i. 1). The whole of the miracle seems, like others of our Lord's works, to have been a parable as well, suggesting spiritual truths. We see here how vain is the labour of man, which is not furthered with the blessing of God. Taking the promise of the former miracle, " I will make ye to become fishers of man," as giving the key-note of interpretation in this, we gather the lesson—which cannot be too deeply impressed, or realized, in the instance of those who minister in the Gospel of Christ—that the energy, and skill, of those who minister in the Gospel of Christ, will, if self-centred, so far as they are concerned, and very much also as concerns others, be unavailing, and unblest, without the aid of Christ; in whom, as well as for whom, they must work. " I can of mine own self do nothing," and, " I can do all things through Christ that strengtheneth me," are the first principles of ministerial training. The passage is sometimes applied to show the uselessness of earlier work in the field of God, to the evangelization of the world at large; for instance, of that of Moses and the prophets. But this application fails in two particulars: their efforts were not directed, like those of the Apostles, to the wide world; and also, in their restricted sphere, they did not fail, for they were immediately under the direction of God. They did not, of themselves, act or speak, but they did fulfil their commission.

6. *Jesus stood.*—Christ is wont to meet men in the ordinary ways of life. He seeks those who are diligent in business, whilst they are absorbed also in devotion. " Not slothful in business, fervent in spirit, serving the Lord," is a threefold rule of right practice. The night of hard work to the disciples was now over; the day of success had dawned; and, as they look to the shore, they see One standing there,

that it was Jesus. Then Jesus saith unto them, Children, have ye any meat? They answered Him, No. And He said unto them, Cast the net on the right side of the

whom they know not, but who knows them right well. There is the same withholding Himself from their recognition, in this instance, as in all others since His resurrection. The inference is obvious, that Christ is present, watching the labours of those who work for Him, long before they are permitted to recognize Him; and that He is there to speak the blessing, which they require, to crown their labours with success. It may be in the early morning of life; it may be as the day of eternity is dawning to them; but there stands the figure of Christ, ready to manifest Himself to them, and to accept their work.

7. *children.*—He addresses them with kindliness and interest, as a stranger might; not, as some say, with apparent curiosity, or as if desirous to buy fish of them. He does not gain from them much response, or confession of their ill success. They are wearied and disappointed with their failure; their right hand had lost her cunning, and they have no heart to meet a stranger's sympathy, though it may have touched them; they simply, and somewhat roughly, answer, "No." The terse roughness, and abrupt speech, of seafaring men, is familiar to us; it has neither intentional rudeness, nor unkindliness.

8. *the shore.*—Ancient writers explain the sea to mean the world, into which the Apostles of Christ, and their successors, cast the net of the Gospel mission. Success is slow, and effort often painful; but Christ gives the word, and results follow, far more stupendous than can be accounted for by their efforts. The fish are explained to be the souls of mankind, saved through their ministrations; the ship is the Church of Christ. Christ Himself stands on the shore of the eternal world, where "there is no more sea," and no more work of probation. He receives His labourers, and welcomes His elect; and makes them sit down together with Him, in heavenly places, and sets before them the feast of the kingdom.

9. *the right side.*—Again the stranger speaks; and, for whatever reason, His direction meets with prompt obedience. They may have thrown right and left before, but in vain; but now they find the fullest success. It is not that they have lost their ancient skill, or their loved lake its abundance; there are fish enough around them, and they are now to draw an unexpected ingathering. And this is the case often, in the experience of those who toil for Christ in the world; they toil "all night" in vain; but there comes the day of an unhoped-for success. It is not that all previous efforts have been thrown away; had they never speeded to labour, they had never known success. The lesson is one of special importance, with regard to missionary enterprise. The connection between work and success is direct; but God gives the word for success, to crown effort in His

ship, and ye shall find. They cast therefore, and now they were not able to draw it for the multitude of fishes. Therefore that disciple whom Jesus loved saith unto Peter, It is the Lord. Now when Simon Peter heard that it was the Lord, he girt *his* fisher's coat *unto him*, (for he was naked,) and did cast himself into the sea. And the other disciples came in a little ship; (for they were not far from the land, but as it were two hundred

cause. The term "right side" has much exercised the ingenuity of commentators. Hengestenberg considers it to mean, that on the right side of the ship the Gentiles are gathered to the Church; whilst they had laboured on the left side in vain for the Jews. But, following the allegorical meaning of the miracle, the opinion of the ancient Church appears to be the best, that on the right side were found the good only (cf. Matt. xxv. 33, 34), and that this was the general gathering of the good and saved into the kingdom; whilst, in the other miracle, we have the gathering of all nominal Christians, good and bad, into the visible Church.

10. *not able to draw it.*—A significant intimation that results should follow, far greater than they could have anticipated, in their day of work; and altogether beyond their powers of management, unaided by the good Lord, who gave the word for success. This issue to the labours of weak and erring men, when applying the gospel of truth and redemption to the necessities of the world, is inexplicable, except by Divine assistance and impulse. The result of individual labour may seem difficult to trace, and long deferred; but it is sure, and far beyond the human power put forth to produce it. (See notes 8, 9.)

11. *that disciple.*—This is S. John's designation of himself; it included the realization of all he hoped for, and of all honour that he could desire. His love detects the Saviour, who so greatly loved him. S. Jerome says that John recognized our Lord, because of the great purity and spirituality of his heart and life; and that he thus realizes the promise, "Blessed are the pure in heart, for they shall see God." We notice "*the Lord,*" as for the first time applied to Christ. He has once before been called the "Lord Jesus" (see i. 12); now the disciples seem to have taken up the profession of Thomas, "My Lord, and my God." He had, previous to his resurrection, been addressed as "Lord," but apparently not in the same sense. (See I. xxiv. c. 14.)

12. *he girt,* etc.—He had taken off this upper dress, which impeded him in his work, and wore only his under garment; for this is the meaning of the classical expression rendered "naked." Our Lord notices his reverential action, in thus reassuming this upper coat before he threw himself into the sea, in his eagerness to be first to reach Him. (See note 27.)

cubits,) dragging the net with fishes. As soon then as they were come to land, they saw a fire of coals there, and fish laid thereon, and bread. Jesus saith unto them, Bring of the fish which ye have now caught. Simon

13. *dragging the net.*—They did not, like Peter, throw everything aside to reach Christ. They were now in the ship's *boat*, at some little distance; and they came more slowly, being hindered by the difficulties arising from their work. They must drag with them the net and the fish, and must come to Christ in the ship. They represent those whose aim and object is to come to Christ; but they come with the distractions of worldly life about them, by which they are much hindered. Yet such persons may serve Christ, with equal faithfulness with those who give up everything to Him, since they consecrate their life's labours to His cause; and out of the entanglements of life, with His aid, they bring to Him, at the last, much treasure won from the ways of life. For we notice that what they brought in with care and toil, were *fish*, the converts of the Gospel net.

14. *a fire of coals.*—This came there, they knew not, and we know not how; probably our Lord alone can answer, for it is His promise to supply what may be necessary, and what man has not. He caused it to be there; it is not *said* miraculously, but, considering the character of this miracle, we are sure that He did cause it to be there, together with the "fish laid thereon, and bread." In the allegorical sense of the miracle, this is considered to represent the heavenly feast, the Supper of the Lamb, the marriage feast of the King's Son, to which Christ invites those who have laboured for Him on earth, and who reach the eternal shore, whither they bring with them the souls they have gained to His Gospel from the world. It is remarkable that, on both occasions when our Lord fed the multitudes, He gave, as here also, *fish* with the bread; early writers explain the broiled fish as emblematic of Christ's body, "burnt up with the agony of His Passion." We know that the fish was an early Christian emblem of Christ's titles; but mystery surrounds the point.

15. *bring of the fish.*—There is some difficulty here. Our Lord desires them to bring of the fish which they had caught. For what purpose is this? Taking the fish to represent the converts gathered by the labours of Christ's agents in the world, and primarily of His Apostles, we see the multitudes of the saved brought before God. The circumstances of the miracle require, that the "fishers of men" should be represented as bringing these converts where Christ is. But the passage reads as if Christ ordered that, of the fish caught by the Apostles, some should be brought, and prepared with those already on the coals; and some writers explain, that this was in order that they should see that those, which Christ is preparing, are not unsubstantial and mystical only, but actually the same as those brought in by the

Peter went up, and drew the net to land full of great fishes, one hundred and fifty and three : and for all there

Apostles; others, that those who labour must find their happiness complete, through the presence of those whom they have brought to Christ. (See 1 Thess. ii. 19.) Others, again, declare that none of these were prepared, or eaten, but only those which Christ showed to them. It would seem unnecessary to press too closely the application, here, of the several features of the miracle, as we must always do those of our Lord's parables. We may, however, take the two lessons as clear: first, that the converts of the Gospel are gathered, and presented to our Lord, in connection with those who have laboured on earth for their everlasting good; and also, that there is illustration of the truth expressed in another figure : "the husbandman, labouring first" (*i.e.* not without labour), "must be partaker of the fruit" (2 Tim. ii. 6). Thus, the reward of the "fishers of men" is partly derived from the result of their work. We need not further entangle ourselves in the difficulty of making the fish at once the converts, and the food; an allegory may well have two independent lines of fulfilment. It may be also that the idea of sacrifice is included, in which both the minister of the Gospel, and those whom He has gained for Christ, are presented before Him, and are accepted through the sacrifice of Christ. (Cf. Rom. xv. 16; Phil. ii. 17; Eph. v. 2, 27).

16. *went up.*—*i.e.* into the ship. He now rejoined his associates, and prominently assisted in drawing the net to shore, which, as it came into shallow water, needed their whole strength.

17. *great fishes.*—The size, and abundance, of the fish in the Sea of Tiberias, are frequently spoken of in books of modern travel. The number, in this instance, has caused much learned speculation. The ancient writers, especially, have various explanations. That of the Greek Fathers is, that the number 100 signifies perfection and multitude, and represents the mighty gathering of the Gentile world; the number 50, the half or inferior number, that of the Jewish converts; whilst the number 3 contains the mystery of the Trinity, through which they are saved. The Latin Fathers interpret differently. S. Augustine makes the three fifties, and also the additional three, represent the mystery of the Trinity; whilst the number 50 itself gives that of the jubilee, when there is rest from labour. S. Gregory takes 10 as the number of the Law, expressed in the Decalogue; and 7 as the number of the spirits of God's might, which together give the number 17; this, multiplied three times, as the mystery of the Trinity, gives 51; and, again so multiplied, gives 153. None of these seem very satisfactory, though they are very ingenious. For, if the number of the fish is that of the saved, it is difficult to say why the mystery of the Holy Trinity should be brought in, as part of the number of the saved. Others have explained that we have here the number of

were so many, yet was not the net broken. Jesus saith
unto them, Come *and* dine. And none of the disciples
durst ask Him, Who art Thou? knowing that it was the
Lord. Jesus then cometh, and taketh bread, and giveth

the kinds of fish in the lake; or the number of the races of earth, to
denote that they are gathered of all nations. There is, no doubt, a
mystery in this peculiar number, which would not otherwise have been
specified; but it is, at present, known only to God. Perhaps we may
safely notice that it is not a complete, or definite, number; and, in this
way, that it represents the great and indefinite number of the saved,
"whom no *man* can number," but which God knows. We must
observe the difference between the fish of this, and of the former
miracle. Those were of various sizes, and were good and bad; these
are all large fish, caught on the right side of the ship, and brought to
land, none being thrown away. Thus the net of the Gospel may be
spread over multitudes, who; may nominally be gathered into it, and
amongst whom separation must be made at the last; but, when gathered
before Christ, only the good will be brought in.

18. *broken.*—In the former miracle, "the net brake;" the contrary
is here designedly noted. Archbishop Trench points out how the
breaking of the net, in the former instance, shows the rents which
schism has made in the present condition of the Church, and that the
sinking ship of the Church, receiving the bad and good together, is
almost shipwrecked by the evil livers within it. (See I. viii. 23.) Here,
however, the good are gathered from the Church, which has reached the
eternal shore; there is no rent in the unity of the faith of the Gospel,
which gathers them in. And the Apostles, representative of an agency,
humanly speaking, so inadequate in strength, have no power given
them, to bring all in safety to the Saviour's presence.

19. *come and dine.*—This, as has been said, is generally thought to
represent the supper of the Gospel, the marriage supper of the King's
Son in heaven. Our Lord Himself comes forth to serve those who sit
at His table in His kingdom (Luke xii. 37, xxii. 30). See the invitation to "come and see" the blessings of Christ's dwellings, in His
earlier call in John i. 39.

20. *durst ask.*—Though Christ had not said so much, and perhaps
still withheld entire recognition, they all felt, and were convinced, that
it was He who was near them; and that none other than He had
wrought the miracle of the fishes, and had provided the meat.

21. *then cometh.*—It is likely that He had joined them in the meal
itself; but this seems distinct from it. He appears to have risen, and,
in some solemn way, to communicate to them of the "breaking the
bread." Some writers, therefore, both ancient and modern, see in this
a sacramental act, if not a celebration of the Eucharist itself. They
also notice the number of the disciples present on this occasion, namely

them, and fish likewise. This is now the third time that
Jesus shewed Himself to His disciples, after that He was
risen from the dead.

So when they had dined, Jesus saith to Simon Peter,

seven; a full and sacred number, as denoting the gathering of all
Christ's faithful labourers at His Supper.

22. *the third time.*—Not in order of His appearing, but of His appearing to the disciples collectively. On only one of these occasions, however, were they all present.

23. *Simon Peter.*—Our Lord now formally renews to Peter his
commission in His Church. The Romish writers lay much stress
upon this passage, in support of their claims of primacy for the see of
Peter. So long as we confine ourselves to the language of the Holy
Scripture, we can find no trace of any rights conferred on Peter, which
could be transferred to his personal successors in any bishopric : and
there are the gravest historical.doubts, as to S. Peter having ever been
Bishop of Rome. The real primacy of Rome, was originally grounded
on its having been the see of the imperial city ; though it is unquestioned
that Peter (though far less than S. Paul) exercised an influence, con-
ceded, naturally, to so eminent an Apostle, over the early Roman
Church. According to the words of Ignatius (Rom. iv., Shorter Ep.) :
" I do not, as Peter and Paul, issue commandments unto you. They
were Apostles." The earliest writers make demand for submission to
Rome, but in virtue of its imperial dignity. Gregory the Great, however, Bishop of Rome, deprecates, in most earnest language, the application of the title of " universal bishop," to his own, or any see. It is
not possible, within the limit of a note, to trace the history of this
usurped and unscriptural claim to its first origin, when, in troublous
days, the orthodoxy and piety of the bishops of the imperial see, and
the dignity of their Church, made reference to their decision, in many
cases, the easiest solution of difficulties ; and when a custom of reference
was thus established, which less worthy men, their successors, am-
bitiously presumed upon. This is the province of ecclesiastical history.
It is sufficient here to notice the firm protest of our own, and other
Churches, against it; and the absence of any such commission in
Scripture. Without interference with the rights of nations, and of
national Churches, there could be no " universal bishop; " and
Christianity never sanctions usurpation of the rights of nations. The
usurpation, which was productive of widespread abuse, and of infinite
complication, even in the Middle Ages, would be simply intolerable in
the present wide limits of the world. It is as much opposed to common
sense (which no ordinance of Christ ever is), as to its common rights.
Some writers appear to be so much afraid of conceding any primacy
to Peter, lest they should take the first steps towards admitting the
usurpations of Rome, that they deny what justly is his right. Peter

Simon, *son* of Jonas, lovest thou Me more than these?
He saith unto Him, Yea, Lord; Thou knowest that I
love Thee. He saith unto him, Feed My lambs. He

was always foremost as a companion of our Lord, admitted to the
greatest intimacy ; he was also the spokesman of his brother Apostles.
His zeal, and energy, won for him the blessings of precedence amongst
them.   After the resurrection, he was the first to plant, both amongst
the Jews and the Gentiles, the Church of Christ; first to nominate the
successor to Judas; first to work miracles; first to exercise the judicial
authority of the Church. But yet, if there was any primacy of personal
position amongst the twelve, it rested with James, who was their
president, and Bishop of the Church of Jerusalem ; not with Peter, as
first leader amongst the Apostles. The present most important passage,
records the full restoration of Peter to the position for which his denial
of our Lord had disqualified him, namely, to equal authority with the
rest of the Apostles in the Church of Christ. It is not a commission of
superiority over the rest.

24. *son of Jonas.*—Our Lord does not use the distinctive name,
which He had conferred upon Peter. His not doing so is a marked
circumstance here.   Peter had forfeited the designation Peter (*the
rock*) ; and was only worthy of being Simon (*the hearer*), the son of
Jonas (*the dove*). There are two points in which Peter is brought to
the remembrance of his denial of his Lord. He had professed an
attachment to Christ, superior to that of his fellow-disciples (Mark xiv.
29). Our Lord now asks him if he does love Him more than His fellow-
Apostles.   And, also, thrice He repeats the question, " Lovest thou
Me?" in unmistakable allusion to the three denials of Peter. These,
coupled with the significant return to his own name, formed our Lord's
rebuke of Peter's sin; its point lay in the fact that Peter did bear to
his Lord that love which he confidently appealed that He discerned
in him.

25. *Thou knowest,* etc.—Peter does not now profess greater attachment than the others; he knows his own weakness, and is humble-
minded and contrite. But the term our Lord uses, does not escape his
notice. Twice Christ asks, " *Lovest* thou Me?" using a term which is
less forcible, being expressive of reverential and Christian regard, rather
than of personal attachment; as is that in which Peter replies, "Thou
knowest that I love Thee," and which our Lord adopts in His third
repetition of the question, thereby admitting Peter's plea of personal
attachment. This change of term, which is lost in translation, is
exceedingly significant in the original.

26. *feed My lambs . . . sheep.*—There is here, again, a difference in
the original word for "*feed,*" in the three passages. In the first
instance, we have a term applicable to the "lambs," expressive of
feeding and leading forth with care, nurturing those young in the faith.

saith to him again the second time, Simon, *son* of Jonas, lovest thou Me? He saith unto Him, Yea, Lord; Thou knowest that I love Thee. He saith unto him, Feed My sheep. He saith unto him the third time, Simon, *son* of Jonas, lovest thou Me? Peter was grieved because He said unto him the third time, Lovest thou Me? And he said unto Him, Lord, Thou knowest all things, Thou knowest that I love Thee. Jesus saith unto him, Feed My sheep. Verily, verily, I say unto thee, When thou wast young, thou girdedst thyself, and walkedst whither thou wouldest: but when thou shalt be old, thou shalt stretch forth thy hands, and another shall gird thee, and carry thee whither thou wouldest not. This

The second expression is suitable to the mature "sheep" of the fold of Christ, and denotes the pasturing and guarding, the oversight and discipline, entrusted to a shepherd of God. In the third instance, the expression first used is repeated. The former word (as Bengel observes) expresses a part of the latter, and fuller, expression, which includes it.

27. *when thou wast young*, etc.—Peter was now of mature age, and full of activity and zeal. Whilst such strength was his, he might, at his will, lay aside his garments, and gird himself again, as he had just done in the exercise of his calling. (See note 12.) And so also, as an Apostle, he might, at will, essay one and another enterprise of missionary labour, throwing aside every weight and impediment to prosecute his work; and then, again, girding himself for new and distant scenes of labour. As God gave him strength and love, so might he labour, as his energetic spirit prompted him. But, in the time of his old age, when he had less power to work, and the fire of his nature was quenched, he should be called to the death of martyrdom—to drink the cup, and share the baptism, of which his Lord had spoken to the brethren James and John (Mark x. 39). Then the executioner should bind him to the cross, upon which his hands were stretched out, and fastened; he should be borne to that death from which flesh and blood must shrink, especially when there is no longer the hot zeal and temper of youth, to dare even death itself. Thus Peter should follow his Lord in earnest and loyal service on earth, as His true disciple; and he should, in his old age, win the martyr's crown, and so follow Him in death—the same bitter death of the cross. We must not lose sight of Peter's zealous profession, "Lord, I am ready to go with Thee, both to prison and to death." Though his rashness was before rebuked, and his fall foretold, yet is not his zeal forgotten, nor his service refused: our Lord here accepts graciously what Peter now fully understood and weighed.

spake He, signifying by what death he should glorify God. And when He had spoken this, He saith unto him, Follow Me.

Then Peter, turning about, seeth the disciple whom Jesus loved following; which also leaned on His breast at supper, and said, Lord, which is he that betrayeth Thee? Peter seeing him saith to Jesus, Lord, and what *shall* this man *do?* Jesus saith unto him, If I will that he tarry till I come, what *is that* to thee? follow thou Me. Then went this saying abroad among the

28. *following.*—No doubt, Peter understood the meaning of the command, "Follow Me;" follow through life, through death, to My kingdom of glory! But yet he rose, and literally followed our Lord's footsteps, who was now apparently leaving them, anxious to hear more, and to speak more. And John, either hearing Christ's words, or anxious to keep near his Lord, went after them.

29. *this man*—John and Peter were united by a strong bond of affection, and in the union of attachment to Christ, who had distinguished them with especial marks of His acceptance. Peter, who had now learnt, and accepted, his own future career, is anxious, perhaps a little curious, to learn what his Master has in store for his loved associate, "the disciple whom Jesus loved;" and asks by what death he, too, should glorify God, and enter into His kingdom.

30. *I will.*—Christ now speaks royally, without reserve or reference. His will is supreme within the kingdom of redemption, and of the resurrection.

31. *that he tarry.*—There are several explanations of these words. Some think that they refer to the natural death which John should die, simply waiting till Christ came to him, in the usual course of peaceful death; rather than that he should be despatched to Christ's presence, suddenly and violently, by the hands of those who took his life, in anticipation of the appointed hour of death. Others say that it refers to Christ's advent to destroy the Temple and Church of the Jews—an advent which John survived by many years. And some suppose that it meant that he should be translated, or at once raised from death; upon which opinion several extraordinary and fanciful legends have been founded. Probably, both the first and second meanings are true; as we generally find more than one meaning conveyed in the terms of Christ's prophecies. (See I. xviii. 9.) Further than this, the inquiry (as also kindred speculations on our own part) is discouraged.

32. *this saying.*—Even in apostolic days, and with their knowledge of Christ, and inspiration concerning His will, there was a misapprehension of the meaning of this declaration; and they took it to mean

brethren, that that disciple should not die: yet Jesus said not unto him, He shall not die; but, If I will that he tarry till I come, what *is that* to thee?

This is the disciple which testifieth of these things, and wrote these things: and we know that his testimony is true.

VII. *CHRIST APPEARS TO THE APOSTLES, AND TO "ABOVE FIVE HUNDRED BRETHREN AT ONCE."*

S. Matt. xxviii. 16–20; S. Mark xvi. 15–18; [1 Cor. xv. 6].

Then the eleven disciples went away into Galilee, into

that John should not share the death of mortals, but be translated; or be on earth alive, when Christ came. John, now at the end of his long life, corrects this misapprehension, so far as to state that Christ neither said, nor implied, such a thing. But he does not say what our Lord did mean; he merely repeats His words, and so leaves the mystery to His solution. It is so far solved, that we know that, long after the destruction of Jerusalem, John died a natural death, in extreme old age. He is said to be the only Apostle who did not suffer martyrdom in death; but he long outlived his fellow-Apostles, bearing his witness to the Gospel (a living martyrdom), into the middle of the next generation, and transmitting, to the end of time, his witness to Christ's truth in his inspired writings, breathing forth his prayer, that Christ should come, as He here said, "Even so, come, Lord Jesus."

1. *the eleven.*—The meeting of Christ with His disciples, on this occasion, appears to have had a more formal aspect than any other. After the Passover festival was concluded, and those assembled in Jerusalem had returned to Galilee (and, therefore, not earlier than the second week after the resurrection), we see that the eleven Apostles went away together into Galilee, to the mountain which Christ had appointed as the place of meeting. They had already seen their Lord, and believed. It was not, therefore, for their conviction that they were ordered to go into Galilee, but, rather, for their public appointment to their life's work. There is a general agreement of authors, that this meeting in Galilee was that large gathering of the whole body of the disciples who could be assembled together at once, of which S. Paul speaks (1 Cor. xv. 6): "After that, He was seen of above five hundred brethren at once: of whom the greater part remain unto this present, but some are fallen asleep." The date of S. Paul's Epistle is

a mountain where Jesus had appointed them. And when they saw Him, they worshipped Him: but some doubted. And Jesus came and spake unto them, saying,

twenty-nine years after this event; and the number still surviving, of those present on this occasion, may have spread abroad the tradition in the early Church, which identifies Christ's appearance to them with that spoken of by SS. Matthew and Mark. S. Chrysostom, and other early writers, explain that Galilee was safer for this large gathering, as being remote from Jerusalem, where our Lord's enemies were so powerful. There is a fitness, also, in this general and formal appearance taking place in the country where so many of His mighty works were done, and so much of His teaching delivered, and where there were so many of the people attached to Him. (See i. 20; I. xxvii. 6.) It is singular that so little is said about the details of this meeting, which was so carefully spoken of, both by the angels, and by our Lord, on the day of His resurrection; and which must have required so much forethought, and preparation, such caution, and so many messages to those summoned, to whom the fact of the resurrection had to be made known—to those, at least, who had left Jerusalem, or had not been present at the Passover, and so were not near the Apostles; and where so many doubts and difficulties had to be met and removed. I. Williams remarks. "It is much to be observed, that on every occasion of our Lord's appearing to the disciples, after the resurrection, it is to confer and delegate various powers: the power of the keys in the upper room; the power of baptism on the mountain, in S. Matthew; pastoral charge to feed the sheep, by the lake, in S. John; power of treading under foot the power of the enemy, in S. Mark."

2. *into a mountain.*—Gk. (more definitely, and more suggestive of pre-arrangement), "*the* mountain." It has been thought by some that this was Mount Tabor; but there appears no reason at all for the supposition. It must have been a low mountain, with a broad and level summit, to accommodate so many as were gathered there. Some authors consider this a special appearance to the eleven only; but the majority of commentators take the view set forth in these notes, that Christ appeared to them, with the five hundred also present.

3. *they worshipped Him.*—The eleven did this, and, probably, the majority of the five hundred; perhaps, subsequently, all of them. Their worship is that supreme adoration paid to God; they, therefore, accepted both the fact of the resurrection, and His Divine claim, so far as at that time this was made clear to them—for the Holy Spirit was not yet bestowed upon the Church.

4. *doubted.*—We cannot but admire the candour which admits that "some doubted," and feel the truth of S. Jerome's remark, "Their doubting has increased our faith." It could not be the eleven that doubted; or, if so, it was not the truth of the resurrection, but whether

All power is given unto Me in heaven and in earth.

He whom they saw advancing was Christ. It was unnatural that *they* should doubt; for, as another early writer states, "those who now worshipped Him had first doubted in Jerusalem." But we must not lay too much stress on the word "*doubted.*" At the most, it argued that such doubts were temporary; but probably they did not doubt the fact of the resurrection, else why had they assembled here to meet Christ! They probably did not at first recognize Him; as so many did not, until He, by revealing Himself to them, taught them that He had none other than the conditions of a natural body. Perhaps (as Paley understood it) those at the distance did not at once recognize Him, until He "came and spake unto them;" or they may have hesitated about His actual corporeity or the identity of His present body with that which was crucified. These were all matters of more, or less, "doubt" to the Apostles themselves, at the first; and very reasonably, therefore, we may suppose that, of this multitude, "some doubted," not the resurrection itself, but details concerning it, until Christ now thoroughly revealed Himself to them. It was, indeed, very much to resolve these, and all doubts, that He now showed Himself to them. Lange takes this expression "*doubted*" in close connection with what precedes; *i.e.* they doubted whether it was right to worship Christ, not concerning His resurrection. His idea is singular. There is a further difficulty to be noticed, in connection with this subject. In Acts i. 15, we find the numbers of the infant Church given as one hundred and twenty only. Did, then, any of these doubters secede from the faith? It is scarcely necessary to suppose so. The five hundred were, most of them, disciples of Galilee, who were engaged there in their own proper duties; the one hundred and twenty were disciples of Jerusalem, who composed the Church there. There was, at present, no Church fund; hence it is unlikely that Galilean converts would be separated from their own home duties, and attached to the Church at Jerusalem.

5, *Jesus came.*—Maldonatus, and Corn. à Lapide, think that this refers to a later scene, namely, that of the ascension; but the majority of the best writers, ancient and modern, are against this opinion. It is difficult to harmonize the accounts of the Evangelists at this point, but the general opinion is, that there is no break of time here in the narrative. Jesus now came nearer, and became personally manifested within the recognition of each individual. There is, also (see note 7), a fitness in connecting the commission now given, with the presence of the multitude of the disciples.

6. *all power.*—The supreme power, as the Son of God, in the kingdom of the eternal Father in heaven; and, also, in the kingdom of earth, which He had won from Satan, and redeemed with His most precious blood. This power is *given* to Him; though, in the one case, inherited by Divine right; in the other, won by Himself. What He gives to man is, in every case, that which was given to Him of His Father.

Go ye therefore into all the world, and teach all nations,

7. *go ye.*—This appears to be a formal commission to the Apostles, with power and authority within the Church of Christ; conferred on them now publicly, in the presence of the assembled disciples, as it had been before explained to themselves, when Christ manifested Himself to them separately. At the same time, the official duties here entrusted to them, are not confined, like their special and miraculous gifts, to themselves personally; but have reference, further, to those who should follow them, in continual succession, to the end of the world. Though at first so strictly confined within the limits of Judea, the Church is now charged to become missionary, and catholic, in the widest sense, over all the world. The successors of the Apostles must continue to *go forth*, until there remains not a nation, where their glad tidings have not been proclaimed, for a witness of Christ's grace and mercy, and God's truth and love; they must go onwards, until Christ's advent ends their commission. (See viii. 14.) But Christ's words have only such a limitation in their primary, and official, sense; for here is the commission, binding on all individual members of the Church of Christ, to do all they can to spread His Gospel amongst mankind. Those whose duty it is, by virtue of their ministerial office, do so by personal service, as missionary heralds; but the duty of the whole Church is, to support, with every material means, the labours of those who, preaching the Gospel, must live of the Gospel. For the mission of propagation of Christ's Gospel is, not the sole duty of the clergy, but of the whole Church of Christ. Had the duty not been thus general, it would not have been publicly enjoined. But the layman may not take upon himself, unauthorized, the special office of the ministry; nor may the ordained minister shrink from his special duties, falling back upon those of the layman. The laity here receive their allotment of work; and in their intelligence and discharge of it, lies the development of vital power in the Church.

8. *teach.*—Gk. "*make disciples of.*" It is important to observe the force of the word, because it is entirely different from that, also rendered "teach," just below. In the first instance, the disciples are to be made, who are to be admitted into the Church by baptism; they are then to be progressively "taught," and trained, in all the commands and doctrines of Christ, and admitted to full membership in the Holy Communion. This "teaching," under the discipline of the Church, and under the illumination of the Holy Spirit, goes on continuously, in due course of our learning Christ, until He comes to reveal Himself to us at the last. S. Mark has a variety of this charge, which is significant: "Preach the Gospel to every creature;" *i.e.* not only to every creature capable of hearing and accepting it, but also the word is used in the same sense as in Rom. viii. 19–22, and elsewhere; where there seems to be allusion to the removal, through the effect of the Gospel, of the original curse which was laid upon earth, and all within it. The

baptizing them in the Name of the Father, and of the

Gospel is more than the mere reversal of Adam's fall; and we may assign very wide extension, rather than bounds, or limits, to its effect; though we know not now, the full blessings of Christ's great victory.

9. *baptizing them*, etc.—This is the authoritative institution of Holy Baptism as a Sacrament of Christ's Church, though not the first mention of it. In our Lord's conversation with Nicodemus (John iii.), He had referred to it, as at the very entrance to His kingdom. The regeneration of water and the Spirit must be had, before a man can even " *enter* into the kingdom of heaven," much less be admitted to its full privileges. We read, also, that the disciples of Jesus, in His Name, practised baptism amongst those who became disciples (John iv. 1, 2). Now, however, the rite is defined as a Sacrament, and made universal ; and Christ orders that upon all who are baptised, should be called the great and holy Name of the Triune God, Creator, Redeemer, Sanctifier of the elect. It is impossible, within present limits, to condense the subject of a treatise ; but there are two points which we may briefly notice here, as of consequence : (i.) As baptism is universal, it must embrace all ages and conditions. Those who are converted from heathenism, will receive it on their admission into the Church, at whatever age they are called. Those born of Christian parents are, by the unanimous consent of the early Church, and the general practice of all subsequent ages, entitled to it, conditionally, as infants. The objections of the Anabaptists cannot be reviewed here ; but we oppose them on the ground of early and universal custom, of charity, and of common sense. Christ does not consider it necessary to specify infants, though so large a portion of His fold, in the general terms of His covenant. Naturally so; for, if He does not consider children too young, at any age, to die, or to be admitted into heaven, so we must believe that He who said, " Of such is the kingdom of heaven," and, " Except ye be converted, and become as little children, ye cannot *enter* into the kingdom of heaven," does not consider them too young to be admitted into His Church on earth, by baptism. The children of Jewish parents were, on the eighth day, admitted to the covenant with God; why not, therefore, Christian children? (ii.) The doctrine of regeneration, in Holy Baptism, is one most clearly stated in Holy Scripture, and authoritatively declared by our Church. Again we cannot review the objections against this doctrine, but merely state it. " S. Paul speaks of us as being ' saved by the washing of regeneration ' (Titus iii. 5), a passage which, like John iii. 5, the whole ancient Church understood of the laver of baptism." (*Bishop H. Browne.*) The term *regenerate*, however, does not imply that those regenerated, must necessarily attain all the advantages of the new birth. Though regenerate, we may neglect and miss the end of our spiritual life ; just as we ruin ourselves, and fail, with regard to the full capabilities of our

Son, and of the Holy Ghost; teaching them to observe

natural life. Those who are regenerate, must constantly experience renewal, or renovation. The distinction here, is well given in the words of Dean Hook: "Regeneration, being a single act, can have no parts, and is incapable of increase. Renovation is in its very nature progressive. Regeneration, though suspended, as to its effects and benefits, cannot be totally lost in the present life. Renovation may be repeated, and totally lost." "Regeneration may be granted, and received (as in infants), when that renovation has no place at all, for the time being." (*Waterland.*) This doctrine of regeneration prevents the repetition of baptism, when it has been administered, either by laymen (see App. XX.), or by those who hold the truth in error, provided the right words of Christ are spoken, and water used; for it is as impossible to be born again as to the spiritual birth, as Nicodemus remarked it was with regard to the natural birth. "The spiritual new birth is a single and complete act, just as the natural birth is a single and complete act. We once receive the natural birth from our mother; so does our mother Church give us the spiritual birth, when once each of us is baptized." (*S. Augustine.*) And, therefore, "in no case are baptized Christians called upon to become regenerate; they are called to repent, to turn to God, to cleanse their hands, to purify their hearts; never to become regenerate." (*Sadler.*) We might as well call on those who are in disease, or who are ruining their life's aim, to be reborn. To this effect our Lord speaks, "He that is washed" (in the "laver of regeneration") "needeth not save to wash his feet, but is clean every whit." (See I. xxiv. c. 11.)

10. *in the Name.*—Gk. "into the Name." The difference is considerable. Baptizing *in* the Name, concerns rather the minister, and is equivalent to his saying, "On the behalf, or with the authority, of the Holy Trinity, I baptize thee,"—into what? Whereas, his saying, "I baptize thee *into* the Name," is the association with the Name of the most holy Trinity; the incorporation of the baptized into that Catholic Church and family of God, upon whom His Name is called. It is difficult to lay too much stress upon our being baptized into the Name of God; for that Name, throughout the whole Scriptures, is but the expression of God's excellencies and perfections; and the revelation of His Name to man, under the early covenant, is the most sacred foundation of all God's revelation and mercy to Israel. It was the distinction of ancient Israel in the world, until Christ came, that the great and terrible Name of the Lord Jehovah had been revealed unto them, and that they were the people "called by His Name." As much, therefore, as "the ministration of righteousness exceeds in glory" "the ministration of condemnation" (2 Cor. iii. 9), so does the Name of the Holy Trinity, now revealed as that into which we are baptized, exceed, in all it confers upon Christians, that which was revealed to Israel. This

all things whatsoever I have commanded you. He that
believeth and is baptized shall be saved ; but he that

essential form in Baptism has been well called "the summary of creeds;"
and no act upon earth, by the hand of God's ministers, can be more
solemn and important, than that of baptizing into the Name of the
triune God. How sad is the neglect of proper teaching, and the want
of right information and reverence, which identifies baptism merely
with the "*naming*" of the person baptized! It is but natural, when
we find many persons thus ignorant and careless, that they should
advance the opinion, that registration by a civil officer is equally effective
with the Church's administration of the Sacrament of Holy Baptism.
Such an agency for recording the name, may so far seem preferable to
such persons, as it avoids, on their part, the sin of profanation of a
Sacrament, and of an irreverence awful to contemplate. We notice
that the term "*name*" is in the singular number ; it denotes the unity
of the Godhead in the trinity of Persons—a doctrine which is thus
associated with our very entrance into the kingdom of Christ.

11. *to observe.*—The three main essentials of Christian life are here,
as in many other instances, enjoined : repentance, faith, and obedience.
Becoming disciples of Christ includes the *repentance*, and refusal of all
other masters ; baptism supposes *faith* in Christ ; and "observing all
things whatsoever He has commanded," is that *obedience* which is a
characteristic of true discipleship.

12. *saved.*—As we know that some who believe fall away from the
faith, and that not all who are baptized are saved, we see that there is
the same limitation here, as in Acts ii. 47. Those who believe and are
baptized, shall be brought within the conditions of salvation (which is
the first meaning of the term "*saved*"), and under the influence of
God's Holy Spirit ; and then, secondly, if faithful unto death, saved
absolutely, and eternally. We should read the awful sentence, "shall
be damned," in the same light, namely, as a state of damnation, from
which God's grace may give repentance of unbelief in matters of faith
and practice, and may renew His great gift of faith ; but, if not, then of
eternal damnation. It is here said, "he that believeth and is baptized
shall be saved," because the covenant of Christ's salvation is with the
baptized only ; but we do not read the converse, "he that believeth
not, *and is not baptized*," partly because unbelief will reject baptism,
and lead to perdition ; partly, perhaps, also, because baptism, under
certain circumstances, may be impossible, as is the case with some
infants of Christian parents, by no fault of their own. Nor, again,
would God bar the door of His "uncovenanted mercies" against those
who *cannot* receive baptism—for then, such as the penitent malefactor
could not enter paradise; nor even against the heathen, who may never
have had the offer of salvation through Christ, or the option of acceptance and rejection. The whole history of missionary labour, is full of

believeth not shall be damned. And these signs shall
follow them that believe; In My Name shall they cast
out devils; they shall speak with new tongues; they
shall take up serpents; and if they drink any deadly
thing, it shall not hurt them; they shall lay hands
on the sick, and they shall recover. And, lo, I am with
you alway, *even* to the end of the world. Amen.

instances where belief has been possible, and lively, but where, from
peculiar reasons, baptism has been delayed, or impossible; instances of
the difficulty of baptism following naturally upon faith, are amongst
the painful experiences of Zenana teaching in India. (See App. XXI.)
But it is clear that the prescribed conditions of the covenant of salvation, are belief and baptism; and that those who wilfully and deliberately reject these, *i.e.* who "believe not" (*i.e.* "*disbelieve*"), or who
refuse to be baptized, will not be saved by any other conditions. Thus,
"he that believeth not shall be damned."   In the words, "believeth
and is baptized," is included the confession of belief made at baptism;
for "with the mouth confession is made unto salvation."   Hooker says,
"If Christ Himself, which giveth salvation, do require baptism, it is
not for us that look for salvation, to sound and examine Him, whether
unbaptized men may be saved; but seriously to do what is required
and religiously to fear the danger which may grow by the want
thereof."   "The argument cannot be deduced from this text, that infants
are incapable of baptism, as being incapable of belief; for then, as faith
is absolutely necessary, they could not, in case of early death, be saved
at all." (*Forster.*)

13. *these signs.*—These signs and gifts were realized in the first ages of
the Christian Church; they were withdrawn when they became no longer
necessary for accrediting the commission of those who preached the
Gospel. In certain Churches (for instance, in that of Corinth), they
appear to have been more than ordinarily necessary, and to have been
bestowed in greater abundance. But these signs are not, like the baptism of repentance, faith, and obedience, perpetually necessary.

14. *I am with you.*—Christ's spiritual presence in the Church to the
end of time, was a promise which was frequently made to the disciples.
(See John xiv. 23, and Matt. xviii. 20, where His presence is promised
even "where two or three are gathered in His name.")

15. *always.*—Gk. "all the days," *i.e.* "every day," without inter-
mission of presence. The expression is thus as comprehensive of time,
place, and persons, as can possibly be.

Holy Thursday.

VIII. *THE ASCENSION, IN THE PRESENCE "OF ALL THE APOSTLES."*

S. Mark xvi. 19, 20; S. Luke xxiv. 44–53; [Acts i. 3–12 ; Cor. xv. 7].

The Farewell Charge.

S. Luke xxiv. 44–49 ; [Acts i. 4–8.]

And being assembled together with them, He said unto them, These *are* the words which I spake unto you,

1. *and being assembled.*—The disciples had again assembled at Jerusalem ; and there had been one other appearance of our Lord, which is not mentioned in the Gospels, but which is recorded by S. Paul in 1 Cor. xv. 7. Speaking of the gathering of the disciples in Galilee, he says, " After that He was seen of James." We are not told of the object of this special personal revelation ; but I. Williams, and others, conjecture, with great probability, that this was James the Less, " the brother of the Lord," who became Bishop of Jerusalem, whom we find, in Acts xv., presiding over the apostolic Church and council ; and that this appearance was to instruct him in that matter. They attach importance to the manner in which the name of James is mentioned in connection with that of the Apostles, as is that of Peter, in the same account by S. Paul : " After that He was seen of James ; then of all the Apostles " (1 Cor. xv. 5, 7). After His appearing to Peter, the gifts, formerly promised to Peter, were conferred on the Apostles generally ; their relative share in that commission must then have been defined to them. The presumption is, that it was so also in the case of James, whose duties with regard to the others, his equals in the kingdom of Christ, our Lord afterwards may have defined. The support of the ancient writers leans towards this theory ; two quotations are alleged which are very important. Theophylact says, " He was seen of James, the brother of our Lord, who was appointed by Him the first Bishop of Jerusalem ; " and Photius : " James the first high priest, who, by the Lord's hand, received holy unction, and the Bishoprick of Jerusalem." Ebrard thinks that the order to assemble at Jerusalem for the ascension, was probably given through James.

2. *the words.*—This is thought by Grotius, and other writers, to be a summary notice of various matters discussed by our Lord with His Apostles, concerning the future prospects of His Church. S. Luke's words (Acts i. 2, 3) are very suggestive ; the " commandments " given to them may (we might almost say *must*) have embraced many things

while I was yet with you, that all things must be fulfilled, which were written in the law of Moses, and *in* the prophets, and *in* the psalms, concerning Me.   Then opened He their understanding, that they might understand the scriptures, and said unto them, Thus it is written, and thus it behoved Christ to suffer, and to rise

afterwards made clear to them by the Holy Spirit. "The things pertaining to the kingdom of God," of which He spoke to them during the "forty days He was seen of them," must have included many points of doctrine, discipline, and practice, which they at once made distinct, as they published the Gospel; such as were "the laying on of hands" upon every baptized person, which is reckoned (Heb. vi. 1, 2) amongst the "principles of the doctrine of Christ;" the orders of subordinate ministry; and other subjects. Whilst, however, the passage is suggestive of a summary, the greater portion of it appears to have been the subject of the special appearance of our Lord—that, perhaps, when "He appeared to all the Apostles," and which terminated, probably, in the procession to Bethany, and in the ascension. He now points, at the conclusion of His life on earth, to the fulfilment of all He has spoken of during His ministry, before His Passion; and to the verification, in His life, and death, and resurrection, of the prophecies and types of Holy Scripture.

3. *law of Moses*, etc.—This is an enumeration of the Scriptures extant in our Lord's day. "They were divided into the law, and prophets, and the Hagiographa—the first containing the Pentateuch; the second, Joshua, Judges, the four Books of Kings, and the prophets except Daniel; the third, the Psalms, and all the rest of the canonical books, Daniel, Esther, Ezra, and Nehemiah being reckoned as one book, and the Chronicles closing the canon." (*Alford.*) (See App. XXII.)

4. *then opened He.*—Our Lord here again confers upon the disciples a special gift. It may be that they did not receive full possession of it until that great day of illumination, when the Holy Ghost was given (John xiv. 26); but this is now bestowed, as the Saviour's gift to them, the power to understand and apply the Scriptures. It was a necessary gift to those who should be the writers of the New Testament, that they should also understand those of the older covenant, and their harmony with the Gospel scheme.

5. *thus it is written.*—The life of Christ, His Passion, and resurrection, are a comment and illustration of the text, "It is written." This formed one-half of their commission as preachers of the everlasting word, especially to Jewish hearers. They were also to preach the Gospel of repentance and absolution in the name of Christ, who had "power on earth to forgive sins," and who now proclaims, by the mouth of His ministers, the word of that power, which He still exerci·es within His Church on earth.

from the dead the third day; and that repentance and
remission of sins should be preached in His Name among
all nations, beginning at Jerusalem. And ye are witnesses of these things. And, behold, I send the promise
of My Father upon you: but tarry ye in the city of
Jerusalem, until ye be endued with power from on high.
For John truly baptized with water; but ye shall be
baptized with the Holy Ghost not many days hence.

6. *beginning.*—" The word of the Lord from Jerusalem " (Isa. ii. 3;
Micah iv. 2). The universal custom of the Apostles, was to preach,
to the Jew first, and then to the Gentile, the unsearchable riches of
Christ. This was the Jews' privilege, as the first-born amongst the people
of God. They thrust it from them, and " judged themselves unworthy
of eternal life; " and, therefore, the Apostles were obliged to turn to
the Gentiles, not merely as graced in their turn with the gift of the
Gospel, but also as to those who were willing to receive what the
elder sons of God refused.

7. *witnesses.*—Eye-witnesses of the earthly ministry of Christ;
witnesses to the truth of all they proclaimed in His name; witnesses,
as martyrs, to His truth.

8. *the promise.*—The Holy Spirit, whose advent was to give life,
intelligence, and the full realization of all that Christ had promised
them.

9. *tarry ye.*—After the ascension, until the Spirit is given you, and
you are inspired with power and wisdom from on high.

10. *with water.*—This refers to the declaration of John (Matt. iii. 11),
that his baptism was but a temporary measure, and should be superseded by that of the Holy Ghost, which was with fire, *i.e.* searching and purifying as fire. His baptism was that of repentance,
preparatory to the first advent of Christ to preach the Gospel; that
of the Holy Ghost was to be perpetual, throughout all ages of the
Church. It was the baptism into the everlasting Gospel of the Saviour,
who had come, and had wrought the salvation of His people; it was,
therefore, " baptism for the remission of sins," baptism into the
covenant already established. The disciples had, probably, all, like
their Lord, received this preparatory baptism of John. It may not,
even in their case, have been superseded by that which, in its earlier
exercise, they had administered in the behalf of Christ (John iv. 1, 2),
and which, in its full institution as a Sacrament of the Gospel, they
were commissioned to exercise solely in future. But henceforward it
would not be enough to be baptized with " the baptism of John " (see
Acts xix. 3–5), as that was baptism into the kingdom now established; but in their case John's baptism of water (an element not
abolished but perfected in union with the Spirit-baptism of Christi-

When they therefore were come together, they asked of
Him, saying, Lord, wilt Thou at this time restore again

anity) was sufficient; and our Lord bade them wait for the baptism of
the Spirit, which was to complete what they, as He also, had originally
received.   The peculiarity of this case is, in itself, a strong argument
against the separation of time between the baptism of water and of the
Spirit, which has been held, by some, as an explanation of the interval
which often elapses between the vital influence of baptism, and what
they term " conversion ; " the truth being that all good which, however
late, exercises vitality within us, is only the quickening of the dormant
gift of the Spirit then bestowed—not any new gift not hitherto ours.
   11. *but ye.*—There is a personal, as well as a general, promise here.
Our Lord speaks of the gift of the Holy Spirit, who, though He should
be sent according to His promise, to abide in the Church for ever, was,
in an especial manner, to be given to the Apostles on the day of
Pentecost.
   12. *at this time.*—Their view was still that of the establishment of
temporal sovereignty in Israel ; but it was now far less material than
before.   The revelation of His prophecy on the Mount of Olives, concerning the destruction of the Temple and Church of the Jews, and
the events of His death, and resurrection, could not have been in vain.
They did not expect that Christ would merely found a temporal
kingdom, in restoration of that of David ; but still they thought that
the kingdom of the Messiah would be of Israel, that Israel should be
the centre of the new spiritual monarchy of the world, and that it
would be inaugurated—as Joel had foretold (see Acts ii. 16–21) —with
the gift of the Spirit of God. We see what a perception they had of the
destiny which had been possible to Israel, as the evangelical and
missionary capital of the world, but which had been rejected, in their
preference for the narrow, and restricted, selfishness of the Judaism of
the day.   Our Lord does not explain to them what it was the office of
the Holy Ghost, at His advent, to make clear; but He gives them a
general caution, against too curiously inquiring into the mysteries of
time, and locality, connected with the development of the purposes of
God.   It would be well that this caution should be remembered, in
these days especially, when there is a superabundance of works upon
unfulfilled prophecy, which contain the most unhesitating assertions
and calculations, many of which time has already frequently shown to
be false conclusions from baseless premises.   The study of prophecy is
encouraged in Scripture, but a deep reverence for God's truth must
inspire it; and those who publish their opinions on such subjects
should, further, be men of deep learning, accurately versed in Holy
Scripture, of profound historical knowledge, and extensive acquaintance with human nature.   It is not for those who publish their
theories, and thus aspire to lead the minds of others, to possess only

the kingdom to Israel? And He said unto them, It is not for you to know the times, or the seasons, which the Father hath put in His own power. But ye shall receive power, after that the Holy Ghost is come upon you : and ye shall be witnesses unto Me both in Jerusalem, and in

piety, and the wish to do good, and facility of writing; they must be men of deeper learning, and profounder thought, possessed of all qualifications, and of power superior to those whom they would lead towards the mysteries of God. Prophecy is God's witness to the generation of its fulfilment, of His knowledge in the past; it is not intended that we should anticipate the day of its fulfilment. He, therefore, who would assert its actual or impending fulfilment, must be full of accurate knowledge of past historical truth, and parallels, and also keen-sighted to detect the signs of the present time; it is not well that he should expose to the world his ignorance and presumption, by hazarding statements which time falsifies, thus rendering subjects of the gravest solemnity matters of popular derision.

13. *His own power.*—There is no connection, but rather a wide difference, and contrast, between this and the word rendered *power*, immediately below: "Ye shall receive power." In this instance, the word implies the independent control, and authority, which God possesses absolutely; the word has other meanings, in different connections, but here it expresses the right and sovereign control, which God restricts to Himself. In the second instance, the word implies that miraculous and spiritual power which God confers. In short, in the first place, Christ declares that God maintains, and reserves, the right of control and absolute authority; in the second, that He will confer upon His Apostles miraculous and spiritual gifts.

14. *ye shall be.*—The course of the apostolic labours is indicated, as primarily to the Jews, and, first amongst them, to the dwellers in Jerusalem. The city which was guilty of the blood of all the prophets, and, finally, of that of Christ Himself, should yet first receive the offer of the gospel of forgiveness and salvation; then it should pass throughout the land of the chosen people, in all the breadth and length of the land, as promised to Abraham—not, as restricted by Pharisaic prejudices, by the exclusion of Galilee, and the coasts of Tyre and Sidon, and the districts west of Jordan. The despised Samaritan, to whom our Lord had ever shown much tenderness, should next have a special mission of its message and blessings brought to him. Lastly, it should go forth into the wide world, amongst all nations under heaven, to every individual, extending its genial influences throughout all creation, until Christ comes. So ever spreads the Gospel, from home, to those near, and to those afar off; from the family to the neighbourhood, in widening circles. Those who advocate

all Judæa, and in Samaria, and unto the uttermost part of the earth.

The Ascension.

S. Mark xvi. 19, 20; S. Luke xxiv. 50–52; [Acts i. 9–12].

So then after the Lord had spoken unto them, He led them out as far as to Bethany, and He lifted up His hands,

missions at home, as a reason for withdrawing from missions abroad, contravene Christ's direction; they also forfeit the blessing promised to those who spread the Gospel. (See Prov. xi. 25 ; Isa. xxxii. 20.)

15. *had spoken.*—This refers to the completion of all that Christ had to say to His Apostles, between His resurrection and His ascension; nothing further remained to be said or explained by Himself. It is, however, in close connection and sequence with what immediately precedes; referring, primarily, to those words just spoken, concerning the promise of the Holy Ghost, and their commission under His power.

16. *to Bethany.*—*i.e.* to some place within the district and precincts of Bethany, "that part of the district which was upon the Mount of Olives." (*Elsley.*) The scene of the few days' last rest upon earth, hallowed by so many personal memories of His presence, and consecrated by so many prayers, is that of the last event of His earthly career. And yet once more shall His feet stand upon the Mount of Olives (Zech. xiv. 4; Ezek. xi. 22, 23). The way thither would lead them past the scenes of His humiliation, and Passion, and of His agony. They might notice this less, as they now went up; but as they returned by the same road to Jerusalem, full of the glorious triumph of the ascension, they must have contrasted with it the past sorrow, and their thoughts of despondency, now gone for ever. Bishop Hall seems to suppose that the one hundred and twenty disciples of Acts i. 15, were witnesses of the ascension; but the general impression is, that the Apostles only were present, as the chosen witnesses, on this occasion. There is nothing stated with regard to any others. Ebrard notices, and reconciles, a difficulty here: "S. Luke places the ascension at Bethany in his Gospel, in the Acts at the Mount of Olives. Bethany stood at some distance from the eastern foot of the Mount of Olives; the mountain, therefore, was between Bethany and Jerusalem. If the ascension took place at Bethany, or near it, the disciples must have returned from the Mount of Olives; and S. Luke says, 'they returned to Jerusalem from the mount called Olivet;' and Bethany itself really belonged to the Mount of Olives, and its environs." (See App. X.)

17. *lifted up.*—No word is spoken, no touch of hand laid upon

and blessed them.   And it came to pass, while He blessed them, while they beheld, He was parted from them, and carried up into heaven, and sat on the right hand of God ; and a cloud received Him out of their sight.

The Message of Angels.

[Acts i. 10, 11.]

And while they looked stedfastly toward heaven as He went up, behold, two men stood by them in white

them ; but in the attitude, and with the gesture, of general blessing, He leaves earth for heaven. He blessed, not them only, but the Church on earth, which He was planting through their ministry. We may gather that, to all to whom He leaves His blessing, and who receive it, He will come in like manner, blessing them with the everlasting blessing of His presence.

18. *carried.*—By angels, who came to conduct Him to His throne. We lose sight of our Lord now; but He speaks again *from heaven* to S. Paul, and to S. John in the Revelation ; SS. Stephen and John both beheld him there, enthroned in the glory of His heavenly state. But we may also behold, in prophecy, the scene of His reception into heaven. The Apostles saw Him rise upward towards heaven. It was granted to Daniel, the man " greatly beloved," to have a vision of His glorious arrival in His kingdom, though the darkness of vision veils his view (Dan. vii. 13, 14). (See notes 24–28.)

19. *a cloud.*—A bright cloud of glory. This connects our Lord with former manifestations of Divine presence : " He maketh the clouds His chariot'" (Ps. civ. 3); and into the presence of God " He came with the clouds of heaven ; " and at His second advent from heaven, "behold, He cometh with the clouds " (Rev. i. 7). It was, indeed, the fitting conclusion of His earthly career, that He should ascend to heaven. As He came down from heaven, so must He ascend thither, and thence shall He return to judgment.

20. *looked stedfastly.*—Their attitude of wrapt amazement is graphically described, both here and in the angels' words, " Why stand ye gazing up into heaven ? " We see them, all unconscious of earth and its claims, with their whole being gazing up whither they cannot now follow their Lord, from the appointed scene of their life's labours, in which they can at present truly follow Him. Even after He had quite passed away from their view, and the distant glory had also passed, they continued thus absorbedly gazing. The spectacle was, to the eye of heaven, as inappropriate as it would have seemed to passers-by of earth. As they were thus forgetful of earth, the mercy of

apparel; which also said, Ye men of Galilee, why stand ye gazing up into heaven? this same Jesus, which is

Christ sent two of His angel escort down, to recall them to their earthly duties. They stood by them, suddenly and unexpectedly, as two angels had stood by those by whom they were seen after His resurrection (Luke xxiv. 4–7).

21. *men of Galilee.*—The angels assign them earthly locality, to remind them of their duties in the world, where they have to lead lives of devotion and labour, after His example. They are thus, also, reminded of His career of goodness and love in this populous district, amongst Jews, and those of mixed race, where so many of His mighty works were done. If they would ascend whither He is gone, they must take up His commission on earth, and His cross. He who came down from heaven, to work amongst men, in these districts for ever associated with His name, and whose dwellers were henceforth men of a famous locality, had never neglected His earthly mission, for all the recollections of heavenly glory where He had reigned. Nor must their glimpse of heaven unsettle them for their true vocation, or they never would follow Him hereafter. They are, therefore, still "men of Galilee," workers in this transitory world; let them remember this, and Christ's example, and follow it, and they shall presently be "of heaven" with their ascended Lord.

22. *this same Jesus.*—"Our Lord did visibly, in earthly shape, ascend to heaven (which to do is inconsistent with the invisible, omnipresent, and immovable nature of God); and therefore he continueth still a man; and, as such, He abideth in heaven, and therefore doth not exist everywhere, or otherwhere. It is the property of a creature to have a definite existence, or to be only in one place at one time; for could it be in divers places at once, it might by reason be in any, or in every place, and consequently it might be immense. Nor can we conceive a thing to be at once in several distant places, without its being multiplied in essence. It is especially repugnant to the nature of a body, at once to possess several places, seeing its substance and quality do not really differ, or are inseparably combined; whence it cannot be multiplied in dimensions, answerable to many localities, without being multiplied in substance. Wherefore, since our Lord as man did, by a proper local motion, ascend, pass through, and enter into the heavens, which must receive Him until the time of the restitution of all things, where He ever liveth to make intercession for us, and whence, in like manner as He went, He shall come again, descending from heaven, and coming in the clouds of glory; our Lord did thus as man, in His flesh, go into heaven, and there perpetually doth abide in glory, until He shall thence return hither to judge the world. We must not, therefore, suppose Him to be anywhere corporally upon earth." (*I. Barrow.*)

taken up from you into heaven, shall so come in like manner as ye have seen Him go into heaven.

Christ's Return into Heaven.

S. Mark xvi. 19; S. Luke xxiv. 51; [Dan. vii. 13, 14].

So then He was received up into heaven.

' And, behold, *one* like the Son of Man came with the clouds of heaven, and came to the Ancient of days, and

23. *shall so come.*—The angels repeat, now that our Lord was gone, the promise which He Himself had so emphatically given before : for all the glory which surrounds Him, He will never forget it; His very occupation amidst that glory, is the perpetual preparation for His return. He was taken up from the disciples, but He shall come again to the hope, and expectation, and to the joyful beholding, of the universal Church, which He has redeemed.

24. *and, behold.*—This prophecy, unlike many which concern our Lord, which are prophecies of what shall be, is a vision of reality. It supplements what the disciples saw, with what Daniel was permitted to see in prophetic vision ; it carries us from where they stood gazing upon earth, into the heaven of heavens, into which Christ had passed as the angels conversed with the disciples ; and, in point of time, seems to be intermediate between this message to the disciples, and the commencement of their labours. It is one scene of the ascension into heaven. There is, therefore, reason sufficient for taking such a vision from its place in ancient prophecy, and inserting it here, amongst the revelations of the ascension.

25. *the Son of man.*—This title was one which the Jews understood of the Messiah; it could not be used of any but of One who was more than a son of man ; it would be an unmeaning designation, if applied to any of the sons of Adam, who was simply that, and nothing more. There was, therefore, great significance in our Lord's use of the term, and in His application of it to Himself. " The title, ' the Son of man,' as employed by our Lord, is the more remarkable, in that He always uses it of Himself, as to His work for us on earth ; no one ventures to use it of Him, except that S. Stephen points to the commenced fulfilment of His prophecy to Caiaphas, ' I see the heavens opened, and the Son of man standing at the right hand of God.' Our Lord called Himself ' *the* Son of man,' *i.e.* He who was foretold under that name in Daniel." (*Pusey.*)

26. *with the clouds.*—Veiling Him from human sight. In that magnificent description of the majesty of God's presence, in Ps. xviii., it is said (*v.* 11), " His pavilion round about Him were dark waters and

they brought Him near before Him. And there was given unto Him dominion, and glory, and a kingdom, that all people, nations, and languages, should serve Him: His dominion *is* an everlasting dominion, and His kingdom *that* which shall not be destroyed.

And [*He*] sat on the right hand of God.

The Apostles return to Jerusalem: they commence their Mission.

S. Mark xvi. 20; S. Luke xxiv. 52, 53; [Acts i. 12].

And they worshipped Him, and returned to Jerusalem

thick clouds of the skies." The mention of these clouds of heaven, and, immediately after, of those who conducted our Lord to heaven, connect their vision closely with the narrative of S. Luke: we see Him arrive in heaven in the clouds, and amidst the angels, of His ascension from earth.

27. *near before Him.*—To receive, at the hand of the eternal Father, investiture of that kingdom to which He had before appointed Him (Luke xxii. 29).

28. *all people,* etc.—"Daniel foretold, not a kingdom in Israel only, not a conversion of the heathen only, but that He who sat above, in a form like the Son of man, should be *worshipped* by all peoples, nations, and languages, and that His kingdom should not pass away. And to whom have peoples, nations, and languages throughout the world, millions on millions, and hundred millions on hundred millions in successive generations, looked to and worshipped as their King, hereafter to be their Judge; whom have they confessed in their Creeds all these centuries since any questioned it, as Him 'whose kingdom shall have no end,' save Him who came in the form of a servant, like a son of man, in Judea? . . . Daniel does certainly foretell of the Christ, that He should be man, and yet more than man: 'One like the Son of man.' He speaks of Him, not as before His birth, nor in His days on earth, but, as He is now since His ascension, at the right hand of God. He speaks of Him, not as 'to come,' but as already come, His life on earth past (for on earth only could He have become a son of man); His days of humility ended; not coming from heaven, but ascended to heaven, and receiving all power in heaven and earth, which, He said on earth, was given to Him on His resurrection. We see in act, what was said in words in David's psalm, which Jesus quoted as written of Himself, 'The Lord said unto my Lord, Sit Thou on My right hand, until I make Thine enemies Thy footstool.' We see that everlasting dominion given to Him, which has now been acknowledged for above eighteen hundred years; and we behold Him receiving the beginnings of

with great joy, from the mount called Olivet, which is from Jerusalem a sabbath day's journey; and were continually in the temple, praising and blessing God.

And they went forth, and preached everywhere, the

that homage, which has been rendered to Him ever since, and shall be rendered to Him for ever, that all people, nations, and languages should serve Him." (*Pusey.*)

29. *worshipped.*—They now, as never before, pay to Christ the full honours of Divinity, honouring the Son, even as they honoured the Father.

30. *joy.*—The expression here is worthy of note; it is in entire contrast with their utter despondency whilst their Lord was removed from them for the three days of His burial. It is also the spirit of their future mien before the world. It was, henceforth, joy and thankfulness with them, even when they faced the terrors of the world's opposition. The promise was already theirs, " Peace I leave with you, My peace I give unto you; " " in Me ye shall have peace " (John xiv. 27, xvi. 33).

31. *sabbath day's journey.*—So near to the bustle, life, and preoccupation of the centres of human life and enterprise, are the deep mysteries of heaven; and, again, it is but a sabbath day's journey from out of the business of life and its anxieties, to the excellence of heavenly converse, to those who can engage in the worship of Christ, upon the Lord's day, with the joy of His presence in their hearts.

32. *in the temple.*—We still see the disciples constant at all the religious services of the Temple; but they trod those courts of the Lord's House, so often hallowed by the Saviour's presence, with far different feelings from those which animated other worshippers there. They saw the fulfilment of type and ordinance in Christ. They had not the restless, and unsatisfied, heart of those who paraded their goodness before God, as did the Pharisee, nor the dread of the conscious sinner; they were " continually praising and blessing God." Their happiness was not to be theirs only; but all who tread the courts of the Lord's House on earth, in our Lord's absence, with like faith in Him, and in His promises, and with like earnest purpose to serve Him in the world, will have the heart to praise and bless God, though there gather around them the difficulties, and troubles, of their earthly calling. Their presence *continually* in the Temple, may find illustration in 1 Chron. xvi. 40, and may imply that they were carefully observant of those services, and laws, which were then ordained.

33. *went forth.*—This expression is suggestive. They went forth from their own prejudices and narrow views, into a more liberal and Christlike mind. They went forth from their sorrow and despondency, now past, and from their gazing up *to* forbidden heights, into earnest and practical work in the world. They went forth from their closed and

Lord working with *them*, and confirming the word with signs following. Amen.

guarded chamber, to the public resort of those before whom they had to maintain the cause and truth of Christ, and to offer to them His Gospel. They went forth from the restrictions of the Law, into the freedom of the Gospel. They went forth from the narrow peculiarities and national exclusiveness of the Jew, into the broad and general brotherhood of the race for which Christ died. They went forth from Jerusalem, into the wide world of God's kingdom upon earth. " They went forth, and preached everywhere."

34. *signs following.*—" Who, then, and what, goes before? The believing preacher, with the word of the Gospel." (*Stier.*) Miracles followed the first utterance of the Gospel; success, in due season, has ever attested it; and the truth that Christ works with those who proclaim His Name, becomes, as the Gospel steadily advances, ever more patent to the world, which, one day, must take up the closing words of the Evangelist, and subscribe to the eternal truth of Christ's religion : " It is truth." Amen.

APPENDIX.

No. 1.

On i. 8.

CHRIST GOING UP TO JERUSALEM.

Heroism is scarcely the right word to apply to Christ our Saviour; but this is a word which finds an echo in every breast; and there is really no one word which can express the sublime and heroic self-devotion which characterized the Son of man, when, as the Evangelists show us, He advanced towards Jerusalem upon His last journey, well knowing all that should befall Him there, and speaking of it in tones which show us how fully He measured the sorrow and the trial which lay before Him, and how steadily He went within the ranges of His adversaries, going straight forward to His martyrdom and sacrifice. In speaking of all this, we seek in vain for a term which can express what is unparalleled and divine; and can only express it by the best we have.

In the words of Dean Milman ("Hist. Christ." I. vii.), "At every step He feels Himself more inextricably within the toils; yet He moves onwards with the self-command of a willing sacrifice, continually dwelling, with a profound but chastened melancholy, on His approaching fate; and intimating that His death was necessary, in order to secure an indescribable benefit for His faithful followers and for mankind. Yet there is no needless exasperation of His enemies; He observes the utmost prudence, though he seems so fully aware that His prudence can be of no avail. He never passes the night within the city; and it is only by the treachery of one of His followers that the Sanhedrim at length make themselves masters of His person."

As He advances towards the end, He constantly, but with a certain reserve, speaks to His disciples of what is before Him; partly with tenderness, as touching their prejudices; partly with the desire to prepare their minds to receive a most painful truth, which, in the want of perfect intelligence of its necessity, they were unable and unwilling to accept.

The following passages from the Gospels will show how distinctly this devotion of Christ is marked by the Apostles :—

1. After Peter's confession of Christ in the name of the Apostles.

" From that time forth began Jesus to shew unto His disciples, how that He must go unto Jerusalem, and suffer many things of the elders and chief priests and scribes, and be killed, and be raised again the third day.   And He spake that saying openly" (S. Matt. xvi. 21 ; S. Mark viii. 31, 32 ; S. Luke ix. 22).

2. After the transfiguration, when, as after the former confession, their faith was strengthened to bear the strain of such an announcement, we read—

"As they came down from the mountain, He charged them that they should tell no man what things they had seen, till the Son of man were risen from the dead.   And He told them . . . how it is written of the Son of man, that He must suffer many things, and be set at nought " (S. Mark ix. 9, 12 ; S. Matt. xvii. 9, 12).

3. Before His leaving Galilee, the scene of so many wonderful works in evidence of His real Divinity.

"And while they abode in Galilee, Jesus said unto them, Let these sayings sink down into your ears : for the Son of man shall be betrayed into the hands of men, and they shall kill Him ; and after that He is killed, He shall rise the third day.   And they were exceedingly sorry.   But they understood not this saying, and it was hid from them, that they perceived it not : and they feared to ask Him of that saying" (S. Matt. xvii. 22, 23 ; S. Mark ix. 30, 32 ; S. Luke ix. 43–45).

4. Before the Feast of Tabernacles, we notice how resolutely Christ prepared for the work before Him ; and with how great caution He avoids doing anything which could afford a handle to the designs of His adversaries, of which He was fully aware, or precipitate their action against Himself.

"After these things Jesus walked in Galilee : for He would not walk in Jewry, because the Jews sought to kill Him.   Now the Jews' feast of tabernacles was at hand. . . . Then Jesus said unto them, My time is not yet come. . . . I go not up yet unto this feast ; for My time is not yet full come.   When He had said these words unto them, He abode still in Galilee.   But when His brethren were gone up, then went He also up unto the feast, not openly, but as it were in secret " (S. John vii. 1–10).

5. Before setting forth Himself, He sends the seventy to prepare His way, giving an additional solemnity to this progress.

"And it came to pass, when the time was come that He should be received up, He stedfastly set His face to go to Jerusalem, and sent messengers before His face.   The Lord appointed other seventy also, and sent them two and two before His face into every city and place, whither He Himself would come " (S. Luke ix. 51, 52 ; x. 1.   See Isa. l. 7).

6. At the Feast of Tabernacles.

"Now about the middle of the feast Jesus went up into the temple, and taught. . . . Then said some of them of Jerusalem, Is not this He, whom they seek to kill ?   But, lo, He speaketh boldly, and

they say nothing unto Him.   Do the rulers know indeed that this
is the very Christ ? . . . Then they sought to take Him : but no
man laid hands on Him, because His hour was not yet come. .. . .
The Pharisees heard that the people murmured such things concerning Him ; and the Pharisees and the chief priests sent officers
to take Him.   Then said Jesus unto them, Yet a little while am I
with you, and then I go My way unto Him that sent Me. . . . And
some of them would have taken Him ; but no man laid hands on
Him.   Then came the officers to the chief priests and Pharisees ; and
they said unto them, Why have ye not brought Him ?   The officers
answered, Never man spake like this man " (S. John vii. 14, 25,
26, 30, 32, 33, 44–46).

   7. On the following day.
   " Jesus went unto the mount of Olives.   And early in the morning He came again into the temple, and all the people came unto
Him ; and He sat down, and taught them. . . .
   " These words spake Jesus in the treasury as He taught in
the temple : and no man laid hands on Him ; for His hour was
not yet come.   Then said Jesus again unto them, I go My way,
and ye shall seek Me, and shall die in your sins : whither I go, ye
cannot come. . . .
   " Then said Jesus unto them, When ye have lifted up the Son of
man, then shall ye know that I am He, and that I do nothing of
Myself ; but as My Father hath sent Me, I speak these things.
And He that sent Me is with Me : the Father hath not left Me
alone. . . . Ye seek to kill Me, because My word hath no place in
you. . . . Ye seek to kill Me, a man that hath told you the truth,
which I have heard of God. . . .
   " Then took they up stones to cast at Him : but Jesus hid Himself, and went out of the temple, going through the midst of them,
and so passed by " (S. John viii. 1, 2, 20, 21, 28, 29, 37, 40, 59).

   8. After leaving the Temple.
   " I am the good Shepherd: the good Shepherd giveth His life
for the sheep. . . . I lay down My life for the sheep. . . . I lay
down My life, that I may take it again.   No man taketh it from
Me, but I lay it down of Myself.   I have power to lay it down, and
I have power to take it again " (S. John x. 11, 15, 17, 18).

   9. On another occasion, in Judæa, and probably in Jerusalem.
   " Then certain of the scribes and of the Pharisees answered,
saying, Master, we would see a sign from Thee.   And when the
people were gathered thick together, He began to say, This is an
evil generation : they seek a sign ; and there shall no sign be
given to it, but the sign of the prophet Jonas : for as Jonas was
three days and three nights in the whale's belly ; so shall the Son
of man be three days and three nights in the heart of the earth"
(S. Matt. xii. 38–40 ; S. Luke xi. 29).

   10. Later, at the Feast of the Dedication.

" And it was at Jerusalem the feast of the dedication, and it was winter.   And Jesus walked in the temple in Solomon's porch. . . . Then the Jews took up stones again to stone Him. . . . Therefore they sought again to take Him : but He escaped out of their hand, and went away again beyond Jordan into the place where John at first baptized ; and there He abode " (S. John x. 22, 23, 31, 39, 40).

11. His progress through the cities and villages towards Jerusalem, which He had prepared for by sending messenger heralds. (See No. 5.)

" And He went through the cities and villages, teaching, and journeying toward Jerusalem. . . .

" The same day there came certain of the Pharisees, saying unto Him, Get Thee out, and depart hence : for Herod will kill Thee. And He said unto them, Go ye, and tell that fox, Behold, I cast out devils, and I do cures to-day and to-morrow, and the third day I shall be perfected.   Nevertheless I must walk to-day, and to-morrow, and the day following: for it cannot be that a prophet perish out of Jerusalem " (S. Luke xiii. 22, 31–33).

12. Christ advances as far as Bethany to raise Lazarus from the dead ; not in the direct line of His progress, for He went back again to resume the tour which was thus for the time interrupted.

" Then after that saith He to His disciples, Let us go into Judæa again.   His disciples say unto Him, Master, the Jews of late sought to stone Thee ; and goest Thou thither again ? . . .   Then said Thomas, which is called Didymus, unto his fellow-disciples, Let us also go, that we may die with Him ". (S. John xi. 7, 8, 16).

13. The result of the raising of Lazarus, and of the converts made by it, on the mind of the rulers.

" Then gathered the chief priests and the Pharisees a council, and said, What do we ? for this man doeth many miracles.   If we let Him thus alone, all men will believe on Him : and the Romans shall come and take away both our place and nation.   And one of them, named Caiaphas, being the high priest that same year, said unto them, Ye know nothing at all, nor consider that it is expedient for us, that one man should die for the people, and that the whole nation perish not.   And this spake he not of himself : but being high priest that same year, he prophesied that Jesus should die for that nation ; and not for that nation only, but that also He should gather together in one the children of God that were scattered abroad.   Then from that day forth they took counsel together for to put Him to death.   Jesus therefore walked no more openly among the Jews ; but went thence unto a country near to the wilderness, into a city called Ephraim, and there continued with His disciples " (S. John xi. 47–54).

14. The last journey towards Jerusalem.

" And He arose from thence, and cometh into the coasts of

Judæa by the farther side of Jordan : and the people resort unto Him again ; and, as He was wont, He taught them again " (S. Matt. xix. 1, 2 ; S. Mark x. 1 ; S. Luke xvii. 11).

15. As they approached Jerusalem.

"And they were in the way going up to Jerusalem ; and Jesus went before them : and they were amazed ; and as they followed, they were afraid. And He took again the twelve apart in the way, and said unto them, Behold, we go up to Jerusalem ; and the Son of man shall be betrayed unto the chief priests and unto the scribes, and they shall condemn Him to death, and shall deliver Him to the Gentiles to mock, and to scourge, and to crucify Him : and the third day He shall rise again. And they understood none of these things : and this saying was hid from them, neither knew they the things which were spoken " (S. Matt. xx. 17-19 ; S. Mark x. 32-34 ; S. Luke xviii. 31-34. See also Isa. l. 7, lxiii.).

16. Christ has advanced as far as Jericho.

"And Jesus entered and passed through Jericho " (S. Matt. xx. 29 ; S. Mark x. 46 ; S. Luke xviii. 35, xix. 1).

17. Introducing the parable of the pounds, declaring in a bold and plain figure His rejection by the Jews, and the vengeance they should bring upon themselves in the success of their present plots against His life.

"And as they heard these things, He added and spake a parable, because He was nigh to Jerusalem, and because they thought that the kingdom of God should immediately appear. . . . And when He had thus spoken, He went before, ascending up to Jerusalem " (S. Luke xix. 11, 28).

18. Christ reaches Bethany, where, at a supper in the house of Lazarus, the anointing took place. The conspiracy amongst the rulers matures.

"Then Jesus six days before the passover came to Bethany, where Lazarus was which had been dead, whom He raised from the dead. There they made Him a supper ; and Martha served : but Lazarus was one of them that sat at the table with Him. Then took Mary an alabaster box of ointment of spikenard very precious; and she brake the box, and poured it on His head, and anointed the feet of Jesus, and wiped His feet with her hair. . . . And Jesus said, She hath wrought a good work on Me. . . . She hath done what she could; for in that she hath poured this ointment on My body, she is come aforehand to anoint My body to the burying. . . .

"Much people of the Jews therefore knew that He was there : and they came not for Jesus' sake only, but that they might see Lazarus also, whom He had raised from the dead. But the chief priests consulted that they might put Lazarus also to death ; because that by reason of him many of the Jews went away, and believed on Jesus" (S. Matt. xxvi. 6–13; S. Mark xiv. 3–9; S. John xii. 1–11).

Then follows the entry to Jerusalem, the results of which are carefully detailed in the notes of Part I.; and the evidences of Christ's perfect foreknowledge of all that lay before Him, and of His free will in action throughout all that is connected with His Passion; and also the continued, and at last successful, proceedings of the Jewish council against Him are pointed out. There is also a continuance of His care not to court danger, now so imminent. (See i. 1, 8, 44; v. 2; ix. 2; xxiii. 3, 5; xxiv. *a.* 1, *c.* 5, 13, 22; xxix. 2; xxxi. 36, 38; and many other places too numerous to detail.)

We see from the above passages how careful the Evangelists are to show that, whilst Christ went deliberately and resolutely to Jerusalem, fully conscious of the proceedings of His enemies, and of all that awaited Him there, in full power to lay down, and to take again, His life, which, else, no man could take from Him, He nevertheless avoided placing Himself in the way of those who sought His life, until the appointed moment, when, His hour being fully come, He advanced to meet them in the Garden of Gethsemane, saying, "I am He."

But though He would not court danger, we see the most distinct intelligence of the minute particulars connected with it; and He spoke most distinctly concerning the death that He should die, sometimes in the privacy of His retirement amongst His chosen disciples, often most openly before the rulers, and before the people; warning them, and declaring plainly that He was the Christ, and that the Christ must suffer. He avoided, indeed, giving occasion to His busy foes, who must have felt the restraining hand of God upon them, in the failure of their plans against Him; but He never ceased to appear openly and publicly, wherever there was a word of warning to be spoken, or a deed of mercy to be done; so that He spoke justly, when He said to those who took Him, in the privacy of the Garden of Gethsemane, and in the darkness of night, "Are ye come out as against a thief with swords and staves for to take Me? I sat daily with you teaching in the temple, and ye stretched forth no hands against Me: but this is your hour, and the power of darkness." And again, before the council, "I spake openly to the world; I ever taught in the synagogue, and in the temple, whither the Jews always resort; and in secret have I said nothing."

No. II.

On i. 29, 44; ix. 3; x. 2; xi. 3.

JEWISH SECTS AND PARTIES.

It is difficult to form a true estimate of the position of the Jewish sects, and their influence on religious society and politics in our Lord's day, without considering them as they are represented to us by Josephus, and in the Rabbinical traditions which have been preserved in writing, as well as in the pages of Holy Scripture. And even then we cannot exactly realize their influence, especially the more salutary aspect of it. For we see them in history as they influenced public affairs; in Scripture as they were to the eye of God alone; and in their writings, so far as they are accessible to us, under circumstances especially distasteful to modern thought,—in none of these exactly as they were to the eye of the people whom they governed.

They were composed of men of high birth, position, and learning; but their learning was, with almost the sole exception of the liberal-minded Gamaliel, confined to the sacred Scriptures, the traditions of the elders, and all writings extant connected with these. They had no dealings with other people; and this must have made them narrow-minded, prejudiced, and self-sufficient, very unlike the rest of the world, and contrasting disadvantageously, and to the disadvantage of their religion, with men of less pretensions to God's favour, but with more knowledge of the world and of mankind. And to our mind, citizens of the world as we are proud to be, though possessing a purer and truer faith than theirs, their exclusiveness of education, and restriction of thought, and isolation of interests, presents them in an uncongenial, if not unintelligible, light. We cannot look on them as on other men; and they demand judgment upon a separate level. The one common ground they occupy with us is the broad one of a common humanity. Their nature is the same as that of all other men, however they differ by education, aspiration, locality, religion, and, above all, by the artificial barriers erected by their narrow pride. And on this ground we must meet them, being especially careful to remember that, as has been said, the true revelation of them in Scripture is that of God's view, not that of their own countrymen and contemporaries. And we must not view them as merely religious sects and parties, but have regard also to their political character; for religion and politics were so closely connected in the actions of the Jewish rulers, as to be almost inseparable.

There are three of the principal sects prominent in the history of the last week of our Lord's life, and each had considerable influence on the events connected with Him. These were the Pharisees, the Sadducees, and the Herodians. Of these, the two former were the two principal religious sects; the last bore the character rather of a political party.

We also frequently meet with the scribes and the lawyers. These two are sometimes confounded, but it is necessary to observe what distinctions may be traced between them.

There was also the great religious council of the nation, the Sanhedrim, which included men of these various sects, and parties, and professions. It is impossible here to give anything like a history of these; but they must each be noticed on the points in which their distinctive opinions brought them in contact with our Lord and His religion. For an excellent sketch of their origin, and the leading features of their opinions, and record of their celebrated doctors, the reader may be referred to the articles in Smith's "Dictionary of the Bible."

Dean Milman thus gives the origin of the first two sects: "Immediately after the return from Babylonia, two sects had divided the people; the Zadikim, the righteous, who observed the written law of Moses; and the more austere and abstemious Chasidim, or the holy, who added to the law the traditions and observances of the latter, and professed a holiness beyond the letter of the covenant. From the former sprang the Sadducees, and Karaites of later times; from the latter the Pharisees."

I. *Pharisees.* The chief peculiarity in their teaching was their value for the oral law; against which the Sadducees maintained the value only of the written law. This oral law was originally a mass of traditions coming down, in the first instance, from the days of Moses (to whom, it was said, it was given on Sinai, as an explanatory appendix to the written law), and from the elders who succeeded him; and gathering bulk as it descended through later generations, until it embraced all that could be raised in the way of question, from the interpretation of the letter of Scripture, and legal maxims and decisions, to the minutest practices of individual life.

1. Their excessive veneration for this oral law, and the perversions and errors with which it flooded the simple truth of God, was one of the chief points which brought them into hostile contact with Jesus Christ. His religion prescribed the prayerful study of the written word of God; and His Gospel, and the doctrines in connection with it, were also carefully reduced to writing by His Apostles, leaving, therefore, nothing necessary to salvation in the corruptible form of human tradition. The Holy Scriptures were therefore the standard of Christ's religion; and, in His exposure of the erroneous system of the Pharisees, there stands in the foreground His stern decision, " *Ye* have made the word of God of none effect through your tradition."

2. The next leading feature of their system, and the second point on which they were at issue with our Lord, was their formalism. They were the most accomplished and thorough formalists which any age has seen. They had prescribed ceremonial for every particular of life, which descended into such extreme, vexatious, and ridiculous minutiæ, that it required a life's study to master them. As the mass of oral tradition obscured the written word of God, and, by subtle tradition, nullified it, so did this elaborate structure of rite and ceremony obscure the simple practice of righteousness prescribed by the law, and substituted a different standard altogether : what ought to have been done for the eye of God, was wrought for the eye of man.

On this point they came at once into collision with our Lord. The rules of Christian practice were few and clear, and the appeal was from sacrifice to mercy—from ceremonial acts to the spirit of religion which prescribed them, as necessary fruits of the law, written by the Spirit of Christ, in the heart and conscience. The whole religion, on the other hand, of the Pharisee, was regulated by ceremonial prescription, in which was the essence of his religion; so that, when sincere as an inquirer after spiritual truth (and there were such amongst the Pharisees), he came to the truth so bound and fettered, that he must be freed, body and mind, before he could attain to it.

The Pharisees would have had Christ graft His ethics upon their system; but the demand required an impossibility. There could be no compromise between Him and them, and their principles admitted of no practical improvement. Neither could men have borne the burden, nor could Phariseeism have borne the strain of the "new cloth," the vitality of the "new wine," of the Gospel. If every little requirement of the scrupulous Pharisee became a matter of heart and conscience, instead of being merely a matter of outward form, when there were eyes to see it, religion, in this aspect, would have been simply intolerable.

3. But more than this : It was scarcely this simple veneration for ceremonial, which was so radically opposed to Christ. With regard to much of what the Pharisees did, He could say, "These ought ye to have done." But the inevitable consequence of such a system as theirs was hypocrisy—it was impossible to act up to the letter of their rules. And they were content to be *thought* religious. There was no heart in their system ; all was on the outside, all was hollow pretence. When the proselyte, allured by their pretended authority and paraded sanctity, joined them, and was initiated into their mysteries, he had not the long-descended veneration for their teaching, derived from his forefathers, to check him. He soon saw the shallowness of that which from afar he had thought so holy, and he presently became "twofold more the child of hell" than his instructors. For he turned back upon his former darkness,

catching only the pretence and hypocrisy of his new creed, missing the restraints of their laws of ceremony, and having nothing to deter him in the way of public opinion ; for a proselyte from abroad to Phariseeism had no personal importance in the eyes of Jewish society.

Never were two principles of religion in more direct and mortal antagonism, than those of Christ and of the Pharisee. They must disown each other ; and only in the extinction of its opponent could the victor live.

The Pharisees were all-powerful with the people, who saw little below the surface of their system ; and venerated them as the holiest of men, living on heights of religious excellence to which they could not attain, but which they did blindly admire. And the Pharisee, in his turn, saw nothing beyond himself. He was blind to the defects of the system in which he had been reared, and which was the acknowledged standard of religious practice, and he turned away from all that could expose it. He used his advantage of position and influence, religious and political, to crush the rise and progress of the spirit of Christianity, and to destroy Christ.

It is sad to think that, of all the sects which survived the over-throw of the Jewish national Church, this has most thoroughly retained its hold upon the Jews. Though not the formalists and hypocrites of our Lord's day, and not bound by the same minutely particular laws of ceremonial, the modern Jews are mostly Pharisees, retaining the tenets of the great doctors of their sect ; and, in the Talmud (which includes the Mishna and Gemaras of their school), holding to the leading principles which the Pharisees taught. And bondage to the traditions and ceremonial laws of a corrupt anti-quity, however alleviated by modern thought, and intelligence, and by association with the outer world, is still one great and radical reason why the Jew of to-day cannot receive the Gospel of Christ.

II. *Sadducees.* There is less to be said with regard to this sect. They were less influential with the people than the Pharisees ; for they were chiefly raised above their level by exclusive tastes, high birth, aristocratic feelings, and great wealth ; so that, in these respects, they came less in contact with Christianity.

Josephus (whose account of these sects, and of the history of chief members of them, is interesting, and important to a right understanding of their weight in Jewish society) thus describes the points on which the Sadducees were at issue with the Pharisees. He also shows us why their opposition to Christianity was less marked, and less powerful, than that of the Pharisees ; though, strange to say, at the last, the Sadducees, rather than the Pharisees, ensured His condemnation and death. Josephus says, "The Pharisees have delivered to the people a great many observances by succession from their fathers, which are not written in the law of Moses ; and for that reason it is that the Sadducees reject them, and say that we are to esteem those observances to be obligatory which are in the written word, but are not to observe what are derived from the tradition of our forefathers ; and concerning these things it is that great disputes and differences have arisen among them, while the Sadducees are able to persuade none but the rich, and have not the populace obsequious to them, but the Pharisees have the multitude of their side." ("Antiq." xiii. 10, 6.)

The points on which they came into collision with Christ were principally their denial of the resurrection, and of the existence of the spirit world. As the resurrection is so leading a feature of the Gospel proclamation, that it was described by St. Luke (Acts xvii. 18) as "Jesus and the resurrection," we see at once the entire antagonism of a sect which denied that primary and vital doctrine. Their denial was founded on the fact that it is not directly mentioned by Moses. Our Lord shows how they should have inferred it from Moses, aided by the light of later and more explicit Scriptures, in which it is directly contained. There is no explanation recorded of their denial of the existence of angels, which is a doctrine directly asserted in the books of Moses.

They possessed high offices of the priesthood in the time of our Lord, and thus it was that they became principal agents in the act of His death. It has been noticed, as an evidence of the decline of real religion at that day, that men holding views so much opposed to the religious standard of the nation, and, if not denying Scripture, at least holding very material and *rationalistic* opinions concerning the greater portion of it, should yet hold the supreme religious offices ; and, though small in numbers, possess such paramount influence upon the destinies of the Jewish Church and nation.

III. *Herodians.* These were scarcely a religious sect. They may have been men nominally attached to the great sects, but whom the stricter members would have disowned ; and they formed a political party, though (as was necessary among the Jews) with peculiar tenets concerning religion. It is said, but perhaps with little foundation, that they affected to consider Herod as the Messiah, as being a king in Judæa. Some of them may have possibly put forward gross flattery of this description, but it can scarcely have been true in any general sense. Josephus does not mention them as a separate sect. They were possibly, in some respects, identical with the Sadducees ; and, in fact, it would do but little violence to the religious opinions of some of the Sadducees, to number themselves further amongst the Herodians. (Cf. S. Matt. xvi. 6 ; S. Mark viii. 15, where, in the former instance, we find our Lord bidding His disciples to "beware of the leaven of the Pharisees and Sadducees ;" in the latter, "of the leaven of the Pharisees, and of the leaven of Herod.")

They were less fanatically bound to the law, less scrupulous about the ceremonial laws which so isolated the Jew from other people ; and their wealth, and privileges of birth, and connections made them decidedly tenacious of their national independence.　It is likely, therefore, that they looked upon the reigning dynasty of Herod, as the best barrier at the moment against the advance of Roman power, and against the absorption of their national life within the vast limits of the Roman empire—a prospect abhorrent to the Jew ; and therefore they were inclined to lend that dynasty all the support they could, and to ignore its vicious example, and its want of real right.　Herod and his family, in their obsequiousness towards Rome, managed to hold Jewish doctrines of religion, in combination with an entire tolerance of the presence and rites of idolatry practised of Rome ; and the Herodians adopted these views, and thus temporized with the supreme sanctions of their religion.　They proposed to "serve God and mammon."

This "leaven of Herod" brought them into immediate antagonism with Christ, who could not for one moment allow such trifling with the law of God.　And if this leaven were tolerated in the system of the Gospel, it would end by its absorption into the idolatries, or, at least, into the rationalism, of the heathen world. If Christians might hold, with the pure doctrines of their religion, entire toleration of heathen rites, and, where it was convenient not to be stricter than the heathen, give way to their standard of morality and practice, there would be as decided an end of Christianity, as either by the hypocrisy of the Pharisee, or the denial of cardinal doctrines by the Sadducee.　If the Gospel could not, in its purity, leaven the world with good, the leaven of the world would penetrate and corrupt the Gospel : " a little leaven leaveneth the whole lump."　The Christian, therefore, must " render to God the things that are God's," however convenient it might be to sink them before the requirements of Cæsar, or of the world.

The principle thus involved placed the Herodians in as direct issue with Jesus Christ, as was the case with any other of His enemies.

The following extract from Dean Milman's "History of Christianity" gives the other side of the question, and shows how Christianity appeared to be antagonistic to the Herodians, and how the Herodians were opposed to the Pharisees, and the character of their united plot against Christ :—

"Some suppose the Herodians to have been the officers and attendants on the court of Herod, then present at Jerusalem ; but the appellation more probably includes all those who, estranged from the more inveterate Judaism of the nation, and having in some degree adopted Grecian habits and opinions, considered the peace of the country best secured by the government of the descendants of Herod, with the sanction and under the protection of Rome. They were the foreign faction, and, as such in general, in direct opposition to the Pharisaic or national party. But the success of Jesus, however it threatened more immediately the ruling authorities in Jerusalem, could not but endanger the Galilæan government of Herod.

"Their object, therefore, was to implicate Jesus with the faction, or, at least, to tempt Him into acknowledging opinions similar to those of the Galilæan demagogue—a scheme more likely to work on the jealousy of the Roman government, if it was at the last Passover that the apprehension of tumult amongst the Galilæan strangers had justified, or appeared to justify, the massacre perpetrated by Pilate. The plot was laid with great subtlety, for either way Jesus, it appeared, must commit Himself. The great test of the Galilæan opinion was the lawfulness of tribute to a foreign power, which Judas had boldly declared to be not merely a base compromise of the national independence, but an injurious infringement of the first principles of their theocracy. But the independence, if not the universal dominion of the Jews, was inseparably bound up with the popular belief in the Messiah. Jesus, then, would either, on the question of the lawfulness of tribute to Cæsar, confirm the bolder doctrines of the Galilæan, and so convict Himself before the Romans as one of that dangerous faction ; or He would admit its legality, and so cancel at once all His claim to the character of the Messiah."

IV. *Scribes ; Lawyers.* These are very generally confounded, as if they were identical, as being merely different names for the same persons. It seems, however, from S. Luke xi. 44–46, that they were not quite identical. It has been supposed that the " scribe " was an official and formal designation ; whilst the " lawyer " was one who was eminently learned in the law, and was an honourable distinction amongst those who were generally designated " scribes."

The office of scribe was an ancient one. They appear to have been of three classes. In the earlier ages of the theocracy, we find them (i.) secretaries of the king's court, and therefore officers of state ; and, again (ii.), officers who kept the muster roll of armies ; but the scribe of our Lord's day was of a different kind, namely (iii.), a writer, classifier, and also an expounder of the law. Some of these were men of great excellence ; as Baruch and Ezra, in ancient times ; and the young scribe of S. Mark xii. 28 (called a " lawyer " in S. Matt. xxii. 35), who brought his question concerning the great commandment to our Lord. In the N. T. we find " the scribes and Pharisees " so closely connected, that we might almost identify them. A Pharisee, however, might be a scribe ; but it was not necessary that the scribe should belong to the sect of the Pharisees. The scribes were a most important body amongst the rulers of the nation ; their professional acquaintance, not only with the law generally, but with the very letter, with even the number of direct and indirect precepts, and with divisions and subdivisions too intricate to follow, gave them great influence. After a long line of great doctors, there came at last to be two principal and rival schools amongst them : those who followed Shammai, who represented the exclusiveness and narrowness, the essence of Phariseeism ; and those who followed Hillel, who was, perhaps, the greatest and best of the Jewish doctors—a man of acute thought, and liberal mind; who gave a regard to the spirit of the law which was truly remarkable, and whose freedom of thought, and breadth of mind, gave to his teaching a forecast of the liberal and genial teaching of Christianity. We may well suppose that the scribes of the former school would be conspicuously opposed to Christianity ; whilst those of the latter would give a more kindly attention to our Lord, and approach Him with deference and respect. And thus we find scribes of the Pharisees' party identical in aim with them ; and also individual scribes of a better class, "not far from the kingdom of heaven," in the more liberal spirit which characterized them.

It was his worship of the letter of the law, to the neglect of its spirit, which brought the scribe into conflict with Christ. It was impossible not to venerate the calling and office of men, to whose devotion to the purity of the text, was owing, under God, the preservation of the ancient Scriptures in their integrity, whose life was spent in teaching and expounding these holy writings. But on the other hand, there is something childish and ridiculous, as compared with the magnitude of their charge, in their counting up, not only books, sections, and paragraphs, but also the number of letters contained in these, and the number of letters contained in the word of God. The Saviour, who "will have mercy and not sacrifice," whose teaching lay "in the spirit, rather than in the letter" of the truth, could not keep terms with a school which had degenerated into idolatry of the letter, which they held with the grossest hypocrisy of life. Far better to be of the thoughtful amongst the heathen, who conscientiously kept to the law of God, "written in their hearts," than of those of the scribes, who could number clause, precept, and letter of the divine oracles, and yet in their hypocrisy denied them ; and in their daily life outraged the holy sanctions of the law committed to them "by the disposition of angels." Christianity might draw the former to the truth, but with the latter there was deadly antagonism.

V. *Sanhedrim.* The origin of this great council of the Jews has been traced by themselves to the days of the seventy elders who were nominated to assist Moses. It can scarcely, however, be proved that that original council continued to exist through the ages of Jewish history, especially under the kings; but if not, there is little doubt that that original council decided the number, and, to a great extent, the office, of the revived Sanhedrim.

It consisted of seventy-one members, who were chosen men

amongst the sects of the Jews, the scribes, and chief priests, *i.e.* the heads of the twenty-four courses of the priesthood. The council was, to a certain extent, administrative ; but it was, very especially, a council of appeal and decision upon religious points, with vast powers of discipline in connection with these. It is said that the power of life and death was taken from the Sanhedrim by the Romans, about forty years before the destruction of Jerusalem ; that is, about three years before the crucifixion. The Talmud is the authority for the statement ; and it agrees with the declaration of the Jews to Pilate, " It is not lawful for us to put any man to death." The instances of the death of Stephen, and of James, are explained as ebullitions of popular fury, in violation of the law, a fury which the rulers well knew when and how to excite. Josephus (" Antiq." xx. 9, 1) directly asserts that the murder of James was a " breach of the laws ; " but the question is involved in too much uncertainty to be easy of decision.

That this great council included Pharisees and Sadducees, Herodians, scribes, and lawyers, is a sufficient proof of its antagonism to Christ. But it is not easy to understand the littleness, malevolence, and murderous intentions with which they deliberately assembled for the suppression of the Gospel ; and for the assassination, and, when that seemed inexpedient, judicial murder of our Lord, whom they all knew to be holy, just, and true, and that He had come from God.

This malevolence makes the history of the Sanhedrim an utterly distasteful subject to all lovers of justice ; and deprives it of that interest which would otherwise belong to a council so venerable, having such prescriptive claims to respect, and before which Christ was arraigned.

No. III.

On i. 29 ; II. ii. 4.

RETICENCE OF JOSEPHUS CONCERNING CHRIST.

The singular reserve of Josephus with regard to the advent of Christ, and the progress of Christianity, has been much noticed. It is, indeed, strange that an historian of so much candour and truthfulness, possessing so many qualifications for giving an impartial account of what was so chief an event of the period of history with which he was contemporary, should so slightly mention this event, as almost to pass it over in silence ; in so entire silence, in fact, as to throw suspicion on the genuineness of the simple passage in which he does directly mention Christ.

We must take it for granted that his silence was intentional. It is impossible that he could possess less information than Roman historians, or that he could accidentally pass over so important a fact of history. It is likely that the spread of Christianity in Judæa itself, in the interval between our Lord's ascension and the destruction of Jerusalem, did not attract any very considerable attention, when contrasted with the disturbed condition of the country ; and we know that Josephus himself was prominently occupied in these troubles. But still it had made very decided progress ; there were Christians throughout the length and breadth of the land. The fact of their conforming at first to the outward observances of the ceremonial law, did not really conceal their separation by their faith from the rest of the nation ; it did not give them the character of being merely a sect of the Jews. It is impossible, therefore, that their peculiar tenets should have escaped the observation of Josephus. And it is most unlikely that he could have been wholly ignorant of the prophecies of Christ which they held, and which enabled them to avoid all the miseries which fell upon their country-men through the Romans.

This silence of Josephus is the more strange, as he so invariably ascribes the miseries which befel the Jews to the direct agency of God, who employed the Roman arm to punish the iniquity of the nation. He even ascribes (on the quotation of several of the early writers) the overthrow of the nation to the punishment which God sent upon them for the murder of James : " These miseries befel the Jews by way of revenge for James the Just, who was the brother of Jesus that was called Christ ; because they had slain him, who was a most righteous person." It is indeed most extra-ordinary that he should thus consider the murder of James, whilst passing over that of Jesus ; whom he merely names, thus showing that he was not ignorant of His history. In the same way, he says (" Antiq." xviii. 5, 2) that " some of the Jews thought that the destruction of Herod's army came from God, and that very justly, as a punishment for what he did against John, that was called the Baptist ; for Herod slew him, who was a good man," etc. With how much greater reason might he not have ascribed these calamities to the fulfilment of our Lord's own predictions, that God would avenge His death and rejection upon that generation of the nation. A man so observant and thoughtful could not possibly have overlooked this consequence, and could scarcely have been unaware of the predictions.

The passage (" Antiq." xviii. 3, 3) in which Josephus directly mentions Christ is a striking one ; and there appears to be fair grounds for accepting it as authentic. Probably it would never have been questioned, but for its decisive character, as contrasted with the historian's otherwise uniform reticence on the subject of Christ. The passage in question has been criticized by Paley (" Evidences," i. 7), whose remarks are valuable. He says, " In a passage extant in every copy that remains of Josephus's history, but the authenticity of which has been long disputed, we have explicit testimony to the substance of our history in these words, ' At that time lived Jesus, a wise man, if it be lawful to call Him a man, for He performed many wonderful works. He was a teacher of such men as received the truth with pleasure. He drew over to Him both many of the Jews and many of the Gentiles. This was the Christ. And when Pilate, at the instigation of the chief men among us, had condemned Him to the cross, they who before had conceived an affection for Him, did not cease to adhere to Him ; for, on the third day, He appeared alive again, the divine prophets having foretold these and many wonderful things concerning Him. And the sect of the Christians, so called from Him, subsists to this time.' "

Paley strongly contends either that the passage is genuine, or that the silence of Josephus is designed ; it being impossible that he could be ignorant of facts which the contemporary Roman historians Tacitus and Suetonius refer to distinctly. He also aptly instances in support of his own view a similar silence of the Mishna (A.D. 180), the Jerusalem Talmud (A.D. 300), and the Babylonian Talmud (A.D. 500).

Designed silence, or even the meagreness of the notice above given, argues that Josephus was full of Jewish prejudices so far as Christians were concerned ; and that, as he did not see the extent of their progress, or foresee the certainty of their triumph, he passed them over in the contemptuous silence of a foe who was assured they would eventually come to nought, but who was too fair, truthful, and impartial to circulate error or falsehood concerning them.

Whiston, however, takes a different view : he declares his firm belief that the passage above quoted, supported by the credit assigned to it by so many of the early writers, is genuine. He cites the evidence of Origen (who says that Josephus did not believe in Jesus as Christ), Eusebius, Higisippus, Jerome, Isidorus, Sozomen, within the first five centuries ; and many more of later date, who (except Origen) quote the passage *verbatim*. But he asserts that Josephus was a Nazarene, or Ebionite Christian, who, like those in Acts xxi. 20, believed in Christ, but without considering that He was more than a man, and who held the necessity of observing the ceremonial law ; and that he held these views secretly, and therefore could not draw attention to Christianity by detailing the progress of the new faith. If his " Discourse to the Greeks concerning Hades" is genuine, this view receives direct refutation ; because he thus quotes sayings of Christ, whom he names as " God the Word," and the Universal Judge. He would, therefore, not have been an Ebionite, but an orthodox Christian.

But the view of Origen seems more probable : at the date he wrote (A.D. 230) he must have heard of tradition of the views held

by Josephus, had he been even an Ebionite Christian; and it
seems natural that a man in high esteem amongst the Romans
(who had not yet taken any active part, as yet, for the suppression
of Christianity, but who were rather treating it with a contemptuous indifference,) should not much concern himself with the progress of a religion which the Romans let alone at the time, and
which, perhaps for the very reason that the Jews persecuted it,
they allowed to develop itself. Whilst, on the other hand, the
absorption of Josephus in Jewish politics blinded him to the earlier
advances of the new faith, and his Jewish prejudices affected to
ignore it. He had nothing to say against it; his integrity forbade
his slandering it; but he did his best to bury it in silence, the
subject being neither an interesting one to his Roman patrons, nor
a welcome one to the Jewish readers of his history.

No. IV.

On iii. 2; xviii. 3.

THE TEMPLE.

The following extract from Dean Milman's "History of the Jews,"
Book xvi., which describes the Temple as it stood at the time of
the destruction of Jerusalem, is so graphic and so full of details of
interest, that no apology is necessary for its insertion :—

"High above the whole city rose the Temple, uniting the commanding strength of a citadel with the splendour of a sacred edifice.
According to Josephus, the esplanade on which it stood had been
considerably enlarged by the accumulation of fresh soil, since the
days of Solomon, particularly on the north side. It now covered
a square of a furlong each side. Solomon had faced the precipitous
sides of the rock on the east, and perhaps the south, with huge
blocks of stone; the lower sides likewise had been built up with
perpendicular walls to an equal height. These walls in no part
were lower than 300 cubits, 525 feet; but their whole height was
not seen excepting on the eastern and perhaps the southern sides,
as the earth was heaped up to the level of the streets of the city.
Some of the stones employed in this work were of the size of 70
feet, probably, in length.

"On this gigantic foundation ran on each front a strong and
lofty wall without; within, a spacious double portico or cloister
52½ feet broad, supported by 162 columns, which supported a cedar
ceiling of the most exquisite workmanship. The pillars were entire
blocks hewn out of solid marble, of dazzling whiteness, 43¾ feet
high. On the south side the portico or cloister was triple.

" This quadrangle had but one gate to the east, one to the north, two to the south, four to the west ; one of these led to the palace, one to the city, one at the corner to the Antonia, one down towards the gardens.

" The open courts were paved with various inlaid marbles. Between this outer court of the Gentiles, and the second court of the Israelites, ran rails of stone, but of beautiful workmanship, rather more than five feet high. Along these, at regular intervals, stood pillars with inscriptions in Hebrew, Greek, and Latin, warning all strangers, and Jews who were unclean, from entering into the Holy Court beyond. An ascent of 14 steps led to a terrace $17\frac{1}{2}$ feet wide, beyond which rose the wall of the Inner Court. This wall appeared on the outside 70 feet, on the inside $43\frac{3}{4}$; for, besides the ascent of 14 steps to the terrace, there were five more up to the gates. The Inner Court had no gate or opening to the west, but four on the north, and four on the south, two to the east ; one of which was for the women, for whom a portion of the Inner Court was set apart, and beyond which they might not advance ; to this they had access by one of the northern, and one of the southern gates, which were set apart for their use. Around this court ran another splendid range of porticoes or cloisters : the columns were quite equal in beauty and workmanship, though not in size to those of the outer portico. Nine of these gates, or rather gateway towers, were richly adorned with gold and silver on the doors, the door posts, and the lintels. The doors of each of the nine gates were $52\frac{1}{2}$ feet high, and half that breadth. Within, the gateways were $52\frac{1}{2}$ feet wide and deep, with rooms on each side, so that the whole looked like lofty towers : the height from the base to the summit was 70 feet. Each gateway had two lofty pillars 21 feet in circumference. But that which excited the greatest admiration was the tenth, usually called the Beautiful Gate of the Temple. It was of Corinthian brass of the finest workmanship. The height of the Beautiful Gate was $87\frac{1}{2}$ feet, its doors 70 feet. The father of Tiberius Alexander had sheeted these gates with gold and silver ; his apostate son was to witness their ruin by the plundering hands and fiery torches of his Roman friends. Within this quadrangle there was a further separation ; a low wall which divided the priests from the Israelites : near this stood the great brazen altar. The great porch or Propyleon, according to the design of the last, or Herod's Temple, extended to a much greater width than the body of the Temple ; in addition to the former width of 105 feet, it had two wings of 35 each, making, in the whole, 175. The great gate of this last quadrangle, to which there was an ascent of twenty steps, was called that of Nicanor. The gateway tower was $132\frac{1}{2}$ feet high, $43\frac{1}{2}$ wide ; it had no doors, but the frontispiece was covered with gold, and through its spacious arch was seen the golden gate of the Temple, glittering with the same precious metal, with large plates

of which it was sheeted all over. Above this gate hung the celebrated golden vine. This extraordinary piece of workmanship had
bunches, according to Josephus, as large as a man. The Rabbins
add that, ' like a true natural vine, it grew greater and greater ; men
would be offering, some, gold, to make a leaf, some a grape, some
a bunch : and these were hung up upon it, and so it was increasing
continually.'

"The Temple itself, excepting in the extension of the wings of the
Propyleon, was probably the same in its dimensions and distribu-
tion with that of Solomon. It contained the same holy treasures,
if not of equal magnificence, yet by the zeal of successive ages the
frequent plunder to which it had been exposed was constantly
replaced ; and within, the golden candlestick spread out its flowering branches ; the golden table supported the shewbread ; and the
altar of incense flamed with its costly perfume. The roof of the
Temple had been set all over on the outside with sharp golden
spikes to prevent the birds from settling, and defiling the roof ;
and the gates were still sheeted with plates of the same splendid
metal.   At a distance the whole Temple looked literally like ' a
mount of snow, fretted with golden pinnacles.'

"Looking down upon its marble courts, and on the Temple itself,
when the sun rose above the Mount of Olives, which it directly
faced, it was impossible, even for a Roman, not to be struck with
wonder, or even for a Stoic, like Titus, not to betray his emotion.
Yet this was the city which in a few months was to lie a heap of
undistinguished ruins ; and the solid Temple itself, which seemed
built for eternity, not ' to have one stone left upon another.'"
(See also Appendix X.; Josephus's " Description of the Temple,"
" Wars," v. 5.)

In contrast with the above account of what the Temple was we
may quote the latest description of its site, so far as modern research has investigated it, from the " Recovery of Jerusalem," by
Capt. Wilson, R.E., and Capt. Warren, R.E. :—

" On Mount Moriah there is now a large open space called
Haram-esh-Sherif. Its surface is studded with cypress and olive,
and its sides are surrounded in part by the finest mural masonry
in the world.   At the southern end is the mosque El Aksa, and a
pile of buildings formerly used by the Knights Templars : nearly in
the centre is a raised platform paved with stone, and rising from
this is the well-known mosque Kubbet-es-Sakhra, with its beautifully proportioned dome. Within this sacred enclosure, the
Sanctuary, as we may call it, stood the Temple of the Jews : all
traces of it have long since disappeared, not one stone has been left
upon another, and its exact position has for years been one of the
most fiercely contested points in Jerusalem topography. The two
theories which have obtained the largest number of supporters are—
first, that which makes the Temple enclosure co-extensive with the

Sanctuary; and, second, that which confines it to a space of 600 feet at the south-western corner of the same place. It is still uncertain which of these two views is correct, and the question can hardly be definitely settled till excavations are made within the Haram walls. On one point all are agreed, that the magnificent triple cloister, the Stoa Basilica, built by Herod, stood on the top of the southern wall, and the appearance of this when perfect must have been grander than anything we know of elsewhere. It is almost impossible to realize the effect which would be produced by a building longer and higher than York Cathedral, standing on a solid mass of masonry almost equal in height to the tallest of our church spires; and to this we must add the dazzling whiteness of stone fresh from the masons' hands."

Beneath the dome of the Sakhra rises a very extraordinary rock; its dimensions are 60 × 50 feet, and its height about 5 feet above the pavement; there is an excavated chamber on the south-eastern corner; in the centre of the chamber there is a slab of marble which seems to mark the mouth of a well. It is disputed whether this rock was that of the Holy of Holies, or that of the threshing-floor of Araunah; or the site of the Great Altar: Fergusson and others declare it the real rock of the Holy Sepulchre. There are also other legends and theories concerning it. See Dean Stanley's "Sinai and Palestine," ch. iii., which says, "This mass of rocks standing where it does must always have been an unaccountable disfigurement of the Temple area. The time for arriving at a positive conclusion concerning it is not yet come. . . . Meanwhile the rock remains, whatever be its origin, the most curious monument of old Jerusalem." (See App. XV. 3.)

No. V.

On iv. 6; xxv. c. 10, 27, e. 26.

THE STEPS OF PRAYER.

The subject of Prayer is one which demands very close attention. It is so immediately allied to that of faith, that we only really understand it in proportion as we possess faith. All men have a general impression concerning it; and at stated times, and on special emergencies, are ready to resort to prayer. But in days when there is so much in the duty of life to distract the mind, when there is so little leisure for abstraction and meditation, when the practical character of the age is apt to give a certain indistinctness and distance to matters of faith, it is increasingly necessary to study the subject of Prayer, and not to rest content with any superficial impression concerning what is so prominent and important in Holy Scripture.

Those fathers of the world's faith whose names stand out like beacons towards the darkness of the ages, in the pages of the Old Testament, were men of simple lives, of astonishing faith, and of earnest prayer; and thus it was that, as princes, they had power with God and prevailed. The customs and habits of their lives may separate them much from ourselves, surrounded as we are by conditions of life so entirely distinct; but they were men of like passions with ourselves: human nature is not different in these our days from what it was in theirs; and therefore, had we their faith, and their prayerful spirit, we should certainly show our spiritual descent as worthy children of those "who through faith and patience inherit the promises."

In the New Testament this subject does not merely present itself to us as illustrated by the lives of eminent servants of God : nor is it only a matter of precept and promise; it is placed before us in no mere outline, as being one of those spiritual truths which are hereafter to be defined to us. It has been gathered into a *regular system* by our Lord, and His apostles. There are its various stages, aspects, and powers distinctly defined before us. The steps by which its importance increases are worthy of very special notice and observation; for not only our full intelligence of the Spirit of Christ's Gospel, but also the direction and success of our lives, depend upon it. These steps are noted here, so far as they may be gathered from the Gospels; they culminate in the interests of the Holy Week. It must be left to the reader who is minded to give attention to the subject of Prayer, as a study, to continue the details where they pass beyond the scope of this work, into the writings of the Apostles.

Early in our Lord's ministry the disciples noticed the stress He laid upon the importance of Prayer; and, after thought and observation, it appears to have struck them that, as in the instance of John and his disciples, the use of a common formula of prayer might be a band of association and unity amongst themselves. Our Lord was prompt to respond to the intelligence of the disciples in this matter : and not only did He teach them a form of common prayer, but, throughout His teaching, He continued to unfold the mysteries, properties, and powers attached to prayer, and dependent on its right use, until the doctrine concerning it was completed in the solemn revelations of the Holy Week.

We may trace the steps of this teaching as follows, taking them chronologically as they occur in the order of the Gospels; and this will make plain to us what we might otherwise not fully perceive, how much of the gospel of Christ depends upon Prayer.

I. *First Year of our Lord's Ministry (i.e. A.D. 28).*

1. The water of life may be had in answer to the prayer of those intelligent of the gift asked for ; a general rule with regard to prayer (S. John iv. 10).

2. Prayer must be sincere, "in spirit and in truth" (S. John iv. 24).

3. The disciples notice that, preparatory to Christ's preaching in Galilee, "in the morning, rising up a great while before day, He went out, and departed into a solitary place, and there prayed" (S. Mark i. 35).

4. Once again, during the same tour, "He withdrew Himself into the wilderness, and prayed" (S. Luke v. 16).

5. Before the solemn choosing of the Twelve Apostles, He "went into a mountain apart to pray, and continued all night in prayer to God" (S. Luke vi. 12).

6. In the Sermon on the Mount, which contains the principles of the Gospel, He gives direct teaching on this point, on which He had before impressed His example on the disciples. Prayer must not be, like that of the hypocrites, for the eye of man ; but solitary, private, apart from the world, alone with God; there must be no "vain repetitions ;" no trust in the length, and eloquence, of prayer ; for "much speaking" they would not be the better heard (cf. Eccles. v. 1, 2) by God, who knows beforehand the necessity which He desires us to express in plain and direct terms ; and therefore in the Lord's House, in the midst of the congregation, it must be abstracted, the heart must be with God (S. Matt. vi. 5–8).

7. The Lord's Prayer is given—1. As the exact words in which prayer should be addressed to God, who recognises, in the comprehensive words of the Son, the intention of His will; and gives answer according to the breadth of that will, rather than to the narrow conception of it possible to him who uses the Prayer. 2. As a model of private prayers, and of public liturgical forms, in which the intimate connection and dependence of the life that is to come upon the life that now is, is kept in prominence (S. Matt. vi. 9–13).

8. The use of prayer is coupled with the condition of forgivingness, on the part of him that prays : and if that condition is complied with, the promise of God's forgiveness of the sins of him that forgives and prays, is added (S. Matt. vi. 14, 15).

9. And further direct exhortation to prayer is given, with promise of success ; and an argument proposed from the readiness of parents of earth to give good gifts to their children, to the far greater readiness of the Heavenly Father, in His absolute goodness (S. Matt. vii. 7–11).

10. There is, however, coupled with this promise, a condition similar to that of No. 7, that we should do unto others as we would

they should do unto us ; the teaching, in brief, both of all that the Law commanded, and that the prophets exhorted (S. Matt. vii. 12).

11. But not the mere saying " Lord, Lord" of nominal profession and formality shall gain entrance for us to heaven, now by petition, afterwards in person ; but actions must correspond with profession, we must do as we say (S. Matt. vii. 21).

Nos. 6–11 have a particular emphasis, as they are included in the Sermon on the Mount.

II. *The Second Year of our Lord's Ministry (i.e. A.D. 29).*

12. After the first miracle of the loaves, and before His circuit through the land of Gennesaret, we read, " When He had sent the multitude away, He went up into a mountain apart to pray, and when the evening was come He was there alone" (S. Matt. xiv. 23).

13. Immediately before the Transfiguration, " He took Peter, and John, and James, and went up into a mountain to pray : and as He prayed, the fashion of His countenance was altered," etc. (S. Luke ix. 28, 29).

On this occasion, and again in the Garden of Gethsemane, we find Him taking these disciples apart for the special purpose of prayer ; as if, before any great crisis in connection with the interests of His kingdom, the united prayer of several might win the grace required. On both occasions those with Him perceived the presence of heavenly visitants.

14. Prayer, and fasting with prayer, are necessary, preparatory to great enterprises, especially to the removal of spiritual power in opposition (S. Matt. xvii. 19–21 ; S. Mark ix. 28, 29).

15. Promise of success in united prayer, and also of Christ's presence amongst those gathered in prayer, whether in the service of common prayer in the House of God, or in the more private assembly of those who meet to pray for any special purpose. " If two of you shall agree on earth as touching anything that they shall ask, it shall be done for them of My Father which is in heaven. For where two or three are gathered together in My Name, there am I in the midst of them " (S. Matt. xviii. 19, 20).

16. United prayer on the part of those associated in purpose for the propagation of Christ's faith necessary before their entering on any missionary enterprise ; the promise, objects, purpose of their enterprise, being clearly defined to their own mind (S. Luke x. 1, 2).

17. Christ's prayer of thanksgiving on the return of the Seventy with joy that their ministry of preparation for His advent had been accredited by God : an example for those who receive the report of men sent forth by them on similar service in their Lord's behalf (S. Luke x. 21).

18. A very important stage is now reached ; the disciples have

learnt the value of our Lord's practice, and have pondered the instruction He has already given on the subject of united prayer ; they have also observed the strength and unity which the disciples of John attained through the possession of a common form of prayer ; they are becoming fit to receive the revelation so soon to be made, that prayer prevails not only when it is a bond of unity amongst themselves, but when it is such a bond of unity also with Christ. The truth concerning the value of a common prayer (perhaps also with some perception that it would constitute a tie of union with Him,) seems to dawn on them, or at least to find expression when Christ " was praying in a certain place, and when He ceased, one of His disciples said unto Him, ' Lord, teach us to pray, as John also taught his disciples.' " He now repeats that comprehensive form which He had before given (see No. 7) as the Christian's prayer, to whom it is for ever consecrated as the "Lord's Prayer." We must notice that the response made to the disciples' request on this occasion is warrant that our Lord will teach the hearts of those who ask how to pray suitably and successfully according to His will (S. Luke xi. 1–4).

19. He adds, to this formal delivery of the Lord's Prayer, no injunction to use " vain repetitions " of it as has been done in the number of *Paternosters* prescribed by the Western Church, but rather an exhortation to perseverance in prayer " in season and out of season." This is given in the parable of the friend desiring three loaves at midnight (S. Luke xi. 5–8).

20. He then, with infinite solemnity, repeats the general injunction to prayer before given (No. 9), and He closes the argument used there in a slightly different way ; He before said that if men, being evil, know how to give good gifts to their children, much more would their Heavenly Father give good gifts to them that ask Him ; He now sums up these " good gifts " in the supreme gift of " the Holy Spirit " (S. Luke xi. 9–13).

21. The success of prayers of intercession is assured in the same parable in which our Lord teaches us that His prayer of intercession comes between the sinner and the stroke of doom, so long as there is hope of repentance and amendment ; the parable of the fruitless fig tree (S. Luke xiii. 6–9).

III. *The Third Year of our Lord's Ministry (i.e. A.D. 30).*

22. Warning against prayer too late " when once the master of the house is risen up, and hath shut to the door (S. Luke xiii. 25 ; cf. S. Matt. xxv. 10–13).

23. The parable of the prodigal son teaches the value and gracious acceptance of prayers of repentance, whilst Christ is still looking out for the return of the sinner, and has not shut to the door (S. Luke xv. 21–24).

24. The lesson of No. 19 is enforced in the parable of the importunate widow, with an explanation of the seeming hesitation or delay in according answer to prayers, being really an incentive to urgency (S. Luke xviii. 1–8).

25. The subject receives a most important light in the parable of the Pharisee and the publican. Prayers of penitence must be humble, must be a confession of sin, with purpose of amendment of life ; must be offered in faith also, and in hope. Thanksgiving must not be of self-satisfaction, of contempt of others, of want of reverence for God ; but of grateful acknowledgment of His bounty. And the rule is a general one, for every one that either humbleth himself, or exalteth himself (S. Luke xviii. 9–14).

26. The miracle of the healing of blind Bartimæus teaches us that it is not enough to cry " Have mercy on us, O Lord ! " even to One " who knows all our necessities before we ask ; " but He will have definite requests for particular gifts expressed in exact terms ; expressed therefore clearly to our own mind, and before Him. If we then pray for the thing we want, our prayer shall be attended to (S. Mark x. 46–52).

IV. *The Holy Week.*

27. Prohibition of all profanation of God's House of Prayer, or even of making any common use of it, however such a use may be for the convenience of the worshippers. " The place where prayer is wont to be made " is guarded, that there may be no distractions of mind to occupy the thoughts of those who come into the House of God to offer the sacrifice of prayer and praise (S. Mark. xi. 15–19).

28. A most emphatic assurance of the success which faith entails on prayer : and a repetition of the condition of forgiveness (S. Matt. xxi. 21, 22 ; S. Mark xi. 24–26).

29. Condemnation of the long prayers of pretence and ostentation of the hypocrite (S. Matt. xxiii. 14).

30. Prayer encouraged for the mitigation of God's judgments, especially when the righteous are involved in the temporal dangers, which the wickedness of their Church or nation draws down : success to such prayers is promised (S. Matt. xxiv. 20, 22 ; S. Mark xiii. 18, 20).

31. Watchfulness and prayer should be constant on the part of those who are surrounded with temptations, and upon whom the Advent of the Lord may come unprepared (S. Mark xiii. 33–37 ; S. Luke xxi. 36).

32. It is incidentally noticed that it was Christ's habit during this week to retire to the Mount of Olives at night ; and, from previous notices of this habit of His, we know that it was *for* prayer (S. Luke xxi. 37).

33. Prayer must be offered *in the name of Christ :* and the most unqualified promise is given that such prayer shall be granted (S. John xiv. 13, 14).

34. The Comforter is given, at the intercession of Christ, to those who keep His commandments (S. John xiv. 16).

35. The doctrine of union with Christ, so vital that separation must entail the death of the spiritual life, is applied to the subject of prayer.   In this union, which is one of spiritual life, and of will, the success of prayer is absolute within the provision of that will (S. John xv. 7).

36. The fruit of such prayer in Christ's Name is permanent (S. John xv. 16).

37. From the date of Christ's departure there will be no personal inquiry, as when Christ was present on earth to answer orally ; but prayer should be made to the Father in His Name ; and acceptance is promised, and the joy of those who receive their requests shall be added (S. John xvi. 23, 24).

38. Christ's Prayer of Intercession (S. John xvii. 1–26).   (See I. xxvi. notes.)

39. Prayer against temptation, with the illustration of Christ's example, a general command to His disciples (S. Matt. xxvi. 36 ; S. Mark xiv. 32 ; S. Luke xxii. 40).

40. The same commands specially given to SS. Peter, James, and John, with the revelation of Christ's agony in prayer, His thrice-repeated agony.   The key-note " more earnestly," as struck in the Liturgy of the Church, in the words, "let us pray," while prayer *is* proceeding, should be that of private prayer (S. Matt. xxvi. 37–46 ; S. Mark xiv. 33–42 ; S. Luke xxii. 41–46).

41.   Prayers of the dying :

        (*a*).   Christ's prayer of forgiveness (S. Luke xxiii. 34).

        (*b*).   The penitent malefactor's prayer of contrition and faith (S. Luke xxiii. 42).

        (*c*).   Christ's prayer in sorrow for the restoration of God's presence (S. Matt. xxvii. 46 ; S. Mark xv. 34).

        (*d*).   Christ's prayer of commendation of His soul into the hands of God (S. Luke xxiii. 46).

It should be noted that the division of the years of our Lord's ministry above specified is not that usually computed by the Passovers : but, as is more convenient for this particular purpose, by the years A.D. of His ministry.

It may be further suggested that the above method of working out and bringing into prominence the systematic proportions of any other leading feature of Christ's Gospel, in its gradual revelations through the successive years of His ministry, would be a study of great profit : such, for instance, as faith, forgiveness, unity, union with Christ, and other subjects.

No. VI.

On viii. 34 ; xiii. 20 ; xiv. 21 ; xvi. 13 ; xx. 26 ; xxv. *d.* 3.

RULES OF THE KINGDOM.

There are a number of brief sententious sayings of our Lord, scattered throughout the Gospels, which appear to bear the character of general rules, because we find them in a variety of applications, and differently illustrated ; or else delivered on different occasions to enforce the same truth.   There are many other sayings of the same sententious or proverbial cast, but which are not thus diversely illustrated, and which therefore scarcely bear the same character.   A list of many of these sentences, which may be fairly called " Rules of the Kingdom of Christ," is here subjoined ; and a comparison of the passages will show how, in their several applications, they are equally decisive ; and we may thence gather that it is our Lord's will they should be considered as His decisions on many other points to which they may be justly applied.

The subject of these *rules* is one of great importance : and the author hopes, at some future time, to be permitted to take them up as a separate study ; and to work out their bearing upon the doctrines of Christianity at greater length than is possible here.

I. Repentance must precede the Gospel message.
    1. Of John the Baptist (S. Matt. iii. 2, 8, 11 ; S. Mark i. 4 ; S. Luke, iii. 3–8 ; [Acts xiii. 24 ; xix. 4]).
    2. Of Christ (S. Matt. iv. 17 ; S. Mark i. 15).
    3. Of the ministers of Christ (S. Matt. x. 7 ; S. Mark vi. 12 ; [Acts xvii. 30, 31]).

II. " Every tree that bringeth not forth good fruit," &c.
    1. Of repentance in days of decision (S. Matt. iii. 10).
    2. Of a religious life (S. Matt. vii. 19 ; S. Luke xiii. 7, 9).
    3. Of severance from Christ (S. John xv. 6).

III. Entrance at the strait gate (S. Matt. vii. 13, 14 ; S. Luke xiii. 24).

IV. " If the salt have lost his savour wherewith shall it be salted ? "
    1. Of Christian teachers (S. Matt. v. 10 ; S. Mark ix. 50).
    2. Of the preservation of a right faith (S. Luke xiv. 34, 35).

V. The right eye, hand, or foot offending, must be severed from the body.
    1. Of natural impediments to individual faith (S. Matt. v. 29, 30).
    2. Of causing impediments to the faith of others (S. Matt. xviii. 8, 9 ; S. Mark ix. 43–47).

VI. " Ask and it shall be given you," etc.
    1. Of prayer simply (S. Matt. vii. 7).
    2. Of special prayer with faith (S. Matt. xxi. 22).
    3. Of importunate prayer (S. Luke xi. 9, 10).
    4. Of prayer in Christ's name (S. John xiv. 13).
    5. Of prayer in union with Christ (S. John xv. 7).
    6. Of prayer offered in the world, through the name of Christ, subsequent to His ascension (S. John xvi. 23, 24).

We notice here, step by step, the expansion of the terms, conditions, and scope of the original simple command and promise. (See App. v.)

VII. " Lord, Lord, open to us."
    1. Such a petition is useless as a mere profession of claim, without the fruit of obedience to prove it (S. Matt. vii. 21 ; S. Luke vi. 46).
    2. May be offered too late (S. Matt. xxv. 11, 12 ; S. Luke xiii. 25).

VIII. " Follow me."
    1. As disciples in life's duties (S. Matt. iv. 19, ix. 9 ; S. Mark ii. 14 ; S. Luke v. 27 ; S. John i. 43).
    2. Notwithstanding natural obstacles (S. Matt. viii. 22 ; S. Luke ix. 59, 62).
    3. Through self-denial (S. Matt. xvi. 24; S. Mark viii. 34 ; S. Luke ix. 23).
    4. In abandonment of the world (S. Mark x. 21).
    5. To the death (S. John xii. 24–25 ; xxi. 19–22).

IX. " I will have mercy and not sacrifice."
    1. Of inviting the sinner to repentance (S. Matt. ix. 13 [see also Hos. vi. 6 ; Micah vi. 6-8]).
    2. Of interpretation of the rules of religion, by the spirit, and not by the letter (S. Matt. xii. 7).

X. " Thy faith hath saved thee."
    1. Of faith in miraculous mercy (S. Matt. ix. 22 ; S. Mark v. 34, x. 52 ; S. Luke viii. 48, xviii. 42).
    2. Of faith on the part of those who brought others to Christ ; or who approached Him with intercession or supplication on behalf of others (S. Matt. viii. 10, ix. 2, xv. 28 ; S. Mark ii. 5 ; S. Luke v. 20, vii. 9. See also S. Matt. xix. 13, 14 ; S. Mark x. 13–15 ; S. Luke xviii. 15–17).
    3. Of faith for forgivenness of sins (S. Luke vii. 50. See also S. Matt. ix. 2 ; S. Mark ii. 5 ; S. Luke v. 20).
    4. Of faith followed by thanksgiving, on the realization of a blessing (S. Luke xvii. 19).

XI. Taking up the cross.

1. In the following of Christ (S. Matt. x. 38 ; xvi. 24 ; S. Mark viii. 34).
2. In the abandonment of the world (S. Mark x. 21).
3. In abandonment of domestic obstacles (S. Luke xiv. 26, 27).
4. To the death (S. Luke ix. 22, 23).

XII. Finding and losing life.
1. In the duties of discipleship (S. Matt. x. 39, xvi. 25).
2. In days of peril and decision (S. Luke xvii. 33).
3. In martyrdom (S. John xii. 24, 25).

XIII. " He that receiveth you receiveth Me," etc.
1. In the name of a disciple (S. Matt. x. 40, 41).
2. For His message' sake (S. Luke x. 16).
3. As an apostle or preacher (S. John xiii. 20).
4. Though but a child (S. Matt. x. 42, xviii. 5, xxv. 40 ; S. Luke ix. 48).
5. Reward even of the cup of cold water given (S. Matt. x. 42 ; S. Mark ix. 41).

XIV. Confessing and denying Christ.
1. Of disciples (S. Matt. x. 32 ; S. Luke xii. 8, 9).
2. Before the world (S. Mark viii. 38).

XV. " He that hath ears to hear let him hear."
1. Of the concurrent voice of prophecy (S. Matt. xi. 15).
2. Of the parable of the sower (S. Matt. xiii. 9-43 ; S. Mark iv. 9 ; S. Luke viii. 8).
3. Of defilement, not in external things, but in the heart (S. Mark vii. 16).

XVI. " Whosoever hath, to him shall be given," etc.
1. Of knowledge in the mysteries of God (S. Matt. xiii. 11).
2. Of talents and opportunities in God's service (S. Matt. xxv. 29; S. Luke xix. 26).
3. Of the measure of hearing God's word (S. Mark iv. 25 ; S. Luke viii. 18).

XVII. Prophecy of Esaias concerning wilful and judicial blindness.
1. Of the closing of the Word of God (S. Matt. xiii. 14, 15 ; S. Mark iv. 12 ; S. Luke viii. 10).
2. Of the rejection of the Gospel (S. John xii. 37-41. See Isa. vi. 1-12'; [Acts xxviii. 26 ; Rom. xi. 8]).

XVIII. "The Son of Man is come to seek and to save that which is lost."
1. Of Christ's anxiety for children (S. Matt. xviii. 11).
2. Of the penitent (S. Luke xix. 10).
3. Not to condemn, or destroy, but to save (S. Luke ix. 56 ; S. John iii. 17, xii. 47).

XIX. The first last, and the last first.
1. Of following Christ (S. Matt. xix. 30).

    2. Of work and reward in Christ's service (S. Matt. xx. 16 ; S. Mark x. 31).

    3. Of obedience to the Gospel call (S. Matt. xxi. 31, 32).

    4. Of religious privileges (S. Luke xiii. 30).

XX. Many called, few chosen.

    1. Of reward in Christ's service (S. Matt. xx. 16).

    2. Of call to the blessings of the Gospel (S. Matt. xxii. 14).

XXI. "The servant is not above his master," etc.

    1. Of experience of the world's treatment (S. Matt. x. 24 ; S. John xv. 20).

    2. As a general rule of service (S. Luke vi. 40).

    3. In discharge of offices of service (S. John xiii. 16).

XXII. The greatest, and the servant, under Christ's Gospel.

    1. Of office in the Christian ministry (S. Matt. xx. 25-28 ; xxiii. 11 ; S. Mark x. 43).

    2. Of rivalry amongst Church ministers (S. Mark ix. 35).

    3. Of Christ's example in this respect (S. Luke xxii. 24-27).

XXIII. "Whosoever shall exalt himself," etc.

    1. In office in Christ's service (S. Matt. xxiii. 12).

    2. Of assumption of superiority (S. Luke xiv. 11).

    3. Before God (S. Luke xviii. 14).

XXIV. "He that endureth to the end," etc.

    1. Of martyrdom (S. Matt. x. 32 ; S. Mark xiii. 13).

    2. In days of general falling away (S. Matt. xxiv. 13).

XXV. The Scriptures must be fulfilled.

    1. By Christ (S. Matt. v. 17, 18 ; S. John xix. 28).

    2. In their testimony to Christ (S. Luke xxiv. 27 ; S. John v. 39).

    3. In their declarations concerning Christ (S. Matt. xxvi. 56 ; S. Mark xiv. 21, 27, 49 ; S. Luke xxiv. 44, 46 ; S. John xiii. 18, xvii. 12, xix. 24-36).

XXVI. All things possible to faith.

    1. Of impediments to faith (S. Matt. xvii. 20 ; S. Mark xi. 23 ; S. Luke xvii. 6).

    2. Of miraculous gifts (S. Mark ix. 23).

    3. Of beholding the revelation of Christ's power (S. John xi. 40).

XXVII. "He that is not against us is on our side."

    1. Of unauthorized ministrations (S. Mark ix. 38-40 ; S. Luke ix. 50).

    2. The same conversely (S. Matt. xii. 30).

XXVIII. "With the same measure that ye mete," etc.

    1. Of our judgments of others (S. Matt. vii. 2).

    2. Of our hearing and obedience in the Gospel (S. Mark iv. 24).

    3. Of our charity (S. Luke vi. 38).

XXIX. " No man can serve two masters," etc.
     Of God and mammon (S. Matt. vi. 24 ; S. Luke xvi. 13).
XXX. Watch.
    1. For Christ's coming (S. Matt. xxiv. 42, xxv. 13;
       S. Mark xiii. 33, 35 ; S. Luke xii. 40).
    2. Watchfulness, with prayer, the way to escape coming
       trials (S. Luke xxi. 36).
    3. Blessedness of those who watch (S. Matt. xxiv. 46 ;
       S. Luke xii. 37, 38).
    4. Watching with prayer against temptation (S. Matt.
       xxvi. 38, 40 ; S. Mark. xiii. 33).
    5. Of vigils of prayer (S. Matt. xxvi. 38, 40 ; S. Mark
       xiii. 33).
    6. Of the general obligation (S. Mark xiii. 37).
XXXI. Peace, the salutation of the Gospel.
    1. By the angels (S. Luke ii. 14.   See also xix. 38).
    2. By Christ's ministers (S. Matt. x. 13 ; S. Luke x. 5, 6.
    3. Amongst Christians (S. Mark ix. 50).
    4. The blessing of peacemakers (S. Matt. v. 9).
    5. Christ's salutation of peace (S. Luke xxiv. 36 ; S.
       John xvi. 33, xx. 19, 21–26).
    6. Christ's legacy of peace (S. John xiv. 27).
    7. The object of Christ's visit to earth (S. Matt. x. 34 ;
       S. Luke xii. 51).

No. VII.

On xvi. 1.

EMBASSY OF KING ABGARUS.

There is an interesting tradition which connects the inquiry of the Greeks, in S. John xii. 20, with a mission which King Abgarus V. of Edessa sent to Jesus Christ. The story is this. The report of our Lord's miracles and teaching had created a strong impression at the court of King Abgarus, and his attention had been attracted by the character and preaching of Jesus, concerning whom faithful accounts had been brought to him ; and he conceived the deepest veneration for Him. Hearing from Palestine how the rulers of the Jews were plotting against His life, and that the time seemed near when these plots would be likely to take effect, he sent an embassy to Christ, which arrived during the last Passover, offering to our Lord an asylum in his country, with the fullest recognition of His claims, and invitation to publish them in Edessa ; and desiring from Christ the cure of a painful malady under which he had long suffered. It is true that a coincidence of date may have suggested the identification of this embassy with the arrival of the Greeks of S. John's Gospel ; but it is exceedingly probable that a neighbouring sovereign should hear of the fame of Christ, and seek His aid ; just as the King of Syria sent Naaman to Elisha, and as the woman of Syrophenicia, hearing of the mercy and power of Christ, crossed the border to plead the cause of her child, and followed our Lord within the confines of her own land.

This embassy bore a letter to our Lord from the king, to which He replied, declining the kindness offered to Himself, it being foreign to the object of His personal mission to earth ; but promising both the cure desired, and the preaching of the Gospel in his land, by the ministry of one of His disciples.

These two letters are preserved by Eusebius ("Eccles. Hist." i. 12), and they have been freely criticized, and are now generally pronounced to be spurious, though extreme antiquity of date is assigned to them ; they are of the third or fourth century, probably of the earlier date. It is to be feared that the tradition which identifies this mission with that of the Greeks may be equally doubtful ; though there remains the strong probability of a mission having been sent to Jesus Christ of such a general character, which tradition presently moulded into this definite form. So much may be therefore true, that, from whatever cause, the Gentile prince despatched messengers with a kindly greeting to our Lord, whose fame must certainly have spread into the countries outside Judæa during the era of His public ministry.

The following interesting particulars are taken from an article in the "Encyclopædia Britannica" :—

"Abgar, or Abgarus, was a name given to several of the Kings of Edessa in Syria. The most celebrated of them was one who, it is said, was contemporary with Jesus Christ ; and who, having a distemper in his feet, and hearing of Jesus's miraculous cures, requested Him to come and cure him. Eusebius, who believed that this letter was genuine, and also a letter our Lord is said to have returned to it, has translated them both from the Syriac, and asserts that they were taken out of the archives of the city of Edessa. The first is as follows :—

"'Abgarus, Prince of Edessa, to Jesus the holy Saviour, who hath appeared in the flesh in the confines of Jerusalem, greeting.

"'I have heard of Thee, and the cures Thou hast wrought without medicines, and without herbs. For it is reported Thou makest the blind to see, the lame to walk, lepers to be clean, devils and unclean spirits to be expelled, such as have been long diseased to be healed, and the dead to be raised ; all which, when I heard concerning Thee, I concluded with myself, that either Thou wast a God come down from heaven, or the Son of God sent to do these things. I have therefore written to Thee, beseeching Thee to vouchsafe to come unto me, and cure my disease.   For I have also heard that the Jews use Thee ill, and lay snares to destroy Thee. I have here a little city, pleasantly situated, and sufficient for us both.—ABGARUS.'

"To this letter Jesus, it is said, returned an answer by Ananias, Abgarus's courier, which was as follows :—

"'Blessed art thou, O Abgarus! who hast believed in Me, whom thou hast not seen ; for the Scriptures say of Me, "They who have seen Me have not believed, that they who have not seen may, by believing, have life."   But whereas thou writest to have Me come to thee, it is of necessity that I fulfil all things here for which I am sent ; and, having finished them, return to Him that sent Me.   But when I am returned to Him, I will then send one of My disciples to thee, who shall cure thy malady, and give life to thee and thine.—JESUS.'

"After Christ's ascension, Judas, who is also named Thomas, sent Thaddeus, one of the seventy, to Abgarus ; who preached the Gospel to him and to his people, cured him of his disorder, and wrought many miracles : which was done, says Eusebius, A.D. 43.

"Though the above letters are acknowledged to be spurious by the candid writers of the Church of Rome, several Protestant authors, as Dr. Parker, Dr. Cave, and Dr. Grabe, have maintained that they are genuine, and ought not to be rejected."

No. VIII. A.

On xvi. 3; xxii. 4, xxiv. *a.* 5, 9, *e.* 1.

THE PASSOVER AND THE EUCHARIST.

This great national feast gathers into itself the mighty events and many interests of the Holy Week.   To this anniversary of it, when Christ fulfilled the type and mysteries included in its celebration, earlier ages had tended.   It is sad to reflect how greatly the purposes of the Divine wisdom, and the designs of those gathered in thousands from all the land to observe the feast, differed.   It was the great day of the visitation of the chosen people; they would not know it, and the glory of God's covenant must now pass away from them.

The Passover was a feast of so much importance, being the standing memorial of a great deliverance, that it attracted many visitors from the Gentile world, who visited Jerusalem annually, or occasionally, at this season.   Some of these became proselytes to the Jewish faith ; but many, though attracted and interested, could never reconcile the might and benevolence of the God of

Israel, with the exclusive spirit and repellent manners of the Jews towards foreigners.

The subject of the Passover has been so amply treated by many writers, that it is scarcely necessary here to do more than refer to some of the leading points under which this feast comes in contact with the history of the last week of our Lord's life; including a short account of the feast as then observed, its fulfilment in our Lord's sacrifice, and the connection there is between the Passover of the Jewish religion, and the Eucharist of the Christian Church.

The following account of the observances connected with the feast is abridged by Bishop Goodwin from Lightfoot:—

"The custom of eating the Passover amongst the Jews was as follows. The Paschal supper began with a cup of wine, which the master of the house blessed, saying, 'Blessed be He that created the fruit of the vine;' and then saying, 'Let us give thanks,' he drank the cup. Then the bitter herbs were set on. Afterwards there was set on unleavened bread, and the sauce called *Charoseth*, and the lamb.

"Then the master of the house blessed God, saying, 'Blessed be He that created the fruits of the earth;' and, taking the herbs, and dipping them in the sauce *Charoseth*, he ate a small portion; and then the table was removed.

"And now they mingled another cup of wine, and the son asked the father—or, if not, the father would himself tell—how much this night differed from all other nights. 'On other nights' (he would say) 'we dip but once; but this night twice. On other nights we eat either leavened, or unleavened bread; on this, only unleavened. On other nights we eat either sitting, or lying; on this night, all lying.'

"The table was now set before them again, and then he said, 'This is the Passover which we therefore eat, because God passed over the houses of our fathers in Egypt.' Then he would lift up the bitter herbs in his hand, and say, 'We therefore eat this unleavened bread because our fathers had not time to sprinkle their meal to be leavened before God revealed Himself, and delivered them. We ought therefore to praise Him, who wrought all these wonderful things, and brought us out of bondage into liberty, out of sorrow into joy, out of darkness into great light. Let us therefore say, Hallelujah, praise the Lord.' And after further ascription of praise, he drank the second cup.

"Then washing his hands, and taking two loaves, he broke one; and, laying the broken upon the whole one, blessed it, and ate it, with bitter herbs. Afterwards he gave thanks over the lamb, and ate also of it.

"Then the supper was lengthened out, and each person would eat according to his fancy; and, last of all, they would eat of the flesh of the Passover a small portion; and after that they would not taste any more food."

This was a singularly solemn and impressive celebration; and we see in it the blessing of the bread, and of the cup, and, finally, the giving of the flesh of the Passover, so intimately typical of the several acts of the ordinance which our Lord founded upon it. It had not, however, merely the force of a memorial rite—it had a constant and present interest; for it represented to the mind of the intelligent worshipper the promise of a perpetual redemption from the bondage of the powers of evil; and we may well suppose that such a worshipper would forecast, however dimly, the glory of the deliverance promised in the Messiah, of which it offered so striking a type and pledge. He must have thought, as he praised God for the deliverance of his nation from Egypt, of the many foes that had menaced Israel through the long ages past of her national life; and how, on her return to God, one after another of these foes had been baffled and crushed, and the nation had come forth from the iron hand of the oppressor; how the fruits of sin were ever as "bitter herbs;" how trouble and sorrow, and many a bitter experience, and repeatedly the tears of bondage and subjection, had been their "meat day and night," until repentance brought them back to God; and how, to return to Him in hope of acceptance, they had had to put away "the leaven of malice and wickedness," the corruptions, or idolatry, or formalism, which had defiled them, and thus to "keep the feast" of God with the "unleavened bread of sincerity and truth," and to present before Him the fruits of righteousness.

And then they might offer before God the lamb of sacrifice. It was slain whole for each family. Thus grouped, a type, really, of each individual, for each must give a sacrifice for his own redemption. And the blood of the sacrifice was accepted, and the flesh of the sacrifice taken away to be eaten in solemn rite, a memorial of the offering for sin; and to become "the food of a better life" to those who partook of it, as "the Lord's Passover," in full assurance of faith, their hearts being sprinkled from an evil conscience "of the folly and degradation of sin from which they were delivered. Thus also they drank of the cup of that true "wine which maketh glad the heart of man," and ate of the unleavened bread of a new and holy life, which indeed "strengtheneth man's heart."

It remains to trace briefly the connection which our Lord maintained between the ordinance of the Passover, and the Eucharist of the Christian Church, which is neither accidental nor faint. It was not merely the fulfilment or supersession of that which was now passing away; nor was it simply a convenient and impressive moment for instituting the new festival. We cannot doubt that our Lord designed to connect the deliverances and promises, in which so many good and holy men of old had rested in hope, with the crowning act of His own redemption of our race from the power of death, and from the bondage of sin, and sorrow, and trouble in life. He gave His life for us, not only to redeem us from death eternal, when we depart this life; but to "redeem our lives from destruction" in all the assaults of the powers of evil, and from the dominion of vice, and from the oppression of life's manifold troubles whilst we are in the world. And therefore He gives us this memorial of a great and complete act of deliverance, and this holy food of a new and risen life, to be constantly celebrated by us until He comes again.

"It is important" (to return to the remarks of Bishop Goodwin on the subject) "to notice this close and unmistakable connection of the institution of the Holy Eucharist with the Passover. It has been observed that the Passover supper, according to the custom of the Jews, concluded with eating a small portion of the flesh of the lamb. The question arises, Did our Lord give His disciples the bread and the wine after the farewell morsel, or instead of it? It would seem most probable that the latter supposition is the true one; that is, that, when they were ready to take the farewell morsel, Christ changed the custom, and gave about morsels of bread instead, and so instituted His own Sacrament. With regard to the wine, there were several cups of wine used by the Jews on this occasion. One of these was especially called 'the cup of blessing,' which was used when thanks were given after supper; and this apparently was the cup which our Lord consecrated and gave to His disciples in the institution of the Eucharist. Indeed, it is notable that S. Paul, speaking of the Holy Sacrament to the Corinthians, directly describes the cup as 'the cup of blessing,' saying, 'The cup of blessing which we bless, is it not the communion of the Blood of Christ?'

"But however these points may be settled as to their smaller details, the general fact of the new relation in which our Lord made His Sacrament to stand to the Jewish Passover feast, is beyond all question. When the minds of the disciples were full of Passover thoughts, their redemption from Egypt, the passing over of their houses by the angel of God on the blood of the lamb being seen on their door-posts, then the Lord took bread and wine, and gave it to them, saying, 'This is My Body; and, This is My Blood.' No conduct could more completely serve to connect the New Testament with the Old, the Gospel with the Law, and to show that He did not come to destroy, but to fulfil. This celebration of the Passover brought the feast to an end. Henceforth there was to be a new feast in the kingdom of God. The celebration of Christ's death was to take the place of the Paschal lamb, and the Blood which reconciles God and man to appear the antitype of all sacrificial blood."

We should therefore certainly connect the blessings of the type with those of the antitype. The promises of the deliverance from

all bondage, of pardon of sin, of entrance and security in the land
of promise, which were celebrated in the observance of the Passover,
are ours in fuller truth, and in brighter excellence, than that feast
could ever convey then.   The Eucharist of the Christian Church
does not only show forth the Lord's death as the memorial of a
fulfilled and abolished ordinance, but there centre in it also all the
promises of God's earlier covenant, with the great act of communion
with the living Christ our Redeemer.   Our Lord did not close, in
His institution, the voices of God's mercy echoing down so many
generations of the old covenant.   He instituted the Eucharist at
the Last Supper, in order that He might most significantly gather
all the blessings of early deliverance into this supreme act of thanksgiving, and give them all to His Church, hallowed and intensified
by the perpetual connection of His ordinance with Himself, in His
devotion to death for our redemption.

No. VIII. B.

On I. xxiv. *e.* 2, 8, 9.

*ON THE REAL PRESENCE, SACRIFICIAL ASPECT, FRE-
QUENCY OF RECEPTION, AND OTHER MATTERS CON-
NECTED WITH THE EUCHARIST.*

The following sound and practical words from Bishop Jeremy
Taylor's " Life of Christ " (p. 290) will repay perusal:—" If we consider how easy it is to faith, and how impossible it seems to curiosity,
we shall be taught confidence and modesty; a resigning our understanding to the voice of Christ and His Apostles, and yet expressing
our articles, as Christ did, in indefinite significations.   And possibly
it may not well consist with our duty to be inquisitive into the
secrets of the kingdom, which we see, by plain event, hath divided
the Church, almost as much as the Sacrament hath united it.   We
see it, we feel it, we taste it, and we smell it to be bread; but Christ
also affirmed concerning it, ' This is My Body.'   Let the sense of
that be what it will, so that we believe those words, and (whatsoever
that sense is which Christ intended) that we no more doubt in our
faith than we do in our sense.   It is hard to do so much violence to
our sense, as not to think it bread; but it is more unsafe to do so
much violence to our faith, as not to believe it to be ' Christ's Body.'
But it should be considered that no interest of religion, no saying
of Christ, no reverence of opinion, no sacredness of the mystery, is
disavowed, if we believe both what we hear, and what we see.   He
that believes it to be ' bread,' and yet verily to be ' Christ's Body,'
is only tied also, by implication, to believe God's omnipotence, that
He, who affirmed it, can also verify it."

With regard to Christ's Body, he continues, "Its being really present does not hinder but that all that reality may be spiritual. I suppose it to be a mistake to think whatsoever is real must be natural; and it is no less to think spiritual to be only figurative; that is too much, and this too little. And if we profess we understand not the manner of this mystery, we say no more but that it is a mystery. In the Sacrament, that Body which is reigning in heaven is exposed upon the table of blessing; and His Body which was broken for us, is now broken again, and yet remains impassible. Every consecrated portion of bread and wine does exhibit Christ entirely to the faithful receiver; and yet Christ remains one, while He is wholly ministered in ten thousand portions."

In his " Real Presence of Christ in the Holy Sacrament " (p. 424), he states, "The doctrine of the Church of England is, that after the minister of the holy mysteries hath rightly prayed, and blessed or consecrated the bread and the wine, the symbols become changed into the Body and Blood of Christ, after a sacramental, that is, a spiritual and real manner; so that all that worthily communicate do by faith receive Christ really, effectually, to all the purposes of His Passion: the wicked receive not Christ, but the bare symbols only; but yet to their hurt, because the offer of Christ is rejected, and they pollute the blood of the covenant by using it as an unholy thing. The result of which doctrine is this: It is bread, and it is Christ's Body. It is bread in substance, Christ in the Sacrament; and Christ is as really given to all that are truly disposed, as the symbols are; each as they can; Christ as Christ can be given; the bread and wine as they can; and to the same real purposes, to which they are designed; and Christ does as really nourish and sanctify the soul, as the elements do the body. It is here, as in the other Sacrament: for as there natural water becomes the lever of regeneration; so here, bread and wine become the Body and Blood of Christ; but, there and here too, the first substance is changed by grace, but remains the same in nature."

2. On the " sacrificial aspect," Bishop Jeremy Taylor says (" Life of Christ," p. 296), "As it is a commemoration and represerment of Christ's death, so is it a commemorative sacrifice: as we receive the symbols and the mystery, so it is a Sacrament. In both capacities, the benefit is next to infinite. For whatsoever Christ did at the institution, the same He commanded the Church to do, in remembrance and repeated rites: and Himself also does the same thing in heaven for us, making perpetual intercession for His Church, the body of His redeemed ones, by representing to His Father His death and sacrifice. There He sits, a high priest continually, and offers still the same one perfect sacrifice; that is, represents it as having been once finished and consummate, in order to perpetual and never-failing events. And this, also, His ministers do on earth; they offer up the same sacrifice to God, the sacrifice of the Cross, by prayers,

and a commemorating rite and representment, according to His holy institution."

After mentioning several passages in Holy Scripture which speak of Christ's manifestation in the Holy Sacrament, he says, " A veil is drawn before all these testimonies, because 'Christ dwelling in us,' and 'giving us His Flesh to eat, and His Blood to drink;' and the 'hiding of our life with God,' and 'the communication of the Body of Christ,' and 'Christ being our life,' are such secret glories, that, as the fruition of them is the portion of the other world, so also is the full perception and understanding of them; for, therefore, God appears to us in a cloud, and His glories in a veil; that we understanding more of it by its concealment, than we can by its open face, which is too bright for our weak eyes, may, with more piety, also entertain its greatness, by these indefinite and mysterious significations, than we can by plain and direct intuitions; which, like the sun in a direct ray, enlightens the object, but confounds the organ."

3. On "frequency of reception" he says, "I suppose this question does not differ much from a dispute whether is better to pray often, or to pray seldom. For whatsoever is commonly pretended against a frequent communion may, in its proportion, object against a solemn prayer." He quotes S. Ignatius, "Hasten frequently to approach the Eucharist;" and S. Augustine, "At least let them receive it every Lord's day;" and S. Jerome, who counsels certain persons to receive it "twice every month." He himself decides emphatically for frequency of reception.

The Church of England directs that "every parishioner shall communicate at the least three times in the year, of which Easter to be one"—a direction which has been abused (through overlooking the words "*at the least*") to limit the occasions of many that do occasionally communicate, to those "three times." This subject may be fitly concluded in the words of Bishop Wilson, of Sodor and Man: "Three times a year! God forbid that any good Christian should make this an excuse for receiving no oftener, if he has an opportunity! And *woe be to that pastor*, who will not give the well-disposed part of his flock more frequent opportunities of testifying their love to Jesus Christ! . . . If therefore you love God and your neighbour, though not so fervently as you could wish; if you have a real desire of being better than at present you find yourself to be; if the fruits of the Holy Spirit, though in a very low degree, do appear in your life; lastly, if you do daily pray for God's grace, that you may, in His good time, be what He would have you to be, and do not live in any known sin; by no means forbear to go to this ordinance, *as often as you have an opportunity*; and depend upon God's blessing, and an increase of His graces."

No. IX.

On xviii. 4.

PLOUGHING THE FOUNDATIONS OF THE TEMPLE.

It is said that the ploughshare was drawn over the ruins of Jerusalem by Terentius Rufus, the general left to carry out the orders of Titus. "But the sentence of Josephus seems conclusive against this as an historical fact; and this devotion of the site of the city does not appear to have been consummated as to Jerusalem after the capture by Titus.

"By a curious coincidence the Roman commander to whom the final demolition of Jerusalem had been committed by Titus, bore the name of Terentius Rufus; the prefect in Palestine at the commencement of the revolt under Barchochab (A.D. 131) was T. Annius, or Tynnius, called by the Rabbins Tyrannus, or Turnus Rufus the Wicked. Thus the two men who were the objects of the deepest detestation to the Jews are perpetually confounded. Rufus is said, at the command of Hadrian, to have driven the plough over the ruins of Jerusalem." (Notes by Dean Milman, "Hist. of the Jews.")

No. X.

On xviii. 5 (see also i. 22, 47, 48); and on II. viii. 16.

CHRIST ON THE MOUNT OF OLIVES. THE LOCALITY OF THE ASCENSION.

The following picture from Dean Milman's "History of Christianity" (ch. vii.) is so striking and beautiful, that it needs no apology for insertion here:—

"It is impossible to conceive a spectacle of greater natural or moral sublimity than the Saviour seated on the Mount of Olives, and thus looking down, almost for the last time, on the whole Temple and city of Jerusalem, crowded as it then was with near three millions of worshippers. It was evening, and the whole irregular outline of the city, rising from the deep glens which surrounded it on all sides, might be distinctly traced. The sun, the significant emblem of the great Fountain of moral light, to which Jesus and His faith had been perpetually compared, may be imagined smiling behind the western hills, while its last rays might linger on the broad and massy fortifications on Mount Zion, on the stately palace of Herod, on the square tower, the Antonia, at the corner of the Temple, and on the roof of the Temple, fretted all over with golden spikes which glittered like fire; while below, the colonnades and lofty gates would cast their broad shadows over the courts, and afford that striking contrast between vast masses of gloom, and the gleams of the richest light, which only an evening scene, like the present, can display.

"Nor, indeed (even without the sacred and solemn associations connected with the holy city), would it be easy to conceive any natural situation in the world of more impressive grandeur, and likely to be seen with greater advantage under the influence of such accessories, than that of Jerusalem, seated as it was, upon hills of irregular height, intersected by bold ravines, and hemmed in, almost on all sides, by still loftier mountains; and itself formed, in its most conspicuous parts, of gorgeous ranges of Eastern architecture, in all its lightness, luxuriance, and variety.

"The effect may have been heightened by the rising of the slow volumes of smoke from the evening sacrifices; while, even at the distance of the slope of Mount Olivet, the silence may have been faintly broken by the hymns of the worshippers.

"Yet the fall of the sacred edifice was inevitable. It was necessary to the complete development of the designs of Almighty Providence for the welfare of mankind in the promulgation of Christianity. . . . The destruction certainly of the Temple, and, if not of the city, at least of the city as the centre and metropolis of a people, the only and exclusive worshippers of one Almighty Creator, seemed essential to the progress of the true faith. The universal and comprehensive religion to be promulgated by Christ and His Apostles was founded on the absorption of all local claims to peculiar sanctity, of all distinctions of one nation above another as possessing any especial privilege in the knowledge or favour of the Deity."

The Mount of Olives (or Olivet, as it is often termed, from the Latin rendering of its name as a plantation or garden of olive trees) has another traditional site of great interest, that of the Church of the Ascension.

"On the top of the middle summit of the Mount of Olives is now the ancient Church of the Ascension, supposed to mark the place whence our Lord ascended into heaven. Whether this church does, or does not, cover the exact spot of earth, on which the feet of our blessed Saviour last stood, is a question with reference to which much has been lately written. It is of more importance to know whether He did or did not ascend from the top of Olivet at all. If He did not, the church is an imposture, or a mistake; if He did, the church cannot be far from, if it does not cover, the exact spot.

"It is stated by S. Luke, that Jesus 'led His disciples out as far as to Bethany; and while He blessed them, He was parted from them, and carried up into heaven' (S. Luke xxiv. 50, 51). But the summit of Olivet is not more than half-way between Jerusalem and Bethany, which seems here to be made the scene of the ascension. But the same Evangelist, in recording the event in Acts i. states that, after they had seen their Lord ascend into heaven, 'they returned to Jerusalem, from the mount called Olivet, which is from Jerusalem a sabbath day's journey.' These texts cannot contradict each other; but how are we to reconcile them? The explanation given by Lightfoot is far the best which has been offered; and it not only removes any apparent discrepancy between these texts, but makes them confirmatory of each other. It amounts to this: that the side of Olivet facing Jerusalem was called Bethphage, and that the other side away from Jerusalem was called Bethany. Bethphage ended, and Bethany began, at the very top of the mount; and when, therefore, a person was said to go from Jerusalem upon Olivet as far as Bethany, he was understood to go to the top of the mount where Bethany commenced." (*Kitto.*)

It is, however, a matter of very grave doubt whether the site which Lightfoot's explanation thus favours, is the true one, though it is one which has been associated with it from early antiquity, and therefore has, at least, the consecration of the devout thoughts of many generations. Dean Stanley ("Sinai and Palestine," ch. xiv.) judges, from the language of Eusebius, that the chapel built by the Empress Helena, about A.D. 325, did not commemorate the scene of the ascension, but the scene of conversations held with the Apostles before the ascension, which conversations he places in a cave now called "the Tombs of the Prophets;" and Dean Stanley adds, that, "even if the Evangelists had been less explicit in stating that 'He led them out as far as to Bethany,' the secluded hills which overhang that village on the eastern slope of Olivet, are evidently as appropriate to the narrative, as the startling, the almost offensive publicity of the traditional spot in the full view of the whole city of Jerusalem is wholly inappropriate, and (in the absence, as it now appears, of even traditional support) wholly untenable." He states also that "the present edifice of the Church of the Ascension on the top of Olivet has no claims to antiquity."

No. XI.

On xviii. 2, 11, 17–20, 53, 55, 57, 59, 66, 67, 82, 83.

FULFILMENTS OF THE GREAT PROPHECY.

The following quotations from Josephus, and other authors, will show some of the fulfilments of our Lord's great prophecy. The subject is one which might be indefinitely lengthened, both as regards the destruction of the Jewish nation, and events of later date. There were many points in which each of our Lord's declarations were fulfilled; it must be sufficient for the present purpose to show one or two only.

1. Stones of the Temple.

" The Temple was built of stones that were white and strong, and each of their length was twenty-five cubits, their height was eight, and their breadth about twelve."　(*Jos.* " Antiq." xv. 11, 3.)

" Of its stones some were forty-five cubits in length, five in height, and six in breadth."　(*Jos.* " Wars," v. 5, 6.)

2. One stone not left upon another.

" For all the rest of the wall, it was so thoroughly laid even with the ground by those that dug up the foundation, that there was left nothing to make those that came thither believe it had ever been inhabited."　(*Jos.* " Wars," vii. 1, 1.)

Eusebius also declares that the Romans drew the plough over the ruins of the Temple, and that he himself saw the ruins (vii. 18). (See also App. IX., " Ploughing the foundations of the Temple.")

3. False Christs.

" While Fadus was Governor of Judea, a certain magician, whose name was Theudas, persuaded a great part of the people to take their effects with them, and follow him to the river Jordan ; for he told them he was a prophet, and that he would, by his own command, divide the river, and afford them an easy passage over it; and many were deluded by his words. However, Fadus did not permit them to make any advantage of his wild attempt, but sent a troop of horsemen out against them ; who, falling upon them unexpectedly, slew many of them, and took many of them alive. They also took Theudas alive, and cut off his head, and carried it to Jerusalem."　(*Jos.* " Antiq." xx. 5, 1.)

This happened about A.D. 45, and therefore is not the insurrection of the Theudas mentioned in Acts v., which took place A.D. 7.

Josephus also mentions many others in the time of Felix; and also one especially, who was a leader of Sicarii in the time of Festus, who committed great excesses ; so that " Festus sent forces, both horsemen and footmen, to fall upon those that had been seduced by a certain impostor, who promised them deliverance and freedom from the miseries they were under, if they would but follow him as far as the wilderness. Accordingly, those forces that were sent destroyed both him that had deluded them, and those that were his followers also."　(" Antiq." xx. 8, 6 ; 8, 10.)

Speaking of the fate of a number of people who were destroyed during the siege, by the burning of the cloister of the Temple, he says, " A false prophet was the occasion of these people's destruction, who had made a public proclamation in the city that very day, that God commanded them to get up upon the Temple, and that there they should receive miraculous signs ·of their

deliverance. Now there was then a great number of false prophets
suborned by the tyrants to impose upon the people, who denounced
this to them, that they should wait for deliverance from God ; and
this was in order to keep them from deserting, and that they might
be buoyed up above fear and care by such hopes. . . . Thus were the
miserable people persuaded by these deceivers, and such as belied
God Himself; while they did not attend, nor give credit, to the signs
that were so evident, and did so plainly foretell their future desolation; but, like men infatuated, without either eyes to see, or minds
to consider, did not regard the denunciations that God made to
them."   ("Wars," vi. 5, 2, 3.)

The above passages show the readiness of the people to follow
false Christs at various periods between our Lord's day, and that
of the destruction of Jerusalem. One more may be quoted, which
shows that these impostors were both numerous, and that they
misled the people by the promise of temporal deliverance exactly
in the way that the temper of the nation preferred to' look for a
Messiah.

After speaking of the Sicarii, and their frequent murders,
Josephus states, "There was also another body of wicked men
gotten together, not so impure in their actions, but more wicked
in their intentions, who laid waste the happy state of the city no
less than did these murderers. These were such men as deceived
and deluded the people under pretence of Divine inspiration, but
were for procuring innovations and changes of the government ;
and these prevailed with the multitude to act like madmen, and
went before them into the wilderness, as pretending that God would
there show them the signals of liberty ; but Felix thought this
procedure was to be the beginning of a revolt ; so he sent some
horsemen and footmen, both armed, who destroyed a great number
of them.

"But there was an Egyptian false prophet that did the Jews
more mischief than the former; for he was a cheat, and pretended
to be a prophet also, and got together 30,000 men that were deluded
by him; these he led round about from the wilderness to the
mount which is called the Mount of Olives, and was ready to break
into Jerusalem by force from that place ; . . . but Felix prevented
his attempt, and met him with his Roman soldiers, while all the
people assisted him in his attack upon them, insomuch that, when
it came to a battle, the Egyptian ran away, with a few others, while
the greatest part of those that were with him were either destroyed
or taken alive; but the rest of the multitude were dispersed every
one to their own homes, and there concealed themselves." ("Wars,"
ii. 13, 4, 5; also vi. 5, 2.)

3. Wars and rumours of wars.

In verification of this prophecy so far as the Jews were concerned,
we may refer to "Wars," ii. 17, 10, where Josephus records an insur-

rection in which several Romans were killed, under Metilius, whose life alone was spared on his promise to embrace the Jewish religion. He says, "The loss of the Romans was but light, there being no more than a few slain out of an immense army; but still it appeared to be a prelude to the Jews' own destruction, while men made public lamentation when they saw that such occasions were afforded for a war as were incurable; that the city was polluted with such abominations, from which it was but reasonable to expect some vengeance, even though they should escape revenge from the Romans; so that the city was filled with sadness."

Following this, in "Wars," ii. 18, 1–8, we read of the slaughter of 20,000 Jews at Cæsarea, which roused the nation to frenzy, so that they broke out into rebellion throughout Syria, and experienced great miseries. At Alexandria also 50,000 Jews were slaughtered.

Quotations of this kind might be multiplied from the same authors; and a further fulfilment shown from contemporary history, in the wars, revolutions, and disaffections in various provinces of the empire.

One more passage, however, may be quoted from Josephus, as it bears upon our Lord's warning to the Christians, to flee when they saw Jerusalem compassed with enemies. It occurred about three years ánd a half before the destruction of Jerusalem. The Roman forces under Cestius advanced in form to lay regular siege to the city, and, "had he but continued the siege a little longer, had certainly taken the city. . . . It then happened that Cestius recalled his soldiers from the place, and . . . without having received any disgrace, he retired from the city, without any reason in the world." (See also Eusebius, "Eccl. Hist." iii. 5.)

The short interval which now elapsed before the final siege, enabled the Christians to recognize the sign given them, and to leave the city.

During the siege itself, a second warning was given, so brief that it verified our Lord's direction in S. Matt. xxiv. 15–18. There was just sufficient time given to escape in haste, when the zealots occupied the Temple (see "Wars," v. 3, 1), and stopped the daily sacrifice, and prevented all exit from the city. This is considered, by many writers, to be the "abomination of desolation;" though the term might find also fulfilment, to many minds, when the precincts of Jerusalem were full of the Roman standards of the army under Cestius.

4. Earthquakes, famines, pestilences.

Josephus mentions an earthquake which affected Jerusalem, shortly before the final siege, during the time that the zealots and Idumæans were rioting in and about the city: "There broke out a prodigious storm in the night, with the utmost violence, and very strong winds, with the largest showers of rain, with continual lightnings, terrible thunderings, and amazing concussions and

bellowings of the earth, that was in an earthquake. These things
were a manifest indication that some destruction was coming upon
men, when the system of the world was put into this disorder;
and any one would guess that these wonders foreshowed some grand
calamities that were coming."   ("Wars," iv. 4, 5.)

This statement finds support in records by the Roman historian
Tacitus, who speaks of earthquakes with which the Jews must
have been familiar. (See "Ann." xii. 58; xiv. 27; xv. 22.) Seneca
also alludes to earthquakes within the province of Syria (Ep. 91, 9).

Josephus, speaking to the visit of Jerusalem of Helena, mother
of Izates, King of Adiabene, who were both proselytes to the Jewish
faith, says : "Now her coming was of very great advantage to the
people of Jerusalem; for whereas a famine did oppress them at
that time, and many of the people died for want of what was
necessary to procure food withal, Queen Helena sent some of her
servants to Alexandria with money to buy a great quantity of corn,
and others of them to Cyprus, to bring a cargo of dried figs; and
as soon as they were come back, and had brought those provisions,
which was done very quickly, she distributed food to those that
were in want of it, and left a most excellent memorial of her of this
benefaction, which she bestowed on our whole nation; and when
her son Izates was informed of this famine, he sent sums of money
to the principal men in Jerusalem."   "Antiq." xx. 2, 5; 5, 2; and
iii. 15, 3.

This was the famine in the reign of Claudius, alluded to in Acts
xi. 28.

The extremities of famine, and of pestilence arising from it,
experienced during the progress of the siege, are spoken of at
length in "Wars," v. 10, 2–4; 12, 1, 3, 4, when they devoured even
human flesh. And yet, as multitudes died from these causes, or
by the sword, their last thought was of the religion which they had
so desecrated in the practice of their lives: "Now every one of
these died with their eyes fixed upon the Temple, and left the
seditious alive behind them."

The miseries of this famine culminated in the instance of Mary
of Pera, who was found to have devoured her own child (thus fulfilling Deut. xxviii. 53–57)—a fact which produced a shudder of
awe, not only throughout the city, but also in the camp of the
besiegers, where it became known.

The fulfilment of our Lord's prediction, in these and foreign
instances, is supported by the testimony of Tacitus ("Ann." xiii. 63,
xvi. 13) and of Suetonius ("Claud." 18; "Nero," 39), who speak of the
frequency of terrible famines at this era, and of the consequent
pestilences produced (as is ever the case with famine) by want of
sufficient and wholesome food, and by the corruption of the dead.

5. Fearful sights, and great signs from heaven.

Josephus says, "There was a star resembling a sword, which

stood over the city, and a comet, that continued a whole year. Before the Jews' rebellion, and before those commotions which preceded the war, when the people were come in great crowds to the feast of unleavened bread, on the eighth day of the month Xanthicus (Nisan), and at the ninth hour of the night, so great a light shone round the altar and the holy house, that it appeared to be bright daytime; which light lasted for half an hour. At the same festival also, a heifer, as she was led by the high priest to be sacrificed, brought forth a lamb in the midst of the Temple. Moreover, the eastern gate of the inner (court of the) Temple, which was of brass, and vastly heavy, and had been with difficulty shut by twenty men, and rested upon a basis armed with iron, and had bolts fastened very deep into the firm floor, which was there made of one entire stone, was seen to be opened of its own accord about the sixth hour of the night. This appeared to the vulgar to be a very happy omen, as if God did thereby open to them the gate of happiness. But the men of learning understood it, that the security of their holy house was dissolved of its own accord, and that the gate was opened for the advantage of their enemies. So these publicly declared, that this signal foreshadowed the desolation that was coming upon them. Besides these, a few days after that feast, on the one and twentieth day of the month Artemisius (Jyar), a certain prodigious and incredible phenomenon appeared; I suppose the account of it would seem to be a fable, were it not related by those who saw it, and were not the events that followed it of so considerable a nature as to deserve such signals; for, before sunsetting, chariots and troops of soldiers in their armour were seen running about among the clouds, and surrounding of cities. Moreover, at the feast which we call Pentecost, as the priests were going by night into the inner (court of the) Temple, as their custom was, to perform their sacred ministrations, they said that, in the first place, they felt a quaking, and heard a great noise, and after that they heard a sound as of a great multitude, saying, ' *Let us remove hence!* ' But, what is still more terrible, there was one Jesus, the son of Ananus, a plebeian and a husbandman, who, four years before the war began, and at a time when the city was in very great peace and prosperity, came to that feast whereon it is our custom for every one to make tabernacles to God in the Temple, began on a sudden to cry aloud, ' A voice from the east, a voice from the west, a voice from the four winds, a voice against Jerusalem and the holy house, a voice against the bridegrooms and the brides, and a voice against this whole people.' This was his cry, as he went about by day and by night, in all the lanes of the city. However, certain of the most eminent among the populace had great indignation at this dire cry of his, and took up the man, and gave him a great number of severe stripes; yet did not he either say anything for himself, or anything peculiar to those who chastised him, but still he went on with the same words which he cried before. Hereupon our rulers supposing, as the case proved to be, that this was a sort of Divine fury in the man, brought him to the Roman procurator; where he was whipped till his bones were laid bare; yet did he not make any supplication for himself, nor shed any tears, but turning his voice to the most lamentable tone possible, at every stroke of the whip his answer was, ' Woe, woe to Jerusalem.' And when Albinus (for he was then our procurator) asked him, Who he was? and whence he came? and why he uttered such words? he made no manner of reply to what he said, but still did not leave off his melancholy ditty, till Albinus took him to be a madman, and dismissed him. Now, during all the time that passed before the war began, this man did not go near any of the citizens, nor was seen by them while he said so; but he every day uttered these lamentable words, as if it were his premeditated vow, ' Woe, woe to Jerusalem!' Nor did he give ill words to any of those that beat him every day, nor good words to those who gave him food; but this was his reply to all men, and, indeed, no other than a melancholy presage of what was to come. This cry of his was the loudest at the festivals; and he continued this ditty for seven years and five months, without growing hoarse or being tired therewith, until the very time that he saw his presage in earnest fulfilled in our siege, when it ceased; for as he was going round upon the wall, he cried out with his utmost force, ' Woe, woe to the city again, and to the people, and to the holy house.' And just as he added at the last, ' Woe, woe to myself also!' there came a stone out of one of the engines, and smote him, and killed him immediately; and as he was uttering the very same presages, he gave up the ghost." (" Wars," vi. 5, 3, 4.)

Tacitus mentions that " of a sudden the doors of the Temple were thrown up, and a voice was heard mightier than that of man, that the gods were departing from it."

It is, of course, possible to refer these portents to the natural desire of the Jewish historian to throw a Divine character round the circumstances which attended the dying glory of his Church and nation; but, on the other hand, we must consider his acknowledged general veracity. The signs related by him were not in themselves more remarkable than those which marked the Saviour's dying hour, when the sun was darkened, and the rocks were rent, the earth quaked, and the graves opened, and the great veil of the Temple, sixty feet in length, and one in thickness, was rent from the top downwards. (See xxxi. 39–42.) We must remember that signs from heaven accompanied the inauguration of Solomon's Temple; and that our Lord Himself foretold that such signs as Josephus declares, should accompany the end; and we cannot but feel that such a supreme event as the destruction of the Jewish Church and nation, so fraught as it was with consequences of the utmost moment to the after history of the world, was a matter worthy of the giving of signs from heaven, indicative of the interference of Providence in these affairs of earth. Truly, as Josephus declares, " the events that followed were of so considerable a nature as to deserve such signals."

6. That these miseries were such as were not from the beginning of the world.

Josephus (Pref. " Wars," 4) says, " It appears to me that the misfortunes of all men, from the beginning of the world, if they be compared to these of the Jews, are not so considerable as they were." And ("Wars," v. 10, 5), " I shall speak my mind here at once briefly :—That neither did any other city ever suffer such miseries, nor did any age ever breed a generation more fruitful in wickedness than this was, from the beginning of the world."

7. Concerning the Gospel being " preached in all the world for a witness," before the destruction of Jerusalem.

Forster, who confines himself to a verification of these prophecies only of the times preceding the destruction of Jerusalem, has the following note :—

"' *Preached in all the world.*' From the most credible records it appears that the Gospel was preached by S. Jude in Idumæa, Mesopotamia, and Syria ; in Egypt and Africa, by Mark, Simon, and Jude ; in Ethiopia, by the converted eunuch, and Matthias ; in Pontus and Galatia, and the neighbouring parts of Asia, by Peter ; in the territories of the seven Asiatic Churches, by John ; in Parthia, by Matthew ; in Scythia, by Philip and Andrew ; in the northern and western parts of Asia, by Bartholomew ; in Persia, by Simon and Jude ; in Media and several parts of the East, by Thomas ; through the vast tract " from Jerusalem round about into Illyricum," by Paul. This Apostle was also in Greece and Italy, very probably in Spain and Gaul, and, we may add also with great probability, Britain ; for Clemens, his contemporary, declares (' Ep. Cor.' 20) that the nations beyond the ocean were governed by the precepts of the Lord. History, in fact, abundantly warrants the assertion that the Gospel has been generally preached throughout the world : in some countries it has been rejected ; in many, where it once flourished, it has been corrupted, or lost ; but still ' God hath called the world from the rising up of the sun unto the going down thereof.'"

No. XII.

On xviii. 37; xxvi. 54.

MISSIONARY LABOUR IN APOSTOLIC AND SUBSEQUENT AGES.

To do justice to such a subject as this should be the aim of an essay of length—a digest, in fact, of Church history of the past, and of the result of modern effort. It may be, however, generally and briefly stated in what respects the experience of the apostolic missionary must have differed from that of his successors, and in what they must be identical.

The missionary of the apostolic age had, in the first place, to surmount various personal disqualifications, and prejudices of early training.

In going forth to the wide world with Abraham's promise, he required much of that grand and simple faith, and of that pure obedience (more akin to that of those who do God's will in heaven, than of those who are chosen to do it upon earth), which prompted Abraham, at the call and command of God, to set aside all the strong and rooted principles of life, which bind men to the homes and customs of their forefathers in the unchanging East, and to seek a new country, and to establish a new religion amongst men of an alien race, founder and heir of a Church and family of which there then existed not a single member. It is difficult for men of the Western world, so liberal in their views of the brotherhood of mankind, so prompt to transplant themselves into any other land in the interests of commerce and civilization, to understand and estimate fully the force of the restriction of Eastern thought and life. These, however, unfold themselves to the view of those who settle in Eastern lands, and attempt to introduce Western ideas, either on subjects of social intercourse, education, or religion. The surmounting of all early influences in the case of Abraham, made him the true father of the faithful to the end of time; of all who recognize no law superior to God's will, no interests more local than those of His Catholic Church, no country of earth more than a place of sojourn to the citizens of heaven. In the case of apostolic missionaries, his descendants lineally, equally rooted to home localities by every association of earthly training, and, in addition, tied to the restricted privileges and hopes of the Jewish religion, there was a necessity for faith in Christ, such as that of Abraham, and for an obedience as unhesitating. He, like his great ancestor, had to lay aside all the ties of locality, nation, and early faith, and to embrace the catholic spirit of the Gospel, which recognized all mankind as the heirs of the promise, and as children of God; and which gathered the Gentile to him in a closer bond of fellowship than ever could the ties of national relationship, even when hallowed and centred in those peculiar to such a religious system as that of the Jewish Church; which made him no longer the citizen of a settled kingdom, and orthodox faith never to be subverted or superseded, supreme under God on earth, but left him, like Abraham, a wanderer, an Hebrew still, seeking upon earth a country and a kingdom beyond this world, and beyond time.

What changes of thought, and feeling, and of aspiration must he have undergone, who, as Christ's Apostle, went forth from Jerusalem, from the land of the promise, from the Jewish Church, and from the Temple services, to preach the Gospel to the Gentiles.

Again, when personal difficulties were surmounted in the inspiration of the Spirit of Christ, he must have become sensible of other disadvantages; those which must fetter an unlearned and ignorant man in going forth with a new and strange doctrine, which must refuse to be engrafted on, or to incorporate, any existing systems of religion, but which must triumph in the abolition of them all, amongst people, the educated chiefs of whom, at least, were infinitely his superior in worldly knowledge, and in all human learning. In knowledge of mankind also, and in acquaintance with the history, habits, and religious systems of various races, they were greatly his superior who came out of a closed and narrow corner of the earth, into the wide expanse of the inhabited world, with a mission to revolutionize human society, more uncompromising and more imperial than that of the empire of Rome. He required, therefore, miraculous power, and a heavenly inspiration to attest his words, and to direct his actions.

He had, however, these advantages: the world before him possessed a common language, which was recognized everywhere as the language of education in all civilized countries; there was also one imperial rule, within which were current the same standard of opinion and code of law. But he was himself educated under a different system, and had been trained to the belief in restricted privileges, which unfitted him to influence the minds of men of world-wide sympathies, and of indifference to, or toleration for, every other creed as well as their own; and he spoke a language almost unknown beyond his own country. He needed, therefore, inspiration with regard to the mode of thought prevalent within the world, and a gift of discernment of spirits, superior to any knowledge of mankind by intuition or study, and a gift of understanding and of speaking languages which he had never learned. There was, perhaps, one other circumstance which gave immediate currency to his word. The hold of ancient religion upon men's minds was not exactly that of devotion, nor yet of superstition; everywhere men of education were laughing at the follies and absurdities of idolatry; and the classes below them were prompted to perceive their growing atheism. The teaching of idolatry did nothing to purify and hallow the relationships of daily life; it had no answer to give to the questions which the schools of philosophy canvassed freely, and treated with infinite wisdom and gravity. The ancient religion had interwoven itself with polite literature; and the beautiful stories of ancient mythology, the poetry, art treasures of the world, all allied to the old belief, must have had a charm for the educated mind of those days, even superior to that with which they have delighted scholars in all subsequent ages, to the present time. And for the lower classes there was the hold which national holidays, and the rites and ceremonies which distinguished them, have ever upon the popular mind. But neither the refined pleasures of literature and art, nor the consecrated license of the holiday, satisfy the deeper longings of the soul of man. And therefore, when the apostolic missionary, accredited by miraculous powers, and inspired with a Divine knowledge of men and of their deeper thoughts, and gifted with many tongues and dialects, came with the offer of eternal peace, answering all the unsatisfied aspirations and intuitions of the soul of man, teaching also a religion which could transform the society of earth into that worthy of heaven, which could purify the lives of men, and hallow the natural and domestic relationships of families, and consecrate the daily work of life—when a simple and true faith was thus placed before men, there were multitudes who turned at once from their superstitions, which they professed outwardly, and inwardly derided, to the truth of the Gospel of Christ. And thus the Gospel spread rapidly in many lands.

II. It was not long before a change took place in the position which advancing Christianity, and retiring heathenism occupied with regard to each other. The age of miracles passed away with the passing of the necessity for miraculous aid; for Christianity soon gathered to itself apologists as keen in thought and argument, and as deeply versed in worldly learning, as were any who maintained the old faith, and contended against the truth. Education speedily, and gradually the subtle powers of refinement, art, and science, passed over to the side of the new faith. It had also assigned her rightful place and revealed her proper duties, to woman; and she, from the first never hostile to Christ, began to train the rising generation to Christianity.

When converts were made, or disciples of Christ grew up, who went forth as successors in the commission of the Apostles to preach the Gospel in other lands, to wild and barbarous nations, they came before men as the modern-missionary does; possessed of superior intelligence, and of the powers of cultivated thought, and of civilization; bringing blessings and offers of this life, together with those of the spiritual teaching of the Gospel, sufficient generally to attest the faith they proclaimed. It was then no longer the contest of

Divine wisdom with earthly wisdom; but of wisdom of the world, illumined with heavenly truth, against the darkness and cruelty of ignorance and error. Henceforward, the best missionary must be the man of intellectual power and attainments, possessed of knowledge of human character, and of tact to influence and mould the thoughts and wills of other men, of love like that of Christ to draw them, and to hold them; he must be a man of high spiritual excellence and energy, and well versed in the Scriptures of truth. It would not be sufficient to have simply a desire to spread the Gospel —the missionary should be a man selected from other men; for the gift of cultivated intellect, and the endowment of the treasures it can amass, must now take the place of that miraculous aid, now denied because no longer necessary to the demonstration of Christ's truth.

III. But there are still gifts which are common to the missionary of Christ in all ages; to the modern missionary equally with him to whom Christ committed the proclamation of the Gospel, in the presence of those five hundred witnesses, upon the mountain of His appearance in Galilee. He must be "*sent*" by Christ upon this high embassy to the souls of other men; and, if sent, graced with the inspiration of the Spirit, and with a true and earnest zeal; accredited, not now with miraculous powers, but evidently in the "demonstration of the Spirit and of truth."

IV. The subject thus briefly sketched must be closed; though, to the author writing in India, the temptation is great to speak of missionary work here; which is, in some respects, an exception to the missionary experience of former ages. Caste, engrossing all conditions of life in this world, and influencing all prospects in the future world, presents a steady front against the advance of Christianity. For it is not only that the convert must be won to Christ, but that means of work and life must be provided now; for when his caste is broken, he is an outcast from his hereditary profession. If the Gospel is offered to the Mahomedan, the difficulties connected with monotheism seem even greater than those of polytheism, or heathenism; as they have been in all ages. That principle of worship which brought the Jew and the Persian into friendly relationship, drives the Christian and the Mahomedan more widely apart than is the severance of heathenism.

And yet there are not wanting indications that the day of a splendid success is about to dawn upon the night of devoted effort, and of small apparent gain—that a mighty harvest will crown the patience of those that have sowed in hope. The impression of this dawning change seems equally present to the mind of the earnest missionary, and to that of the heathen amongst whom he is labouring; one by one the barriers of progress are disappearing, and truth and light advancing.

It remains that those who work for Christ in this especial commission, should work in more thorough accord and union—should actively associate with themselves, and in their work, the sympathies of their fellow-Christians, both clerical and lay; avoiding the hindrances which must arise where men, engaged in a special work, become so engrossed in it, and so bonded with those similarly engaged, as to form sometimes almost a Christian caste. The missionary must be in the van, leading the efforts, and commanding the help, of all Christian men. His must be the common enterprise and interest of all; and he must be the first to make it so. Then, in the united effort of all, the work must go forward and prosper.

No. XIII.

On xviii. 37.

IMPORTANCE OF A LEARNED MINISTRY.

It would seem scarcely necessary to point out that, though Christianity owed so much, in the earliest ages, to the efforts of "unlearned and ignorant men," who were miraculously aided by many excellent gifts of the Spirit in their evangelistic labours, it should owe little now to men so disqualified to meet the trained wisdom of the world, except the example of a godly life in the position assigned to them by Providence.

But yet the argument is sometimes advanced, in the present day, that the plain speaking, of plain and unlettered men, is most convincing and acceptable to the masses; and that the clergy of the Church of England, or any other learned ministry, are, to a certain extent, unfitted to deal with the ignorant, in consequence of their superior knowledge; which, it is affirmed, unfits them to understand the ways of thought of ignorant men, and to apply telling arguments to those who are so far below them in cultivation and intelligence.

This is really a fallacy. The plain ministrations of an uneducated man may attract a certain attention, and cause *excitement* for a time; in itself an unwholesome substitute for deep religious conviction. The impression, however, must be chiefly personal, owing its strength to the individuality of the man himself. It is not a part of a combined and sustained effort; it is, therefore, only under very exceptional circumstances that the effect so produced could be at all permanent. Earnestness always carries weight; but earnestness wanting proper authority, liable to all the errors of uninformed zeal, and stepping outside its own proper sphere of influence, is not likely to work much lasting good—it only excites a craving for such irregular ministrations.

On the other hand, inexperience of the habits of life and thought of the labouring and working classes, may, for a time, and to a certain extent, disqualify a very young clergyman for his pastoral work; but assuredly not to the extent alleged. Any one who casts his mind back upon the experience of his early years in the ministry of Christ's Church, will remember much more of the kindness, forbearance, sympathy, help of these uneducated classes, than of their distance from him; of their giving the right hand of their simple fellowship to the young labourer, rather than of their standing aloof from him because of his superior learning.

And does ever, can ever training in argument, science, learning, disqualify a cultivated mind from fathoming depths of which he has as yet no practical experience? Cannot sound argument, wielded by a trained and cultivated mind, be applied in plain language, and urged by homely illustrations; and so be brought exactly within the comprehension of the unlearned? It surely cannot be of necessity (however it may suit presumptuous persons of inferior powers to assert it) that learning should be unable to descend into the ways of common life, without the adjuncts of scientific phraseology; and be powerless to express and circulate itself effectively, without a previous preparation on the part of those to whom it addresses itself. The truth is, that sound learning. and the advantages of a cultivated mind, are thoroughly appreciated by those of lower estate, very many of whom are endowed by God with as excellent natural gifts of intellect, and as much natural ability, as those of the classes above them. They may not, indeed, be able to define the laws of thought and argument; but they are well qualified to understand sound argument, and lofty thought, when addressed to them in familiar terms, and with unaffected earnestness. There must be intelligence of each other between those who are studying each other in sympathy of heart; although the one may come from his college hall to preach, and the other from his fields, or his shop, to listen.

The author remembers the disgust with which, in his early service amongst such classes, he heard that a " ranter " of local notoriety, a small butcher, who left his week-day stall to go and " preach *the Gospel* " on Sundays, used to boast, " Thank God, I never read a Commentary! " and he remembers, too, how those who told him shuddered also at the man's pride, self-sufficiency, violence, and errors, and at the way in which he was misleading foolish and ignorant men, whilst glorying in his own ignorance.

But arguments of this nature against an educated, and in favour of an unlearned, ministry for uneducated people, should be carried into other provinces. It should be shown that superiority of education unfitted the ruling classes to govern; but that the best man to govern the labouring classes was one of themselves, the man of the people. It should be proved that the leaders of thought, invention, and social progress, as well as those of religious instruction, should be deposed in favour of some demagogue from the ranks of those for whose welfare they think and plan. The truth is, that the masses of the people appreciate, and canvass keenly, the most brilliant projects and successes of the politician; that they are ready to apply, and can intelligently use, the most subtle developments of science and of mechanism; and that they rise at once to meet, intelligently and gratefully, the hand which is extended to raise and improve them, in whatever of their life's difficulties it may greet them. To themselves, the real "man of the people" is not one who presumptuously pushes himself out of his proper sphere, into one for which he is by nature and education unfitted, but one who studies to use the brightest intellectual gifts, the most cultivated intelligence, and even the highest advantages of birthright, for their best interests.

No! there can be no learning which, in itself, unfits a man to cope with ignorance, and to dispel it. And if, in the most sacred of all earthly callings, the learning of this world is applied in subordination to that which is from above, it cannot but be useful and fruitful in the cause of Christ. In days when miraculous powers are withheld, and supernatural aid is not granted, those who work for Christ can afford to dispense with no natural advantages or powers which God has given; and with no cultivation and training of these, which can give influence, and command success, in dealing with men. It is not without reason that both Scripture and history are silent upon the subject of the successes and labours of those "unlearned and ignorant men," who were first chosen to propagate the gospel of faith. With one or two exceptions, their evangelistic labours are unrecorded, and their arguments are not produced, their method is not detailed, for the imitation of Christ's ministers who succeed them. The record of the apostolic age is mainly the life, labours, preaching, and teaching (with little mention of miraculous agency) of the polished and learned Paul, the scholar and the gentleman, the trained and experienced disputer; who could wield the world's wisdom against those who were equally versed in its schools of thought, and who was yet the Apostle of the uninformed barbarians; and whose writings are equally the text-book of the scholar, and the standard and study of those untaught and unversed in the subtleties of schools.

Most communities of those who are not in the communion of our Church, feel this necessity of learning, and its power amongst the people, in the present day; and they take praiseworthy pains in the training of their ministers; and we feel how this their care is, in itself, helping to bridge over the chasm which separates us. It gives them a truer information of the grounds on which rest the claims of the Church, and of their own differences; and thus is paving the way, under the providence of the God of unity, for that union which is the very principle of Christianity, and the dear object of all who embrace the cause of Christ.

One other advantage to the nation, derived from the learning and social position of the clergy, must not be overlooked; namely, the force of their example, in the country towns and villages of the land, upon thought, conversation, and actions of the classes below them. It is impossible to calculate, but not difficult to conceive, the advantage to public morals, and also to the cause of godliness, which is derived from there being, at any rate, one resident family of intelligence and position in every such community, which may set the example of an household regulated by the standard of the Bible; and the example gains strength from the fact that there is known to be, in every neighbouring community, the same example under the same circumstances. It is a matter of notoriety that the example set by the sovereign, and members of the royal family (circulating through the local influence of the nobility and large landowners who have access to the Court, and who retire from scenes of public life and metropolitan society into the seclusion of their country homes), does very materially affect the moral and religious life of all classes of the people, down to the lowest. And alike, where his influence strengthens the good example of the great landlord, or where there is none other resident of high education and position than himself, the social example of the parish clergyman and his family is of very great importance.

No. XIV.

On xviii. 115; II. iv. 17.

POWER OF THE KEYS.

The doctrine of the Church of England on this point has been fully stated in the notes referred to; but the want of space there obliged the omission of any counter statement to the claims which Rome has founded upon the original grant of our Lord, and also any citation of authorities (and here they must be few) as to the nature of that absolution which is still valid in the commission of the Church.

1. The testimony of the ancient Fathers is strong and general as to the equal sharing of the Apostles in this power, which S. Peter, on his confession in their name, obtained for all; he being thus (as S. Cyprian shows) a figure of the Church in her unity; and also as to the point of its transmission, through them, to the later Church. The following quotation of S. Augustine is very striking, as it shows the opinion of the ancient Church in his own, and from earlier days, as to the claims of S. Peter:—" The declaration, ' I will give thee the

keys of the kingdom of heaven,' includes the whole Church, which
in these days is shaken by various trials, but falls not because it is
founded upon the Rock (*Petra*), whence Peter (*Petrus*) derives his
name.   For the Rock (*Petra*) does not take its name from Peter
(*Petrus*), but Peter from the Rock; just as Christ is not from Christian, but Christian from Christ.   Therefore, since the Lord says,
' Upon this Rock (*Petra*) will I build My Church,' because Peter
(*Petrus*) had declared, ' Thou art the Christ the Son of God,' he
says, Upon this Rock (*Petra*) which thou hast confessed will I build
My Church.   For that Rock (*Petra*) was Christ; upon which foundation even Peter (*Petrus*) was built, for ' no other foundation can
any man lay than that which is laid, which is Jesus Christ.'   Therefore the Church, which is founded on Christ, has received from Him,
in Peter, the keys of the kingdom of heaven, that is, the power of
binding and loosing sins."

This passage is a very valuable comment on the original text; in
which the Church of Rome misses the grand distinction, so clear is
the original between the word *Petra* (the living *Rock*) and *Petrus* (the
stone, hewn from it and built upon it); and, meanwhile, certainly
places herself in the false position denounced in the verse with
which S. Augustine concludes his statement of doctrine.

II. With regard to the extent in which the Church still claims this
power originally conferred on the Apostles, the following few quotations from authors of repute, will be useful in support of the statement made at considerable length in the notes above referred to :—

From Hooker, vi. 6, 5, 8 :

" The sentence of ministerial absolution hath two effects; touching sin, it only declareth us free from the guiltiness thereof, and
restored unto God's favour; but concerning right in sacred and
divine mysteries whereof through sin we were made unworthy,
as the power of the Church did before effectually bind and retain us
from excess unto them, so upon our apparent repentance it truly
restoreth our liberty, looseth the chains wherewith we were tied,
remitted all whatsoever is past, and accepteth us no less, returned,
than if we had never gone astray.

" For inasmuch as the power which our Saviour gave to His Church
is of two kinds, the one to be exercised over voluntary penitents only,
the other over such as are brought to amendment by ecclesiastical
censure; the words wherein He hath given this authority must be
so understood, as the subject or matter whereupon it worketh will
permit.   It doth not permit that in the former kind (that is to say,
in the use of power over voluntary converts), to bind or loose, remit
or retain, should signify any other than only to pronounce of sinners
according to that which may be gathered from outward signs; because
really to effect the removal or continuance of sin in the soul of any
offender, is no priestly act, but a work which far exceedeth their
ability.   Contrariwise, in the latter kind of spiritual jurisdiction,

which by censures constrained men to amend their lives, it is true that the minister of God doth more than declare and signify what God hath wrought."

" The act of sin God alone remitteth, in that His purpose is never to call it to account, or to lay it unto man's charge; the stain He washeth out by the sanctifying grace of His Spirit; and concerning the punishment of sin, as none hath power to cast body and soul into hell fire, so none hath power to deliver either besides Him. As for the ministerial sense of private absolution, it can be no more than a declaration what God hath done; it hath but the force of the prophet Nathan's absolution, ' God hath taken away thy sin.' "

From Hook's " Church Dictionary," Art. *Absolution.*

" The true doctrine is this, and must be this—for the consolation of His Church, and particularly of such as class with the penitent publican in the gospel, Christ hath left with His bishops and presbyters, a power to pronounce absolution on the condition of faith and repentance in the person or persons receiving it. On sufficient appearance of these, and on confession made with these appearances in particular persons, the bishop or presbyter, as the messenger of Christ, is to pronounce it. But he cannot search the heart: God only, who can, confirms it." (*Skelton.*)

" We may infer, that the power of any sacerdotal absolution is only ministerial; because the administration of baptism (which is the most universal absolution), so far as man is concerned in it, is no more than ministerial. All the office and power of man in it is only to administer the external form, but the internal power and grace of remission of sins is properly God's; and so it is in all other sorts of absolution." (*Bingham.*)

" It is plain that the Apostles exercised the power (Acts ii. 38; 2 Cor. ii. 10), and gave their successors a charge to use it also (Gal. vi. 1; James v. 14, 15); and the primitive histories abundantly testify that they did so very often, so that they must cancel all those lines of Scripture and records of antiquity also, before they can take away this power. Nor can they fairly pretend it was a personal privilege dying with the Apostles, since the Church hath used it ever since, and penitents need a comfortable application of their pardon now, as well as they did then; and whereas they object with the Jews that ' none can forgive sins but God only ' (Luke v. 21), we reply that God alone can exercise the power in His own right, but He may and hath communicated it to others, who did it in His Name, and by His authority; or, as S. Paul speaks, ' in the person of Christ ' (2 Cor. ii. 10). So that S. Ambrose saith, ' God Himself forgives sins by them to whom He hath granted the power of absolution." (*Combe.*)

" Our Church maintains, appealing to Scripture for the proof of it, that some power of absolving or remitting sins, derived from the Apostles, remains with their successors in the ministry; and, accordingly, at the ordination of priests, the words of our Saviour, on which the power is founded, are solemnly repeated to them by the bishop, and the power at the same time conferred. We do not pretend it is in any sort a *discretionary* power of forgiving sins, for the priest has no *discernment of the spirits* and hearts of men, as the Apostles had; but a power of pronouncing authoritatively, in the name of God, who has committed to the priest the ministry of reconciliation, *His* pardon and forgiveness to all true penitents and sincere believers. That God alone can forgive sins, that He is the sole Author of all blessings, spiritual as well as temporal, is undeniable; but that He can declare His gracious assurance of pardon, and convey His blessings to us, by what means and instruments He thinks fit, is no less certain. In whatever way He vouchsafes to do it, it is our duty humbly and thankfully to receive them; not to dispute His wisdom in the choice of those means and instruments; for in that case, 'he that despiseth, despiseth not man, but God.'" (*Waldo.*)

"In the primitive Church absolution was regarded to consist of four kinds: sacramental, by Baptism and the Eucharist; dedicatory, by word of mouth and doctrine; deprecatory, by imposition of hands and prayer; judicial, by relaxation of Church censures."

From Bishop Pearson, "On the Creed," Art. 10:

"The Church of God, in which the remission of sin is preached, doth not only promise it at first by the laver of regeneration, but afterwards also upon the virtue of repentance; and to deny the Church this power of absolution is the heresy of Novatian."

From Sadler's "Church Doctrine Bible Truth:"

"When accused by His adversaries of usurping the prerogative of God, Christ neither softened nor explained away His words. Nor did he assert that, as God, He possessed an inherent right to forgive. On the contrary, He claimed the authority, not as the Son of God, but as the Son of Man; 'that ye may know that the Son of Man hath power on earth to forgive sins.' He claimed then, on this occasion, to exercise not an inherent, but a delegated power; and this delegated power He, in His turn, delegated to the Apostles. 'All power,' He says, 'is given to Me in heaven and in earth, go ye *therefore*;' 'As My Father sent me, *so* send I you;' 'Whose soever sins ye remit, they are remitted unto them.'"

"It is incredible that a power against sin, or for the consolation of sinners (which the power was), should be confined to the time when the age was the purest, *i.e.* the most free from sin. As one of our greatest divines, Jeremy Taylor, has well asked, 'When went it (the power of remitting and retaining) out? When the anointing and miraculous healing ceased? There is no reason for that: for, forgiveness of sins was not a thing visible, and, therefore, could not be of the nature of miracles, to confirm the faith of Christianity first, and, after its work was done, return to God that gave it; neither could it be only of present use to the Church, but as eternal as sin is; and, therefore, there could be nothing in the nature of the thing to make it so much as suspicious that it was presently to expire.' "

"Absolution of course can only be a means of grace to sincere penitents, and so is exactly on the same footing as the two sacraments. It was no doubt given, from the very first, to those who appeared sincere in their profession of repentance ; but the responsibility as to the right reception of it lay wholly with the men who applied for it."

No. XV.

HOLY PLACES.

1. Gethsemane. On xxviii. 1.
2. Calvary. On xxxi. 1.
3. The Holy Sepulchre. On xxxii. 8.

1. *Gethsemane.* "Occupying part of a wide open space between the brook Kedron and the foot of Olivet, we find what is now considered the Garden of Gethsemane, memorable as the resort of our Saviour, and as the scene of the agony which He endured on the night He was betrayed. There is little, if any, doubt that this is the real place of this solemn transaction ; it seems to have been an olive plantation in the time of Christ, as the name Gethsemane signifies an oil-press. That which is now pointed out as Gethsemane is probably but a part of the ancient garden. It is about fifty paces square, and is enclosed by a wall, of no great height, formed of rough loose stones. Eight very ancient olive trees now occupy the enclosure, some of which are very large, and all exhibit symptoms of decay clearly denoting their great age. As a fresh olive tree springs from the stump of an old one, there is reason to conclude that, even if the trees which existed in the time of our Saviour have been destroyed, those which now stand sprang from their roots. But it is not incredible that they should be the very same trees. The olive tree lives to a great age, and these eight trees are certainly very old. Dr. Wilde describes the largest of these as being nearly twenty-four feet in girth about the root, though its topmost branch is not thirty feet from the ground. M. Bové, who travelled as a naturalist, asserts that the largest are at least six yards in circumference, and nine or ten yards high, so large indeed that he calculates their age at 2000 years. The garden, as now enclosed, is too small to satisfy all the conditions of the Gospel narrative ; and it is more than probable that the ancient garden occupied also some of the space now covered by several

similar enclosures adjacent, some of which exhibit olive trees equally old." (*Kitto.*)

It has been argued that these eight trees cannot have been standing since the time of Christ, because the Roman army cut down every tree near Jerusalem. But every traveller who has seen an Eastern encampment knows the value of trees; and if Gethsemane, or the eight special trees, formed shade or protection over the quarters of Roman officers during the protracted siege, their being cut down would be extremely improbable.

Dr. Farrar ("Life of Christ") writes : " The traditional site, venerable and beautiful as it is from the age and size of the grey gnarled olive trees, of which one is still known as the Tree of the Agony, is perhaps too public (being, as it almost always must have been, at the angle formed by the two paths which lead over the summit and shoulder of Olivet) to be regarded as the actual spot. It was more probably one of the secluded hollows at no great distance from it, which witnessed that scene of awful and pathetic mystery. But although the actual spot cannot be determined with certainty, the general position of Gethsemane is clear; and then, as now, the chequering moonlight, the grey leaves, the dark brown trunks, the soft greensward, the ravine with Olivet towering over it to the eastward, and Jerusalem to the west, must have been the main external features of a place which must be regarded with undying interest while time shall be, as the place where the Saviour of mankind entered alone into the valley of the shadow."

" In spite of all doubt that can be raised against their antiquity, or the genuineness of their site, the eight aged olive trees, if only by their manifest difference from all others on the mountain, have always struck the most indifferent observers. They will remain, as long as their already protracted life is spared, the most venerable of their race on the surface of the earth; their gnarled trunks and scanty foliage will always be regarded as the most affecting of the sacred memorials in or about Jerusalem, the most nearly approaching to the everlasting hills themselves in the force with which they carry us back to the events of the Gospel history. (*Stanley*, " Sinai and Palestine.")

2. *Golgotha, Calvary*; "the place called a skull" (S. Luke xxiii. 33). There has been considerable debate on the subject of the origin of this name. (i.) It has been supposed that it was derived from the form of the ground, which was a low eminence, and rounded like the top of a skull. There is *now* no proof that it was a hillock; the name Mount Calvary, as applied to the site now shown as that of the crucifixion, is foreign to its present appearance; but it is not quite certain that there never was such a rising on the ground as would justify the use of the term. The enemies of Christianity in early ages, did all that man could do to obliterate the traces of

these sacred sites, defacing them with idolatrous shrines, levelling what was rising ground, and heaping stones over what was depressed. So that, whilst it is likely that the undying interest of the Christian world through successive generations, may have preserved with fair accuracy the tradition of the genuine sites, it is equally probable that neither Calvary, nor the Sepulchre (especially as they were adjacent objects for the destructive zeal of the heathen), present now any resemblance to their former appearance. There seems to be no explanation of the term more probable than this.

(ii.) It has, however, been supposed that the name was derived from its use as a cemetery, where the bones of those executed were buried upon the spot where they were put to death. But against this simply gratuitous supposition the words of the Evangelist seem to be a protest; it is not a place of *skulls*, but " the place of a skull," or, as S. Luke specifies it, simply " the place called a skull," which agrees with the former explanation. The great care taken against defilement by the dead, especially by dead criminals, would argue against such a cemetery being allowed to exist on the spot where the road passed into the city (S. Matt. xxvii. 39).

(iii.) Least probable is the idea or tradition, preserved by several of the ancient writers, that Adam's skull was buried there. They mention it as a tradition, but diverge at once into the mystical associations which thus connect the memory of the first and second Adam upon the same spot, rather than vouch for its truth.

3. *The Holy Sepulchre.* It has been supposed during the greater (that is, the earlier) part of the time which has elapsed since the Saviour's burial, that the site of His entombment is correctly marked by the church known as the Church of the Holy Sepulchre. In later days a theory has sprung up, which certainly has some strong recommendations in its favour, which identifies the Sepulchre with the remarkable rock (see App. IV.) beneath the dome of the Sakhra. The most elaborate statement of this claim has been made by Mr. Fergusson, whose architectural knowledge gives great weight to his arguments. He brings forward an array of early authorities in support of the theory; but his view is strongly disputed by Captain Warren, whose local discoveries demand, perhaps, superior credence. And, on the other hand, the opinion of most travellers inclines to the authenticity of the site covered by the Church of the Anastasis above referred to; and this opinion has received the support of the officers engaged in the excavation of Palestine. Captain Warren (in the " Recovery of Jerusalem ") enters carefully into the theory proposed by Mr. Fergusson, and brings forward many ancient authorities to disprove it, including several of those cited by Mr. Fergusson, whose testimony he reads differently. The advantages of experience and knowledge gained in the service of the " Exploration Fund " are on Captain Warren's side, who professes himself as greatly im-

pressed by the arguments of Mr. Fergusson, until the progress of investigation compelled him to abandon them.

The following description from the " Recovery of Jerusalem " (p. 10) is exceedingly interesting:—

" Nearly in the centre of the Christian quarter lies the Church of the Holy Sepulchre, which is said to contain within its walls the Tomb of our Lord. At the time of the crucifixion, the Sepulchre was without the walls; it is now well within them. Some critics explain this by saying that, after Constantine built his Church of the Resurrection, the town spread out and surrounded it; whilst others are equally certain that the present site must have been within the limits of the ancient city, and that we must look elsewhere for the Sepulchre, and even for the church built by Constantine. The solution of this difficult question depends on the course of the second wall which surrounded the city; if it ran to the east of the church, there is no reason why the present tradition should not be correct; if it ran to the west, it must be wrong. Up to the present time (1870) no one has seen any portion of this wall; the point from which it started, and that at which it ended, are alike unknown. It was, however, ascertained, during the progress of the survey, that the old arch near the south end of the bazaars, called the gate Gennath, was a comparatively recent building, and that the ruins near the Church of the Holy Sepulchre, which had been pointed out as fragments of the second wall, were really portions of a church."

The following extract is from Dean Stanley's " Sinai and Palestine : "—" Underneath the western galleries of the church, behind the Holy Sepulchre, are two excavations in the face of the rocks, forming an ancient Jewish sepulchre as clearly as anything that can be seen in the Valley of Hinnom, or in the Tombs of the Kings. . . . The existence of these sepulchres proves, almost to a certainty, that at some period the site of the present church must have been outside the walls of the city, and lends considerable probability to the belief that the rocky excavation, which perhaps exists in part still, and certainly once existed entire within the marble casing of the Chapel of the Holy Sepulchre, was at any rate a really ancient tomb, and not, as is often rashly asserted, a wooden structure intended to imitate it."

In his introduction to Captains Wilson and Warren's " Recovery of Jerusalem," Dean Stanley sums up the results obtained up to that date as follows :—" The course of the ancient walls, on which hung the much-disputed question of the possible authenticity of the Holy Sepulchre, still remains unsolved; or, rather, so much additional progress has been made towards its solution, that as far as the excavations have as yet gone, they disparage, rather than confirm, the alleged proof that the walls excluded the site from their compass, and therefore admitted of its genuineness."

This spot, whether it retains or loses its chief interest, must remain an object of attraction, hallowed, as it has been, by the worship and devotion of so many generations, and as the centre of attraction to which all Christendom looked in the time of the Crusades. It seems dangerous to hazard an opinion, much more decision, as to the identity or otherwise of the site, with the sepulchre in which our Lord lay; and it would be loss of space here (though the study is a deeply important and interesting one), to review the arguments historical and topographical for and against it, when shortly we may hope that the question may be finally set at rest, or, at least, very conclusive light be thrown upon it, by the indisputable evidence of excavation of sites.

No. XVI.

On xxx. *d.* 4–6, 21, 24, *f.* 3, 5, 12, 13, 15, 24, 40.

PILATE'S EFFORTS TO RELEASE CHRIST.

The desire of Pilate to release Christ is evident. He did not, however, dare to take the one fair and manly course open to him, namely, to give his judicial order for release at once, on his pronouncing the innocence of Christ. Still, we must make allowance for the pressure put upon him: the life of one man, against whom the chief rulers of his people clamoured, and against whom the voice of the nation was raised desiring His death, could be of little moment in the eyes of a Roman judge. It was "*expedient* that one man should die;" and against this was only Pilate's sense of justice, which was not very acute, and his unwillingness to be driven to act as the Jews pleased. He was not able to resist their expression of will beyond a certain point; he was already too deeply compromised at Rome, and he feared the consequences of a complaint by the rulers at the emperor's court; where they had, at that time, interest enough to be formidable enemies, especially in the reign of an emperor so distrustful of his lieutenants, and so ready to listen to accusations against them, as was Tiberius. Their threatened complaint was exactly one which the emperor would most readily have listened to, and acted on. Christ was accused, by the high dignitaries of the nation themselves, of sedition against Rome, and of the proclamation of His own sovereignty; and Pilate would be arraigned for having treated such a charge of treason with haughty indifference, knowing that all the traditions of the nation pointed to the rise of a King such as Christ claimed to be, who should throw off the Roman yoke; and already, repeatedly, great trouble had been given by pretenders to His character. There was certainly every reason to suppose that such a charge would be re-

ceived; it would, at least, be a matter of expedient policy to entertain it; and that Pilate's fear of it was not groundless is shown by
the fact, that when, a few years later, he was accused by the rulers
upon much less plausible grounds, he was at once recalled from his
government, and disgraced. Our Lord made allowance for the
difficulties of his position, though He clearly stated his sin, when
He said, " He that delivered Me unto thee hath the greater sin."

The following will show distinctly the various efforts made by
Pilate for the release of Christ: the question is of importance, as it
bears strongly upon the innocence of Christ, and the determined
malice of His enemies, and their resolution to put Him to death by
means of the Roman power. The clearing of Pilate's character
from some of its blackness is a matter of secondary importance, in
the case of so worthless a man; but the tracing of the steps by
which a feeble, irresolute, and unpriucipled man very often
proceeds to crime, and gives effect to the crime of others after the
same fashion, cannot be without use.

I. From the first, Pilate showed his reluctance to have anything
to do with the case. Probably his indignation at the insolence of
the Jewish rulers in refusing to cross his threshold, "lest they
should be defiled; " in compelling him to come out to them; and
then so plainly showing their opinion of his character, in assuming
that judgment would be given in their favour without a hearing of
the case, roused the spirit of the Roman, if it did not also the
judge's sense of the claims of justice, and of the respect due to his
tribunal.

He requires a formal accusation, distinctly specified charges,
tangible evidence; he will take nothing for granted, and permit no
irregularity in his court.

II. On the hesitation of Christ's accusers, he sternly desires them
to take Him away for trial in their own courts.

III. When the Jews altered their bearing, and pressed a charge
on which Pilate must act, he examined Christ; and being perfectly
satisfied as to tho harmlessnoss of His claims, so far as Rome was
concerned, and struck with His dignity, and being well aware of
His life and actions, in awe also of His Divine character, he pronounced Him innocent.

IV. The Jews pressed their case, and Pilate gave no order of
release, though his sentence was pronounced; but he caught at the
statement that Christ was of Galilee, and, under pretence of respect
to Herod, but really in hope of getting rid of the case, and its em-
barrassments, he sent Him to Herod for trial.

V. Herod sent Christ back with the greatest contempt; showing
clearly that his opinion coincided with that of Pilate, as to his
having committed no political crime. Here was the accused again
on his hands; he might have taken advantage, as he evidently
wished, of the contempt with which the native sovereign treated

the charge, to order the immediate release of Christ; but he temporized, and lost the opportunity.

VI. There was a custom that one prisoner should be released at the Passover, in memory of the release from bondage i n Egypt. The Romans had observed this custom, and now Pilate, knowing how many acts of goodness Christ had done, and how many recipients of His grace were now in Jerusalem, expected that the popular voice would be in His favour; he therefore proposed that Jesus should receive His release at their hands. But the rulers had provided for this, and Barabbas was chosen for release—a pseudo-Christ, really guilty of the crimes alleged against Jesus; and the people were persuaded to clamour for the crucifixion of Christ.

At this crisis, the messenger came from Procula Claudia, Pilate's wife, earnestly warning him to have nothing to do with the blood of Christ, concerning whom she had been deeply impressed by a dream; and the superstition of the Roman at once took alarm.

VII. Pilate, however, still temporizes, using the term, "King of the Jews," as an appeal to the national pride of the people. It was in vain. And then he pleads that he has already examined the case, and finds no ground of capital charge. But still he hesitates.

VIII. Pilate tries another appeal: he pronounces Christ a "*just person*" (echoing the significant tone of his wife's message, and showing the influence of her dream upon his mind); and washes his hands before them of the stain of blood and judicial murder. The sight of the judge of the highest court in the land, using a national mode of expressing his desire to free himself from what he pronounced a great judicial crime, should surely check the more reasonable amongst them, and raise some reaction in Christ's favour. It only elicited the cry, contemptuous alike of Pilate and of Christ, "His blood be on us, and on our children!" And then Pilate gave way: he "gave sentence that it should be *as they required*."

IX. He now tries an appeal "*ad misericordiam:*" he scourges Jesus, which was clearly an outrage on justice in the case of an innocent prisoner; but he hoped that when the mob saw Christ thus degraded and suffering, they would pity Him, and be satisfied with what was done. But the sight only whetted their thirst for blood, and they redoubled the cry, "Crucify Him!"

X. Yet he makes one last effort and appeal. He is awestricken and fearful when he hears that Jesus claims to be the Son of God; and now he labours earnestly for His release, and to unwind the bonds with which he has fettered himself. The rulers see it; they discern his conflict of superstitious awe, and sense of justice, and pride of his own position, and hatred of themselves; they understand, also, his dread of their misrepresentation of his acts; and so they play, against his now-awakening resolution, their last threat, "If thou let this man go, thou art not Cæsar's friend!" Perhaps he had

discerned some hesitation when (see VII.) he spoke of Christ as the
" King of the Jews." He brings Him forward once more when derided,
spit upon, beaten, and clothed with the trappings of mock royalty;
surely their malice will be satisfied, they will take affront at the
degradation of the sacred title, and for its sake release Christ: he
may be still "Cæsar's friend," and yet spare the claimant of
Hebrew royalty. "Shall I crucify your King?" he asks. "We
have no king but Cæsar" is the final decision, and the solemn truth
henceforth; and Pilate dares no longer resist the menacing expression of their will, and gives the formal order for Christ to be
led to execution.

No. XVII.

On xxxi. 23, 24.

THE MARYS.

The following is the tenth Fragment of Papias, who was a disciple
of S. John, and personally acquainted with many Christians who
had conversed with our Lord, and with His Apostles. It distin-
guishes between the different Marys mentioned in the New Testament, and connects them with the Apostles. Its authenticity is not
certain :—

"1. Mary, the mother of our Lord.
"2. Mary the wife of Cleopas, or Alphæus, who was the mother
of James the Bishop and Apostle, and of Simon, and
Thaddeus, and of one Joseph.
"3. Mary Salome, wife of Zebedee, mother of John the Evangelist, and of James.
"4. Mary Magdalene.
"These four are found in the Gospel.
" James, and Judas, and Joseph were sons of an aunt (2) of the
Lord's.
" James also, and John, were sons of another aunt (3) of the
Lord's.
" Mary (2), mother of James the Less and Joseph, wife of Alphæus,
was the sister of Mary, the mother of our Lord; whom John names
'of Cleophas,' either from her father, or from the family of the
clan, or from some other reason.
" Mary Salome (3) is called Salome, either from her husband, or
her village. Some affirm that she is the same as 'Mary of Cleo-
phas,' because she had two husbands."
The " one *Joseph* " here mentioned is known in the Gospels as
Joses. Some confusion is caused by the fact that two sisters (1)
and (2) bear the same name, Mary. It has been pointed out, how-

ever, that the name of the Virgin, is, on the authority of the best
MSS., given generally as *Mariam*, whilst her sister, Mary of Cleophas
(properly " *Clopas* "), is *Maria*. There seems to have been a close
companionship, as well as sisterly affection, between these two
sisters; and it is probable that they resided together, being widows
(Joseph and Alphæus being dead), according to a tradition which is
supported by the silence of the Gospels concerning their life.

Some critics identify Mary Salome with the sister of Mary, our
Lord's mother, mentioned in S. John xix. 25; if so, there was close
relationship between the three. But the identification of Mary
Salome with Mary of Cleophas, mentioned in the Fragment of Papias,
is not supported by the opinion of critics.

It may be noticed that Mary, the sister of Lazarus, is not mentioned in the Fragment of Papias. It may be that she is thus
identified with Mary Magdalene; but the great opinion of the early
Fathers is against this identification. It was, we know, supported
by the Church of Rome in the Middle Ages, which leaned to that
view; but it is now universally rejected.

This identification (if it be so) of Mary Magdalene and Mary the
sister of Lazarus, would, as it is contrary to the view of the early
Fathers, throw suspicion on the authenticity of this fragment; to
which, indeed, a late date has been assigned.

No. XVIII.

On xxxi. 36.

NECESSITY OF DEATH TO MAN.

It might be an interesting subject of inquiry (though the data
must be insufficient, and the merest digest of authors, scientific and
theological, voluminous), whether death would be a necessity to the
bodies of men; whether, had Adam remained unfallen, the death
which was passed as a penalty, might have ensued through natural
causes.

It is certain that death was present in the world before our era,
as may be gathered from the various remains, fossil and other,
which have come down to us; and therefore, if death could affect
animal life, might it not have affected the animal life of man? Could
the body of man necessarily have withstood the many accidents
incidental to residence on earth? Would not a falling tree, a land-
slip, a falling rock, have utterly crushed and destroyed life, as it
must have mutilated the body? Could it ever have been possible
to such a body as ours to live in water, to withstand fire, to exist
in entire vitiation of air? Could it, supposing its accidental pre-
vention from obtaining food, have lived on without natural food?

And the possibility of dangers and accidents such as these, or similar in effect to them, may have lurked in the groves, amidst the rivers, and in the glades of the plain of Eden. This body of ours was not a spiritual body before Christ, the first Adam of the resurrection of life; it had the limitations, and was subject to the laws, of bodies formed from "the dust of the earth." Does not the very necessity of eating argue a necessity of replenishing vital powers; and therefore, in the failure of proper food, a possibility of death? Could it ever have been possible to man to distil from the herbarium of earth, which formed his original grant of food (Gen. i. 29), the elixir of immortal life?

It may have been, however, one of the privileges bestowed on those whom God created in His own image and likeness, to be exempt from the action of the law of death. There was around them, we know, the protection of ministering spirits. "The tree of life in the midst of the garden" of Eden, may have had properties which were necessary for the sustentation of life even there; or was a sacramental emblem, as the ancient writers thought, of such a gift. At any rate, the fact of there being such a tree, endowed with the properties ascribed to it, is suggestive of immortality not being naturally inherent in man's body, but dependent on the use of some gift of God external to himself, and dependent on the will of God.

It is declared distinctly and invariably in Holy Scripture, that death came into the world by sin, and that "death passed upon all men, for that all have sinned;" but we can scarcely argue from this that man's body must otherwise have been endued with immortality, and that it could not possibly have become subject to death.

It seems that man's body was not in itself suitable for existence in the heaven of heavens, amongst the inhabitants of the spirit world. Before he could be admitted into another state of being, beyond earth, he must be " *translated* " (whatever change that word expresses) by the power of God. Enoch and Elijah, that we know of, were thus *translated*, because they pleased God. The change to the spiritual body of the resurrection may have passed upon them, either in anticipation of, or, far more likely, after our Lord's resurrection; at any rate, they retained their bodies of earth without losing them by death. It appears, however, that before Christ's entrance into heaven, they had not ascended up into heaven; and must therefore have remained, embodied, amongst the disembodied saints of the world of saved spirits. (See Essay, "The Descent into Hell.")

We see from their case that it need not follow that man *must* die. The longevity of the antediluvian world proves that considerable limits of extension could be assigned to the bodily life, even after its subjection to the law of death; what may not, therefore, have been possible before the entrance of that mortal law? It is enough, however, to ask if man *could* be mortal before Adam fell; whether it was his privilege to escape death by "translation" in God's time; and whether his punishment was his subjection to a natural law, to which it had been his happy destiny to be superior; or was it a new law, to which his unfallen nature could not possibly, under any circumstances, have been subjected?

Does not Christ's death further suggest the exercise of a law always *possible* to our animal body? Our Lord's body was not mortal by Adam's sentence; yet, at His permission (permission, we gather from Holy Scripture, not compulsion), it experienced natural death; and at His will passed under the action of the law now universally reigning in the world. In all things connected with His human body, we find our Lord subject to the will of the Father, dependent on His preservation, and obedient to His rules of life, and, finally, "obedient unto death."

It is declared that life and immortality were brought to light, by our Saviour Jesus Christ, through the Gospel (2 Tim. i. 10)—a statement which suggests powerfully that these were not previously necessary conditions and properties of the body of man; they may have been gifts destined and held in reserve for him, but not, even in his unfallen state, his by necessity of being. He had an immortal soul; but was it not always, for residence on earth, the tenant of a body to which mortality was possible?

We cannot decide these points, which neither revelation has unveiled, nor science can certify to us. We may, however, be permitted to suppose that death *might* have befallen man (even as now it *must*); but that the law of man's access to heaven would probably have been by "translation" in God's good time; and that then, by God's gift, he could have been endowed with a more abundant life than that of his earthly sojourn—with, in fact, the spiritual life which Christ "brought to light," and which became revealed to him from the date of the resurrection of Christ, who reversed, and more than reversed, the sentence which had passed on the human race through the fall of Adam; that, in short, unlike the existence of the soul, immortality of the body must always have been the special gift of God, even as now we are told the crowning blessing and "gift of God is eternal life, through Jesus Christ our Lord."

No. XIX.

On xxxi. 37; xxxii. 18; II. i. 6.

INSEPARABILITY OF CHRIST'S NATURES.

On this point, the orthodox writers, both of ancient and modern times, are explicit, and are agreed. They declare that the Divine and human natures are inseparable. Their being held separable would involve the capital heresy of the Nestorians, who asserted that there were two distinct persons, as well as natures, in Christ; and it would affect the great doctrine of the Atonement. For, if severed from the Godhead, the manhood could not of itself atone for the sins of the whole world; for then *Christ* would not have died for the sins of the world, as, in His human nature, He did die. But, God and man being one Christ, "God so loved the world, that He gave His only begotten Son," not merely a sinless human form taken up for the occasion, and disunited from the Divine Son by death; but the God and man, which were thus one Christ.

Hooker, after discussing the union of the two distinct natures of God and man in one Christ, thus sums up the teaching of the Church on this point : "These natures, from the moment of their first combination, have been, and are for ever inseparable. For even when His soul forsook the tabernacle of His body, His Deity forsook neither body nor soul. If it had, then we could not truly hold either that the person of Christ was buried, or that the person of Christ did raise up itself from the grave. For the body separated from the Word can, in no true sense, be termed the person of Christ; nor is it true to say that the Son of God, in raising up that body, did raise up Himself, if the body were not both with Him, and of Him, even during the time it lay in the sepulchre. The like is to be said of the soul, otherwise we are plainly and inevitably Nestorians.

"The very person of Christ, therefore, for ever one and the self-same, was, only touching bodily substance, concluded within the grave, His soul being only thence severed, but by personal union His Deity still inseparably joined with both." ("Eccles. Polity," V. lii. 4.)

Bishop Pearson says, "Christ raised Himself from death, according to His express prediction; for the union of the two natures (the Divine and human) still remained; nor was the soul or the body of Christ separated from the Divinity, but still subsisted, as they did before, by the subsistence of the second Person of the Trinity."

On xxii. 11; II. i. 2.

THE SABBATH AND THE LORD'S DAY.

The change of the world's day of rest from the seventh to the first day of the week, is a very extraordinary one. It must have been by the direct order of Christ Himself that the change was made. No human order could have rightly superseded the obligation of that ordinance, which, in the beginning, God appointed in memory of the great work of creation. No sanction of the Christian Church, within the power of binding and loosing upon earth, could affect the rights which all mankind, within and without the pale of that Church, have in the original grant of the sabbath. God alone could declare that the work of redemption was greater than that even of creation, and man's real interest in it higher; and that therefore the Lord's day should take the place of the sabbath as blessed by Him, and hallowed. Certainly, in no way more significant could we have decided the relative magnitude of His great works.

The command itself is not stated in express terms; but from the date of the resurrection until the canon of Scripture closes, there is not only a cessation of the reference, so common in the four Gospels, to the observance of the sabbath, but also one continuous evidence of the Lord's day as the great day of Christians; and the conclusion is irresistible as to the truth of the testimony of ancient writings, and of tradition, that our Lord Himself ordained the observance of His own day.

Isaac Williams traces the coincidence between the act of the creation of man, and that of His ransom from death upon the sixth day of the week; of Christ's resting the seventh day from His work of grace, and rising again, as the " light of life," on the day when light was originally created. He quotes the opinion of Origen, that, " as two kind of creatures were formed on the Sunday, both animals and man, the animals were created on the forenoon of that day, and afterwards, perhaps at the sixth hour of that day, God said, ' Let Us make man in Our image,' which time, therefore, would correspond with the time of our Lord's dying upon the cross, and His Church being formed from His side. So that," he continues, "in the afternoon we were first created; and at the same period of the same day were redeemed and created anew in Christ. On the seventh day God rested from the work of creation; and on the same day Christ rested from the work of redemption in the grave. On Sunday God created the light; and on Sunday, Christ, the true Light of the new creation, came from the grave. That sabbath, also, on which our Lord rested in the grave, is like our whole condition throughout our stay in this world, wherein we die to sin, and mortify the flesh, and are buried with Christ, and wait for a new resurrection. But as our Lord said of the sabbath, 'My Father worketh hitherto, and I work,' notwithstanding the rest of that hallowed day; so also it is with the sabbath which is fulfilled in us; for our old man is laid at rest, and dead with Him in the sabbath of the grave; but we have also a new sabbath wherein the new man is renewed daily in His likeness, wherein He and the Father worketh. It is to us also the sabbath with regard to that which is to come, inasmuch as ' there remaineth a rest for the people of God ; ' and, therefore, that rest is not yet attained." (See Heb. iv. 9.)

The character of absolute rest, which was so distinguishing a mark of the Jewish sabbath, does not belong so directly to the Lord's day.   There are not (it must be owned, by the strictest advocates of Sabbatarianism) the same restrictions and penalties ever spoken of with regard to the observance of the " first day of the week," as those which fenced the sabbath days of rest. Our Lord's observance of the sabbath day during His ministry upon earth, gives frequent and significant intimation of a new and genial law of liberty, whose first principle should be that God hallowed the day as one for the peculiar work and exercise of that spiritual life newly communicated through Christ; and the second that this "sabbath was made for man, and not man for the sabbath," as was too much the appearance of the Jewish view of the holy day. The words above quoted from the Epistle to the Hebrews, may furnish a key to the spirit in which the Lord's day should be observed—not simply as a day of rest, for there "*remaineth*" (unattained as yet) "a rest for the people of God." The practices of the Apostolic Church show that it was devoted to the exercises of religion, and especially to the receiving of the Eucharist, and to such kindly, charitable, and brotherly association as would make the religious assembly of this day a foretaste of that of the Church in heaven.   Not as its first and essential principle, but so far as it may be promotive of these great objects, the Lord's day borrowed from the sabbath its sanction of *rest*—for men must rest from worldly duties, and employments, and pleasures, to engage rightly and heartily in those proper to the Lord's day.   And as our Lord declared, " My Father worketh hitherto, and I work," so is the proper work of the Lord's day certainly the most important work in which we can engage on earth ; and we cannot rest from it until we enter upon the rest remaining for us in heaven.

There is a happy unanimity with regard to the observance of the Lord's day by Christians, which is of great force amongst heathen men. We are familiar with the ancient divisions of the Church with regard to the observance of Easter ; how the want of unity on this point between the early Church of our own land, and the Roman missionaries, led to most unhappy consequences; and the record of the strife serves to illustrate the strong impression which must be produced, by the universal observance of one great day by all Christians. It was this which attracted the attention of the world to the Jewish religion.

There are differences of opinion with regard to the strictness with which the Lord's day should be kept sacred, especially with regard to the *rest* enjoined upon it. It is unnecessary to enter into the question here, further than to observe that, on the one hand, as the day is the special day of public and private devotion, any licence and craving for holiday pleasures, which interfere with the primary duties of the day, must tend towards error and irreligion; and that, against the argument sometimes advanced, that the hard work of the world increasingly requires that the Lord's day should be a day of liberty and amusement, we must oppose the principle that this very increase of worldly work, and its absorption of the mind's powers and interests, show that the religious occupation of the Lord's day is all the more vitally necessary for those who would, from the work and tribulation of this life, rise to the life immortal. On the other hand, whatever tends to make the Lord's day a day of gloom, and restraint, and austerity, is equally to be deprecated, as hurtful in its consequences to the cause of Christ; for it makes, especially to the minds of the young, the day of religion a day of uncongenial and disagreeable restraint, from which a sad reaction must naturally ensue.

It has been noted that the observance of the Lord's day is very striking in its effect upon the heathen. An illustration of this may be found in the experiences of residents in India. Much has been said about the unhappy effect upon the native mind of the differences of Church and sect; but the native mind is quite familiar with these subdivisions of religious opinion within the limits of their own creed, and though they are certainly weaknesses displaying themselves in the advancing army of Christian truth, their influence is a good deal overrated. Far stronger is the effect produced, happily, by the united observance of the Lord's day—it serves to combine, to the native eye, all Christian men in a bond of brotherly unity. The "*great day*" of Christians is a recognized mark over the extent of our empire.

The obligation to rest upon the Lord's day from such public labours as are foreign to the duties of the day, is one of the few points on which law in India has been able, without interference with the faith of the land, to advocate Christianity without constraining the opinions or interfering with the work or occupation of our Hindoo or Mohammedan subjects. Upon a day which is no sacred day of their own, the law directs that government work shall be suspended, except in cases of necessity; and there is an appeal to the consciences of Christian residents in India, to support this law by the influence of their own individual example and practice.

It is, however, sad to notice, in many parts of the country, the growth of evasions of this just and religious principle. There is often a want of care in letting the sub-contracts of work—no clause is inserted in these, no prohibition given, against work being carried on on the Lord's day; and the native sub-contractor is left at liberty to do as he pleases. If remonstrance is addressed to the overseer in charge—if one who is careless in the matter—he says that he cannot prevent it; either he has no right to interfere with what a native chooses to do on a day that he does not hold sacred; or else, that if he did interfere, the men would throw up their work, and seek it elsewhere. The latter threat is now not uncommon, because native workmen find that there are those who will permit them thus to evade the government order on this point.

The growth of carelessness in this matter is followed by (or, perhaps, it may be rather said, is the consequence of) a corresponding carelessness on the part of private employers of native labour; and the impression is gaining ground that the rule on this point is being relaxed. We clearly have no right to interfere with what our native subjects do *themselves* on a day which is no holy day to them. But, on the other hand, we have no right to take advantage of this to get them to do work *for us* which we think it wrong to do ourselves; and they have no right to consider it a hardship if, in giving them daily work, we except the day which we hold sacred as a day of rest.

The matter is one which directly concerns the work of the clergy in India; especially of those who, being in government service, represent, in their respective stations, a department of the Imperial government. It has been the author's good fortune to have received invariable support, in agitating this subject, from government officers, and to have succeeded in every instance, except one, in which he has interfered to stop the evasion of this rule, and that without any unkind feeling being produced by his recommendation of a stricter enforcement of the existing law. With regard to its infraction by private persons, the matter is one of greater difficulty; and it is also one for deep regret, because the growth of public laxity on this point must neutralize the effect of law, which rests for support upon public opinion: if it is a matter in which Christian residents themselves are indifferent, the reason for the interference of government is less evident.

The subject is one of very vital importance, and the author, writing in India, may be permitted to dwell upon it with a particularity to which it would have no claim here, except as an assertion of a general principle applicable to all countries where the Christian colonist lives in the presence of heathen. The author's own views with regard to the Lord's day are decidedly anti-Sabbatarian; but he feels distinctly that the day is one for rest from worldly duties, and for religious exercise and special private devotion. How

strictly, or otherwise, these are to be observed to the exclusion of
"seeking our own pleasure on God's holy day," is a matter of
private conscience. Doubtless there is very much that is innocent
and allowable, which the Jew, and perhaps the Puritan, would have
condemned as "sabbath-breaking." But this does not make it
right, or lawful, to allow the day to be classed amongst days of
worldly work, either for ourselves, or those whose labour we employ
in our behalf. No wrong is done to the native by our not furnish-
ing him with Sunday work, in opposition to the rule of the government, and of the Divine law, that the stranger that is within our
gates may rest as well as ourselves. Probably there are not a few
who think that the advantages secured to themselves, make it not
unfair that they should allow the day's pay, to the servant whose
work is not of necessity on the Lord's day; that he may draw no
comparisons unfavourable to their religion between them and
himself.

It must be remembered that God does not at all recognize the
right of men to do as they please upon the day which is His own.
It is not the right of Christian men only to rest upon the Lord's
day; the day is the right of all men, "*specially* of them that
believe;" and in advocating its outward observance, so far as we
are concerned, we should not merely say that we do so because it
is *our* day; but because, from the beginning, God appointed the
day as one common to mankind (common, also, in their degree,
even to the brute creation, who have their appointed rights and
interests in it). False religions may have dropped and forgotten
the day, its rights, and its claims; had they not done so, they
would not have forgotten the true God; but these should be remembered and put forward by Christian men. And on this point it
is a just act on the part of a Christian government in heathen lands,
and one acknowledged by as early a precedent as the edict of the
Emperor Constantine upon this point, that, whilst compulsion is
not exercised contrary to the religion of the land, God's original
law should be publicly recognized, and maintained amongst those
who are professedly bound by it; and as witness to the rights
and privileges of all mankind.

And if the united observance of this holy day by Christians has
so marked an influence upon the surrounding heathen, we may
fairly argue that any indifference to, or neglect of, its obligations is
a most serious wrong to the faith of Christ. It is a manifest sin
that the Christian should take pattern from the heathen in this
matter; it is also a grievous hindrance to the spread of the Gospel,
and to the labour of the missionary. For, as nothing has been
more repulsive to the Gentile mind than the Judaism which expresses itself in narrow and intolerant Sabbatarian views; so the
genial, earnest, spiritual exercises of this day draw that mind, even
in its most idolatrous or atheistic manifestations, to see that God is

in His holy Temple, amidst those who worship in spirit and in truth; that it is good for men to be with Him there; that in the purity and earnestness of our religion lies the secret of our worldly might, and moral excellence; and that there is in truth before us that eternal life, and that heavenly kingdom, to which we aspire in the world to come.

No. XXI.

On II. vii. 9, 12.

LAY BAPTISM.

Though the ordinary ministration of the Sacrament of Holy Baptism is restricted to those lawfully appointed to minister in holy things, yet the Church has always acknowledged the validity of lay baptism in cases of necessity; "Baptism by any man, in case of necessity, was the voice of the whole world." Hooker is disposed to admit even the baptism of infants by women, in very extreme cases, as justifiable; it is allowed by the Church of Rome, against whose example, in this respect, there is no room for prejudice; and by various reformed Churches. He thus sums up the arguments in favour of lay baptism, including that by women: "Whereas general and full consent of the godly learned in all ages doth make for validity of Baptism, yea albeit administered in private, and even by women, which kind of Baptism in case of necessity divers reformed Churches do both allow and defend; some others which do not defend, tolerate; few in comparison, and without any just cause, do utterly disannul and annihilate; surely, however, through defects on either side, the Sacrament may be without fruit (as well in some cases to him which receiveth, as to him which giveth it), yet no disability of either part can so far make it frustrate, and without effect, as to deprive it of the very nature of true Baptism, having all things else which the ordinance of Christ requireth. Whereupon we may consequently infer that the administration of this Sacrament by private persons, be it lawful or unlawful, appeareth not as yet to be wholly void." ("Eccles. Polity," V. lxii. 22.)

The experience of the clergy in India, and in the Colonies, particularly of missionary clergy, must convince all of the charity of this opinion, against which the Church of England has wisely concluded to lay no bar of prohibition, though she has not thought it right to express any direction of allowance. It has often happened that children born in places distant from the station of any authorized minister, or even at the out-stations of his charge, which are only occasionally visited, have been of necessity baptized by laymen; often by the person accustomed to read Divine Service to the residents on Sunday, sometimes by the medical officer in attendance, sometimes by the child's parent, according to the urgency of the case. There have been cases also, in which the mother, or nurse, in very extreme necessity, has baptized the child, hoping that God would forgive the irregularity of administration of the Sacrament, for which He has specified no exception of requirement. It would be impossible for the Church to lay down regulation for such cases, but it is charitable to hope that Christ, " seeing their faith," would say to the child thus brought to Him for the remission of sins, " Thy sins be forgiven thee."

Two cases of this nature, within the author's experience, may be cited in illustration of such necessity. In the first instance, there was a body of troops, with the women and children belonging to them, on the last day's march towards a large military station. The women were left behind on the road, all the men being engaged in making provision for crossing the Ganges into the station. Whilst so left, one of the women was confined prematurely, and the child only lived to die. She called for water, and, with her own hand, baptized the child, which forthwith died. In the second instance, the chaplain had just arrived from his visitation of a distant out-station, when he was hurriedly summoned to baptize a dying child. With all expedition, he arrived too late; and the nurse in attendance, a Roman Catholic, stated that she had baptized the child in accordance with the rule of her own Church, which, she stated, was peremptory in such cases. In both these instances, the essential form and words prescribed by our Lord were correctly observed; and the chaplain, whilst pointing out the irregularity, could not but admit the plea of necessity; and he so far acknowledged the validity of the act, as to declare that he should not have rebaptized the children had they lived to be brought for admission into the militant Church; and both children received the only recognition possible, namely, interment with the service of the Church of England.

In India, also, greater irregularities than these have happened, and their occurrence affords a strong argument for the most liberal and charitable construction of the validity of baptism by women, in extreme cases. In the Zenana mission work, now so extensive and as yet so imperfectly defined, converts are frequently made; but the stringent social rules of the country forbid the convert to receive baptism from a clergyman. The Zenana teachers hesitate, in the absence of proper authority, to administer the Sacrament; and a most painful dilemma ensues: either the lady missionary must acknowledge the impossibility of compliance with the positive rule of Christ, or she must lay stress on the necessity of faith, and avoid the subject of baptism.

Two instances, within the author's knowledge, of the settlement of this question by the convert herself, may be stated as examples of what may be more common than is supposed or can be known. Some years ago, the wife of a native gentleman of very large fortune and of high caste, became a convert to Christianity. Her unusual abilities, great beauty, and admirable personal character gave the greatest weight to her opinions. She fell ill; and just before her death, saying she was a Christian, and dared not die unbaptized, and calling upon Christ to forgive what she saw was an irregularity, even to being sin, she baptized herself with water, using the form in S. Matthew's Gospel. After her death, her husband inquired into, and finally embraced, Christianity; and founded a Christian family of great importance to the fortunes of the native Church of that part of India. The second instance was the performance of the same act by a Zenana convert, who asked in vain for permission to receive baptism in the hour of death, and, seeing no alternative, baptized herself, rather than not comply with what she said she understood was an absolute command, without exceptions.

In these cases, there can be no doubt that the validity of the administration of baptism by those still, except in faith, heathen, cannot be recognized; and that, if the question were pressed to decision, the answer must be that such baptism was not only irregular, but, within the discretion of the Church on earth, entirely unallowable. But we have here one of the difficulties of an infant Church, irremovable until the progress of the truth puts down the barriers of caste, and of social seclusion, unless the administration of baptism by an authorized Zenana teacher can be sanctioned; and such a permission would, at any rate at the first, close all Zenanas against Christian teachers. We can only trust that Christ, who ordained the rules within which His Church on earth may bind or loose, may see in such instances special individual cases, in which, whilst His Church must hesitate authoritatively to bind or loose within the terms of His commission, He reserves to Himself powers of dispensation; and that when those already His by confession of a right faith, have come into His presence, He has accepted their faith, and excused their construction of His command, and granted the inward and spiritual grace, of which the outward and visible sign was so utterly irregular. His acceptance of one, who, on His failing to receive the usual washing of water from those who ought to have rendered this service, washed His feet with her tears; and of her, who, failing her attendance at the burial of her Lord, yet accepted His saying that He must die, and, in that belief, anointed His body beforehand to the burial, and thus did " what she could " (S. Luke vii. 37-50; S. Mark xiv. 3-9); may justify our charitable hope of His acceptance of these cases also.

The difficulties which are thus shown to surround the subject of

Holy Baptism, in the earlier stages of Gospel progress—in places, at least, where the duties of life carry Christians beyond the central stations and residence of authorized clergy—may plead for the most charitable construction of such cases as those for which even Hooker, living in a country enjoying Christian ordinances, and himself most sensitive of any licence or irregularity, in writing of recognized rules, and of exceptions permissible under them, has ventured to pronounce justification.

And with regard to such exceptional cases as those of Indian experience, we must feel that the difficulties of the progress of the Gospel in that country, have, in many points, no resemblance to, or parallel with, those of early ages. But certainly Christ's one and catholic religion was not destined to find an exception, in the social or religious customs of this large portion of the habitable globe, to the rule of universal prevalence. Nor is there, in India alone, any restriction of the limits within which the apostolic commission must work out the evangelization of "all the world." Therefore, whether, as it is the mission of Christianity to purify and remodel the laws of caste, it may be also to put down the domestic *purdah* of female seclusion—to such an extent, at least, as was the custom amongst the Jews; or whether this ancient and general institution of the East is to be retained, within limits recognizable by the laws of the Church, time and the progress of Christianity must show. Meanwhile, these are questions for the most earnest deliberation, not simply of missionaries, but of the Fathers of the Church; and though we may hesitate to allow that the principal Zenana missionaries should be permitted by authority (as has been proposed) to administer the Sacrament of Baptism, in special cases; yet we must feel the demand for our sympathy in these difficulties, and see the call for our prayer that Christ, whose work it is, will be pleased to remove the barriers of female seclusion, and of caste, as He has all other difficulties apparently irreconcilable with the fulfilment of His absolute command to "make disciples of all nations," and to baptize every convert.

No. XXII.

On II. viii. 3.

ANCIENT DIVISIONS OF THE HOLY SCRIPTURES.

A wider division than that mentioned by our Lord, is given in the following passage from Josephus (against Apion. I. 8):—" We have not an innumerable multitude of books among us, disagreeing from, and contradicting one another, as the Greeks have; but only twenty-two books, which are justly believed to be divine; and of

them, five belong to Moses, which contain his laws, and the traditions of the origin of mankind till his death. This interval of
time was little short of three thousand years; but, as to the time
from the death of Moses till the reign of Artaxerxes king of Persia,
who reigned after Xerxes, the prophets, who were after Moses,
wrote down what was done in their times, in thirteen books. The
remaining four books contain hymns to God, and precepts for the
conduct of human life. It is true, our history hath been written
since Artaxerxes very particularly; but hath not been esteemed of
the like authority with the former, by our forefathers; because
there hath not been an exact succession of prophets since that
time. And how firmly we have given credit to those books of our
own nation, is evident by what we do; for, during so many ages as
have already passed, no one has been so bold as either to add anything to them, or to take anything from them, or to make any
change in them; but it becomes natural to all Jews, immediately
and from their very birth, to esteem those books to contain divine
doctrines, and to persist in them, and, if occasion be, willingly to
die for them."

The above passage is interesting, as being probably the earliest
record of the Jewish canon; and also for its distinction between
the Scriptures held as inspired, and those known as the Apocrypha.

The subject of the canon of Holy Scripture is too voluminous for
notice here; but the articles " Bible," " Canon," " Scripture," in
Smith's " Dictionary of the Bible," may be referred to as containing
an exhaustive summary, and as offering a groundwork for distinct
study of this question.

INDEX.

B.

C.

K.

L.

M.

N.

O.

P.

LONDON: PRINTED BY WILLIAM CLOWES AND SONS, STAMFORD STREET
AND CHARING CROSS.